WHAT YOU DON'T KNOW

Merry Jones

FILLES VERTES PUBLISHING

COEUR D'ALENE, ID

Merry Jones/Filles Vertes Publishing
PO Box 1075
Coeur d'Alene, ID 83814
www.FillesVertesPublishing.com

Publisher's Note: This is a work of fiction. Names, characters, places, and incidents are a product of the author's imagination. Any resemblance to actual people, living or dead, or to businesses, companies, events, institutions, or locales is completely coincidental.

What You Don't Know/ Merry Jones. -- 1st ed.
ISBN 978-1-946802-40-8
E-BOOK ISBN 978-1-946802-45-3

To Robin, Baille, Neely, as always

WHAT YOU DON'T KNOW

Merry Jones

FRIDAY, AUGUST 10, 2018

The screams came from Sophie, and they were serious, not the kind that happened in a game, or even in a fight. These were the kind that happened when someone severed a digit, when their hair caught fire. Nora jumped to her feet, slamming her coffee mug onto the table, noting the dark splash on the placemat, the stain that was already forming.

"Girls?" she bellowed as she ran to the playroom, images pulsing in her head. A finger crushed, an arm broken. An intruder at the sliding doors. With a knife, with a gun. Oh God.

Nora swung around the newel post, flew down the half-flight of stairs, took the left past the laundry room into the den. Her socks had no traction, so she skidded over the hardwood floors into the room. Her eyes darted left to right, right to left, searching for blood, for damage, for a stranger. Only when she saw her children intact and uninjured did she allow herself to breathe.

"What?" she panted.

At the sight of her mother, Sophie stopped screaming. She halted her stomping and flailing on the sofa as if only now remembering that she might get scolded for jumping on the furniture. Hopping down, she crashed into the coffee table and knocked her plastic tea set onto the floor.

Nora thought Sophie would barrel into her arms, but no, she stopped beside Ellie, who was crouching behind the sofa's armrest, eyes gleaming and intense like Tommy's. Seeing how much Ellie resembled Tommy was disturbing. Nora almost heard him chuckle.

"Mom! Do something!" Bug-eyed, Sophie raised a hand and pointed at the floor near the sliding glass door.

Nora blinked Tommy away and stepped farther into the room, her gaze following the trajectory of Sophie's finger, unable to understand the panic.

"Goodness," she began. "What's the big—"

Nora stopped mid-sentence, her blood halting its circulation, her skin erupting in goose bumps. Some primal sense took over, some paleo-revulsion, and she recoiled, stepping backward, stumbling over her own feet.

The spider was huge.

Nora's shoulders hunched and her throat tightened. Damn. Her knees dissolved, so that for a few seconds, she couldn't move.

Sophie shouted, begging her to kill it.

Ellie hugged herself and stared.

Of course, yes. She would have to kill it. But, God, it was ugly. And as big across as Sophie's hand, with long pointed spindly legs. Looking at it made Nora's stomach wrench and her skin writhe, yet she couldn't look away.

"Kill it, Mommy!" Sophie screamed. Or maybe it was Ellie. It could have been either of them.

For a few heartbeats, the playroom was silent, electric with tension. Six eyes gawked at the spider. And then Ellie burst into a high-pitched constant keening that reverberated in Nora's bones.

"Get it, Mom!" Sophie yelled, covering her ears to muffle Ellie's wails. When had her daughters become so casual about killing? Was it too much television? She'd have to monitor what the girls were watching and talk to Dave about it. Then again, he'd only tell her she was being overprotective, that the girls had to be prepared for the world they'd live in.

"It's coming closer!" Sophie cowered behind Ellie, hands still over her ears.

"Ellie!" Nora barked. "Cut it out. I can't think with that noise."

"Mom said cut it out!" Sophie yelled into her sister's ears. "Be quiet!"

"Sophie, don't yell in her ears," Nora yelled, then softened her voice. "In fact, don't yell period. And Ellie, hush."

Finally, Ellie stopped screaming. She stood up, rapt and silent. The spider didn't move.

Nora edged over to the bookshelf and retrieved a wad of drawing paper. She held her breath as she rolled it up and held the makeshift tube at the ready—a slugger waiting for the pitch.

"Mom, hurry. It's going to get away!"

Nora half hoped it would. She watched it. An alien being without bones, without a brain. Was it even aware that it existed? That it was in danger? She stepped closer, her body wracked with disgust. And definitely, without a doubt, she didn't just see but felt the spider tense, preparing all its several limbs for battle. Oh God. How did it know? Could it hear her heartbeat? Was it watching her?

A vague memory surfaced about spiders' eyes, that they were made up of dozens of smaller eyes scrunched together, compressed into one organ. Or maybe that was insects, not spiders. Bees, maybe. Tommy would have known. God, the thing was ugly. Her nerves pulsed with the urge to crush it. Why was she resisting? Killing it was no big deal. It was just a damned spider.

The girls were losing it. Sophie's pigtails had come loose, her curls dangling over one ear. She clutched Ellie with both arms, hugging her, comforting her sister when, really, it was she who needed comforting. Ellie stared, white-faced, chewing her lip. Her hands grasping Sophie's.

"Kill it, kill it," their little voices chanted.

Kill it, Nora's mind repeated. She imagined herself a bull-fighter—the spider, her toro. Or no. She was more like a Nazi, and the spider some arthritic old Jew. No, what was she thinking? She was neither *torero* nor Nazi. Her victim was a spider. Nothing.

So why was she hesitant to kill it?

Maybe she should let it go. She could find a jar to capture it and then dump it outside in the garden. That would show the girls that all creatures have a right to live, that the spider was nothing to be afraid of, that he was just being a spider. Yes, that's what she should do. And it's what she would have done if the spider had given her the chance.

Instead, it made its move.

It jumped. It leapt through the air, landing inches from where it had been. And it didn't stop. It took off running on all eights across the hardwood floor.

The girls' shrieks shattered the air. They glommed onto each other in terror, Ellie bellowing, Sophie squealing. Nora grimaced. Why hadn't she just killed the damned thing? Why had she allowed the situation to heighten to this level?

She jumped into action, overcoming her fear, chasing after it like a mama bear protecting her cubs, stooping to the floor, pounding the thing with the roll of drawing paper. She struck once. Again. And again, and again, sending pieces of spider legs skittering across polished wood. Spider insides pasted the paper. The corpse itself shriveled to a tiny ball, its remaining legs curled up as if trying to protect themselves.

For a moment, there was silence. Nora stood, panting. Unsteady.

Ellie scurried over and gripped the back of Nora's jeans, peering at the small mess. "Ew."

Nora asked Sophie to get a tissue. Sophie dashed from the room and brought back a handful. Nora tried to stop shaking, to act casual as she scooped up the remains, took them to the toilet, and flushed them. She watched the tissue swirl around the bowl and disappear.

"That was gross." Sophie's giggle was high-pitched and tight.

"It was this big!" Ellie spread her arms a foot apart, unsteady, unsure. Measuring herself by Sophie's mood, imitating it.

"I think it was furry," Sophie added. "And it had teeth." She bared hers, making spider faces that were less than scary since she was missing her front teeth.

"This is how Mommy smooshed it." Ellie imitated the moves, slashing the air. Again. And again.

Sophie laughed.

The killing was already becoming family lore. Nora would be the hero of the story, and the spider, the hideous villain.

The coffee Nora had been drinking came back up. She swallowed, forcing it down, hugging the girls and pushing away memories. Wondering if bullfighters felt sick after a kill. But never mind. It was done. On some level, she marveled at how easy it had been. How, at the moment of impact, she hadn't felt any resistance, might as well have been striking the empty floor. She wadded up the piece of drawing paper, stained with spider remains, and tossed it into the trash can.

"Girls." She steadied her voice. "Clean up your toys and wash your hands."

It was almost dinner time.

SATURDAY, JULY 19, 1993

Nora's tongue pushed against her upper lip as she concentrated on bending the red string behind the blue. She tied a knot and repeated the step with the red string behind the black. Red behind yellow and then purple. The row looked good.

Before starting a new one, Nora leaned back and gazed out the sliding doors. In the yard, the leaves of the apple tree and dogwoods were perfectly still. Nothing moved, not a squirrel or a bird. Even her mother's wind chimes hung limp and silent. Earlier, she'd heard the boys next door shooting baskets in their driveway, but not now. Now, it was too hot even for them. Nora stared at the trees, wondered if they felt the heat. Did they get thirsty? Lonely? Bored? Did trees feel anything at all?

Canned laughter drew her attention to the TV, a *Saved by the Bell* rerun that Nora hadn't really been watching. She had seen the episode tons of times. But she liked the show, the way all the kids got along, the ease of their friendships. Their acceptance of Screech even though he was annoying. Not to mention that Zach was *so* cute. And sweet—like now, when his arm was around Screech's shoulders, reassuring him that he wasn't a total loser.

A commercial came on. Nora went back to bracelet weaving. Checking the tape that secured the finished end of her bracelet to the coffee table, she repositioned herself on the hardwood floor, her back against the sofa, her legs sprawled out. Holding four strings taut, she worked the fifth through them, following a pattern she'd learned at camp. Blue behind black, knot. Behind yellow, knot.

She was tying blue behind purple when Tommy clumped down the stairs. She hesitated mid-knot, tensing.

Shoot. Why did he have to come down where she was? Why couldn't he stay upstairs in his dark room developing his bug pictures, or in his dark stuffy bedroom doing whatever he did in there with the door closed all by himself? She steeled herself, preparing. If he messed with her, she'd ignore him. This time, she would pretend he wasn't even there until he got bored and went away. She wouldn't get mad: that's what he wanted.

"Yo, pissface." Tommy never called her by her name. Mostly, he used a variety of terms reflecting bodily waste. If she reacted, he got encouraged and even more obnoxious. So she didn't react.

He joined her, plopping his skinny annoying self onto the sofa, setting his ant farm smack on top of the tape that secured her strings, taking his camera out of its case.

Nora tried not to cringe. Why why why had he brought his stupid bugs with him, let alone dumped them exactly and precisely where she was knotting? Stupid question. He did it because he was Tommy. Her older brother lived to bother her, gross her out, scare or make fun of her. Well, she wasn't going to let him. She would ignore the farm and concentrate on her knots. Where was she? Yellow behind purple?

But Tommy wouldn't let her ignore him. Holding his camera, he climbed off the sofa and hunched on his knees right beside her, so close that she could feel his body heat and smell his peculiar odor, a combination of sweet and stale, musk and warmth. She could even smell his breath. He must have had bologna for lunch.

"I know you don't like them." He aimed his lens at the plexiglass case. "But I don't get why. Look at them. See how nice they are? Nobody's stuck up or thinks they're better than anybody else. Nobody gets in fights. Not like people. Ants are actually better than people."

Only her brother would say a thing like that. The more odious they were to others, the more Tommy loved them. He watched his ants the way she watched *Saved by the Bell.*

She kept knotting, sorry that she'd looked at them. They made her itch, the way they never stopped moving, scurrying through their tiny tunnels, digging, crawling with all those legs. Yuck. But she couldn't let Tommy know that. If he knew, he'd stick them in her bed or her underwear drawer. Tommy repositioned himself, shooting their pictures from various angles.

Why couldn't he go hang out with his friends and leave her alone? Oh. Right. Because Tommy didn't have any friends. Because he was the weirdest, most annoying, dorkiest kid ever. And he had nothing better to do than torment his younger sister.

Tommy stopped shooting and frowned. He put his camera down and, without asking, peeled Nora's tape off the table. Nora held onto her strings with one hand and smacked him with the other.

"Don't—Tommy, leave that alone!"

He reattached the tape a few feet away. "Your string's ruining my shots."

"So? Go take your stupid pictures someplace else. I was here first."

"Tough. The light's good here."

Nora reached for the tape, peeled it off, and replaced it where it had been.

Tommy didn't comment. He watched until she was finished, then unfastened the tape and moved it away again.

Okay. So that was how it was going to be? A silent move-the-tape fight? Should she engage? Escalate things by moving his farm? Nora's heart pounded out her anger, but she resumed knotting, determined not to lose track of her pattern, refusing to get distracted by her older brother, his tense bony frame, his thick matted curls with the permanent cowlick on the crown of his head, the angry pimples blossoming on his fuzzy, bristly, unshaven chin, the strange musty sweet smell of his body, his clicking camera. Nora concentrated on strings, on colors, on pattern. She knotted black with yellow, purple, red, and blue. But no matter how hard she tried, she couldn't ignore the persistent movement of hundreds, maybe thousands, of tiny swarming creatures just a few feet away. Their motion nagged at her, and the nagging grew until she felt them crawling—not just *on* her skin, but *under* it—as if she herself, her body, was the ant farm and the tiny things were swarming inside her.

Ridiculous. She needed to ignore them. But the itching wouldn't stop. Nora held the strings in one hand, scratched her arms and legs with the other. She stretched her neck, took a breath, and assured herself that no bugs were on her, let alone in her limbs. She couldn't let Tommy get to her. One of her mother's homilies rang in her head: *Don't make a mountain out of a molehill.* Or an anthill?

Tommy knelt, adjusted his f-stops, clicked the camera again and again.

Nora wove the next row with purple, forming fours and tying knots. But—oh God—her neck tickled. Her back. *Cripes.* Holding her threads in place, she checked the farm. It was intact. No bugs had escaped. She'd just had a tingle. An unrelated itch.

Tommy nudged her arm, leaning over her to take a shot. She shimmied away, swallowed the urge to pound him, and tied red behind blue. Wait, that wasn't right. Shouldn't it have been purple behind red? Crap. She'd messed up her strings, all because of

Tommy with his stupid camera and ants. What was he doing? Why was he so close?

She looked up, came face to lens with Tommy's camera. "What—are you taking my picture? Don't." She turned away.

But Tommy scooted around the table, tracking her movements and clicking pictures. "That's great. You look really annoyed. Now look at the ants. I want to get your expressions."

Nora took a breath, closed her eyes. Do not react, she told herself. Do not let him see that he's getting to you. She made her face placid and calm, opened her eyes and focused on her string.

"I said, look at the ant farm."

She didn't.

Tommy stopped taking pictures. He picked up the television remote and turned off *Saved by the Bell.* Aiming the camera at her, he clicked a few times. He was trying to provoke her into making faces so he could take embarrassing photos, but Nora was on to him. She ignored him, sorted her strings, and began a new row of purple.

Tommy picked up the ant farm and held it up to Nora's face. "I told you to look at the ants!"

Nora closed her eyes but sensed thousands of tiny legs, their incessant motion. She heard Tommy breathe in his bologna breath. And without looking, she pushed the farm away.

Tommy pushed back, harder, crouching now, pressing his weight against hers so that the farm was caught between them.

Nora dropped her string and used both hands, thrusting her weight against his. Tommy leveraged his position, using his whole body to shove the ant farm into her face. He was taller, weighed more. She couldn't resist for long. The muscles in her arms trembled, her shoulders burned. Finally, she simply let go.

Tommy fell forward against her. They rolled backward, Tommy half on top of her. The ant farm, launched by the force of his weight, flew across the family room and crashed into the bookshelf, slamming onto the hardwood floor. For a moment, neither of them moved. They lay stunned, out of breath. Then Tommy's eyes went wide.

"No!" He bellowed and ran to the farm. "Look what you did, you little shit! Go get a jar or something!"

Nora looked across the room. The plexiglass wall of the ant farm had come loose, spilling sand and a legion of ants out onto the floor. Tommy was frantic, trying to block their progress, to scoop them up and force them back into the broken farm. But it was no use. They were free, their line heading directly toward Nora. She clambered onto the couch.

"Nora! Get me a fucking jar."

When she didn't, he spun around, swinging his fists, pummeling her arms and torso. Nora curled into a ball, protecting herself until, finally, he stopped pounding, grabbed a fistful of ants, and dashed upstairs. Nora fought tears. The punches hurt, but she wouldn't let Tommy make her cry. Damn him and his stupid bugs. Eyeing them, she backed toward the stairs, but stopped as Tommy ran down with a saucepan. He brushed past her and, kneeling over the ants, he cupped his hands, trying to recapture them and drop them into the pot. Ants crawled all over his arms.

"Tommy, they'll get all over the house."

"I know that. Don't you think I know that, you fucking turd?" He swung the pan through the air, yelling, "Look what you've done!"

"What I've done? You're the one who shoved—"

"Shut up! You just shut up!"

The ants were halfway to the coffee table. Nora's knees felt weak; she hugged herself, toes curling.

Tommy was wild eyed. He dropped some more into the pot. Brushed a few from his arms, scrambling to rescue them.

Nora eyed the advancing column. Soon, ants would be up the walls, on the shelves, the table, the sofa, the stairs. Tommy sat defeated, watching their escape. But only for a moment. In a flash, he was on his feet, clicking his camera, recording the shattered ant farm, the parade of survivors.

Nora had no choice. She'd have to fix this herself. Grimacing, she leapt off the sofa and didn't stop, didn't look down. She dashed out the sliding doors into the heat, past the silent wind chimes and motionless trees, to the garage where she grabbed the bug spray, and hurried back into the family room, dreading what she'd find. She expected Tommy to fight her, but he didn't. Tommy was fully engaged, hopping and kneeling around the room, bending low, capturing shots and snapping images, while bugs crawled onto and over him.

Stomach churning, Nora held the can high and aimed. She blasted them all, even the ones on Tommy, who kept shooting, recording the slaughter as one by one, ants shriveled and died, including the big, gross, fat one still in the broken farm that must have been the queen.

When she was finished, Nora took a deep breath and counted until her mind went blank. She deposited the broken farm into the trash and brought back a broom to sweep up the corpses before their parents got home from work. Tommy didn't help. Without a word, he took his camera and went upstairs to his room.

In the commotion, Nora forgot all about her bracelet. Hours later, she found it on her pillow. All that was left of it was an unraveled, tangled wad of string.

FRIDAY, AUGUST 10, 2018

When her phone rang, Nora ran up the steps to the kitchen and grabbed it off the counter. Her hands were still shaking as she checked the caller ID.

"Dave?"

Early in their marriage, he'd call without a reason. He'd talk about nothing in particular, saying he just wanted to hear her voice. Back then, they'd been more connected. Now when Dave called, it was most likely to say he'd be home late. He had client appointments, partner meetings, depositions, trials. Lots of reasons to miss dinner.

"Nora, what's wrong?"

How had he known something was wrong? All she'd said was his name.

"Nothing." Adrenaline still pumped through her body, but she wouldn't take up his time talking about a spider. Not while he was at work.

"So, don't count on me for dinner tonight. Depositions to prepare for the Langdon case. It's a nightmare."

Nora knew Dave's voice as well as she knew her own, and she recognized the lie. The almost undetectable tensing of his vocal cords was as clear to her as a fire alarm. Nora bit her lip. She held the phone, not speaking, and gazed out the kitchen window. She could almost see the heat. The children's swings hung completely still. The weeping willow drooped; the oak tree's leaves didn't rustle. The lawn needed mowing. And moss covered the slabs of slate along the garden path. Theirs must be the most unkempt yard in all of Bryn Mawr. When were the mowers coming? Tuesday?

She remained silent, deciding not to make it easy for him.

"I'll be as early as I can."

Nora still said nothing. She remembered other times that he'd lied. Painful and pointless confrontations had resulted from calling him out. Havoc caused by some trivial fib like a bill being paid late, or a doctor appointment that wasn't kept. And then came the bigger lie, the one when she'd been pregnant with Ellie. Afterward, he'd sworn he'd never cheat again, so this lie wasn't like that one. This lie, whatever it was about, had to be insignificant, not worth cornering him.

The girls stampeded into the kitchen. Sophie's curls had come completely free of their elastic bands and bounced as she ran.

"Nora? Okay?" Dave asked. As if it mattered what she thought. As if her opinion could alter his plans.

"I'll try to make it home before bedtime. If not, kiss the girls for me."

Nora told him that of course she would and hung up, bothered.

Almost five-year-old Sophie stood beside her, tilting her head and blinking her wide, quizzical eyes. Sophie often looked at Nora this way, wordlessly asking, "What's wrong?" As if Nora would define the world for her, explaining the significance of each individual incident that occurred. At that moment, Sophie's eyes were a mix of violet and red, matching her purple T-shirt. In the morning, they'd been yellow like her pajamas. Her eyes were chameleons, constantly changing, mirroring whatever was close to her.

"Were you talking to Daddy?" she asked.

"Yup."

"Why are you mad at him?"

Lord. Had she sounded mad? Was she that transparent? She'd have to be more careful with her voice.

"I'm not mad." Nora made herself smile. "Why would I be mad at your daddy?"

"Because I bet he's not coming home for dinner again," Sophie said.

"Daddy never comes home for dinner." Ellie's voice was matter of fact, disinterested. Her eyes were brown, like Nora's. Steady and deep, they seemed the opposite of Sophie's, not emitting light but sucking it in, drinking it.

"He comes home when he can, pumpkins. He works hard to take care of us, and he wants to be here for dinner. But tonight, Daddy has to work late. I'm disappointed, not mad." Nora continued to smile as she wiped her hands on a dishtowel.

"You looked mad when you were talking to him."

Christ. Couldn't she let down her guard for a single moment? Why did Sophie always have to be watching her, missing nothing? She tossed the dishtowel onto the counter.

"Sad and mad. Mad and sad," Ellie repeated in singsong. A year older than Sophie, she often sounded younger.

Don't count on me for dinner tonight.

Why was she so bothered that Dave wasn't coming home? Probably she wasn't. Probably she was still upset about the spider and its eight long leaping legs.

"So. Supper." Nora cleared her throat and gave a cheery grin. She tried not to think of arachnids or where Dave would be at dinnertime. "Go wash your hands."

"Chicken fingers?" Ellie sat on one knee, chewing her thumbnail.

"Ellie, stop that." Nora raised an eyebrow. Ellie's hand shot away from her mouth and stayed behind her back as she followed Sophie to the powder room.

Nail biting was only one of Ellie's issues. She also was afraid of the dark, of being alone, of bad dreams—so much so that she couldn't sleep in her own room and instead stayed in Sophie's. Ellie didn't mix easily with other kids, often preferring to play by herself. Nora assured herself that all of these behaviors were merely developmental, nothing to worry about. After all, the girl was not yet six years old.

Even so, Nora did worry. Because, before the nasty, mean-spirited, teenage Tommy, there had been a young, shy, quirky and quiet Tommy who had been a loner, playing by himself, never having a single friend that she could remember. Unless she counted insects.

Never mind. Ellie was nothing like Tommy. God, no. Nora took chicken fingers out of the freezer as Ellie, back from washing her hands, began folding dinner napkins into perfect rectangles, seams straight, corners aligned.

No, it wasn't the spider. It was Dave. The lie in his voice. *Don't count on me for dinner.* What was he lying about?

Nora needed to relax. She handed Sophie forks and knives to set out and asked Ellie to get a box of macaroni from the cupboard. She filled a pot with water.

While they waited for the water to boil, she and the girls washed nectarines and grapes. They peeled and sliced bananas and cut a cantaloupe for fruit salad.

As supper took shape, Nora was oddly conscious of her movements. Kneeling, reaching, lifting, turning, slicing. She held her stomach tight and her shoulders erect as she took out a bowl for the fruit salad. She dumped macaroni into bubbling water, performing her role as mom even as she kept hearing Dave's voice with its subtle tautness. *Don't count on me for dinner tonight.*

"Why didn't you tell Daddy about the spider?" Sophie watched the macaroni boil.

Nora saw it again, leaping through the air, scampering over the floorboards. Her back rippled and arched. "He was busy."

Her hands trembled as she stirred milk and powdered cheese onto the noodles. How absurd to be so affected by a smashed spider. People killed things all the time. Mosquitoes, flies. Mice. And how about meat? Eating a chicken finger required killing a chicken. Killing was a normal part of daily life. Carefully, Nora opened the oven and took out the cookie sheet. She placed pieces of chicken onto plates. When she turned off the stove, she heard the gasp of an expiring flame.

There was no deposition. Dave had lied. In fact, lately he'd been lying a lot.

Nora dished out fruit salad with a sprinkling of shredded coconut. If she were less sure of Dave, she might suspect that her husband, whose intense gazes could still roast her flesh, was having another affair.

But he would never. Last time, he'd wept. For a full six months he'd begged her forgiveness, promising his eternal love, fidelity, and honesty until she'd finally taken him back. Knowing what was at stake, he wouldn't risk cheating again. No. It had to be something else. She and Dave were fine.

Even so, the syllables burned: *af-fair.* Nonsense. Not possible. Dave was devoted to her.

She poured two glasses of milk. Sophie asked for ketchup, so Nora squirted some onto her chicken.

*Don't count on me. Don't count on me. Don't count on me.
Don't count on me.*

When was the last weeknight Dave had been home for dinner? She couldn't remember. Damn. Nora stood at the kitchen counter, her mind taking off, showing her pictures of Dave pressing himself against some other woman, kissing her, unbuttoning her shirt, reaching inside and sliding his fingertips under lace. Acid spread through Nora's throat, burning her lungs and stomach, dissolving her marriage, her life. *Don't count on me for dinner—*

"More mac and cheese, please!" Ellie called. "Mac and cheese, please!" She pounded her fists and rattled the dishes, laughing and yelling. "Mac and cheese, please!"

"Ellie! For God's sakes, stop!" Nora's voice sliced the air. She spun around, her eyes narrowed. She'd been louder and shriller than she'd intended. Her hand rose, grabbed a chunk of her hair.

Ellie went silent and pale.

Sophie stared at Nora, stunned, as if she'd been slapped.

Oh God. What had she done? Nora ran to hug them, first one, then the other. "Sorry. I'm sorry, Ellie. I didn't mean to yell."

No. She hadn't meant to yell. Not at them, never at them. She kissed Ellie's cheeks and held Sophie's head to her chest, inhaling the blend of herbal shampoo and kid sweat. She assured them that Mommy loved-loved-loved them and was just tired. Everything was fine. Of course they could have more mac and cheese. Only next time don't bang the table. And guess what? After supper, they could have ice cream from the truck when it came by. Nora made herself sound cheerful as she released them. She pushed her hair behind her ear and gave Ellie a wink. Watched her girls eat with gusto.

What had she just done? Inventing scenarios that got her upset and then snapping at her children? Dave's late nights were legitimately about work. He was a lawyer with a demanding practice. She'd overreacted because his phone call had come right after she'd battled that hideous arachnid. She'd transferred her adrenaline-soaked fury onto poor, over-worked, loyal, lovable, sleep-deprived Dave.

Yes, that was what had happened. Silly woman.

Nora got herself a fork and put the extra mac and cheese into a cereal bowl. She sat with her girls and chatted about camp, swimming lessons, and mosquito bites. She refilled their glasses of two percent and smiled, not letting on that she kept seeing a grotesque creature dodge and contort as it tried to escape her blows, or that she kept replaying the actual kill, wondering at how easy, how darkly exhilarating it had been.

Was that Craig Treschler? Oh God, it was.

Nora slumped down in her seat, trying to be invisible. What was Craig doing there, on the day camp bus, wearing a Main Line Tadpoles T-shirt? Only counselors wore those. Wait, was he a counselor? At her camp? How? Why? She couldn't breathe, couldn't move. Yes, it was him, for sure, sun-tanned and muscled, looking chipper even now at the end of a long, blistering hot day. Chatting with the driver before starting down the aisle.

Don't sit with me. Don't sit with me. Don't even look at me. Keep walking. Why was he stopping? Oh God. He was grinning, baring his big white teeth. The better to eat you with. What was he grinning at? Was it her? She froze, dreading what he'd say or do. Had he recognized her? Would he mock her? "Why, look who's here, it's the scumbag's sister!"

Nora clung to her camp bag and looked out the window. Was he still standing there? What if he grabbed her camp bag? What if he taunted her?

Out in the parking lot, parents had lined their cars up to collect campers who didn't ride the bus. One or two at a time, the camp director escorted kids into back seats and buckled them in, their faces red from exertion or their hair damp from the pool.

Nora stared but didn't see the kids, their mothers in their cars, or even the bus. Instead, she saw herself on her bike after school on a June day. She had stopped at the corner before crossing the street as a bus growled slowly up the hill, spewing black exhaust.

It was the Lower Merion high school bus—Tommy's bus. As it passed, she heard shouting and saw a commotion inside, something zooming over the kids' heads, arms reaching to grab it. Were the kids playing catch? On her bus, everyone had to sit still and be quiet. They couldn't shout, let alone play games. Was it different in high school?

Something flew out a window and crashed onto the bushes along the curb. A book? It couldn't have been. Who would throw a book? She turned, saw that it was, yes indeed, a book lying open on top of an azalea bush. As the bus chugged up the hill, another book tore through the air, pages flapping and fluttering until it flopped into the gutter in front of Mrs. Carlson's house.

What was going on? In the excitement of playing catch, had someone's books fallen out the window? Puzzled, Nora rode up the steep street, racing the bus, so she could tell the driver that someone had lost their books.

"How'd you like soccer today, dude?" Craig's voice startled her, brought her back to the present. He was standing next to her, talking to a little boy in the seat directly in front of her.

The kid wasn't scared though. He beamed, telling Craig about his game, how he'd scored a goal and almost scored another one. Nora kept her head turned toward the window, told herself that Craig wouldn't recognize her. And if he did, he wouldn't pick on her, not here, not in front of the little campers. Not with the bus driver able to hear.

Although the bus driver had done nothing for Tommy.

And there it was again, the memory. Nora had waited at the bus stop to tell the driver about the books, out of breath from racing her bike uphill.

The bus doors folded open and the driver yelled, "No more roughhousing, you two. Next time, you'll walk home, the both of you."

And, oh God, Tommy tumbled out backwards into the street, landing on his butt and scuttling backwards like a panicked crab as Craig Troeschler jumped off and followed after him, swinging Tommy's empty backpack. Tommy raised his hands, protecting his head. The doors closed and the bus chugged away with a dozen noses pressed against the windows.

Nora tried to stop remembering. She concentrated on the parking lot. On the yellow Volkswagen door opening for a girl about seven years old, dressed in magenta and white striped leggings and an orange tie-dyed tank top. Focus on those stripes, Nora told herself. On colors and patterns. On mismatched clothes. Or cars. But while the Volkswagen's door closed, her memory played on, and Craig's voice boomed at Tommy.

"Don't ever take my seat again! Hear me, you sorry piece of shit? Next time you see me standing on the bus, what are you going to do?"

Craig whapped the backpack at Tommy's hands and head, and Tommy turned away, dodging and cowering. His face flushed crimson, even darker where black fuzz grew in unshaven patches along his jaw.

Tommy muttered something.

"What? I didn't hear you." Craig's grin gleamed, vicious. He kept swinging the canvas bag.

"I said I'll get up and give you the seat." Tommy hunched, arms protecting his head.

"You'll give me the seat?" *Slap.* "What else will you do?" *Whap.* "Say it."

"I'll go away."

"Wrong!" Craig bent over him, growling. "What will you do?"

"Crawl. I'll crawl away." Tommy's voice was husky. A swallowed sob.

Craig stopped smacking and jeered. "That's right, crybaby douchebag. You'll get on the ground with the rest of the dirt and crawl out of my sight." He threw the book bag at him, spit at the ground, and sauntered off across the street.

Toward Nora.

Nora didn't move, couldn't. What had just happened? Craig Troeschler was an older kid who lived in a red brick house up the street. What did he have against Tommy? And the driver—he and all the other kids on the bus must have seen what Craig was doing. Why hadn't they stopped him? Unless—

The realization hit like a slap. It appeared like a rewind, like scattered shards unshattering and reconnecting into an unbroken whole. In a short, silent moment, Nora knew that the game she'd seen on the bus hadn't been catch. It had been kids playing keep-away with Tommy's books, tossing them back and forth and, finally, out the window.

It was why he hid in his room and never invited anyone over. Why he slunk around without making a sound. She'd known he wasn't popular or cool. But the truth was far worse: Tommy, her big brother, was the brunt of jokes. He was a wimp who got bullied. A loser. A freak.

Nora's whole body went numb. She wished she hadn't seen what happened. It wasn't her business. She wasn't part of it, had nothing to do with it, had stumbled into it by chance. What should she have done? Intervene? Stand up for her older brother and confront an even older, bigger Craig who had just acted meaner than anyone she'd ever seen before, who even on that warm spring day was wearing a black biker leather jacket that matched his greased-back shoe-polish-black hair? Nora didn't know what her role should be, how she should act, so she did nothing. Even when Craig walked right up to her, standing at the bus stop with her bike, she said nothing. For a flickering heartbeat, she thought, oh God, he was going to pick on her for just standing there, witnessing, or for being Tommy's sister. Did he know she was his sister? But he passed her by without the merest glimpse, not even a grunt.

Tommy looked up, then, probably to make sure Craig was gone. For an endless, permanent, never-to-be-forgotten moment, brother and sister stared at each other in silent recognition of Tommy's humiliation, his perpetual victimization, his tormented hopelessness. When finally Tommy wiped his eyes and climbed to his feet, Nora didn't go to him. When he brushed himself off and started down the hill to reclaim his books, she didn't help. Later, at home, they didn't tell their parents what had happened. Neither of them mentioned it, not ever.

But months later, Craig was on her camp bus, a counselor where she was, at twelve, just a counselor-in-training. He wore no gel in his hair and gave cheerful high fives to a little kid. Would he recognize her from the bus stop? Connect her to Tommy? Taunt her for the whole ride home?

Nora pictured her brother hunched in the street, promising to crawl in the dirt for Craig. Letting Craig defeat him. Something surged in her belly, searing and sharp. She sat straight and looked directly at Craig, catching his eye.

"How ya doin'?" He winked and took a seat across the aisle.

She narrowed her eyes. Nora wasn't like Tommy. Just let him mess with her. She wouldn't cower. No, if Craig picked on her— if he said one mean word, she'd fight back and make him bleed.

"Wait, don't I know you?" He sat back, half smiling.

She ought to tell him who she was and what she'd seen. Her hands went clammy and her belly somersaulted.

"Don't think so," she said instead, half-smiling back.

"I'm Craig." His smile broadened, revealing straight white teeth. He was actually kind of cute. Dark and hunky. Mischievous sparkling eyes.

Tommy had groveled at Craig's feet. But she wasn't like Tommy, didn't want to be like him. Silently, she counted. One, two, three... until she shoved her nerves aside.

"Nora," she said, as if she didn't even know Tommy or anyone else with that name.

FRIDAY, AUGUST 10, 2018

The girls had been fed, bathed, tucked in, and read to. Their bathing suits had been washed and the dishes were done. Nora was in bed, reading. Well, not really. Really, she was staring at page thirty-something, picturing Dave in various sexual positions with the Other Woman, who she'd again imagined might possibly exist. She wondered how late he'd be and whether she'd work up the nerve to ask him about it. She imagined that conversation, what he would say. He'd be surprised, of course. Would he deny it? Or would he laugh at the absurdity of the idea and reassure her? More likely, Dave would be baffled by her suspicion but flattered by her jealousy. He'd take her in his arms and hold her, promising that he was hers and hers alone, that she could trust him.

But what if he didn't? What if his eyes grew somber and his shoulders slumped, silently admitting it? Would he beg for forgiveness again? Or pack a bag and leave? Lord. Nora closed her eyes, told herself to stop being ridiculous and dramatic. She had no reason to imagine such a dire and unlikely scene. Dave was neither having an affair nor leaving. Their marriage was solid. Nora clutched her book, and stared at the words, the letters shimmying on the page.

The girls were still awake, whispering and giggling in Sophie's room across the hall. Nora hoped they'd continue to be close, no matter who got custody. *Good Lord.* Where had that come from? She was out of her mind. Had she really imagined a divorce? She needed to stop. There was no other woman. End of story.

Bullshit. If he really loved Nora, he'd have come home for dinner not just tonight, but all the nights he'd stayed out late. She'd forced herself to be cheerful, meal after meal, while his seat at the dinner table remained vacant. She'd pretended, for the girls' sake, that it was normal for daddies to stay at work into the night, that everything was fine. But the girls weren't stupid. They sensed something was off—after all, Ellie was biting her nails and Sophie was always asking questions, picking up on Nora's moods even when Nora tried to hide them.

Across the hall, Sophie shrieked.

"Sophie," Nora called. "Quiet down."

"But Ellie said another spider might be here."

"Don't worry. There's no spider in there."

"There might be." Ellie sounded certain.

"Mommy!" Sophie shouted. "What if one climbs in my bed?"

Nora took a breath and set her book on Dave's side of the bed. She got up and crossed the hall. Her daughters made her turn on the light. They got out of bed and huddled behind her while she examined their sheets, the floor under both beds and dressers, the closet, shelves, curtains and windowsills. Finally, as she tucked them in again, she heard the front door close.

It was barely eight-thirty. Very early for a passionate date. Unless his girlfriend had to get home. Maybe she was married, too. Maybe she had kids. Who the hell was she?

She wasn't anybody, damn it. She didn't exist.

"Hello?" Dave's baritone barreled up the stairs. "Where are my girls?"

"Daddy! Daddy!" Ellie and Sophie jumped out of bed, screaming, ran to him and leapt into his arms.

Nora stepped back, watching, caught off guard by the open affection of her family. Obviously, she was wrong about the affair. Dave really was working extra hours. Without thinking, she offered her cheek for him to peck as he passed. The girls trailed as he tossed his suit jacket, briefcase, and phone onto their bed. Sophie and Ellie chattered about their day at camp, about Sophie doing big arms in the pool and Ellie learning the frog kick. They pulled his hands, dragging him to their room. Dave glanced at Nora long enough to shrug and roll his eyes in feigned help-lessness, a captive of his manic, adoring daughters.

Nora smiled, not so much at Dave as at the delight the girls took in capturing their father. Who could blame them for being so excited? It was a rare night when daddy was home before they were asleep. For a moment, she listened as they each offered to read to him, vying for his attention. Then she went back to bed, climbed into her side, and picked up her book.

And noticed his phone lying beside her on the crimson floral comforter.

TUESDAY, JULY 22, 1993

Warm water poured over Nora's head, rinsing pineapple-coconut scented shampoo bubbles over her eyes. As she soaped her legs, she wasn't thinking anymore about Craig, how friendly and outgoing he'd been on the bus, or how awkward she'd been in her hesitant response. Nor was she thinking about her two best girlfriends, Natalie and Charisse, who were both away at sleepover camp for six whole weeks, leaving her alone with her pathetic counselor-in-training job and her dorky brother, whom she also, for sure, was not thinking about. No, as Nora stood sudsy in the shower, the single thought in her head focused on the evil-demon poison ivy rash above her ankle. It raged and itched like a plague from hell even after a whole week. Nora could deal with being friendless for a summer. She was okay with being a CIT, herding four and five-year-old kids back and forth to the pool, playground, bathroom, arts and crafts room, or bus. She didn't even mind that she wasn't getting paid one single dime. But poison ivy? That, she minded.

Her ankle screamed to be scratched, but she wouldn't give in. She had learned that scratching made it worse. So she held the rash directly under the shower spray, hoping that the water might soothe and quiet the itch. Instead, the pulsing aroused it. The itch surged to life, exploding into a furious rampage. Even then, Nora resisted. It took all her will power, but she didn't scratch. She turned the knobs and made the water hotter, with any luck, hot enough to scald the rash and sear the itch away. How could she have known that the rash would feed on the heat, guzzling and swallowing it, licking its lips, swelling, burgeoning, intensifying until finally, it crushed Nora's resolve. She squatted, her fingers hungry like talons, reached for her ankle, tore at her flesh.

Beyond the shower curtain, something clattered.

Nora stopped scratching and listened, heard only the splash of water against the tub. Something—maybe her hairbrush—must have slipped off the counter. Except brushes didn't just fall on their own. Nora leaned forward and peered around the shower curtain. The mirror, clouded with steam, showed no reflections. Her towel was draped over the counter, and a clump of dirty clothes remained on the floor. Her hairbrush was beside the sink.

She turned the water off, reached for her towel. Watched the last soapy bubbles swirl around the drain. Her ankle no longer itched, but blood dripped where her nails had ripped skin.

Something clicked. A door closing?

Nora whisked the shower curtain open. Steam fogged the room, dimming a shapeless damp ghost that blurred her brother's form. Nora screamed and, in a heartbeat, covered her body with the towel.

Tommy wore his idiot grin, amused.

"What the hell, Tommy?" she shrieked, securing the towel.

"It's about damn time you get out of there."

"Get out!" she sputtered. "What are—Why are you in here?"

"Why do you think? I'm waiting for a bus?" Clutching the strap of his camera case, he took a step back. "I needed to piss."

She could always tell when he was lying. His eyes shimmied and his lips pursed ever so slightly.

"Are you kidding? While I'm in the shower?"

"I had to go."

"Bullshit." She clutched the towel.

"Why else would I come in here? To sneak a peek? What, at you?" He forced a laugh. "Don't make me puke."

"Wait—" She eyed his camera. "Were you taking pictures?"

"I'd rather eat glass than look at your flat chest and skinny butt. You're insane." He stepped toward the door, his hand tight around his camera strap.

She didn't move, just stood there holding up her towel. "Where are you going? I thought you needed to use the bathroom."

He stopped, didn't look up. "I did."

"What? While I was in here? Liar. You didn't. You spied on me in the shower. Admit it."

"You're full of shit." His smirk failed, and his face reddened. "So what if I came in? I had to take a piss and couldn't wait three hours for you to get done with one of your Guinness book showers."

Something hot and furious erupted in Nora's chest. She wasn't a little kid anymore. She was twelve years old. She'd already had two periods and owned a training bra. How dare he?

Nora charged into her room and slammed the door. Her mother would be home from work any minute, so she practiced what she'd say. She phrased it carefully so that her mother wouldn't dismiss her as a tattle tale, pronouncing that everything was okay, and Nora was just overreacting. That Tommy hadn't done anything wrong, that family was family and Nora had to be flexible. She rehearsed in front of her mirror, revising and rewording until she came up with lines that she thought worked.

"Mom, I'm uncomfortable about something and need to ask you how to handle it." Starting that way didn't blame Tommy for anything, might even flatter her mom because Nora was asking her advice.

By the time her mother came home from work, though, Nora had begun to doubt herself. Maybe she was overreacting. Maybe she really did take long showers and Tommy really had needed to use the toilet. Maybe he hadn't sneaked a peek or taken pictures. Maybe she was going to get him in trouble for no reason.

She replayed her shower, the itching, the steamy heat, the unexplained sounds. The look on Tommy's face when she'd opened the curtain and found him standing there, tongue-tied for an excuse. No, she wasn't wrong. For sure, he'd done something sneaky. Nora took a last look in her mirror, practiced her lines once more, and headed down the hall to deliver them.

Her mother was in her bedroom, still in the rumpled clothes she'd worn to work. Her rose-colored slacks matched the paint on the walls, the print on the floral bedspread, and the tones of her nail polish and lipstick.

"Mom?" Nora began. "Something's bothering me." She hesitated when her mother didn't look up.

Her mom stood beside her dad's open closet, one of his suits draped over her arm and a piece of paper in her hand. She stared at the paper, her shoulders wilting, hair hanging limp around her cheeks. Nora couldn't see her face.

Nora began again. "I need to ask your advice."

Still her mother didn't move, didn't answer. What was so important about that piece of paper? Was it a phone message? A receipt?

"Mom, Tommy spied on me. In the shower." Well, so much for rehearsing. The words had burst out on their own.

Her mother looked in Nora's direction but seemed to be looking into the distance, not at her. Her face was gray, her mouth slack. Her hand grasped the paper.

Nora's chest fluttered. "Mom? Are you okay?" Had something bad happened? Had someone died?

"What? Yes. Of course, I'm fine." Finally, her mother registered Nora's presence. She stuffed the paper into the pocket of her slacks. "Take my advice, Nora. Don't look for trouble unless you're prepared to find it."

Nora blinked. Was her mother trying to say that by telling on Tommy, she was looking for trouble?

"I'm not the one looking for trouble, Mom. Tommy is. Can you talk to him?"

Her mother's eyes jolted, refocusing on the clothes she was gathering. "Nora, can we talk later? I've got to get your father's suits to the cleaners."

"Mom. He came in while I was in the shower."

"I'm sure he had a reason, dear. Don't be so dramatic." She rifled through the closet, removing a blazer. She paused for a nanosecond before reaching into its pockets.

"Dramatic? Tommy follows me around with his stupid camera. I get no privacy—"

"Nora, stop." Her mother tossed the suit and blazer onto her bed and ran a hand through her hair, exposing the gray roots. "I work all day and come home to cook and do chores. All I ask of you is that you get along with your brother. You're not little kids anymore, I can't referee and solve all your petty disagreements. If you and Tommy have a problem, you're old enough to work it out yourselves."

Nora's mouth hung open. Was her mother serious? "He doesn't listen to me—"

"Why doesn't he? If you want him to work with you, Nora, try being nicer to him. You aren't exactly an angel here."

"What did I do?"

"Really? You want a list? How about breaking his ant farm?"

"But I didn't—"

"A word to the wise: you can't catch flies with vinegar."

No, Nora supposed that she couldn't. But she didn't want to catch flies. And neither vinegar, nor fly-catching—nor Tommy's ant farm—had anything to do with her problem.

"I just want him to respect my privacy."

Her mother seemed harried, distracted. She scooped the clothes off the bed and drew a deep breath. "Nora honey, it's time you learned. In a relationship—any relationship—you have to pick your battles."

"What battle—"

"Your brother has a brilliant, inquisitive mind. He's not your average kid, he's unique. You need to appreciate him and stop wasting energy on small stuff. Communicate. Compromise. Always be willing to give more than you get. That way you can coexist in peace." Promising to be back in half an hour, Marla hurried out of the house. The edges of that piece of paper peeked out of her hip pocket.

Nora, riddled with advice, was on her own.

FRIDAY, AUGUST 10, 2018

Nora set her book down and eyed the phone, half-hidden in rumples of rose floral comforter. From across the hall, she could hear Dave reading Dr. Seuss. He'd be busy for a while.

But no, she wasn't going to be that kind of wife, one who checks up on her husband, who monitors his phone calls. If she did that, soon she'd be reading his texts and email, or stalking him when he went out.

Don't look for trouble unless you want to find it.

How many times had her mother given her that warning? A thousand? If it wasn't the most frequent Marla Quotation, then it was definitely in the top three. Nora could see her, her crimped chin-length hair dyed medium ash-brown, her nails filed into rose-colored ovals, and her lips painted a shade of rose, always rose, never a deeper red or lighter pink.

A memory surfaced of Marla standing in her bedroom with a piece of paper clutched in her fist. "Don't look for trouble," she had breathed, "unless you want to find it."

At the time, Nora had been, what, eleven years old? Twelve? She'd walked in on her mother examining the paper, had watched as her mother's fingers tightened around it, crushing it. What had that paper been? A receipt for a hotel room? For jewelry? A love note? Nora couldn't imagine. Her father, Philip, had been a pharmacist, a balding guy with glasses and a voice like talcum powder. Not a player.

So why had her mother's nostrils flared and her eyes glowered? Why had she sighed so deeply before uttering her advice? *Don't look for trouble.*

Probably she hadn't glowered, sighed, or slumped. It was more likely that Nora had embellished the memory, turning it into some unsolved parental mystery. Besides, her advice was hardly unusual. Marla had had tons of adages: If you expect nothing, you won't be disappointed. Let well enough alone. Don't cry over spilt milk. Don't rock the boat. What you don't know can't hurt you. Things can always get worse. No matter what, family comes first.

Nora rattled through half a dozen more before realizing how utterly sad they were. Had her mother been depressed? What had Marla been like as a young woman, before she'd been a mother spouting tired adages? Back in the '70s, as a teenager, had she been popular? Had her heart ever been broken? Or had Philip been her first love? Had she been happy in her marriage?

What had she found in his pants pocket?

Across the hall, Ellie pleaded, "Now read this one, Daddy. Please?"

"No, Ellie! My turn to pick!"

Dave explained that it was already past their bedtime and overruled their argument that, in summer, they had no bedtime. The girls begged and cajoled, not letting him go.

But he was finishing up. Time was running out. Nora eyed his phone. All she had to do was pick it up, turn it on, and press an icon or two to see if anyone was habitually calling or texting him. And if the habitual caller/texter was a woman, Nora would find out who she was and what she was texting.

Don't look for trouble, Marla's voice echoed.

But her mother hadn't followed her own advice. She'd taken the paper from her husband's pocket. Besides, wasn't it better to know the truth?

Nora picked up Dave's phone. Pushed the button that lit the screen saver. Younger versions of Sophie and Ellie popped up. They were standing in front of a Christmas tree wearing Santa hats, Sophie's mouth open in laughter, Ellie's stretched into a clownish grin. The shot had been taken by a professional photographer a few years ago, back when they'd still sent Christmas cards. How old had the girls been then? Two and three? It was sweet that Dave had this picture as his screensaver, with Sophie's curls pressed into Ellie's cheek and their eyes catching the light. Nora's finger went to the picture, tracing the line connecting their faces, gently touching their noses, their chins.

Raucous laughter erupted across the hall. Dave's baritone growled, playing a monster. Were the girls out of bed again? Would they scamper into her room, trying to escape bedtime by hiding under her covers?

If she was going to learn anything, she had to act now. She punched in Dave's password. She'd known it since Ellie had been a baby, since the day a car had run a stop sign and T-boned them, crushing the driver's side door. Ellie, in her car seat, had been unharmed. Dave had taken the brunt of the impact—a dislocated shoulder and a cracked rib—so Nora had used his phone to call for help. Where had they been going that day? The mall? The grocery store? Nora didn't remember, but she remembered the password: Stolilime.

Bingo. Dave's phone came alive. Now, all she had to do was press an icon.

She hesitated, fingers shaky. How harmless the phone seemed, tiny enough to fit in a pocket. Looking at it, no one would guess that this sleek, skinny rectangle could be life-shatter-ing. At least, marriage-shattering.

Don't—her mother's rosy lips whispered—*look for trouble.*

Nora took a breath. Her mother was wrong. Finding trouble was different than causing it. If Dave was cheating, his cheating was the trouble, and it would still be trouble whether she found out about it or not. Wouldn't it?

Maybe not. Didn't she already know everything she needed to know about Dave? He was home now, earlier than she'd ex-pected. His presence meant something, didn't it? Even if he was having an affair, which he wasn't, not after last time, but even if he was, he wasn't letting it keep him from his family. It must only be a phase and it would pass.

After all, Dave was committed to Nora. He depended on her. She'd helped him prep for his bar exam, picked out the suits he'd worn to interviews. She'd given birth to his children, after labor-ing and popping hemorrhoids and enduring his peppy relentless coaching for twenty-three and seventeen agonizing hours. When his father died, he'd clung to her, weeping. No flimsy affair would be enough to destroy or even dent their marriage, that's how closely their shared history bound them.

They'd barely recovered last time. It had taken years. After that, after what they'd been through, he would never. She was almost absolutely sure.

Nora clutched the phone, her hand stiff like a crow's claw. Her throat closed, refusing to take in air. Her children's voices faded, sounded far away.

Thunder rumbled outside. Nora turned toward the window, surprised to see rain slashing at the pane. The day had been cloud-less. Where had the storm come from?

Across the hall, Dave's reassuring voice was saying goodnight. "Remember," he said, "you're safe. There's nothing to be afraid of."

Nora glanced at the phone, the doorway, back at the phone. Just before Dave walked in, she pressed the off button and put it back exactly where he'd tossed it. Instead of snooping, she would simply muster the nerve to ask him straight out. She had a right to know. She was his wife.

When he walked into the room, Nora made herself smile. "What a storm—"

"They told me what you did."

What? Her eyes went to the phone. How could they know?

Dave scowled as he unbuttoned his shirt. "What were you thinking? Were you trying to scare them?"

What was he talking about?

He sat on the bed and took off his shoes—shiny black slip-ons with tassels. "For God's sake, Nora. You didn't have to slaughter it."

What? Oh. The spider?

Lightning flashed, overpowering the lamplight and for a moment turning the room and Dave ghostly white.

"They said you freaked out."

She'd freaked out? The girls had been hysterical, screaming for her to kill it.

"It was really big."

"They showed me how you kept pounding it after it was dead. They said pieces of it were flying everywhere."

Well, that was true. Nora cringed, remembering. "It took all my nerve, Dave. You should have seen it. It was gigantic. It actually jumped, and then it ran. I was afraid it would get away."

"You should have let it go," he said. Dave stepped out of his slacks, hung them up. If she looked in a pocket, would she find an upsetting piece of paper? Nonsense. Dave's side of the closet was open, displaying his suits, hand-made and expensive, arranged in a neat row, organized by color and fabric. Nora's favorites were the charcoal pin stripes that complimented his graying temples. But today, in the heat, he'd worn a taupe shade of summery wrinkle-free linen. He hung the jacket over the pants.

"I should have let it go loose in the house? Are you kidding?"

Thunder clapped outside, sharp and followed by another flash of lightening.

"No, I'm not kidding. Why kill it? It was only a spider." His face was severe. Gravely serious. Why did he care so much about a stupid spider?

"Only? Oh my God, Dave. It was huge. You weren't there. The girls were screaming—"

"Oh, come on, Nora. We've talked about this. We agreed to teach the girls respect for animals—all animals."

He had nothing on now but his briefs. Some men looked silly, but Dave looked good in underwear. His shoulders were wide and muscled. His abs were still discernable under a belly just soft enough to be considered mature. His chest and legs were solid and dusted with just the right amount of soft brown hair. Best of all, though, was his butt. Tight, round, and not too narrow. Nora wondered if the Other Woman appreciated that butt. And thinking of her, how was Nora supposed to broach *that* subject while Dave was fixated on the assassination of a spider? Maybe this wasn't the right time. Besides there was no Other Woman. Dave's persistent lateness was because of depositions and various client meetings, just as he claimed, and his crankiness was due to stress.

Dave's phone lay exposed on the comforter beside the briefcase, feigning innocence.

"Nora, seriously. You know how sensitive and impressionable they are. Ellie's so nervous she bites her nails and won't sleep in her own room."

"Dave. The girls are fine."

"Really? Can't you see how your behavior today affected them?" He stood beside the bed with his arms extended, as if arguing a case before a jury in his Jockeys.

Nora kept her voice low so the kids wouldn't hear. "Of course I see. I showed them how to face up to fear and take charge even when they're scared."

Dave smirked. "I don't think so. I think you showed them that it's okay to slaughter an innocent creature."

What? Why was Dave seriously making an issue out of a dead spider? Nora wasn't going to apologize. Nor was she going to defend herself and mention that she'd actually considered setting it free until it jumped and scared the bejeebies out of her. She ran her hand through her hair, and a lock flopped into her eye. "Dave. Get over it. It was a spider."

"Exactly," he gestured grandiosely, exhibiting his biceps and triceps. "A living thing that had just as much right to live as a parakeet or puppy—"

"So, what would you have done, Doctor Doolittle? Pick it up and pet it? Invite it to tea?" She crossed her arms, tilting her head up to meet his eyes.

"I'd have picked it up, yes. I'd have carried it outside and let it go free. I certainly wouldn't have gone postal on the thing."

Nora fumed. "Fine. Next time I see a mosquito biting you, I won't swat it."

"I'm just saying you could have made an object lesson out of it."

"So, I guess we're vegans now. You wouldn't want to encourage the slaughter of an innocent chicken."

"Come on, Nora. All I'm saying is you should try to set an example, okay?"

Another clap of thunder. A flash of lightning spilling through the windows.

Nora's brows furrowed. What was Dave doing? Why was he so being critical? He couldn't really care that she'd killed a spider. She listened to the water running, to the brushing of his teeth, the rinsing, the spitting. She waited, preparing. When he finally came to bed, she'd plain out ask him. She practiced the words in her mind: Are you having an affair?

Rain pelted the windows. Lightning flashed yet again, casting stark light over the room. In an eyeblink, Nora saw the rumples in the comforter, Dave's shoes on the floor, the doorway out to the hall. The phone.

No, she couldn't ask him outright. Maybe she should rephrase her question. What's the real reason you were late tonight? Or, Dave, are you hiding something from me? No. Both were too accusatory. However she phrased it, Dave would react poorly. Already irritated about the spider, he'd declare that he was working his ass off and that, instead of appreciating the stress he was under and encouraging the effort he was making to support their family, his wife was accusing him of hiding things from her. He'd turn it around, blaming her for being suspicious. "Dammit, Nora," he'd snap. "I'm doing my best. I love you. Why isn't that good enough?"

But what if, as he proclaimed his love, she detected a dishonest quiver to his voice? What if she saw a lie in the small muscles around his eyes, a minuscule twitch or twitter?

The toilet flushed, the water ran again. In a moment, he'd come in.

Nora lay back against her rose-colored pillowcases, closed her eyes, breathed deeply, and told herself to stop inventing trouble and trust him. She waited to feel his weight on the mattress, to share a goodnight kiss.

"Mommy?"

Nora lifted her head. Sophie stood at the door, her eyes wide, head tilted as if asking, "Mommy, what should I think? How should I feel? What's going to happen?"

The storm had frightened her, she said. But Sophie was intuitive, and Nora suspected that the storm that scared her daughter wasn't the one raging outside.

Nora guided Sophie back to her bed and stayed with both her frightened girls until their eyelids drooped and their breathing steadied. When she came back to her own room, Dave was on his side, softly snoring.

In the morning, Nora recalled that his phone had rung sometime deep in the night. Dave had taken the call into the hall, whispering so he wouldn't disturb her. Or so she wouldn't hear.

FRIDAY, AUGUST 6, 1993

The first time Annie asked Nora to her house, Nora stopped breathing. Her face got hot and her heart somersaulted so violently that she was almost unable to answer. It wasn't that Nora had never been to another kid's house. She'd gone to Natalie's or Charisse's a hundred times, ever since first grade. But Annie? Annie was the coolest girl going into sixth grade, if not in the whole middle school.

Annie had long, straight, dishwater-blonde hair, usually French braided. She was taller than Nora and could do cartwheels. She had neon pink braces on her upper teeth. And—how cool was this—she wore a regular bra. Most of the girls at school were jealous of her. Every single boy had a crush on her. Nora hadn't been in her class last year, but she'd ridden the same school bus, never imagining that the last week of camp where they were both CITs, Annie would notice her and want to be her friend.

Somehow, Nora had managed to articulate the word, "Sure."

And, once at Annie's house, Nora did her best to cement a friendship. She acted like Annie, mimicked Annie's hushed way of speaking, laughed when Annie laughed, even took almost an hour to fix a French braid just like Annie's. Her efforts seemed to work. Annie began confiding in her, gossiping about other girls, telling Nora what boys she liked, complaining about her strict parents and three older sisters. Annie even admitted that her bra was filled with tissues and gave Nora one of her sister's bras so Nora could do the same.

As weeks passed and middle school started, Nora began to trust the friendship. She shared homeroom and English class with Annie and spent less time with Natalie and Charisse, who, by comparison, were dull and immature. But when she was at Annie's house for the fourth or fifth time, Annie said a few words that threatened to ruin everything.

The visit had started off fun. Annie's sisters had friends over too, and while everyone was distracted, Annie motioned for Nora to accompany her upstairs. Nora followed Annie into a long white-tiled bathroom that reeked of hairspray and was cluttered with brushes, hair dryers, toothbrushes, lotion bottles, deodorant, nightgowns, and damp towels. She felt a pang of jealousy, imagining what it must be like to live there, to have sisters—normal siblings who got along, who she could actually talk to, or even have fun with. Annie opened a cabinet and took out a jazzy pink razor and a spray can of foam.

Nora watched with trepidation as Annie pushed the shower curtain back, sat on the side of the tub, slathered her legs with shaving cream, and ran the razor along her skin. She rinsed and dried her legs under the faucet and then held out the can of shaving cream for Nora.

Annie's laugh was the tinkle of a bell. Light glowed in her eyes. "Your turn."

Nora heard her mother scolding. *What's your hurry? You're too young. Don't rush things.*

But the situation was clear. Nora had to choose: Did she want to be cool like Annie or not? She pictured Tommy, alone with his bugs and his camera, friendless, the butt of jokes.

With the sense that she was doing something terribly wrong, she took the can and sprayed foam onto her leg. It tickled, especially around her poison ivy. She tried to keep her hand steady as it slid the razor up her leg like a plow through snow, leaving a bare track.

She told herself that her mother wouldn't notice. When was the last time she'd looked at Nora's legs? And Annie was laughing, saying how sexy Nora's legs were. They slathered on skin lotion and ran their fingers up and down each other's smooth, silky skin. Giggling, they checked under each other's arms to see if there were any hairs there to shave. They discussed the other hair sprouting between their legs, even peeked into each other's panties to compare.

"I'd be dead if Heather found out I shaved my legs." Annie put the razor away.

"Heather?"

"My mother."

"You call her Heather?"

"That's her name, isn't it? My father is Kirk. Why? What do you call your parents, Mommy and Daddy?" She asked it as if the idea were absurd.

Nora imagined calling her parents by their names. Marla and Philip? They would freak if she addressed them that way. Still, why shouldn't she? Those were their names, weren't they?

"I'm serious," Annie went on. "I'm the baby, and you wouldn't believe how strict my parents are with me. Thank God they're so clueless."

They went back downstairs and were eating fresh banana bread when Annie said those few unexpected, devastating words. "Next time, let's go to your house."

Let's go to your house. The words hurdled at Nora, bashing her face, ricocheting inside her skull. Nora stopped chewing. Banana bread stuck in her throat, almost choking her. She should have anticipated this situation, should have been prepared. All these weeks she'd pretended to be just like Annie, when really, she was nothing at all like Annie, whose house was always full of cool kids and noise and the aromas of cakes baking and roasts roasting.

What should she say? Sorry, no. I don't want you to see my brother? What would Annie think? She'd think Nora was weird and creepy. She'd stop being her friend. Nora fumbled, didn't know what to say. So she said, "Sure."

Annie gulped milk and asked her to describe her room. She asked what her house looked like, what it was like to be an only child. Nora's stomach twisted, and she stumbled over her words, changing the subject before she had to tell Annie that she wasn't the only child, that she had a brother. Talking instead about boys, a topic Annie never tired of. Making up a story, that she'd heard Luke liked Christine. Anything to change the subject.

It worked, for now. But sooner or later, she'd have to figure out a reason that Annie couldn't come over.

Cripes, it wasn't fair. It wasn't her fault that Tommy was so embarrassing that she'd never even mentioned him to Annie. If Annie came over, Tommy would sneak around, peeking and snapping their pictures. Annie would hear all of Tommy's gross names for her, like Piss-face. He'd barge in with his disgusting bug collections. Or he'd just slink around with his musty smell and unshaven, zitty face, and uncombed hair, showing Annie that Nora wasn't her caliber. That she was the sister of the neighborhood loser, the kid everybody picked on no matter what, always had, always would. The kid that got tossed out of the school bus. It wasn't right, wasn't fair that Tommy was her brother. *He's unique. He has a brilliant mind. He's not like average kids.* But she wanted him to be average. Or at least not so embarrassing.

Why should she have to miss out on a normal life just because of him?

By the time she got home that night, Nora was determined to set things right. Her mother—no, Marla—was dipping pieces of flounder into milk and breadcrumbs. Nora didn't hesitate. After all, her cause was righteous.

"I want to invite my friend Annie over."

Marla kept dipping. "Okay."

"But I don't want Tommy around."

"Well, that's kind of unreasonable." Her mother turned to her, holding a limp piece of fish. Milk dripped onto the floor. She lowered her voice. "Your brother lives here, too—"

"Tommy Tommy Tommy Tommy." Nora's voice was too loud. "Everything's always about Tommy. Let's build him a dark room. Let's buy him a freezer for his bugs. What about me? Can't I ever have anything just for myself, without Tommy ruining it?"

"Nora, what's got into you?"

"He's weird. Face it. Nobody likes him."

"Nora—"

"Nobody. But he doesn't like them either. He just likes his bugs."

"That's enough."

"Kids make fun of him."

"Nora, stop—"

But Nora couldn't stop. "He smells bad. He doesn't use deodorant—"

Upstairs, a door slammed. Had Tommy been listening? Well, tough if he had.

"And I don't want people judging me because of Tommy."

"Okay, that's it." Her mother slapped the fish onto the plate, sent breadcrumbs flying. "Who exactly do you think you are, some perfect, flawless princess? Too good for your family? Let me remind you something, Miss Fancy Prima Donna. Tommy is different because he has a unique and brilliant mind. More important, he's your big brother. Your blood. Which means you stick up for him no matter what. Friends come and go, but family is forever."

"Why should I stick up for him? He only cares about himself."

"How can you say that? Tommy loves you."

"No, he stalks me. He pinches me and calls me names."

"That's how he shows affection. He's at an awkward age, Nora. He's having a rough adolescence and doesn't know how to act. But he'll grow out of it and be amazing. Besides, who are you trying to impress? I don't know this girl Annie, but if she's really your friend, she'll accept your brother the same way Charisse and Natalie do."

Nora rolled her eyes. "Charisse and Natalie are so lame."

Marla's eyebrows rose. "Oh? Since when? You've been friends forever."

"Not for ages. I've outgrown them." The conversation wasn't going as planned. Nora's eyes filled with tears. "Look. All I'm asking is to have a friend over without Tommy messing it up. Why can't he schedule a driving lesson that day? Or stay in his room with his bugs."

"I'm not banishing him, Nora. Invite your friend over, she's welcome in our home. But it's Tommy's home, too."

"That is so not fair!"

"Hello? Life isn't fair." Breadcrumbs caked her mother's fingers as she picked up a towel and glared.

From his room upstairs, Tommy thumped on the floor, doing God knew what.

Nora spun around and left the kitchen, stomped up to her room.

Her mother's voice followed, telling her to wash up and set the table. Dinner would be ready in fifteen minutes.

Later that evening, Nora called Annie and said she was sorry, but when they'd talked earlier, she'd forgotten that her house was being renovated and men were working inside. So, it wasn't a good time to have friends over and wouldn't be for a few months. Nora stopped breathing, waiting for Annie's reaction. Annie accepted the lie, suggesting they go to the mall instead. Still, angry tears blurred Nora's vision.

SATURDAY, AUGUST 11, 2018

On Saturday morning, Dave dropped the girls in Gladwyne at his mother's for their weekly visit and went to his tennis match. Despite having a heart condition, Edith loved having the girls, baking cookies, setting out good china for tea parties, making ragdolls, helping them dress up in her old clothes and high heels. Nora didn't go along, respecting her mother-in-law's time with her grandchildren.

Instead, Nora welcomed these mornings as time for herself. Usually, she tackled chores or hit the gym before going to book club or brunch with friends. But that day, she sat on the sofa doing nothing. Just listening to the faint electric hum of the house, its appliances, its air conditioning. Watching rays of light pour through the windows onto a sea of tiny floating flecks of dust. Staring at the rich hardwood floors, the Persian area rugs and baby grand that had been her grandmother's, the pristine crystal and porcelain pieces that had been handed down through generations. Replaying Dave's departure.

He'd rushed the girls out the door, shouting an abrupt goodbye. Had he taken his racket case? Of course, Nora had seen it in his hand. But had she caught a whiff of his cologne? Why would he wear cologne to a tennis game? He wouldn't. She must have imagined it.

Good God, was this her new normal, doubting Dave's every move?

No. She wouldn't. She wasn't going to be that kind of wife. She would take her husband at his word. Dave said he was playing tennis, so he was playing tennis. He loved tennis, played every weekend with Ted Oliver, his doubles partner. She needed to stop fixating on this imagined infidelity, get off the sofa, and stop watching dust settle. Get dressed. Exercise before book club.

Fine, yes. She'd do all that. But first, maybe she'd just call Ted's house and check to see that he was playing today. She could pretend that Dave's phone was turned off and she had a message for him—like she wanted him to pick up some milk on the way home. Except, no. She couldn't do that. It was embarrassing, underhanded. She didn't need to check up on her husband.

Nora headed into the kitchen, telling herself that she was going for a cup of coffee, not for her phone which happened to be on the counter beside the coffee pot. But as long as it was there, she picked it up and punched in her code.

Don't look for trouble, her mother hissed. But Nora ignored her, imagining the conversation instead.

"Hi, Jeanie," she'd say when Ted's wife answered. "Hey, did Ted leave yet?" And when Jeanie said, yes, he'd gone, Nora would say, "Okay, sorry, never mind. It's nothing important."

But what if Jeanie said, "Leave? No, he's right outside washing his car." Or mowing the lawn. Or sleeping. Or whatever.

In that case, Nora would stutter and fumble, having uncovered a heart-swallowing lie.

Better if she didn't call. Better not to know.

Nora set her phone down and poured coffee, carried the mug to the table, sank onto a chair. Eyed the remnants of breakfast. Half a bowl of soggy corn flakes afloat in two percent. A crust of toast smeared with grape jelly. An empty juice glass.

A banana peel.

Nora's shoulders eased. Her stomach unknotted. Dave always ate a banana and a granola bar before tennis. The banana peel testified that he hadn't lied, that he was indeed playing tennis. That there was no affair. Which of course she'd known all along.

Nora danced around the kitchen, clearing breakfast dishes, arranging them in the dishwasher, wiping jelly stains off the counter. She took comfort in the mundane normalcy of chores, the way they underscored her roles as wife, as mother. When she finished, she headed upstairs.

In the shower, she scrubbed until her skin was ruddy. She would not be the kind of woman who suspected her husband was cheating. She would be proud, confident, self-assured. She would not doubt Dave. His word was gospel. His love, a given. Nora blow dried her hair, carefully dabbed foundation onto her face, applied eyeshadow, mascara, and just the right shade of plum lip gloss. She selected a bright floral print sundress that covered her still-after-almost-five-years-not-totally-faded stretch marks and showed off the definition in her upper arms, the muscled length of her legs. She stepped into strappy sandals. Ensemble complete, she stood in front of the full-length bedroom mirror, pretending to meet herself for the first time. What would her impression be of the woman in the mirror? Was she too noticeable in bold yellow, magenta, green, and purple? Was the fabric too flimsy for a strong body with ample breasts? She stepped closer to the mirror, examining the chin-length, almost black hair, the occasional strands of white. The deep brown eyes. Were they too intense? Were the eyebrows too thick? The nose too thin? And the lips—were they just a tad too wide? What did all these parts add up to? Was she pretty? Would women admire her? Would men find her attractive? Would Dave, if he saw her for the first time today?

Nora stood straight, twirled, struck a pose looking over her shoulder at the mirror. Turned, stuck her hip out and posed again, pretending to be saucy. She practiced a broad smile that would seem confident and proud. The secure smile of a woman adored by her husband, children, relatives, and friends. When she was sure she could be convincing, she grabbed her bag and phone and hurried downstairs.

SATURDAY, AUGUST 11, 2018

The bloody mary at Don's Firehouse was a meal in itself—rich with horseradish, a big stalk of celery, and juicy, fat olives skewered on a toothpick. Nora checked the time on her phone. Where was Dave now? Had he finished with tennis? Was he having a beer? Calling his girlfriend? Stop it, stop it, she scolded herself. What's wrong with you? Be with your friends.

Barbara was disheveled, having arrived late. She sat across from Nora, all harried and flushed and apologetic. Barbara stood out in the group, partly because she wore a diamond ring the size of an avocado pit and looked like a runway model, but mostly because her husband was a newly-announced candidate for the U.S. Senate. Barbara didn't flaunt it though. If anything, she seemed to treasure the company of her run-of-the-mill suburban mom book club friends.

"Sorry." She swung her highlighted hair behind her shoulder. "It was Oliver's fault."

Oliver, their new seventeen-hundred-dollar Welsh Corgi puppy, had chewed up a pair of Paul's fifteen-hundred-dollar Italian loafers. Paul had been furious, yelling and threatening to turn the poor thing in to the SPCA. The kids had cried hysterically, and the nanny had been unable to calm them. It had been a complete meltdown with little Colin and Harry locking themselves in the bathroom with the puppy until Paul relented. He ended up promising on his mother's life not to get rid of Oliver. After that, she'd had to fight traffic on the Schuylkill to get into Philadelphia.

Barbara ordered a mimosa, thought about it, then called to the waiter to bring two.

Nora tried not to stare at Barbara or let on that she doubted her story. But she did doubt it. She didn't know Barbara's husband, Paul, very well—he was always out of town for business or, lately, his campaign—but she doubted that a public figure like him would so easily lose his temper. And, from what Barbara had said, Paul had been raised on a Main Line estate where he'd had menageries of animals—horses, cats, dogs. Surely, he'd know how to deal with a puppy and wouldn't have allowed it near his good shoes. But why would Barbara go to the trouble of concocting such a story?

Nora studied Barbara's strong cheekbones, her freckled, sunburned, surgically-perfected nose. Her sparkling, highlighted hair. Her jingling, gold bangle bracelets.

Barbara must have felt Nora's stare. She turned to her with twinkling eyes and a startlingly cheerful smile. Nora smiled back and looked away, refocusing on the conversation, preparing to say something about this month's book.

But no one was talking about *Where the Crawdads Sing*. It had been Katie's choice, and Katie wasn't even there. She was home with a sick kid. But it didn't matter, because club members seemed disinclined to discuss the book. They were more interested in discussing some television series that Nora hadn't watched. Nora positioned her lips into a pleasant smile and let go of the conversation. She scanned the half-full restaurant, looking especially at couples. Were they on dates? Married? Had one of them ever cheated? Were they cheating now? A man noticed her and met her gaze. She averted her eyes as if she hadn't been studying him. Overhead, a huge wooden rowing shell was suspended with—she counted one, two—eight extended oars. Under it, the front walls of the restaurant had been folded back, opening the place to tables on Fairmount Avenue. Nora wondered how they kept the heat from flowing in. She thought of Dave, playing tennis in that heat. Where was he now?

"Bottom line, I just can't stand her acting," Patty said. "She's totally flat. Her face never changes. She never shows emotion or raises her voice."

"You want your lemon?" Alex plucked it from Nora's drink before she could answer.

"That's deliberate. She keeps a poker face so no one can tell where she stands." Barbara spread cherry compote on a corn muffin.

Patty nodded. "Well, she's doing a good job. You can't tell if she's happy or sad, telling the truth or lying, guilty or innocent, friend or enemy."

"But that's her character," Barbara said. "She's a lawyer. They're all like that."

Nora raised an eyebrow. "What do you mean, 'they're all like that'?" She looked from one face to another. They all knew her husband was a lawyer.

"She's talking about the show." Patty dismissed the question. "She didn't mean real lawyers."

"You'd get it if you'd watched the show." Barbara crinkled her perfect nose, scrunched her shoulders. Nora didn't understand the body language. Was Barbara trying to be cute?

Alex reached over and gave Nora's hand a squeeze as if to say, "Hang in there, we'll be done with television talk in a minute."

Meantime, they discussed the upcoming series finale, predicting which plot points would be resolved and what the cliffhanger might be. Nora only half listened. She sipped another bloody mary and chomped a piece of ice. Did her friends really think lawyers were dishonest? Did they think Dave was? Was he? Would he have been more honest if he hadn't become a lawyer, if he'd been, say, a dentist? She pictured him in a white jacket, probing a patient's mouth with an instrument. The patient became a woman, and the instrument his tongue. Nora shut her eyes, shivered just a little. She was being irrational, beginning to obsess.

"I wish she'd dump him," Alex said. "How many affairs has he had now?"

What? Who? Was everyone thinking about affairs? Smiles and nods.

"Too many to count." Patty began listing the women.

Barbara sipped mimosa number three. "His wife is just about the only one he doesn't screw."

Everyone laughed, then paused to chew biscuits and corn muffins, to sip drinks.

Nora toyed with her wedding ring. "So, you're saying she should divorce him?"

Three heads turned to her.

"Catch it on Netflix, Nora." Patty swallowed her biscuit. "You know the actor—Steve Harding."

Nora wasn't sure who that was. She pictured someone tall and handsome who strongly resembled Dave.

"The guy has political ambitions, and he uses everyone, especially his wife," Patty said.

Nora glanced at Barbara whose husband also had political ambitions.

"But she can't divorce him," Patty continued. "I mean, deep down he loves her."

"Seriously? He doesn't love anyone. He loves power." Alex reached for another muffin.

"No, he loves her," Patty insisted. "He always comes back to her."

"Because he can. Because she doesn't have the balls to confront him." Alex bit off a chunk of celery.

"She knows he's cheating?" Nora asked.

Nobody answered. Patty munched. Alex scowled. Barbara shrugged.

"Not sure," Alex said. "I mean, she should. But like they say, the wife is the last to know."

"Bull," Barbara spoke with authority. "If wives don't know, it's because they prefer denial to facing the truth. If your husband is cheating, you've got to know something's off."

"But on the show, she doesn't see it even though it's right in her face." Patty popped the rest of a biscuit into her mouth.

"The only reason she doesn't dump him is that it's a television series and they need to keep the tension up for like, thirteen episodes. In real life? She'd have sent him packing three seasons ago." Alex crossed her arms.

"Is anyone else cold? Think they'd turn the air down?" Barbara asked.

No one else was cold. Patty told Barbara that being cold was her punishment for being thin. She needed to put on weight like the rest of them. Body fat would keep her warm. Barbara gave Patty the finger. Alex gave Barbara her cardigan.

Nora finished the bloody mary and watched drops of red juice slide over the last of the melting ice. "Let's say it wasn't a TV show. Would you still think she should kick him out?" She directed the question to Barbara.

Barbara blinked. "But it is a TV show."

"Right. But in real life, should an affair end a marriage?"

"Oh God, Nora. You're not having one, are you?" Patty gasped.

"You can tell us, if you are." Alex lowered her voice. Her eyes seemed hungry.

The three of them leaned forward, resting their elbows on the table, blinking at Nora like starving crows. None of her friends had any idea about five years ago, what Dave had done, what Nora had forgiven.

"Of course not." Nora made herself laugh. "I'm just asking."

"She's thinking about it," Barbara told the others. "Well, take my advice, Nora. Don't do it."

"How can you tell her not to?" Patty grinned. "You of all people."

Wait, was Patty joking? Had Barbara had an affair?

"Shut up, Patty." Barbara slapped Patty's arm. "Don't be a bitch."

"Seriously," Nora pressed on, facing one friend, then another. Smiling to make her questions seem harmless. "I mean, Barbara, if Paul had an affair, would you kick him out? Patty, would you divorce Ronny?"

The women started tittering.

Patty scoffed. "Ronny? No mere woman could lure him from his beloved recliner."

Alex said that, between his plastic surgery practice and training for marathons, Ed had no time for one woman, let alone two. "Plus, he's too disorganized to make a haircut appointment. How could he arrange secret trysts?"

"Paul would never." Barbara's husband was campaigning for the Senate, so despite his good looks and opportunities, he wouldn't risk bad publicity. Besides, he openly doted on Barbara, sending her flowers and love notes, calling her several times each day even when he was out of town.

"Fine, so none of them would cheat," Nora said. Was she the only one whose husband had strayed? Was she a chump for staying with him? "But what if they did?"

The others looked at her, losing their laughter as if they sensed her urgency. Patty's eyes narrowed. Alex stared at Nora, brow furrowed. Barbara sat at attention, studying her drink.

"I wouldn't want to know," Patty said. "I'd hope Ronny would make sure I didn't find out."

"Really? You'd want to be lied to?" Nora's chest tightened. "Because for me, the lying would be even worse than the cheating. How could you ever trust him again?"

"If I didn't know about it, it'd be the same as if it weren't happening. At least as far as I was concerned. What's the old saying? What you don't know can't hurt you?"

Alex shook her head. "I'd want to know. If Ed's keeping secrets that big, the marriage is over. Isn't it?"

"That's what I'm asking." Nora tried to make her voice sound playful. "I mean, could a marriage survive?"

"Not mine," Barbara said. "Paul would never cheat. And if I did, the marriage wouldn't survive, and neither would I. Paul would kill me."

Alex laughed. "For sure, murder would be involved at my house too. I'd kill Ed's ass."

"Not me," Patty said. "What good would Ronny be if he's dead? I'd divorce him and take every cent he ever earns."

"No, you wouldn't," Barbara said. "You'd never divorce Ronny."

Patty folded her hands and sighed. "You're right. I'd stay with him and make his life hell. He'd spend the rest of his days trying to win my forgiveness."

The waiter delivered two Caesar salads with grilled chicken, a barbecued brisket sandwich, and Nora's black-eyed pea soup. They ordered more drinks. Around them, the room buzzed with conversation and the clinking of utensils on plates.

As they ate, Patty told them to come clean. Had any of them ever cheated?

Nora set down her soup spoon, wondering. Her gaze moved to Patty's familiar round face and heart-shaped mouth. She'd known Patty since high school. Patty would never cheat, could never keep secrets, especially big ones. Alex was a tennis player, a golfer, a dieter. A stickler for the rules, so she was also a no. What about Barbara? Nora wasn't sure. Barbara was an unknown, with her perfect hair, enhanced breasts, elegant jewels, and perfectly manicured nails. She'd met Paul when she'd been a dealer at a casino, mingling with high rollers. *Hmmm.* Maybe.

Nobody volunteered anything.

"Okay, so no one's admitting actual cheating," Patty went on, "but has anybody been tempted?"

Alex sat back and straightened her arms, as if pushing the question away.

Barbara studied the remains of her salad, folding her hands on her lap. "Don't you guys think we should talk about the book?"

"Screw the book," Patty said. "Don't dodge the question."

Alex cleared her throat. "Of course, I've been tempted. Who hasn't? Hot men are everywhere. I mean, have you seen the butt on our waiter?"

Laughter. Nods. Admissions. Flicks of hair and bites of lunch.

Nora put on a grin but didn't say anything. Her friends probably wouldn't believe her, but she'd never been tempted to cheat on Dave. Sure, there were men she considered sexy—Barbara's husband, Paul, for example. But Paul's sexiness was merely a fact, like his eye color or profession. It didn't involve her.

"So, if we're playing truth or dare," Barbara swallowed mimosa, "I'll need a few more drinks."

Everyone laughed, maybe nervously.

"With Paul around, why would you ever look at anyone else?" Patty asked. "He's a heartthrob. It's like he stepped off a GQ cover."

Patty and Alex listed bellies, baldness, hairy shoulders, and other reasons as to why their husbands would never adorn magazine covers. Barbara remained silent.

They all had too much to drink. By the end of lunch, Nora was shocked to learn that Patty had lost her virginity to Mr. Kohl, their high school swim coach. Alex had had an abortion sophomore year of college. And before Paul, Barbara had partied with her share of high rollers and done lots of cocaine.

When Nora's turn came, she searched for a secret that would match the level of their confidences. Tommy shot into her mind. "Why not tell them about me?" But Tommy was a secret she would never share. So, she had nothing.

Her other secrets were mundane—shaving her legs even though her mother had said she was too young. Or junior year of college, getting an extension on a term paper because of her dog's death when she hadn't had a dog. *Yawn.* Boring. Nora needed something juicy. But what? She thought of Dave and his secrets. He must be done playing tennis. Was he in a hotel room with another woman, his tennis racket lying beside the bed? Stop it, she told herself. Just stop.

Finally, she told a partial truth about experiencing serious post-partum depression after Ellie. Nobody seemed impressed so she embellished, telling them of a day when, exhausted, sore from breastfeeding, and drowning in diapers, laundry, and baby throw-up, she'd thought seriously of suicide.

Patty's mouth dropped. "God, Nora. Why didn't you call me?"

Nora's face got hot. She'd gone too far, made her story too extreme, made herself sound over-the-top too different. *Weirdo. Freak.*

Patty looked stunned and hurt that Nora would have kept such a big secret from her. She promised that she would have been there and made Nora get help. Nora wanted to back up and erase her story, replace it with something more normal. But she was committed to it now. She reached across the table and took Patty's hand, explaining that, back then, she hadn't been able to articulate her feelings. By the time she could, her depression had lifted and there was nothing to talk about.

Patty's face relaxed. Nora's remained hot, flushed with shame for lying. But she'd wanted to fit in with her friends, to provide a story that made her seem as interesting as they were. And her contemplation of suicide had worked, because afterward, they started telling stories about their own lowest moments.

They shared who'd taken antidepressants, which ones, and for how long. Discussed seasonal depression, light therapy, hormones and PMS. Going to work or staying home with the kids. Nora drifted, offering occasional comments so that she'd appear to be engaged. Lifting the corners of her mouth so she'd seem light-hearted. Glancing at her phone to check the time. Eventually, Alex reminded them that they had yet to discuss the book they'd read, and everyone laughed.

"I liked it," Barbara said.

"Me, too."

They'd all liked it.

"Good. Anybody got anything else to say about it?" Patty asked.

No one did.

"Next time, we should stay on topic," Alex said.

Patty reminded everyone what the next book was and where they would meet.

Nora got home around three, after three bloody marys. Dave's car wasn't there. The girls were still at Nana's. Alone with floating dust particles and faint electric hums, she put her handbag on the table in the foyer. She didn't allow her face to relax and her shoulders to slump until she was upstairs, in the privacy of her room.

THURSDAY, SEPTEMBER 23, 1993

Home. Finally. Alone. No need to say the right thing, hang with the right group, or stand, walk, sit, smile, yawn with the right attitude. Hot, crampy, and eager to lie down, Nora lugged her book bag up the front porch, past the empty, unused, wicker rocking chairs and the wind chimes that made no sound in the stillness of the simmering, unnaturally exhausting, late September afternoon. She unlocked the front door, went straight to the kitchen and opened the refrigerator for a drink. The lemonade pitcher was empty. Of course it was. Stinking Tommy must have finished it and been too lazy to wash it out. She left the pitcher there. Maybe Marla would be annoyed when she saw it. Maybe she'd even scold him for once, though probably not. Tommy was her angel. *He's brilliant and unique, not like other kids.* Nora settled on water. She took out the ice while dreading her math homework, a full page of stupid repetitious multi-digit problems of division and multiplication, same kind they'd had to slog through last year. It was an annoying, boring, waste of time that the teacher justified as review. She gulped the water so fast that her brain froze, and while she waited for the pain to pass, she considered calling Natalie and doing the problems together, splitting them up the way they had last year and all the years of math homework before that.

Except no, she couldn't call Natalie. Something fundamental and irreversible had occurred that day and because of it, Nora knew she would never call Natalie again, not ever. She started upstairs, lugging her bag, her throat tight, chest roiling with sorrow, or maybe guilt. But why should she feel bad? She hadn't done anything wrong. True, she and Natalie had eaten lunch together all through elementary school, but this was Welsh Valley Middle School. And she hadn't asked Natalie to save her a seat. Neither had she asked Annie to. But both of them had, on opposite sides of the cafeteria aisle. She'd had to make a choice on the spot, in a flash, a heartbeat. And now she couldn't stop seeing the look on Natalie's face. Shattered. Deflated like a leaky balloon. Bereft like an abandoned puppy. *God.* What had she done that was so awful? It wasn't like she and Natalie had been going steady and Nora had cheated and left her for a new love. So why had it been such a big deal? Why did she have to feel guilty about making a new friend? Why was it her fault that Natalie wasn't cool enough to fit in?

And why was her bedroom door open?

Nora dropped her book bag, stepping toward her room. She always shut her door when she left for school. Someone else had opened it, and her parents were at work. So it had to be Tommy. He'd gone into her room. Was he still in there?

She leapt forward, bursting through the doorway.

Tommy stood at her dresser with his back to her.

"Damn it, Tommy! What the hell are you doing?"

He jerked as if startled but didn't turn around.

Her underwear drawer was open.

"Answer me." Something hot surged in her chest, seared her insides.

He still didn't face her. "You're home early."

"Why are you in my room?" Her voice was low, a growl. Her fists tightened.

She stomped toward him. He turned away from her, hunching. Why wouldn't he look at her? What was he doing? Was he sliding something into the drawer? Taking something out? She grabbed his forearm to see what he was holding, but he moved faster, yanking his hand away and punching her arm so hard that she stumbled backward against the bed.

"Get away from me!" he squawked. "I'm just looking for my sock."

His sock? "In my dresser?" She righted herself, took a firm stance just out of his reach. "You're full of shit."

"I think it got mixed up in the laundry."

"So? You could ask me to look for it." Her hands were on her hips so he wouldn't see them trembling. "You don't get to come in here and go through my stuff. Besides, that's not even my sock drawer."

His neck was crimson. "How should I know which drawer it's in?"

"It's not in any of them. Who cares about a stupid sock? Just get out of here." She lunged at him, grasping the back of his shirt.

He pivoted and smacked her arm again.

"Get out!" She tried not to show her pain and pointed at the door. "Don't come in here again. Ever!"

"Since when do you tell me what to do? I'll come in if I want. Whenever I want." Tommy went on taunting. "Loser. You're on the rag, aren't you? I can smell it."

What? "Shut up. Just shut up!" Could he really smell her? Her period had started that morning. God. Did she smell bad? Had she smelled at school? Her face sizzled at the thought. She would die. But no, it wasn't possible—Annie would have told her. In fact, Tommy probably hadn't smelled anything either. He'd probably seen her pads in the bathroom and was just being a dick. Even so, she inhaled deeply through her nose, smelled a faint perfumy scent, but nothing else. "Know what, Tommy? I get why nobody likes you. You're such an asshole. Get out."

"Or what, you'll tell Mommy? Go on. Tell her I went into your room. Big freaking deal. You're always doing shit to me, but I don't whine about it."

"I don't do anything—"

"No? What about my ant farm? You never even apologized, let alone paid me for it. I bought that with my own money. And what about all the stuff you make up, like that I spied on you—"

"I didn't make that up and you know it. God. Just go away. You're such a freaking loser!"

"I'm a loser? Really? You think you're better than me?" Tommy finally wheeled around and faced her. He stepped close and stood over her, speaking softly as if telling a secret. "You think you're Miss Too Cool to Breathe the Same Air as her Brother! Well, news flash, you're not cool, little sis. You will never be. Oh, you'll try to be. You'll put on acts, pretend, fake it, cozy up to the right people, but underneath, you are, always were, and always will be, the same as me. A misfit. An oddball. A freak."

His last word was almost a whisper. His breath tickled her face, smelling of bologna, and of something else. Something familiar.

"Out. Now." She pointed at the door. Tried to stop hearing his words repeat in her mind. She was not like him. *Misfit. Oddball. Freak.* He was the oddball and freak, sneaking into her room when she wasn't home, coming into the bathroom while she was in the shower, liking bugs better than people. Who does that?

"I only came in for my sock."

"Out!" She kept pointing until he left. Then she went to her dresser. Again, she smelled a trace of something, something sweet. Their mother's Chanel? More likely, it was just the smell of clean clothes, laundry detergent. Her underwear drawer was a mess. Tommy was such a jerk. She slammed the drawer shut and flopped onto her bed. Had he really been looking for a sock? Doubtful. So what had he really been doing?

Nora bolted back to the dresser. She emptied the drawer out, searching for dead bugs or some other token of Tommy's appalling creepiness. But no. Her underwear drawer was insect-free.

She straightened the underwear, then scanned the room to see what else he'd meddled with. Her window was undisturbed, the lacey drapes limp in the breezeless heat. Her closet was just as she'd left it in the morning—jeans and T-shirts piled on the floor where she'd tossed them, deciding what to wear.

Maybe he hadn't messed with anything else. Still, he'd been in her room.

Nora's arm ached where Tommy had punched her. Probably she'd get a bruise, but she'd held her tears, wouldn't give him the satisfaction of making her cry. Crampy and tired, she grabbed her book bag, climbed onto her bed, arranged her pillows, and leaned back, taking out her math homework. With an unexpected pang, she pictured Natalie sitting by her phone, doing the problems alone.

SATURDAY, AUGUST 11, 2018, 7 P.M.

Saturday evenings, Dave and Nora usually got a sitter and went out with other couples—Dave's clients, partners, tennis buddies, or pals from law school. If they didn't have plans with any of them, then they'd do something with friends or Dave's brother, Don, and Don's wife, Sheila.

This night, they were headed to dinner in China Town. Don drove along Kelly Drive, Dave beside him in the front seat, talking sports or work or cars or some other mind-numbing topic. Nora didn't pay attention. She shared the backseat of Don's newly-leased Prius with Sheila, who kept folding and refolding her hands.

"You okay?" Nora smiled. "You seem…"

Sheila lowered her voice. "We're thinking about a second child. Dan says Henry needs a sibling. But I'm not sure."

Henry was two years old and the sole focus of his mother's attention. The owner of every toy and piece of toddler equipment available, he was a master of tantrums and manipulation.

"You talking baby?" Don must have heard them whispering.

"Don't eavesdrop," Sheila said. "I'm asking Nora's opinion."

Don stopped at a red light and shook his head.

"You guys want another kid?" Dave asked.

"Tell her, Dave," Don said. "Kids need siblings. How would you have survived without me?"

"I'd have had fewer bruises and one less broken arm."

"And no one to wrestle or mess around with. Or to stay up and order pizzas to that horrible teacher—what was her name again?"

"Mrs. Sullivan."

"Right. To her house at two a.m.? Or to sneak vodka from the liquor closet—"

"Or take the blame for all the things you did."

"What?" Don turned to face him, eyes wide and feigning innocence. "Time out. You're not still mad about the Philly's game. Because it was the other way around. That was all you."

"Hell if it was. It was your idea to ditch school, but I was the one who took all the heat. And what about Dad's missing golf clubs?"

"Not fair. That wasn't entirely my fault."

The light had turned green. The car behind them honked, and Don drove on. "Without me, who'd have covered for you when you snuck out at night to smoke pot or drink beer or hook up with some girl?"

Sheila and Nora exchanged looks.

Dave grinned, stretching his arm around Don's shoulders. "We had some fun, didn't we, little bro?"

"Still do."

"Good times."

"And bad."

"Thick and thin." Dave pinched Don's cheek.

"Fine," Sheila said. "I get that you guys have a never-ending brother-love-fest. But you aren't typical siblings."

"Really?" Dave twisted to face her. "Look at Ellie and Sophie. They're inseparable. Right, Nora? The girls sleep in the same room by choice. They're best pals."

Nora nodded, edging closer to the window. Her own sibling popped to mind. Tommy was grinning, baring his braces clogged with food bits, holding jars of dead bugs. "Our kids are close," she smiled, "but still, each family's different. No way to predict how Henry and the new one would get along."

"True enough, Nora," Don said. "But however they get along, it's worth it. Poor you. As an only child, you really can't imagine what a big deal it is having a brother or sister."

Dave's gaze flicked to her. She met his eyes, wordlessly thanking him for saying nothing. He accepted that Nora didn't talk about Tommy and had never even mentioned him to Sheila and Don.

"Right." Nora held her smile but set her jaw.

Dave reached back for her hand and squeezed.

Sheila went on, talking about studies she'd read about the psychologies of single children versus those with siblings. But Nora couldn't listen anymore. She focused on the pressure of Dave's hand, his smooth golden wedding band and sturdy warm fingers. She tried to get rid of Tommy, but it was no good. Now that she'd pictured him, Tommy wouldn't go away. His memory crowded between her and Sheila in the back seat, big as life in the khaki pants and blue checkered shirt that their mother had bought by the dozen because he'd refused any other fabric or color even though kids at school taunted him. *Hey, Tommy. Don't you ever change clothes? Do you sleep in those?* They'd jeered him right to his face, called him weirdo, freak, creep. Mocked him with jabs as solid as punches, and with solid punches too.

"Well, I'm sure you two lovebirds will make the right decision." Dave winked at Nora as he tried to change the subject. "Meantime, how about them Phillies?"

Don said, "I got tickets next home game. You in?"

Tommy crossed his legs, getting comfortable. Go away, Nora begged him. *Weirdo, freak, creep.* But he settled in, filling the back seat with his long skinny limbs and musty smell. Nora looked out the window, and the conversation faded into a dull buzz. They drove past houses, parks, the river. But Nora didn't see any of that. All she saw was Tommy.

Tommy. He was like a recurring bad dream, a wart that kept growing back. He reappeared even though Nora never spoke about, even tried not to think about him. Sometimes he showed up with bruises, split lips, and torn books. Other times, he'd have a note from school because kids in gym class had stolen his sneakers or hidden his clothes or cornered and taunted him in the locker room, cafeteria, staircase, or study hall. Tommy hadn't been simply unpopular. He'd been a pariah. An outcast who'd taken his anger out on his younger sister. Nora had lived in terror, not just of Tommy, but of the likelihood that as his sister, she'd likewise be shunned, judged, teased and tormented. As far back as she could remember, whenever other kids were around, she'd pretended not even to know him.

Family comes first. Your brother is your blood.

And Marla and Philip? They'd been no help. They'd doted on Tommy, encouraged his eccentric hobbies, and claimed that he was a genius, a unique gift to the world. By contrast, Nora had felt uninteresting and overlooked. Marla's parenting had taken the form of hasty clichés. *Pick your battles. Don't rock the boat. You can't catch flies with vinegar.* Other than the oblique guidance gleaned from remarks like these, Nora had pretty much been left to raise herself, had made drastic decisions with irreversible consequences.

So, no. Nora didn't talk about him. Had never mentioned him even to Dave, until he had seen Tommy in family pictures on her mother's spinet.

"Who's this?" On his first visit to her parents' house, he'd picked a framed school portrait of a little boy from the piano.

"Oh, that's Tommy." Marla had taken Dave's arm and gazed over his shoulder at the photo. "Nora must have told you about him. He's her brother."

Dave had frowned, no doubt confused.

"He passed away." Marla had sighed as she picked up another photo. "Here he is with his father and Nora at a science fair. He was twelve."

Nora winced, remembering. She clutched her seatbelt, heard the rhythm of Don and Dave's banter, and forced a smile at Sheila.

The picture had been snapped moments before a boy—his name escaped her—had run by and rammed right into Tommy, knocking over his entire exhibit. The boy had apologized, said it was an accident, but Tommy, accustomed to being victimized, had been convinced he'd done it on purpose and lost it. He'd barreled into the boy, swinging. Their father, Philip, had put his hands up, flustered and stuttering, his face cardiac red, as he'd pleaded with Tommy to back off. A small crowd had gathered, the science teachers clucking and flapping. Nora had backed away, mortified, until finally, someone had separated the boys and helped restore the exhibit. By then, the boy's arm had been twisted, Tommy's face had been scratched and his shirtsleeve torn.

In the picture, though, Tommy's blue plaid shirt was neat and intact, and he stood proud and unscratched with his cowlick at attention beside his display of impaled bugs on poster board.

"Hold on." Dave had wanted clarification. "This is your brother?"

Nora had felt his gaze asking, what the hell? Why didn't you tell me you had a brother? What happened to him? All those questions and more had flashed in his eyes, so she'd avoided them and moved away from the piano.

But Dave, being Dave, hadn't let the subject go. He'd asked her mother about Tommy, prying out details of his life and tragic, untimely death.

And Marla had been happy to provide them. "It was years ago. Not as much was known then about depression." Marla had set the picture down, her hands thin, freckled, lined with blue, swollen veins. "Certainly, Philip and I didn't know much. And as a young boy, he wasn't depressed at all. He was gifted. Probably a genius. He talked at ten months—used whole sentences by his first birthday. He taught himself to read. Did addition and subtraction at three years old. Oh yes. He was way beyond his grade level in school, so Philip and I helped him pursue his interests independently—"

"Mom, how's dinner coming?" Nora's whole body had tensed. "Can I do anything?"

"No need, dear." Marla had waved a hand, dismissing Nora's question. "Anyway, there was a downside to Tommy's brilliance. Because he was so far beyond other children, he had no one to befriend. Other children probably bored him. I believe that over time, his lack of companionship became problematic. As intelligent as he was, he was... how should I put it? Socially awkward? Introverted. He never said it, but in hindsight, it's clear that he was lonely. I suppose that's what led to depression."

Marla had kept talking, telling Dave that Nora had been Tommy's best, possibly his only friend, even though she was several years younger. That when Nora wasn't around, Tommy locked himself away with various entomology projects or photography.

As Marla spoke, Nora had pasted a placid smile on her face and refilled her scotch. She'd suggested that Dave didn't really need to hear about Tommy's projects and that they talk about other things. Like the weather.

But Dave had persisted, asking outright, blatantly and without apology, "So what happened? How did he die?"

Nora had clutched her glass, chewed her lip.

Her mother had taken a seat in her brocade wingback chair. How small she'd looked, how frail. A hollowed out gray-haired doll with a thread-thin voice. "Well, he didn't intend—It was a terrible accident."

Nora had gulped more scotch, bracing herself. "Please. Let's not go through it."

Dave had apologized, saying he shouldn't have asked, that Marla needn't go on.

But Marla wouldn't stop. "You should be told. After all, Tommy was Nora's blood."

Nora had stared into the fireplace, trying not to listen but hearing every word, seeing Tommy climb the steps to the attic and shut the door.

"It was his sophomore year. Of high school." Marla paused and fiddled with the thin gold ring on her liver-spotted hands. "It was late at night and we were all asleep, so we didn't hear him walking around the house."

Except that Nora had. She'd lain in bed, wondering what Tommy was doing. She'd gotten up and found him on his way to the attic. She'd never told anyone, though. Hadn't seen the point.

Dave had started to say something, maybe that Marla shouldn't continue.

But Marla interrupted him, "My husband found him in the morning."

"There's no need to go on. Please. Tommy killed himself." Nora had blinked, but the image hadn't faded.

"Nora. You know very well that the detectives said it wasn't necessarily suicide. It could have been an accident."

"Mom—" Nora had pleaded.

"It's nothing to be ashamed of, Nora. Tommy was just a regular teenager discovering himself. He was experimenting, testing various methods of—"

"For God's sake, Mom." Nora had tried to end the discussion. "He hanged himself."

"But maybe by accident. It turns out that choking can create particularly intense and stimulating... sensations. He probably didn't intend to die."

Nora had shaken her head and kept quiet.

Dave had expressed his condolences and apologized for resurrecting painful memories.

Marla had assured him that she'd come to terms with the loss long ago.

What's done is done. Don't cry over spilt milk.

Later, when they were alone, Nora had made it clear that the subject of Tommy was off limits. That she couldn't talk about him. And after that night with her mother, she hadn't, even though she knew that silence wouldn't free her of him, that Tommy would continue to appear unpredictably in her thoughts and dreams.

She never mentioned the dreams to Dave. One in particular recurred fairly often, in varying forms. Tommy would follow her doggedly until finally, she'd turn and shove him away. With a pained look, Tommy would fall to the ground, where he'd shatter into hundreds of crawling pieces.

When they were home in bed, Dave reached for her, and finally, Nora relaxed. The talk of siblings had dominated dinner, with Don and Sheila debating the merits of having a second child. As if invited, Tommy had pulled up a chair and sat among them, the candlelight flickering on his braces.

Nora sipped wine, kept smiling politely until, as she helped herself to General Tso's, Dave mentioned his mistress.

And she dropped her chopsticks.

They clattered onto her plate, and everyone looked at her.

"Jesus, Nora. It was a joke." Dave blinked. "I was kidding. Because I'm working so much that it's almost like I have one."

"One" meaning a mistress. She fumbled with her chopsticks. How should she have responded? With a laugh? The others had chuckled, their mouths stuffed with rice and tofu and garlic sauce. What had been funny about the idea of Dave cheating?

But the evening was finally over—thank God—and she was home in bed, wrapped in Dave's arms. At least in this most basic way, she could reconnect with him. She let herself forget about siblings, and the nonsense about Dave cheating. Just lay with him and let go. After more than ten years, she knew his body and would find comfort in the pattern, the steps to their familiar sexual dance.

Except that Dave wasn't doing that dance. His rhythm had changed from a waltz to a samba. What was his mouth doing? His kisses felt staccato, his lips breezing over her quickly, lightly.

When had his fingers become so aggressive? So accurate? Oh God. She squealed, almost in pain, then moaned in unexpected, unprecedented pleasure. After he sent her reeling, spinning, actually yelping in blinding orgasm, Nora lay back on the pillow. What had happened to her husband? Where had he acquired those new lovemaking techniques?

Ask him, she urged herself. Before he falls asleep, while your bodies are still entangled, ask him. The longer you wait, the harder it will be. It's better to know than to wonder.

Fine. She'd ask him as soon as her heartbeat steadied. As soon as she could find her voice. Nora took a breath and swallowed: one, two, three. "Dave?"

"Hmmm?" His voice was groggy, almost asleep.

She needed to know and couldn't wait. In the morning, the kids would be all over the both of them, and then he'd be off to tennis again. Unless "tennis" was actually some babe. Which it wasn't, of course, but she needed to hear him say it. This was her only chance until who-knew-when.

"I need to ask you something."

No response.

"Dave?" She shook his shoulder. "Dave?"

"Hmmm." His eyes didn't open. His arm sprawled heavily over her hip. His breathing was slow and rumbling.

Not two minutes after they'd finished making love, Dave was sound asleep.

How was that even possible? How could he—*poof*—be asleep? His mind just switched off, untroubled. She watched the quiver of his exhaling lips.

Moonlight beamed through the window blinds, washing everything with stripes of grayish blue: the room, the bed, the sheets,

Dave's face, the muscles of his shoulder, the length of his arm. Nora's hip. Even her thoughts, her urgency, her dread.

Predictably, Dave began snoring, belting out long guttural, grating snorts. Nora couldn't lie there anymore. She lifted his arm, got up, and stepped past the hulking dark bureaus, the cushioned divan, the crossed slats at the window and the slices of glowing moon beyond. She checked on the girls, inhaling their sweet shampoo when she kissed their foreheads. She tiptoed down the staircase. Maybe she'd make some chamomile tea.

On the way to the kitchen, though, she passed through the foyer. And the console table where Dave had left his wallet, his keys. And his phone.

She hesitated for a heartbeat, long enough to decide that she wouldn't hesitate. Dave's phone would answer all her questions, would tell her which numbers he called most frequently, which ones called him. It would show her the texts he'd received and the ones he'd sent. Unless he'd deleted them, which he might have if he were actually hiding an affair. But then again, he might not have, since he had no reason to think she'd check his phone. Dave trusted her. He'd never consider that she might sneak or pry.

And normally, she wouldn't. But this situation wasn't normal. She had to get the absurd cheating idea out of her head. So she wasn't snooping, exactly. She was simply reaffirming and solidifying her trust.

Nora snatched up the phone and hid it in the fold of her nightgown. She looked over her shoulder, checking to make sure she was unseen. Then, holding her breath, she crept toward the kitchen.

Don't look for trouble, Marla scolded.

But Nora didn't waver. What choice did she have? Hadn't Dave been "working" way too much? Hadn't he somehow learned definitely new ways of making love?

No, she wasn't looking for trouble; she'd already found it, was sinking into it. Trouble was already up to her knees. Or her neck. Some body part, it didn't matter which.

Nora turned on the kitchen lights and, soundlessly, set the phone on the table. She took a seat and, scarcely breathing, stared at the little piece of technology. A convenience. A weapon of treachery.

With jarring clunks, the ice maker deposited fresh cubes into the freezer tray, shattering the silence. Startled, Nora ran a hand through her hair, took a breath. She picked at a hangnail on her middle finger. Scratched at a water stain, wiped crumbs off the table. Why was she hesitating? She would put the phone back where she'd found it. Dave would never know.

Fine. Nora picked up the phone, unlocked it with Dave's password. Clicked on the phone icon, checked recent calls first. Good God, there were a lot them. So many names and numbers. Of course there were. Dave was a busy man, used his phone for work.

Nora leaned in and studied the screen, scrolling through the list, catching several recurring numbers. Probably clients or other attorneys. Tennis buddies. Then she got up and went to the junk drawer, rifling through rolls of tape and takeout menus until she found a pencil and a notepad. She brought these back to the table and reviewed the list of names and numbers, eliminating men's names and those she knew were impossibilities—Lois, one of the people Dave and Ted played mixed doubles with, for example, was gay. And Cynthia, a partner at the firm, was about twenty years older than Dave. Several calls, though, were listed not by name but by numbers. And one in particular showed up frequently—seven times, in fact, in the last two days. Nora read the number out loud as she copied it down. Her heart pounded, and her mother's voice repeated its warning. *What you don't know can't hurt you.*

It wasn't too late. She could still stop. She could assume the number was a client in trouble, someone who'd called because they were about to be arrested or sued. But no matter how her heart beat or her mother's advice battered her, Nora was determined to pursue the truth. She returned to the menu page and clicked on the text message icon.

The number she'd written down was at the top of the screen, along with a text. She clicked on it. "After I left you, I saw Nora and fought the urge to tell her. But you're right, it's better that she doesn't know."

Nora's blood went cold, froze in her veins.

Shivering, she read the message again. Then again, slowly, one word at a time. Then again rapidly. No matter how she read them, the words didn't change. Nor did their meaning.

The texter had seen Dave secretly. And was someone Nora knew.

Nora's hands shook as she scrolled to another message. "I called but you didn't pick up."

Dave replied that he'd been in court. He asked what was up.

"Got time to see me today?"

He said that he'd make time. Asked where, when.

Nora stopped, bit her lip. He'd make time? The man who was too busy to come home to his family for dinner would make time for this, this secret slimy text-sender who knew her and was setting up trysts with her husband? Nora was blinking too fast, breathing too rapidly. She needed to slow down but couldn't. Her finger trembled as it touched the phone screen once more.

"My place? Any time. Paul's still away."

Paul?

Nora knew only one Paul. The Paul who was Barbara's husband, the handsome, wealthy, candidate for Senate, Paul. The Paul who traveled a lot, who was often away.

She shivered, hugged herself. Looked away from the phone, up at the wall, the waxy crayon pictures of rainbows, trees, a dog, or maybe a pony. Ellie's perfectly symmetrical flowers. Their house. One, signed by Sophie with a backward e, showed a family of stick figures: three in red triangular skirts and a larger one with black pants and big hands standing higher than the others. Their family.

She read it again. "Paul's still away." Stop it, she told herself. The name didn't mean anything. There were dozens, hundreds of Pauls, not just the one married to her friend. But who else but her friend would write, "After I left you, I saw Nora"? She continued to scroll. Saw that Dave had agreed to a place and time.

Nora stared at the tiny screen, shivering. She returned to the text she'd read first and read it again and again until her eyes ached: "It's better that Nora doesn't know."

SATURDAY, AUGUST 11, 2018

It had to be Barbara. Her friend. Her Barbara. What other woman with a husband named Paul would have seen her and not want her to find out that she was seeing Dave?

Nora looked at the number she'd written on the memo pad. It didn't look familiar, but of course it wouldn't. She didn't know Barbara's number by heart, didn't have any of her friends' numbers memorized. Her phone knew all the numbers. All she had to do was punch up her contact list and touch a name. She'd go get her phone and compare the numbers.

The hallway tilted, off balance. Nora held her hand against the wall to steady herself. Barbara? The day before, she'd shown up late to book club, flushed and distracted. Was that flush the afterglow from a tryst with Dave? Nora heard a thud, a small crash, and registered a flash of white pain as she collided with the hall table. Damn. She hadn't been paying attention to where she was going, had stubbed her toe on the table leg and knocked her phone and Dave's keys to the floor. She hopped, cradling her toe, cursing the angry, explosive pain. Had the noise awakened anyone? She crouched, rocking back and forth, waiting for the throbbing to ease, and looked up the dark stairs. The landing was empty. She held still, listening to the night sounds, distant traffic, crickets, humming appliances. But no one startled awake by a thud and a crash. Or a heartbreak.

Nora pictured Barbara kissing Dave with her silicone-enhanced lips. Dave twisting his fingers through her perfectly gold highlights. Barbara panting steamy air from her freckle-dotted, surgically turned-up nose. Everything about Barbara's body was altered, fake. Maybe Dave was attracted to her height? Barbara was five inches taller than Nora, almost as tall as Dave. Facing him, Barbara would meet him eye to eye, nose to nose, breast to breast, hip to hip. They'd fit together. Oh God. Nora grabbed her ears and squeezed. How was it possible? Barbara? Fucking her husband? When had it started? Who'd initiated it? Had Dave? Had he approached her at, say, the book club Christmas party, and laughingly, playfully, teasingly whispered some tired line into her ear, maybe that she looked good enough to eat? Had Barbara's body inspired those new movements of Dave's tongue, the patient, nuanced motions of his fingers?

Nora let out a small wail, high-pitched like a choking hamster. She stood and hobbled into the kitchen, favoring her sore toe, and stood in front of the refrigerator with her phone in one hand and an empty glass in the other. When had she taken the glass off the shelf? She didn't remember. Damn. Nora turned, saw a bottle of scotch beside Dave's phone. She didn't remember taking out the scotch, either. Damn. Nora shivered. Was she having lapses? Losing it? She was clearly getting ice and making a drink. She opened the freezer, reached into the ice tray, the cubes so cold that they stuck to her fingers, ripping at her skin as they fell, clinking into her glass. Pain shot through her toe as she stepped back to the table and slid into her seat, eased as she raised the aching foot onto the chair beside her. Situated, she reached for the scotch bottle, opened it, poured, and drank. Poured another. Seethed.

She'd first met Barbara in playgroup. Ellie and Barbara's son, Colin, had been about a year old. Colin had been a bruiser, twice the size of the other babies. Barbara had shown off the biceps she'd developed from lifting him, joking that she was used to handling big men at the casino where she'd worked before marrying Paul.

Paul's still away.

He'd been a regular at her table. Had tipped well.

It's better that Nora doesn't know.

Nora took another swig. Playgroup had turned into a support group for moms. Back then, chasing her toddler and pregnant with Sophie, Nora had hungered for adult companionship. But even in playgroup, Nora had felt different. When all the moms had sat on the floor in a circle, their babies on their laps, singing songs with hand motions, Ellie had squirmed to get off Nora's lap and sat alone.

Ellie, in fact, had never been inclined toward group activities. When the group was adding muffin ingredients to a huge bowl, Ellie had wandered over to play with building blocks. While the others finger painted, Ellie had drifted over to the dolls. Nora had tried not to worry that her daughter would be friendless forever, that she'd become an outsider like Tommy.

Barbara had been the one to notice Nora's concerns and offer support and insight. She'd assured Nora that she shouldn't worry, that Ellie simply wasn't a follower, that she was independent. Nora had appreciated the comments. But now, looking back, it seemed that Barbara had seemed overly interested in Ellie, including her in whatever she and Colin were doing— puzzles, books, the jungle gym—and upon learning that they lived only a mile apart, making playdates for Colin and Ellie. At the time, Nora had thought Barbara was just being friendly. But now, she wondered. Had Barbara had her eyes on Dave even then? Had she met him before she'd met Nora and been curious about his wife and child? Was it possible that the affair had been going on all these years?

Nora covered her eyes, her jaw tensed. Her stomach churned. No. It wasn't possible. She ran her fingers through her hair. She fidgeted, trying to stop jumping to conclusions and condemning Barbara prematurely. Lots of women were married to men named Paul. And she hadn't compared the phone numbers yet, couldn't be sure that Barbara was actually the woman texting Dave.

Nora stared at the pair of phones, lying on the table side by side, his and hers. The answer was right in front of her. All she had to do was look. Her heart ricocheted against her ribs, bruising itself on her bones. But she had to find out.

She steadied her hand enough to reach for her phone, click the contact icon, and scroll down to her friend's name. Barbara's number appeared in big bold digits. Nora bit her lip. She eyed the scotch bottle, the melting ice in her glass.

She stalled, looking around the room, noting the girls' drawings. Ellie's dark-colored rainbows. Sophie's picture of her family, four stick figures hand in hand. It was coming loose from the wall, the tape losing its stickiness. Nora would have to fix it. Tomorrow.

Finally, she picked up Dave's phone and looked again at his texts.

The numbers were the same.

SATURDAY, SEPTEMBER 30, 1993

For once, Nora was glad to have Tommy beside her in the family room. Pouring over some insect book, he was breathing too loud, making maddening little whistling sounds through his nose. But what mattered was that Tommy was the same as always, wearing the same checkered shirt and khaki pants, emitting his same musty, stale, and faintly sweet smell, sprouting the same dark fuzz on his chin and upper lip, erupting the same red pimples, and growing the same matted patch of dark curls and stubborn cowlick. Tommy's presence was comforting. As familiar as the aging leather sofa cushions and the tired La-Z-boy chair, as unchanging as the slatted patio and patchy lawn outside the sliding doors, as homey as the aroma of roasting onions and beef wafting down the steps.

Luckily, he didn't look at her. If he had, he might have noticed her over-bright eyes and red, chafed lips.

From upstairs, Marla called Nora to set the table for supper.

Oh man. What if her mother asked about the red patches around her mouth? Nora began concocting stories about walking into a pole, or how the redness must be an allergy. Or, even better, she could pretend that she had no idea that her skin was red, let alone why. But wait, she probably wouldn't need to explain, because what were the chances that Marla would even notice? Absorbed in slicing pot roast and mashing potatoes, Marla would only glance at Nora—if she looked at her daughter at all.

Besides, the redness might not be all that noticeable. It must have faded by now. Half an hour had passed since she'd removed the wadded-up tissues from the bra Annie had lent her, un-snapped it and given it back. And that was after she'd scrubbed her face—especially her lips—with the harsh green hand soap from the mall's ladies' room, rubbing herself dry with rough paper towels until her skin was raw.

Even now, sitting with Tommy in the family room, her face burned. She touched her mouth, felt the stab of a split lip, the sting of Annie's laughter when she'd found Nora bent over the sink, scrubbing.

"God, Nora." Annie had stared. "What are you doing?"

As if Nora had been doing something bizarre and outlandish—which she had been, kind of, scrubbing her face off.

All Nora had known was that she had to get clean, wash off what had happened, and get back to the way she'd been before. So she'd rubbed her mouth again with a fresh paper towel and started over with yet another glop of bitter and unforgiving soap, even though she'd seen in the mirror that the makeup was gone completely. Because even if the makeup had washed away, the kiss, its taste and smell, lingered and tingled, clinging to her still, and so she'd scrubbed, desperate to get it off.

In a way, it was Annie's fault. No, not in a way. It was totally Annie's fault. Annie had been the one to suggest getting decked out and going to the mall. Annie had been the one to spot the boys in the food court, two of them, way older than they were—probably as old as Tommy. One was tall and dark-haired and had worn a letter jacket from Cardinal O'Malley High. Annie hadn't hesitated. She'd grabbed Nora's arm and headed toward the boys, stopping a few yards away, pretending she hadn't noticed them.

"I'm dying. We need to find some fun." She talked just loud enough for the boys to hear.

In a blink, the boys had joined them. They'd stood so close that Nora had had to crane her neck to see the tall one's face, let alone to talk to him. Not that she'd had anything to say. She'd stood silent and awkward, not sure what was happening or what she was supposed to do. She'd copied Annie, her smile, the cock of her head, the way she put her weight on one foot and thrust her hip out. Nora had laughed when Annie laughed, and lied along with her when the boys asked where they went to school, pretending to be a freshman at Kingsley, three years older than she really was. Acting as if she knew what she was doing even as her stomach had flipped.

It flipped again as she sat next to Tommy, remembering what had happened at the mall, so she concentrated on the rhythm of his breathing. His stillness. Beside him, she began to relax.

He was probably the same age as those boys.

"Nora!" Marla called again, impatience clipping her words.

On the way to the kitchen, for a second, not much longer, Nora allowed herself to picture Tommy as a normal older brother, someone she could talk to. Someone cool, on the swim team or track, maybe even football. She imagined him as a high school senior, wearing his letter jacket to the mall. But the image of Tommy faded, replaced by that of Rick, the tall, cute one.

Rick's blue eyes had twinkled when he'd said that he thought he'd seen Nora before. Maybe at Belmont pool? And she'd said something outlandishly stupid, that no, she'd just moved here from Maine. Maine? Really? When she'd said that Annie was actually her first friend in the area, her face had burned with lies and panic. But Rick hadn't noticed, had asked her how long she'd lived here and whether she missed Maine. But while Nora was inventing an answer, Annie had slid between her and the guy named Rick. Annie had laughed, blinked her eyes, taken over the conversation and, a few awkward moments later, walked off with him, leaving Nora speechless and alone with the other one.

In the kitchen, Nora took plates out of the cabinet and silverware from the drawer. She answered Marla's questions. Yes, Tommy was downstairs. Yes, he was reading. Yes, she'd remembered to put out the water pitcher. Did her mother really think she'd forget how to do what she did every single night?

Nora pressed her burning lips together and felt a throb. She should have walked away. Should have come home. But, she hadn't. On unfamiliar turf and without Annie to give her cues, Nora had been paralyzed. She'd stood there with tissues wadded and crumpled into her borrowed bra and borrowed makeup painted on her face, wondering where Annie and Rick had gone, when they'd be back. And what she was supposed to do in the meantime.

But the other boy, the shorter, not-so-cute one with gelled hair and a smattering of forehead pimples, had taken her hand. His palm had been damp, and Nora's breathing had become rapid and shallow, rabbit-like, as if her body was standing beside this boy but she was out of there, gone, having left it behind. She'd hoped that that feeling—of exiting her body—was a sign that she was going to faint. Not that she'd ever fainted before, but she'd wanted to, because if she had, then that sweaty hand would have let go of hers. People in the mall would have noticed her passed out and come to her aid. The guy—his name had been Anthony—would have backed away.

Anthony had smelled dizzyingly, cloyingly, sickeningly of the ocean, of geranium, a blend of salt and sweet. He led her out of the food court to the adjacent long hall near the restrooms. Into a corner, where he'd pressed her against the wall and said, "Welcome to the neighborhood, Nora from Maine."

He'd clasped her butt, tightly, painfully, and at the same time crushed his lips stiffly against hers. The smell of cologne had mixed with his lunch (Chinese food?), and his tongue had jabbed her mouth, tasting of half-digested egg roll and something with soy sauce. Nora hadn't been able to breathe. She'd turned her head for some air, and he'd snickered.

"What? Come on, little frosh. Nobody likes a tease." He'd laughed then, revealing silver braces with tiny yellow chunks of food caught in the wires.

"I don't feel well." Nora had gasped and pushed him away. She'd hurried down the hall to the ladies' room where she'd huddled on a vinyl upholstered sofa for an immeasurable time, shaky and sickened, not sure when it would be safe to go back out. Where had Annie gone with Rick? And how was she supposed to reconnect with her? Should she just forget Annie and go home? And how would she ever get rid of the smell of Anthony's cologne, or the feeling of his wormy tongue, or the taste of his Chinese food?

Nora was filling water glasses when her father walked in, announcing that there had been a detour on his drive home. He'd had no idea they were digging up Old Gulf Road. Her mother pecked his lips and said she hadn't either. But never mind, he was just in time for dinner.

Nora steeled herself for a meal with her family. She'd act as if nothing had happened. Well, in a way, nothing had. It wasn't as though she'd been mugged or mauled or kidnapped. But her face still hurt, a reminder of how she'd scrubbed to wash off that kiss.

She wasn't sure how Annie had found her. Maybe Anthony had told her that Nora had run to the bathroom, sick. Or maybe Annie had just wandered in. Either way, Annie had appeared in the ladies' room, unconcerned at finding Nora with soap suds across her mouth and soggy used paper towels all over the countertop.

Annie had laughed, not waiting for an explanation, and kind of danced toward Nora and the row of sinks. "How cool was that? They really believed we were in high school!"

Her lipstick had been smeared, her hair and shirt disheveled. She'd made no apology for stranding Nora with Anthony, the butt groper with braces, no excuses for claiming Rick, the tall good-looking one that Nora had been talking to. Annie had not hesitated, had just led him away as if Nora hadn't been in the middle of telling him about winters in Maine and how she loved skiing. But it was no big deal. They'd just been goofing around, playacting that they had boobs and were freshmen.

Tommy shoveled chunks of beef and potatoes into his mouth, lips smacking with each bite. Her father helped himself to seconds, asking Nora to pass the green beans. She did. He asked how her day was. She said fine. He asked for the salt. Marla and Philip exchanged news of their days. Everything was like always, except for Nora. She chewed the pot roast, still unable to re-inhabit her body. She'd ventured into territory where she hadn't belonged, and from which she couldn't quite return. She felt sullied. Stained. Worse.

But she was overreacting. She needed to move on and forget the whole thing. Really, it had been nothing. Neither she nor Annie would ever see those boys again.

Still, she couldn't stop reliving it, replaying what had happened. The revolting wet tongue. Annie stranding her. And worst of all, Annie stealing Rick from her without a thought or apology, on a whim, for no reason. Just because she could.

So. It was Barbara. For a while, Nora didn't move. She stared at the phone number, redefining memories and reinterpreting moments. Barbara had complained at book club that she had no time for herself. Had she meant that she had no time to sneak off with Dave?

Nora stiffened, tightened her jaw. How long had Dave been lying to her? He knew she couldn't bear lies, had sworn he'd never lie again. But how many late meetings had been with Barbara instead of clients? How many "tennis matches" had been preceded or followed by a traitorous sexual tryst? Had they met at Barbara's while her boys, Colin and Harry, were in preschool and Paul was out campaigning? Or had they gone to a hotel? Nora hadn't noticed room charges on their credit card, but Dave would surely have been more careful, charging the rooms to his firm. Which hotel? The Hilton on Columbus Boulevard—no. The Ritz Carlton. Had they laughed about their secret while tangled up in the sheets of a plush, king-sized bed? Mocked her for trusting them? For being so profoundly clueless? Had they made fun of Paul for being so easily duped?

Nora pressed her fingertips against her eyelids, imagining Dave caressing Barbara's shoulders and back, his wedding band glowing, molten. How did the ring not sear his skin? How could he wear it while touching her? And what about her? Were Barbara's breasts freckled like her nose? Did they feel real? Oh God. What about that announcement Barbara had made at book club? While they'd been discussing that television show instead of their book, she'd yelped and breathlessly laughed, "I just had an orgasm."

She'd explained that, at Paul's request, she'd gone to the spa and had a wax—not just on her legs. She'd bragged, lowering her voice to add that now, sensations were much more intense, so that walking—even sitting with her legs crossed—could cause a climax.

Nora had laughed along with the others then. But now, as she pictured Dave's hand between Barbara's smooth waxed thighs, she clenched her teeth, no longer amused.

She swallowed scotch, censored the image. Honestly, she needed to stop. Barbara and Dave? The idea was absurd. Impossible. Barbara's husband was not just the best-looking man in Philadelphia and possibly the Commonwealth of Pennsylvania; he also adored his wife. Plus, he was nearly a U.S. senator, far ahead in the polls. Why would Barbara cheat on him? She wouldn't. And if she would, why would she pick Dave? He wasn't even close to the caliber of Barbara's husband.

And for another thing, Dave wouldn't cheat. Not again. He wouldn't. There had to be another explanation for the texts.

Nora struggled to find one. Her fingers fumbled, touching icons on the phone, punching up texts, scanning them. On Friday, they'd made plans to meet at Barbara's at noon. The day before, Barbara had sent him a link to Paul's campaign schedule. Then she had asked if Nora knew anything, and Dave had assured her that Nora had no clue.

Of course she didn't. She was clueless, as dull as a cabbage. Predictable, plain, old, boring Nora. No one special. She was, after all, Tommy's sister. *You'll always be the same as me: a misfit, an oddball, a freak.*

She read on, the knots in her stomach tightening with each text. There were dozens, going back weeks. Finally, she made herself stop. She'd seen too many, couldn't stop seeing them. I'll make time for you, Nora has no clue, Paul's still away, Come by this afternoon.

She didn't remember leaving the kitchen or climbing the stairs, but somehow, she made it back to her bedroom where she was standing over Dave, watching him sleep. Nora knew all about his sleep, the rhythm of his breathing, the warm, dusky smell of his skin, the harsh cracks of his snores, the peace on his face. How could he sleep so deeply, not troubled by his deceit? Not bothered by her absence, not even noticing that she wasn't in bed? Who was this man whose jaw hung slack, who looked like, slept like, and smelled like, but somehow wasn't her Dave?

Nora's whole body hurt. Each breath felt as though razors were slashing her lungs. Dave's face was untroubled and at ease. She had to be mistaken. Maybe she could erase the last hour, climb in bed beside him and wrap herself in his arms. Pretend she'd never looked in his phone.

But she couldn't. The texts wouldn't allow it. They flashed in her head in neon red, the evidence stacking up against Dave, showing him to be a liar. A cheater. She wanted to pummel him, tried to make fists but couldn't because she still held the phones. Tossing them into the folds of their comforter, she clenched her hands and stared at him until her eyes burned. When finally she looked away, the room had drifted out of reach, intangible as a memory—the mahogany bureaus, the velvet divan, the moonlit windows, the fluffed pillows, and the half-naked liar, cheater, heartbreaker, marriage-destroyer husband.

She ought to kill him.

The thought volunteered on its own, unsolicited, offering an outlet for her shock and rage. She could slam the lamp base against his head. How many hits would it take? She pictured the impact, the spattering blood, warm on her nightgown. Dave's eyes opening in shocked confusion. The satisfaction of hearing bones shatter, of whispering into his ear as he died that, guess what: Nora had a clue.

Dave stirred and rolled over, his back to her.

Nora watched his sculpted shoulders, the slope of his back. Her life hung in shreds. Killing him would accomplish nothing unless he knew why she was doing it. She ought to wake him up, demand to hear the truth, and kill him afterward.

"Mommy?" Sophie was beside her. When had she come in? Her eyes glistened in the dim light. "I heard a noise."

Nora knelt to meet Sophie's eyes. "Sorry. It must have been me walking around," she whispered. "I can't sleep."

Sophie's head tilted. "Did you have a bad dream? Is that why you're crying?"

Crying? Nora touched her face. Indeed, it was wet.

"It's just a dream, Mommy. Don't be scared. Know what I do when I get one?"

Nora took Sophie's hands. "You come and get me?"

Sophie nodded. "And sometimes, I climb in with Ellie." She furrowed her little eyebrows. "Mommy, why don't you climb in with Daddy?" She hesitated, then smiled. "Or, if you want, you can climb in with me."

Oh my. Sophie was mothering her. Nora had become so pathetic that a not yet five-year-old felt compelled to help her. She wiped her tears with the back of her hand and thanked Sophie, giving her a kiss. Actually, it was a good offer. If she went back to her own bed, she'd stay up all night staring, thinking of ways to murder Dave, maybe even doing it.

So she led Sophie back to her room and cuddled up beside her. She lay still, watching a kaleidoscope of images: ants in a farm, spider parts in a tissue, Barbara in her flashy BMW, Tommy in his coffin, Dave with a freshly smashed skull. She held on to Sophie through the night, as if her child's warm scent and deep, steady breathing could sustain her.

SUNDAY, AUGUST 12, 2018

While birds were first chirping, Nora slipped away from Sophie and went back to her own bedroom. The phones were where she'd left them. She picked them up and sat on the side of the bed, still aching.

Nora's grip tightened around the phones as she stared at her sleeping husband. His breath was a steady rumble. Knowing what she knew, aside from killing him, what could she do? Yell at him? Stop cooking for him? Run up credit card bills? Her options were laughable. At best, they would irritate him. They certainly wouldn't rip Dave's heart to ribbons the way he'd ripped hers. No, Dave held the power. He was in control.

It had been better not to know. If only she hadn't looked at the texts. On cue, her mother whispered, *I told you not to look for trouble.*

Dave snorted and turned over, sprawling his legs across her side of the bed.

She ought to try to sleep. She wouldn't be able to think or figure out what to do unless she had rest. She climbed into bed but couldn't relax. Instead, she turned onto her side and imagined what she would say when Dave woke up.

The moment he opened his eyes, Nora would be ready.

"Dave," she'd say. "I know."

He'd blink a few times and rub his eyes. Then he'd pretend to be too groggy to comprehend. "What time is it?"

She would hold up his phone.

He would be confused, not understanding why Nora was awake or why her face was so grave. His first coherent thought would be that something was wrong with the kids. "The girls?" He'd start to get up.

"The girls are fine."

Dave would settle back against his pillows, rub his eyes again. That's when she'd slam him. "I know about Barbara."

"Huh?" He'd stall, probably look at the clock. "It's barely five o'clock." He would say this as if the time explained everything. As if it justified his affair.

He'd get up and use the bathroom. When he came back, he'd rustle his hair and sit on the edge of the bed, looking half-asleep.

"So, what's wrong?" He'd act as if she hadn't mentioned Barbara and ask again why she was up so early. He'd reach for her hand, and that's when he'd finally notice what she was holding in it. His brows would furrow, and his gaze would linger on the phone as his mind began scrambling to figure out how much Nora knew, how he might slither out of trouble.

Nora would bring up the texts from Barbara about Dave coming over, about Paul being away. "Tell me about these."

Dave would squint at the screen. The delicate skin around his eyes would twitch.

"Tell me." She would want to throw the pillows at him, tear the sheets out from under him. But she wouldn't risk waking the children.

His eyebrows would rise, his hand would rustle the soft hairs of his chest. His head would tilt with a question the way Sophie's so often did. His gaze would travel from Nora's face to the phone. He would realize there was no escape; he'd been caught. But, being Dave, he wouldn't surrender or apologize. No, like a cornered animal, he'd attack.

"What the hell, Nora. You've been reading my texts?" He would steer the conversation straight at her, mowing her down.

"That's your response?" Nora would hiss. "You're screwing my friend and you're pissed—"

"I'm what? That's crazy!"

"—that I looked in your phone?"

"You bet I'm pissed." Dave would stand, gesticulating as though he were arguing a high-profile case. His nostrils would flare, righteously indignant. "I use that phone for my practice, Nora. It contains privileged conversations—"

"It sure does."

"Give me the phone." Fully awake, Dave's would switch to his stony, unemotional lawyer voice. "Nora. Now." He'd hold his hand out.

"Tell me the truth," she'd insist. "How long have you been fucking her?"

"The phone." Dave's eyes would be ice.

Nora would plop the phone into his palm, unable to speak. Her throat would have clamped shut. She would sit stiff and wordless, aware that she had accomplished nothing, learned nothing, that all she'd managed to do was admit she'd been prying.

Dave's jaw would ripple as he scrolled though the messages about Paul being away, about meeting Barbara secretly, about not letting Nora know. But he would not admit anything.

"I'll change my password," he'd growl. "And don't ever even think of looking at my texts again." He'd glare at her as if the rage in the air belonged to him.

That's how it would go.

By Dave's logic, the snooping would be the issue, not the affair. He'd counter every charge Nora presented as if he were speaking to a jury. He would insist that the messages not be admitted into evidence since she'd had no right to see them in the first place.

Nora closed her eyes, rubbed her forehead. No. Confronting Dave about the text messages was a bad idea. He was a professional arguer. He knew how to dodge, deflect, defend, distract, and maneuver. Having been caught, he would deny everything. Isn't that what he advised his clients? Deny deny deny.

Nora flopped onto her back, stymied. Would she really let him dismiss her that way? Not even addressing her suspicions or feelings?

She got up, put the phones on the dresser and got back in bed. Dave's face was smooth and unlined, as still as a mask. Nora shivered beside him, not knowing what to do with her limbs or how to position herself.

See? I warned you not to look for trouble. Now that you've found it, let it go. Don't rock the boat.

"Nora?" Dave's face crinkled as he squinted at her. "Can't you sleep?" He blinked a few times, rubbed his eyes.

She shook her head and hugged herself, still shivering.

"Come here." He reached for her, pulling the comforter up so that she could slide closer to him.

Nora's belly churned. She ached to rest her head against Dave's chest as if she'd never read a single text.

He watched her. "You okay?"

She nodded. Fine. Peachy. Perfect. Nora was tired, her mind groggy. She should just ask him about Barbara and give him a chance to explain. But would she believe his answers? Damn. Trust was a circle.

I told you. I warned you. Don't rock the boat.

Dave tugged at her. "Come on, Nor. We can still grab a couple hours." His eyes were soft, his voice warm. She took a breath, aware that it might be her last before life as she knew it collapsed. Then, she asked him what she wanted to know.

SUNDAY, AUGUST 12, 2018

"What?" Dave leaned on his elbow, not fully awake. "You think I'm having an affair?" He rubbed his eyes. "With Barbara?"

"I read her texts." Nora waited for him to explode, to accuse her of snooping and invading his privacy.

"You read her texts? In my phone?" He didn't sound angry. He sounded baffled. He scratched his head, turned the lamp on, and looked at her with his head tilted, the way Sophie did. "Why would you do that?"

Nora's hands tightened. Her eyes darted from side to side, up and down. Her mind went blank, and she tried to remember. Why had she done that? Oh, yes. Because Dave had been gone so much, worked so late. Because he'd had a lot of phone calls. And because he'd made love differently. Would any of that justify what she'd done? Prying. Invading her husband's privacy. Becoming the crazy possessive, jealous wife. Dave had every right to be furious.

He sat on the side of the bed. Silence billowed between them, thick and tangible, as seconds passed.

Nora considered apologizing. Or backing up, trying to unsay what she'd said. She wanted a do-over, starting from when Dave told her to climb into bed.

"Why did you look at my phone?" Dave's voice was soft. "That's private."

"I know." Nora cut him off. "But I had to."

"I don't get why you think I'd cheat." His shoulders straightened. His voice became brusque and wounded. "I mean, why? After all this time. I gave you my word, Nora."

"I remember."

"Do you think I don't love you?"

Nora couldn't think of what to say.

"I do, Nora. More than ever."

She studied his face, puffy from sleep, no signs of a lie—no tiny tics or twitches.

"To be honest, I'm stunned that you'd suspect me. And more than a little bit hurt. It's been five years since the thing with Steph—"

Nora's hand went up. "Do not say her name."

"And I promised then that I would never lie to you or cheat again."

Nora nodded and looked away. Saw the wedding photo on the dresser. Dave had promised to be faithful that day, too.

"So? What is this about? Doesn't my word count for anything? Don't you trust me?"

"I do trust you." Her face burned, and she didn't trust her voice, so she paused until she knew it wouldn't crack. "I mean I did until—"

"Until you didn't. So, instead of discussing your doubts with me, you decided to launch an undercover investigation." Even now, even at this intimate moment, Dave talked like a lawyer.

"I meant to talk to you." She paused, took a breath. "I should have."

"Yes."

They were quiet for a moment. Nora chewed her lip.

"But if you're not having an affair, why does Barbara invite you over while her husband's away? And tell you to make sure 'Nora doesn't know'?"

Dave sighed and scratched his belly. "Damn it, Nora. I see how it looks, but you'll just have to trust me. I can't go into it other than to say that it doesn't concern you."

She raised her chin. "I'm your wife." She kept her voice down, struggling not to shout. "How does a secret relationship between you and my close friend not concern me?"

Dave was on his feet, pacing around the room. He crossed his arms, breathing heavily. Finally, he sat beside Nora. "There is no affair. You have my word. Understood?"

"Then what is it?"

Dave paused. "I'm helping Barbara with some confidential matters. Of a personal nature." His words sounded measured, calculated.

"She's your client?"

He pressed his lips together, hedging. "Unofficially. Informally. In some capacity, I suppose you could say so."

"What?" Nora leaned so that she could get a better look at him. "You're representing Barbara?"

"Not technically. But, sort of. I'm assisting her."

Nora stood and faced him. "So. You're saying that you and my friend *are* and *are not* working together, that you *do* and *do not* represent her, and that, whatever it is, neither of you thought it would be appropriate to mention it to me. In fact, you agreed to keep it secret and carry on behind my back." She grabbed her arms, hugging herself, digging her nails into her skin.

"I understand how it looks." Dave stood and pulled her to him. He kissed her forehead. "But believe me, nobody's conspiring against you. It's a matter of Barbara's privacy and best interests."

Nora didn't resist his embrace, but neither did she return it.

"Look." Dave kept holding her, stroking her back, gazing gently into her eyes. "This entire discussion has been based on a monumental misunderstanding. I should have been more forthcoming with you. And you should have told me what you suspected. Can we just agree to be more open in the future, put it aside and try for a few hours' sleep?"

He was right. Nora nodded and climbed into bed. Lying beside Dave under their plush floral comforter, she tried to quell her sense of betrayal. But couldn't quite. Because even if there was no affair, even if Dave and Barbara had been doing legitimate legal business, they'd been conducting that business behind Nora's back. Sharing secrets. Meeting privately, exchanging texts. And that was almost like cheating.

Dave's arm fit snugly against her, his breathing slow and even. In moments, Nora drifted. She slept, but her sleep was neither deep nor restful. When the girls woke her up, it was after nine, and Dave had already gone to tennis.

SATURDAY, OCTOBER 2, 1993

Nora woke up to her dad's off-key rendition of "I've Been Working on the Railroad," and the smell of smoky bacon. On Sunday mornings, Philip often cooked. He'd wear an old flowered apron over his jeans and flip pancakes while the coffee brewed, no doubt hoping the aroma would lure Tommy out of his room for breakfast. Nora hoped it would, too, because if the aromas didn't lure Tommy out of his room, she'd be enlisted to bang on his door, waking him to convey the message that dad had cooked, and the food was ready. Which meant, she'd be on the receiving end of Tommy's gruff and indecent replies.

When the phone rang, Nora answered on the upstairs extension. "What's going on there? Is someone singing?" It was Annie. Apparently, she could hear her father.

Nora dragged the phone into her bedroom, told Annie that it was the television and that she'd turn it down.

"So?" Annie asked. "Can you go? How's two o'clock?" She was probably in her room, sprawled across her unmade four-poster bed.

Nora lowered her voice. "I can't. My dad's making a big deal out of having a family day."

"Family day? What's that? Do you have to stay home and play Scrabble? Have a game of catch? Gawd. Family day. That is so lame."

Yes, it was lame. But it was the only excuse Nora had been able to think of when Annie suggested they go back to the mall and maybe meet some new guys.

"Trust me, Nora. After a couple hours, your dad'll be as sick of it as you will."

Downstairs, her father sang on. Her mother called for her to wake up Tommy. God, couldn't she have a single phone call in peace? Not that she knew how to handle this one. Why why why why did Annie insist on going to the mall again? Why couldn't she be happy rollerblading or bike riding or just hanging out watching a video?

Annie was still talking. "Besides the food court's where all the high school kids hang. And, honestly? I wouldn't mind running into that Rick guy again." Her laughter tinkled, sharp like shattering porcelain. "I should have given him my phone number."

"Well, thanks for leaving me with his creepy friend." Nora's stomach twisted at the thought of him, his smell, his braces jammed with pieces of food, his fat gross tongue.

"Creepy? Come on, Nora. It wasn't his fault you got sick. You probably wouldn't have liked Johnny Depp that day. Trust me. He was totally biker hot."

Biker hot? What did Annie know about bikers? She was just turning twelve. Down in the kitchen, her father blared a verse from another of his favorite tunes, "Someone's in the Kitchen with Dinah."

"Nora? Is Tommy up? Come set the table." Her mother's voice was shrill now, annoyed. Why couldn't the woman set the table her own damn self? Why was everything always Nora's job?

"I gotta go, Annie."

"Okay. So, I'll call you at a quarter of two. By then, your dad will be sick of whatever it is he's planning, and you'll have played dutiful daughter long enough, so you'll be able to sneak off for a little. Sound good?"

"I can't promise—"

"You'll see. It'll be fine."

"Nora!" Her mother clomped up the stairs. "Where are you?"

"Great. Okay. Later." Nora hung up and called down to her mother. "I'm here. Getting Tommy."

Marla reversed directions, muttering. Nora let out a breath and chewed the inside of her cheek. How was she going to deal with Annie? What kind of family activity could take all afternoon? She approached Tommy's door with trepidation, bracing for one of his typical greetings, like, "If you knock one more time, I'll smash your face," or "Shut up or I'll come shut you up." Or the always popular, "Drop dead, shit head."

She hesitated at his door, braced herself, knuckles poised for knocking. During other Sunday wakeups, she'd sustained twisted arms and nasty pinches. This time, she'd knock and call his name, then take off, not sticking around for him to come out. She took a breath, rapped on the door.

"Tommy!" She kept her voice soft, hoping to irritate him less. "Get up."

She waited, but Tommy didn't answer. Was he still asleep?

"Tommy, Dad made breakfast. Come down and eat!"

Nothing.

Nora stared at the door, turned and looked at the stairs. What was she supposed to do? Why was Tommy her responsibility? It wasn't her fault he wouldn't wake up. Even so, she tried again, pounded this time, not with her knuckles, but with her fists.

"Tommy. I know you can hear me. Are you going to get up or what?"

Silence.

In a minute, Mom would yell upstairs, impatient with her. "I don't ask much," she'd say. "Is it too much for you to get your-selves out of bed?" She'd go on, not considering the fact that Nora and Tommy were two separate people, that Nora was unfairly being blamed for Tommy's behavior. Well, for once, she wasn't going to get chewed out for his laziness. Nora pressed her ear to the door and, hearing nothing, turned the knob and pushed the door open wide.

"Tommy, get up—" She stopped mid-sentence because Tommy wasn't there.

His bed was rumpled but empty.

"Tommy?"

She didn't want to go into his room, to enter his world of mounted butterflies and crawly things, his posters of caterpillars, his blown-up photographs of roaches, locusts, and June bugs. She stood in the doorway. The curtains were closed, the light dim, the air musky and stale. Yesterday's clothes festered on the floor. Books and folders spilled out of his book bag beside his bug freezer.

But no Tommy.

Nora checked the bathroom but didn't find him. She called his name again, but heard no response. She was angry now. He must have heard her, must be deliberately ignoring her. Why would he do that—unless he didn't want her to find him. Which meant he was somewhere he shouldn't be.

Nora's teeth clenched as she darted out of his room and down the hall to hers. Whatever he was doing in there—probably leaving a dead bug or some other sick creature to scare her—it didn't matter. He had no right to be in there. She burst in, ready to attack.

But Tommy wasn't there.

She checked her pillow and sheets. Found no grisly surprises. Looked at her bookshelf. Nothing.

"Tommy?" She stepped out of her room cautiously, worried now. What could have happened to him? Had he run away? Her imagination kicked in and she pictured him taking off before dawn, hitchhiking, maybe accepting a ride in a pickup truck driven by a kidnapper or killer.

"Nora! Tommy!" Her mother's tone was definitely angry now. "Breakfast is on the table. Dad and I are eating."

"Mom, I can't find—" Nora didn't finish saying that she couldn't find Tommy because just then, he appeared at the end of the hallway, slinking out of their parents' bedroom with his camera in hand.

"What?" He wasn't dressed yet, wore the undershorts and T-shirt he'd slept in.

"Why didn't you answer me? I've been calling."

"Didn't hear you."

She didn't believe him: His face was crimson. Why? Was he embarrassed? What had he been doing? An image flashed in her mind: her mother clutching a piece of paper from her father's pocket, her face turning that same deep red. "What were you doing in Mom and Dad's room?"

He shoved past her toward his room. "Like it's any of your business."

"Like it's Mom and Dad's business."

"So what? Go on. Tattle on me. Tell them I was in their room. Big fucking deal."

"Fine. I will." She wheeled around, headed for the stairs.

"Hold on, what's the big deal? I was just taking pictures. Of their furniture."

Pictures of their furniture? Nora stopped and faced him. "Why?"

"You wouldn't understand. It's—I'm experimenting. With light. And texture. The wood in their bedroom set has an interesting grain."

He was lying. His tongue tripped and his words didn't flow right. But being hungry, and without time or interest in calling him out, she started down the steps.

"Wait. So, why were you looking for me?"

Seriously? Why did he think she'd look for him on Sunday morning when the house smelled of bacon and hot maple syrup?

"Breakfast."

She was almost at the landing when he called after her, "For real. I was just getting shots of the furniture."

Nora didn't respond. Tommy hurried after her, was on her heels, tailing her nervously into the kitchen. Their father was draining bacon grease, while their mother poured orange juice into their glasses. The pancakes were already on plates.

Everyone sat down.

"So, how's the weekend going?" Dad asked. "Either of you have plans for later?"

Nora almost rolled her eyes. Did he really believe Tommy might have plans? "I might go to my friend Annie's house."

Her mother's eyebrow raised. "You've been spending an awful lot of time with that girl. Why don't you ever get together with your other friends, like Natalie or Charisse?"

Nora shot her a look. How could her mom disapprove of Annie? She'd never spent five minutes with her and had no idea how immature, by comparison, Natalie and Charisse were.

"What was that for?" Her mother stopped eating and glared at Nora.

"What was what for?" Her father was sipping coffee. He looked up, clueless.

Her mother scowled at him. "You saw that. You know exactly what."

Nora helped herself to bacon strips.

"What?" He shrugged.

"Are you completely oblivious, Philip?" Marla's hands were on the table. "This is what I mean. This is the attitude I get. Didn't you notice how she looked at me?"

Wait. *This is what I mean*? They'd discussed her? Her attitude?

Tommy had drowned his pancakes in syrup and was shoveling forkfuls into his mouth, smacking his lips as he chewed.

Nora's father turned to her, frowning. "Nora, apologize to your mother."

"Apologize?" Nora bit into a piece of bacon. "For what? I didn't do anything."

"You sassed me."

What was going on? Nora had hardly said a word, nothing close to what she'd wanted to say, what she had every right to say, what she knew even though nobody would admit it. The truth was that her mother was ashamed of Tommy, of what a total loser he was, of how he had not a single friend with less than six legs, of how he slunk around with his camera snapping photos of things that crawled in dirt. But her mother would never admit those feelings, so blame got shoved onto Nora for being normal and having actual friends. Nora was sick of bearing the brunt of Mom's dark little secret about Tommy Tommy Tommy Tommy.

"All I said was I wanted to go to Annie's—"

"Philip." Her mother snapped, her eyes sharp on her husband.

"Nora," Her father sounded bedraggled. "I'm afraid you're not going anywhere today."

"What?"

"You were rude to your mother, so you're staying home."

Marla looked at her coffee cup, her face smug.

Tommy chugged orange juice.

Nora said nothing. She sat at the table, thinking of how unfair her mother was, how clueless her father was. The good news, though, was that she didn't have to worry about what to tell Annie about going to the mall. This day was going to be spent home with her family, after all.

SUNDAY, AUGUST 12, 2018, 11:00 A.M.

As if from a distance, Nora watched herself move through the morning, getting the girls ready to go to Barbara's backyard pool where they'd meet Patty, Alex, and their kids. She got Ellie into a pink swim suit, Sophie into yellow. She packed a bag of towels, caps, goggles, sunscreen and hairbrushes, and brought it downstairs, wondering if Barbara had texted Dave again. Damn. What kind of person conducted a secret relationship—even about business—with her friend's husband? What was so personal and private that Nora couldn't be allowed to know? Unless—was it something about Barbara's past, something coming back to haunt her? Or something about Paul? Maybe he'd done something sleazy to rise in politics so fast. Maybe it was something so shady that Barbara needed a lawyer to protect her own interests. Did it involve the IRS? The Mob?

"Mommy, can we go now?" The girls were waiting by the door. How long had they been there, watching her?

"Yup. Off we go." Nora smiled. She tussled Ellie's hair, tugged Sophie's pigtail before herding them into the car.

It's just a legal matter, she told herself. Nothing that concerns you.

But it—whatever it was—did concern her. Friends didn't meet secretly with each other's spouses. Not innocently, anyway. And Nora wasn't going to allow it. She'd confront Barbara. Face her. Make her tell the truth.

And then? What would she do if Barbara leaned her freckled nose close and admitted that, yes, Nora was right, she'd been seeing Dave, that, no, it wasn't for legal advice at all. That in fact, they'd been having an affair for some time—six months? A year? Five? They'd been keeping it secret for the sake of the children and had no intention of ending their relationship. What then? Would Nora slap her? Scream at her? Poison her chicken salad?

But that was ridiculous. It wasn't an affair. Dave had said it wasn't. He wouldn't have lied to her.

If only she could go back to yesterday, before she'd read the texts. Nora ached for ignorance, for the dumb, smug comfort of oblivion. She liked being married to Dave, simply being Mrs. Dave Warren. But apart from Dave, she liked being a Mrs. It offered prestige and pedigree. It gave her admission to the private, exclusive club of Married People. Barbara wouldn't try to take that away from her. Barbara was her friend.

Then again, was she? They'd had kids in the same playgroup and had bonded over Ellie's and Colin's infancies. Over toddling, teething, toilet training, Colin's climbing skills, and Ellie's quirkiness. They'd sung "The Wheels on the Bus" together, complete with hand signals. They'd taken their kids to the park and the zoo, and talked about when to get pregnant again or whether to get a dog, and later, to keep in touch with other playgroup moms, they'd both joined the book club. But were they friends? Was anyone her friend?

You're the same as me: a misfit, an oddball, a freak.

Nora drove past the gas station, the supermarket, the drug store, the bank. Ellie and Sophie were belting out a song she didn't know, one with animal sounds, probably from camp.

Patty was her friend, for sure. They'd known each other since seventh grade. But was time enough to make them friends? And what about her neighbors, Carol and Yasmin? And Dave's partners' wives, or the volunteers at the hospital auxiliary? The moms at the school? There were lots of women in her life. They laughed together, shared lunches, gossip, bottles of cabernet. But were they friends, or had they come together because of convenience? Because they lived close by, or their husbands worked or played tennis together, or their kids had been born at around the same time? Did she really know any of them? Did she trust them? Did she actually *like* any of them?

The girls sang a nursery rhyme in the backseat. "The cow, it goes: Moooo Moooo!" They bellowed the animal sounds, then erupted into giggling fits.

Nora made a left at a stop sign, but her mind was still on her friendships. And she wondered, did any of her friends actually like her? Why should they? Of course, in an emergency, she'd watch their kids or bring a lasagna. She hosted dinner parties. Raised money for charity. She made phone calls, playdates, and plans for lunch. But underneath, what did she really offer them?

"The pig, it goes: Oink Oink!"

Nora watched them in the rearview mirror and glimpsed a segment of her own face there. Nora Field Warren. Mrs. David Warren. Mother of Ellie and Sophie Warren. Who the hell was that? Did she let anyone know what she thought or felt? Except for that truth or dare game at the last book club, when had she last confided in anyone? Oh, but wait. Even then, she hadn't confided. She'd embellished a fib to make it juicy while concealing her real true past. Wasn't that what she always did? Hide the truth and take cues from her environment, mirror the behavior of others. Performing the roles of her life: wife, mommy, co-chairman of the school's Family Fun Day committee, room mother, carpool driver, country club member, charity board member, bake sale coordinator, et cetera?

"Your turn, Mommy."

Her turn? She stopped at a red light, tried to figure out what Sophie was talking about.

"Pick. We already did chicken and pig and cow."

Oh, the song. She recalled their shouted "moos" and "clucks."

"How about a horse?"

"Yes!" Sophie squealed, and they began again. "Out on the farm, out on the farm, there's a horse on Grandma's farm..."

Nora drove through a yellow light, pulled onto Barbara's street, and parked in front of the house as her daughters finished neighing, then reminded them: "No running. No pushing. No swimming by yourself. No deep end."

Out of the car, Sophie bounced and chattered, taking Ellie's hand. Together, they skipped toward the backyard gate. Nora tried to remember a time when she'd felt like that, immersed in and excited about the moment. Growing up with Tommy, it hadn't been very often. Happy times had been squelched by his gloom, fun drowned by his misery. *Weirdo, creep, freak.* She'd spent her childhood trying to get out from under Tommy's shadow, trying to distinguish herself from him. But what had that meant? Who had she been? Who was she now? Was she kind? Funny? Curious? Generous? Was she friend-worthy? Was she anything at all?

Maybe that was what had led Dave to drift away. Unlike Barbara, with her casino-dealing, cocaine-snorting, high-rolling past and body-waxing, bling-wearing, laugh-out-loud present, deep down, stripped of her roles and concerted efforts to be appropriate in each situation, Nora was nobody in particular.

The girls spotted Patty and her kids on the patio and scampered away. Nora waved and followed, hauling the bag of extra towels, dry clothes, hair brushes, caps, goggles, sunblock and snacks over her shoulder. With a smile.

Barbara was in her usual spot, under a tree near the shallow end of her expansive heated pool, wearing a gold bikini, a wide straw hat with a gold and black polka dot band, and an oversized, even for her, gold bracelet.

She waved from behind big black sunglasses. "Have a seat." She gestured at half a dozen chaise lounges.

Nora wanted to slap her. How could Barbara act so happy-to-see-you cheerful? Didn't she feel the least bit awkward? Planting her towels on three lounges, settling in, she avoided Barbara by keeping busy with the girls. Sophie hopped around, grabbing her goggles and swim cap, impatient to join Harry and Colin in the pool. Patty's boys dropped their gear and took off yelling, flying into the water. Patty hollered at them to slow down, but her voice was lost in their shrieking and splashing. Nora rubbed sunscreen onto Ellie and Sophie and reminded them to stay in the shallow end. They raced to the pool where Ellie entered inch by inch, skittish at the chill, and Sophie jumped in, howling.

They were both fine.

Nora adjusted her chair, angling it so she could more easily keep eyes on Barbara, who leaned sideways, listening to Patty. Their conversation was mostly lost to Nora, drowned out by pool noise, but the brim of Barbara's hat bobbed as she nodded in agreement. She gestured as she replied, her diamonds glaring in the sunlight. Nora didn't know what they were talking about. It didn't matter. What mattered was that Barbara was basking in the sun as if she and Nora were the best of friends, while still believing that she was sharing a secret with Nora's husband. How could she pose there, all smiles and freckles? How could she offer a pitcher of fresh mimosas?

Nora felt like a spy. No, a hypocrite, smiling as if nothing had changed, not letting on what she knew. She watched the children, drank mimosas, watched Barbara's glossed lips, eyed her tanned, flat, stretchmark-free belly.

I'm helping Barbara with confidential matters. Personal matters.

From time to time, one of the children called out for their mothers to watch them swim a few strokes, or jump off the side, or dunk and hold their breaths. At those times, Nora would turn with the other women and dutifully observe the performances, praise the skills. But for the most part, her gaze, concealed by sunglasses, was aimed at Barbara. Nora lay back on her lounge and seethed, deciding when to corner the vixen, what exactly to say.

She saw the bruise by accident. While she was refilling her juice glass, Barbara reached into the ice bucket and dislodged her bracelet, exposing an inch or so of skin above her wrist.

At first, Nora thought it was a birthmark, violet and intense, irregular at its edges. She glimpsed it for two, maybe three seconds before Barbara saw her staring and shoved the bracelet back into place, thrusting her arm behind her back so abruptly that she flung melted ice onto Nora's leg.

Nora looked up, met her eyes.

Barbara forced a laugh and apologized. She reached for ice again, but with her other hand. Their silence extended, became just long and prominent enough to be awkward, until Barbara began to yammer about Nora's bathing suit, how good Nora looked in it, how she must be working out.

But Nora interrupted, pointing at the arm behind Barbara's back. "I don't remember that bracelet. Can I see it?"

Barbara stiffened, her right arm and its heavy gold cuff held stiffly behind her back. For a heartbeat, her eyebrows lifted, and she looked at Nora as if asking how much she knew, why she was forcing a showdown. But she recovered quickly, adding a lilt to her tone.

"Oh, this old thing? It's the same one I always wear." She held her arm out to display it and pulled it back, stepping away before Nora could actually look at it.

Nora thought back, remembering Barbara at book club, at the pool, at parties. She hadn't always worn that bracelet, might actually have never worn it. In fact, Barbara usually wore a diamond tennis bracelet or a set of thin gold bangles. So, if Barbara had a giant purple birthmark on her wrist, Nora would have already noticed it.

Patty stood up. "I'm going for a dip. Coming?"

Nora shook her head. "In a while."

"Maybe later." Barbara was standing poolside with her arms crossed. On impulse, Nora walked over and stood right beside her, intimately close.

"I know." Her voice was low, hard to hear under all the pool noise.

Barbara took a breath, put a hand to her chest. "Sorry, what?"

"About Dave."

Barbara's mouth opened. She hesitated, eyeing Nora. "You know?"

Was she going to deny it?

"Mom!" Sophie yelled. "Watch! I can do a head stand!" Sophie pushed her head down into the water and kicked at the surface. Not exactly a headstand, but she emerged looking proud.

"Good job!" Nora grinned and gave her daughter a thumbs up. Then, she waited for Barbara to respond.

Barbara fixed her gaze on the children, their bobbing and floating. "How much do you know? What did he tell you?" A breeze sent loose strands of hair fluttering against her cheek. Her arms hugged her chest.

Nora said nothing.

"Surely, not everything?" A purple blot of flesh peeped out from the rim of Barbara's bracelet. Definitely not a birthmark.

"He told me enough," Nora said.

They stood side by side, hips almost touching. The heat of the sun, shrieks of children, and splashes of water faded away.

"Good," Barbara let out a breath. "I'm glad. I hated keeping it from you."

Then why had she? "Let's talk." Nora nodded to the picnic table under the trees beyond the pool.

Nora called to Sophie and Ellie, telling them she'd be watching them from the picnic table. Reminding them that lunch would be ready soon.

Barbara didn't shout anything to her boys. She gripped her bracelet and walked silently to a picnic table, and sat with her back straight, her hands folded. She didn't try any more to conceal the bruise. It spilled out from under the bracelet, ugly and dark. When Nora sat opposite her, Barbara lowered her sunglasses, revealing a matching bruise under her eye.

Nora was aghast, speechless. Abuse? Was that the confidential personal matter Dave had been helping with? No. How could it be? Paul adored Barbara, doted on her. He lavished her with jewelry, foreign cars, exotic trips, designer fashions. Paul, an Ivy Leaguer, had attended Princeton, or was it Yale? He was a gentleman—charming and impeccable and handsome. She hadn't seen him often, but whenever she had, his nails had been manicured. His teeth blindingly white. And for God's sake, he was running for the U.S. Senate. No way would Paul Ellis beat his wife.

And yet.

Barbara replaced her sunglasses. "He wasn't always like this," Barbara began. "When I met him, he was thoughtful and sweet. My knight on horseback. Prince charming." She paused, absently picking at slivers on the picnic table. "I don't know what happened, when he changed."

"Why didn't you tell someone? You could have come to me. Any of us."

"You don't get it. Paul is... He's not who he seems to be."

"So let's call the police. Now. Today. Have him arrested for spousal abuse."

"Nora." Barbara smiled sadly. "That would ruin him."

"What do you care? The man beats you!"

"Shh!" Barbara stopped picking slivers and glanced around to make sure no one had heard. "Look, Nora. You have no idea what I'm up against or what kind of man he is."

"I know he's the kind of man who hits his wife. That's enough."

"No." Barbara stiffened. "I have the boys to think about. He'd take them. He'd make me seem unfit. If I do anything to stand up to him, he'll go after me. Trust me, it's been building for a long time. Since I was pregnant with Harry. I was big as a house, swollen ankles, barely able to walk, and he accused me of cheating. I laughed. I thought he was joking until he slapped me. He still imagines that every man who looks at me is my secret lover."

Nora swallowed a gasp. She thought back to first meeting Barbara at playgroup with little Colin, how she'd sparkled, standing out among the other moms with their limp hair and baggy sweatpants. Nora had been jealous of her energy, toned body, perfect makeup, highlighted hair. When Barbara's designer tees and jeans got spattered with glue or finger paint, she exuded nothing but happy nonchalance. Had Barbara really been abused, even then? Had she been faking her cheery pep, covering a terrible secret?

"The last few years, ever since Harry's birth..." Barbara paused. Her fingers again found the rough patch on the table and resumed picking at it. "Paul's been unbearable. Possessive and, oh my God, controlling. He questions my every move. He doesn't trust me and checks on me, makes me call him every two hours to make sure I'm not out with some other guy. Nora, it's hell. I never know who he's going to be. One minute, he's romantic and giving. The next, he's jealous and possessive. I can't win, Nora. If I reassure him and tell him I love him, he accuses me of trying to charm and manipulate him. If I don't reassure him, he accuses me of sleeping around and calls me a slut and says I'll shatter his political future. Yesterday, I begged him to go with me to counseling." She bit her lip. "Well. You've seen his reaction."

She held up her wrist, displayed the bruise.

"You have to leave," Nora said. "Take the boys. Today. Stay with us."

"I can't."

"Why not? What are you afraid of? What can he do to you after you're gone?"

Barbara rolled her eyes and swatted tiny sweat beads off her freckled nose. She looked around again, making sure no one was close by. "I know you mean well, Nora. But if leaving were easy, don't you think I'd have done it by now?" She pushed her hair back, stiffened. "Look, you don't even know him. You've met him, what, three times at crowded parties? And he's been delightful and witty, right? Suave? Gallant? Trust me, Nora, you know nothing about my husband, so don't presume to give me advice."

Nora bristled, stung. She'd meant to be supportive, didn't deserve to be snapped at. Obviously, Barbara didn't appreciate her input. So what should she do, get up and walk away? She started to stand, but hesitated. Barbara had been hurt. Fierce, angry bruises mottled her skin. Nora couldn't just leave her. She sat again.

"Sorry." Barbara sniffed, wiped at her nose with diamond-clad fingers. "You're only trying to help. I don't mean to sound ungrateful."

Nora reached across the table and squeezed Barbara's hand. "It's okay."

A few quiet moments passed. Barbara dabbed at her eyes, checking for mascara, calming herself. Nora gazed at the pool. Patty swam laps, and the children played. She looked up at the trees around them, their leaves almost motionless. Dead bare branches hiding among the foliage. Finally, her gaze settled on the table. And she noticed that the wood was moving. No, not the wood—tiny red dots on top of it. The dots scurried over the surface of the table and benches. Immediately, Nora's legs and arms began to itch, and she thought of Tommy and his bugs, his ant collection on the loose.

"Barbara…" She was about to point out the dots—they were probably tiny spiders—when Barbara leaned across the table, her face inches from Nora's.

"Here's the deal. I might as well say it. I haven't left Paul because Paul will not let me leave. Ever. He's sworn he'll stop me, and he means it. He'll find me and lock me away somewhere. No one will ever find me. He'll make me disappear. This…" she held out her bruised wrist, "is nothing. Even if I somehow managed to get away, he'd use his connections to find me and bring me back."

Nora eased to the edge of the bench, hoping there were fewer bugs there. Maybe she could stand and talk? "Can't you get protection? A restraining order?"

Barbara scoffed. "An order through the courts? Make no mistake, Paul will not allow a scandal. He's running for public office and has a family-man image to keep up."

"Piffle. Lots of people separate and get divorced. There's no stigma anymore."

"Like I said. You don't know Paul. He won't allow even an innuendo of imperfection. He's the ideal husband with the perfect family. And I am his perfect wife."

"That's medieval. It's bull. You don't have to—"

"He is a powerful man. Party bosses and big money supporters don't pick nice guys to run for the Senate. They back ambitious, sociopathic egomaniacs, like Paul. Trust me, leaving him is not a matter of packing a bag and driving off."

Barbara's polished nails ripped splinters out of the tabletop. Miniscule red dots scurried everywhere, helter-skelter.

Nora tried to absorb what she'd heard, to redefine Paul as a bullying bastard and Barbara as a victim. "I don't know what to say," she said, finally. "I had no idea."

"I hide things well, don't I? Anyway, now you know why I turned to Dave for help."

No, actually, she didn't. Why Dave? Why not the police or a divorce lawyer? Why not a bodyguard? "But Dave doesn't practice domestic law."

"No. But more importantly, he has no connections or obligations to Paul. And I can trust him." She paused, scratched her arm, then her leg.

The bugs were on her. Nora couldn't interrupt Barbara's life-altering talk, but neither could she sit still and let the things bite them. So, casually, as if to shift positions and stretch, she stood.

Barbara grabbed her arm. "Nora, I hope you understand why we've been so secretive. And I have to ask—to beg. Please please please. Don't say anything to anyone. Not a peep. As far as our friends know, I'm a blissfully happy, loving wife who waxes her privates for her sexy, adoring husband. Okay?"

Nora blinked. What had seemed erotic days ago seemed hor-
rifying now. "Of course. Not a word."

Barbara smirked and stood, scratching her thigh. "I'm glad
you know. It's a relief not to hide this mess from you anymore.
The way Dave and I have been sneaking around, I was afraid
you'd think we were having an affair."

Really. What an absurd idea. Nora tried to laugh, couldn't.

"Oh, damn." Barbara stood. "What time is it? I have to call
and check in, and my phone's back on my chair. 'Scuse me." She
dashed back to her lounge chair.

Nora watched Barbara run off, backside jiggling. She wondered if there were bruises there, too. How was it possible that
Barbara—sassy, confident, striking, strong Barbara—had been so
brutally victimized? How was it that that stunning, sleek, smooth,
prominent candidate Paul could have caused those ugly purple
marks? Across the deck, Barbara dug her phone out of her bag,
hurrying to call her husband on schedule—how revolting.

But how was Dave going to get Paul to change? Argue with
him? Sue him? Threaten to leak the story to the media? Dave was
just a criminal defense lawyer, not a power broker with heavy
duty political clout. It seemed futile.

But still, Dave, her sweet husband Dave, was doing his best to
help. Nora had had so little faith in him, had suspected him of
cheating, when actually he'd been rescuing her friend. She
flushed with a mixture of pride and guilt. And love. For sure, she
owed Dave an apology. More than that. She owed him her trust.

Nora headed back toward the pool, absorbed in scenarios. She
imagined Dave helping Barbara and the boys sneak away in the
night. And Paul coming after them. No, not Paul himself. He
played in the major leagues, so he'd send a hitman after them—
not just Barbara, but her helpers as well. Oh God. Paul would

never. Except that he might, if he was as controlling and ruthless as Barbara had said. As her black eye and purple arm had proved. Maybe Dave could negotiate with him. Provide Paul with an incentive of some kind, and a cover story to explain the separation without a scandal. Maybe Colin or Harry had asthma and needed to recuperate in the fresh air of the Alps.

"Mommy, no one will give me a turn."

Nora had been so deep in thought that she hadn't noticed the dab of pink fabric and small limbs huddling on the lounge chair beyond Barbara.

Ellie sat alone, doing nothing. "Everyone likes Sophie better."

"I'm sure that's not true." Except she was sure that it was. Sophie was easier, lighter, jollier, and Nora knew that as well as anyone. Just as everyone had known the differences between Nora and Tommy. But this situation had nothing to do with Tommy, and Nora would not compare him to Ellie. They were nothing alike.

Still, no one was playing with Ellie.

Nora made herself sound cheery. "Well, never mind. It's time for lunch anyway." She asked Ellie to call the others to come eat, and Ellie hopped off, pleased with her important job. Tommy would never have done that.

Nora turned to ask Barbara about her phone call, but Barbara was lying on her lounge chair with her wide straw hat covering her face like a big, round, Do Not Disturb sign. Had something happened during the call? Was she seething? Crying?

Patty returned from her swim just before the kids scrambled out of the water. She and Nora handed out dry towels and a picnic of sandwiches, peaches, chips, and juice. Nora kept moving, passing napkins around, switching apple juice for grape, making sure that Ellie didn't eat alone, that Barbara remained

undisturbed. She chatted and smiled as if she were a normal suburban mom relaxing at her friend's pool on a hot summer day,
munched celery sticks as if she hadn't just learned the shocking,
terrible, intolerable secret Barbara had entrusted to Dave, and
now, to her. As if she didn't recall how dangerously out of control
big secrets could get.

FRIDAY, JUNE 2, 1993

The warm night breeze fluttered through the curtains, carrying with it the chirping of crickets so loud and dense that it almost drowned out the voices of Nora's parents upstairs in the study. Nora heard phrases, random words out of context.

Her mother hissing, "Hussie!"

Her father snapping, "...pocket... snooping..."

Another argument. All these months later, were they still fighting about that piece of paper her mother had found in her dad's pocket? What could he have been carrying that would cause this recurring battle? It had to be someone's phone number. But whose? A girlfriend? Ew! Nora couldn't believe anyone would want to flirt with her father. That Philip, with his heavy glasses and thinning hair, could attract another woman. Apparently, her mother could believe it, though, as she brought it up whenever they argued, whenever she was mad. Which, lately, was pretty much always.

Nora tried not to listen. She had the television on but wasn't watching. She thought of Annie, of her perpetual half-smile that made her look as if she knew an amusing secret. Nora was practicing that semi-smile, wondering how it looked on her.

Tommy sat beside her in his usual spot on the sofa, peering through his camera lens at a jar of newly caught fireflies. After supper, as the sun had been going down, he'd gone outside with Philip. Nora had seen them running around the yard, hooting and acting goofy, chasing lightning bugs, cupping them one by one in their hands and dropping them into a jar. Afterward, Philip had punched air holes in the lid, and Tommy had put in a leaf for them to climb on and a drop of water for them to drink. There must have been half a dozen of them trapped in there, and Tommy was fixated. Once in a while, he turned the jar or moved his camera to change perspective. Nora watched him watching them, amused by his close observation. Tommy never noticed the stubble on his cheeks, his raw red pimples, the tired smell of his two-day-old shirt, or the swatches of thick, cottony hair dangling over his forehead and curling down his neck. He never noticed anything about himself, but when it came to bugs or photographs of bugs, no detail escaped him.

Times like this, when Tommy was quiet and concentrating, absorbed in thought, Nora felt a curious fondness for him. He intrigued her, this odd person with whom she shared parents. When he wasn't picking on, snooping, or embarrassing her, Tommy was all right. But even then, he remained a puzzle she couldn't solve. What compelled him to surround himself with insects? Why didn't he have any friends? How had he become such an outcast? When had it begun? She had no idea what had happened to Tommy, how he made it through his days, what he hoped for. Tommy was at once a stranger and the person she was most closely connected to in the whole world. She sat beside him, repeated the word "brother" in her head, trying to make sense of it.

"Okay, hang on." Tommy snapped off the lamp and the television.

They sat together in the dark, ignoring the percussive muffled anger upstairs, feeling the warm summer breeze, not talking, not moving, quietly watching bright, phosphorescent glows blinking on and off, flashing signals in some unreadable code.

"So cool," Tommy whispered. "That's how the guys attract girls. By flashing them."

"What?" Nora didn't know if he was serious.

"I'm serious," he said. "Bioluminescence. Watch the way they light up, for how long, in what pattern—each is different, but they're all trying to get a date."

The lights magically flickered on and off. Nora understood how girl fireflies would like it. She liked it, too.

After a while, their parents quieted, and the chirping crickets outside became the only sound. Nora and Tommy sank into the sofa cushions, lulled and relaxed, breathing in rhythm. Nora saw what Tommy saw. The on and off, the bright and dark. She felt what he felt. The peace. The mysterious beauty.

"Think they'll get divorced?"

Tommy's question startled her. She couldn't reply.

"Because I do."

She saw the silhouette of his unruly, untrimmed hair. "What are you talking about?"

"Are you deaf? Do you not hear Mom and Dad fighting all the time?"

"People fight, Tommy. That doesn't mean—"

"Not this much. Not unless they hate each other. Listen to them. They're vicious."

Nora felt punched, stunned. She didn't know what to say. She'd mostly tuned out her parents' fights, accepting their bickering as just something parents did. Which it was. Of course it was. Tommy was wrong. Nobody was getting divorced. Besides, what did Tommy know about arguments, let alone marriages? He'd never had a girlfriend, had no idea how couples acted, unless they had six legs and their butts lit up.

"If they split, I got dibs on Dad. You can stick with the witch."

What?

"But I'm pretty sure they'll wait 'til I'm out of high school—"

"Stop it, Tommy. Shut up!" She shoved him.

"What's that for?"

"It's not true, that's what." Her chest felt tight, her throat thick.

"Shit. You seriously don't know? How blind are you? Can't you see what's happening in your own house?" Tommy flipped on the light. "There. See better now?"

Nora squinted, eyes adjusting. "It's just a fight." Her voice was choked.

"Don't act like this is the first one. It's been going on for months."

"It has not." She tried to sound definite but heard a whiny sniffle, a build-up of tears.

"What planet do you live on? Oh, shit—you're going to cry? Crap." He stood, started toward the stairs. "What was I thinking, trying to talk to you like you were actually mature enough to discuss something that affects us both? I should have known better. Never mind. I'm going to bed."

"Fine! Go! Just so you shut your stupid mouth!"

Nora remained on the couch, watching the jar of fireflies. With the lights on, their magical glows were gone. They were just bugs.

Her parents were fine. They were not getting divorced. She wiped her tears. Tommy had just been trying to get her upset, saying stuff to unsettle her. It was her own fault for letting him. She'd let her guard down and relaxed, trusted the calmness. Trusted Tommy. *God.* She was twelve years old, she should have known better. She closed her eyes and counted, putting the conversation behind her, waiting for her breathing to settle down.

SUNDAY, AUGUST 12, 2018, 10:15 P.M.

After the girls were in bed, when they were alone in their bedroom, Dave sat her down.

"Nora. When are you going to tell me what's wrong?"

She bit her lip. He could always read her mood, no matter how she tried to cover.

"Nora?" He waited.

She felt his eyes on her. The air didn't move. Nothing did. The universe held still, waiting for Nora to say out loud, in words, what had happened that day.

She might as well get it over with, just tell him.

Dave's body shifted. "You saw Barbara?"

Nora explained that, yes, but not just Barbara. Patty, too, and all the kids.

"But Barbara and I went off to talk. And it came up about, well, you know." She stumbled over her words, avoided his eyes.

"Huh? What came up?"

"About. About how you're helping her."

"What?" Dave stood, glaring at her. "Nora, you repeated what I told you?"

"Of course not. I just said that I knew you were working with her. But—"

"For God sakes, Nora. Why did you do that?" He ran his hand through his hair. "I told you about Barbara in confidence—and only because you pressured me. And the first thing you did was run out and tell her that I'd discussed her situation with you?" He spun around, turning his back.

"I—I didn't..." Nora sputtered, searching for words, not knowing where to start, not prepared for this reaction. "Dave, I didn't say anything specific."

"But why would you say anything at all?" He faced her again, heat radiating from his eyes.

Nora took a second to recall the sequence, the reason she and Barbara had gone to the picnic table.

"It's a matter of ethics, Nora. Can't you see that? I trusted you to—"

"It was the bruises." Nora saw them again, dark and angry.

Dave stopped lecturing. His eyebrows furrowed, head tilted. "The what?"

Nora told him about the gold cuff that couldn't quite cover the one on Barbara's wrist. And the sunglasses hiding the one near her eye. "He hurt her because she asked him to go to counseling."

"Son of a bitch!" Dave's fists tightened and he slumped next to her on the bed.

"She's really scared of him, Dave. I told her to leave and bring the kids to stay with us, but she said he'd come after her." Nora twisted her wedding ring. "All this time, I thought Paul worshipped her. Our friends all envy her, being married to him. God, those two are local aristocracy. No one would believe what's really going on. It's incredible."

Dave rubbed his eyes and sighed. "I guess I can be candid with you, since Barbara has been. The fact is that, despite his public image and popularity, and despite his promising future in politics, Paul Ellis has a dangerous dark side. Secrets that could ruin him. Now that he's likely to be elected to the Senate, he's afraid of negative publicity. A scandal that could ruin him. Possibly even criminal charges."

"Criminal? Like spousal abuse?"

Dave hesitated. "There's more to it than that. Donations from questionable sources. Business deals with questionable characters—"

"Like the Mob?"

Dave shook his head. "Look, I can't get into all that. My concern is Barbara and the kids. Their well-being."

Yes, Barbara and the kids. "She needs to leave."

"Right. But, as she told you, that's a complicated procedure. You're either with Paul or against him."

"So what if she's against him? What'll he do? Divorce her?"

"This is way bigger than simply a divorce. He won't allow it."

"But she can't stay."

"She and the boys are going to disappear and emerge elsewhere, safely. With new identities."

What? "Like witness protection? That's crazy."

"So is Paul Ellis."

"Wait. What are you saying?" Nora's hand went to her face. "I won't even know her name? I'll never see her again?"

"Nora." Dave spoke slowly, his hand on her shoulder. "Barbara needs to get away where no one, not just you, but none of her husband's cronies, can find her." Dave made Paul sound like the head of the Mafia.

The whole idea was astounding. Barbara, leaving everything behind? Her big house, her cars, her club memberships, all her charity boards, even book club?

Dave explained that he'd spent months amassing and transferring funds—small chunks at a time. He'd managed to obtain new identities and was about to take Barbara to look at homes in rural upstate New York.

Rural? Nora couldn't picture Barbara, with her plumped lips, designer fashions, and gelled nails, living anywhere rural. Then again, Nora couldn't picture Paul hitting Barbara either. Paul was nationally known, appearing on political ads and talk shows as a rising star. Women found him charismatic and irresistible. Men found him articulate and wry.

Nora found him monstrous.

"Hold on, Nora. You said she had a black eye?" Dave frowned. "He's never hit her anywhere that would show before. Certainly not in the face." Dave stood. "Damn."

"What?"

Dave's nostrils flared, something they did only when he was livid. He began pacing.

"Dave?"

"Son of a bitch is escalating, becoming less careful about concealing his abuse. More impulsive, less controlled. Which makes me think something's happened to trigger him." He stopped pacing and turned to Nora. "In your conversation, did Barbara indicate that Ellis is suspicious? Does he suspect she's planning to leave?"

Nora thought back, saw tiny spiders scurrying, Barbara leaning toward her, Nora's own dark reflection warped in the lenses of Barbara's sunglasses. *Paul will never let me leave.*

"No. Nothing I remember."

Dave crossed his arms, his nostrils flaring even wider than before. "Think harder."

She did. She replayed the conversation, the pool noise in the background. The relentless, glaring sun. "No. She didn't say anything about that."

Dave huffed and shook out his shoulders. "Look. Nora, whatever you do, don't say a word about this to anyone."

"Of course not. I would never—"

"Not anyone." He held her gaze for a long moment, then headed for the door.

"Where are you going?"

"I don't know. Nowhere." He turned in a circle, took a couple of steps toward her, a couple away. Crossed his arms. Uncrossed them. Looked toward the hall, then back at Nora. "But I can't stay still. I guess I'll go to the study and make sure everything's in order so she's ready to go. Go on to sleep. I'll be a while."

After he left, the silence felt jagged. Nora went to the window. The trees were still, undisturbed on a windless night. No one was outside. The streetlight cast motionless shadows. The neighborhood looked calm. The only sound was the singing of crickets.

TUESDAY, OCTOBER 13, 1993

Usually, Nora's bus came about fifteen minutes before Tommy's, but not always. When it was late, they had to wait on the same corner.

It wasn't just them, of course. Other kids were there too. Pam from down the street and Roger from across the street. And a few high school kids, waiting for Tommy's bus. She only knew one of them by name: Craig.

She focused on the view up the street, pretending not to see Craig, not sure if he'd remember her from the camp bus. But if he did remember her and said, 'hi,' she didn't want Tommy to see her being friendly to the kid she'd seen tormenting him. And, to be honest, she didn't want Craig to see that she was Tommy's sister. Probably she was a terrible person. Probably she'd go to hell. But it was true; she was ashamed of her brother. *Family comes first.*

The morning was windy, the air nipping with a hint of autumn. Kids stood apart from each other, everybody in their own early-morning sphere of please-don't-bother-me. A few faced down the street, watching the corner where the buses would appear. Nora was one of them. She couldn't wait for the bus so she could get on and sit with Annie.

As usual, she had a list of things ready to talk to her about, things she needed Annie's insights on before starting the day. Middle school was still pretty new. So many new faces. So much homework. So many hallways to navigate, full of kids Nora often thought she'd seen in her classes but wasn't sure, couldn't remember because they changed rooms for each subject. The worst part was that, apart from lunch, she didn't have a single class with Annie. And at lunch, their table was a zoo with lots of kids vying for Annie's attention, so they couldn't really talk. The bus ride was their only chance during the day for time alone. It wasn't enough, though. Nora often felt lost, still unsure what the rules were or how kids measured each other in this realm, and she yearned to look over and check out Annie's reactions, to see if she should be friendly or aloof, stand straight or slouch, act attentive or bored. Unmoored, she held on, waiting for the bus rides to and from school to sit with Annie, get her bearings and feel anchored.

But the bus was nowhere—twenty minutes late now. She gazed down the street, willing it to appear. Tommy wandered over and stood right next to her. Oh God. She didn't look at him. Instead, she edged away, just far enough to make it seem like they weren't together. His cowlick stood at its usual attention. His hair clumped onto his forehead, wadded like black steel wool. His back slumped under the weight of his backpack.

"Where's your bus?" Tommy asked.

"How should I know?" She shrugged.

"Might have broken down."

"Hey, Bozo! You bothering that young lady?" Craig strutted over. "Because you're out of your league."

Tommy shrunk, hung his head.

"It's fine." Nora slid between them. "He's fine." She didn't say he was her brother.

Craig skirted around her to get to Tommy. Tommy turned vivid red. His eyes darted from side to side as he backed away.

"You're supposed to wait over by the street sign, away from normal people. How many times have I told you not to bother anyone?" Craig moved forward, and Tommy moved back as if in an ominous, tuneless cha-cha. "I warned you to keep out of my sight, you turd." Craig's lips curled into a smile, his eyes gleaming, hair fluttering in the wind.

"Leave him alone," Nora spoke up. "He didn't do anything." But she didn't mention, didn't say out loud, that Tommy was her brother.

Some of the other kids knew, of course: Pam and Roger. They all lived in the same neighborhood. Most everyone at the bus stop knew who everyone else was, which house they lived in, who was family. Maybe Craig knew, too. Maybe she didn't have to tell him.

Before she could decide, Craig darted, grabbing Tommy's jacket, yanking it so hard and fast that Tommy fell to his knees. Craig pounced, pushing Tommy down and mounting him like a pony.

"Stop!" Nora said. Or meant to. Her mouth opened, but she had no air. She needed to move, to grab Craig and stop him, but her limbs froze, and she stood stunned and silent, doing nothing for her brother.

The other kids gathered around Craig and Tommy, watching. Saying nothing, doing nothing.

"You make me sick, you turd. Bothering that nice girl. You make me puke! Apologize to her. Now!" Craig smacked Tommy's rear. "I didn't hear you! Say you're sorry!"

Tommy wriggled and bucked, trying to knock Craig off of him.

"Craig." Nora found her voice. She stepped closer and put her hand on his shoulder. "He didn't bother me. Let him be."

But Craig didn't let him be. As he climbed off Tommy, he hissed, "Stinking piece of shit."

Tommy tried to get up, but Craig shoved him down again.

Nora turned to the other kids. Roger. Pam. The other, older kids whose names she didn't know. All their faces had changed, become rapt and savage. Craig seemed spurred on by their attention, his shoulders bulged, jaw rippled, fists tightened. He loomed over Tommy like a coiled snake, poised to strike its prey.

Nora couldn't breathe. Craig wasn't going to stop. Tommy was breathing hard. She needed to do something besides repeat, "Craig, let him alone." She might have thought of a way to intervene, but right then, as she was desperate to stop the confrontation, her school bus pulled up. She hadn't heard it bluster and snort up the street, so she'd been surprised when the circle of onlookers split to reveal the bright yellow monster, idling with its doors flapping open.

Craig looked up, his fist hanging in the air, aimed at Tommy's jaw.

The moment hushed. Nobody moved. Leaves stopped rustling because even the breeze held still.

"Everything okay out there?" Sally, the overweight bus driver, craned her neck to see what was going on, but the kids climbing onto the bus blocked her view. Nora didn't follow them; she didn't dare get on the bus and leave Tommy undefended.

Family comes first.

Who knew what would happen, how far Craig would go? Even with the bus driver watching, he was leaning over Tommy, lip curled and sneering, aching to hurt him.

"Craig? What are you doing?" someone shouted from the bus.

It was a girl's voice. Nora wheeled around. Annie leaned her head out a window, scowling. "Don't be a bully. Let him up and come over here."

Craig's eyes softened, his sneer eased into a grin. "Hey, Annie! How's it goin'?" He hurried to Annie's window, stood chatting and laughing.

Wait. Craig knew Annie? Annie knew Craig?

Nora helped Tommy to his feet. His nose was bleeding, so she gave him a tissue. He didn't answer when she asked if he was all right, didn't even look at her. Leaves and dry grass clung to his clothes. He recoiled when she tried to brush him off.

Sally called out, "Anyone else getting on? Last call."

Nora spun around and hurried to the bus, leaving Tommy alone. But it wasn't her fault he'd been hurt. And she had no choice; she had to go to school. She ran up the steps, rushing to ask Annie about Craig, how she knew him, why she was friends with him, how much she'd seen of the scuffle with Tommy, how much she knew about the kid he'd been pounding. *Weirdo. Creep. Freak.* She ought to tell Annie about Tommy being her brother. The longer she waited, the harder it became to fess up. Besides, Annie had stuck up for Tommy even without knowing who he was. She might not care that he was Nora's brother. And it would be a relief not to keep the secret anymore. Annie was her friend, no matter what.

She was halfway up the aisle before she noticed the red-headed girl. Nora stopped, stung as if sucker punched. For the first time that school year, Annie hadn't saved her a seat.

MONDAY, AUGUST 13, 2018, 8 A.M.

Nora hadn't slept, being haunted by Barbara, her bruises and fear, trying to figure out ways to help her. First thing Monday morning, she called, but Barbara didn't answer. She tried again after half an hour. Still no answer. Probably, she had an early appointment at the day spa, getting a facial, a pedicure. Another Brazilian wax. Probably, she'd muted her phone. But Nora worried. Had Paul become violent again? Had he beaten her so badly that she couldn't talk? Not in the middle of a campaign.

Nora reassured herself that Barbara was fine as she got the girls ready for camp. She scrambled eggs, searched for lost sneakers and forced curly hair into pigtails, all the while repeating to herself that she shouldn't worry, that Barbara was all right. She'd been all right yesterday, and what could have happened since yesterday? Nothing. But Nora called again while packing lunches, and again ten minutes later, hanging up before voicemail picked up. Barbara was at the salon and her nails were wet, that was why she couldn't answer. Nothing was wrong.

The camp bus honked. Nora kissed the girls and ushered them outside. She watched from the door as Sophie skipped away, pigtails bouncing, and Ellie dragged her feet on the walkway.

As soon as the bus pulled away, she called again. Got no answer.

In fact, Barbara didn't answer all morning.

She called Patty and tried to sound casual, asking if she'd heard from Barbara.

"Why? We just saw her yesterday."

She called Alex, then Katie. Neither had talked to Barbara.

Nora told herself that she was upset over nothing. But the fretting continued even as she went to the gym for a spinning class. It was still there when she came home and ate granola and yogurt, as she showered, and threw a load of laundry into the washer. It lingered, like ominous background music, as she went to the market and got steaks to grill for the next day's dinner. And through it all, she called Barbara every half hour.

She hadn't heard anything from Barbara when the girls came home from camp, thirsty, hot, tired, and cranky. Nora set them up in the playroom with lemonade and crayons, suggesting that they relax and draw something for Daddy.

While they colored, Nora eyed her phone, resisting the urge to call yet again. She shifted the laundry load, emptied camp bags, listened to voicemails from Sheila, Alex, Katie, and telemarketers, but not from Barbara. She sat on the playroom sofa with her eyes closed, trying to sense her friend's whereabouts as if she were a psychic. Was she near water? A parking lot? A garbage dump?

She told herself to stop obsessing. Barbara was fine.

When the pictures were finished, Nora hung Sophie's pony and Ellie's flowers on the refrigerator for Dave. Hands got washed. Ellie folded napkins. Sophie helped roll ground beef into meatballs. Nora called Barbara again, got no answer.

Maybe Barbara's phone was broken. Or her battery died. Maybe she'd dropped it in the bathtub. She'd ask Dave what was going on. He'd know. Why wasn't he home yet?

Sophie finished making meatballs. Nora helped her wash grease off her hands, listened for Dave's car in the drive, his key in the lock. The spaghetti was boiling and the meatballs bubbling in sauce when Nora's phone rang. Ellie was setting out forks and knives. She didn't look up, just said, "Daddy's not coming home."

Sophie said, "Big surprise."

Nora dried her hands and grabbed the phone. Saw Dave's name on the screen.

"Nora—Hey, look. I'm sorry. Things have come to a head real fast."

"What do you mean? Where are you?" She turned the burner down. Red sauce popped and spurted onto the stovetop, spattering in small clots.

Dave talked fast. "Go ahead and eat without me."

"Why? What's going on?" And then she remembered. "I can't reach Barbara. Are you with her?"

"Don't worry. We'll talk later. Everything's coming together."

She took that as a yes. A horn honked in the background. So, Dave was in the car with Barbara.

"Kiss the girls for me. I'll be back as soon as I can." His voice was stiff. Guarded.

Back? From where?

"Mom." Sophie tapped her arm. Nora put up a hand, telling Sophie to wait a minute.

"But why are you—"

"It's happening," Dave interrupted. "Imminently. Faster than expected. We're locking in the final details. They're going this week."

This week?

"Got to run. Don't wait up."

Sophie tugged at Nora's T-shirt. "Can I talk to Daddy?"

Nora asked if he had a minute for Sophie, but Dave had already hung up.

Humming softly, Ellie unfolded his napkin and put his silverware back in the drawer.

Nora gazed out the window at the night. The wind had died down, the stifling humidity was no doubt rising. Crickets screeched. Moonlight flickered starkly through the heavy leaves of trees. But inside, the air was light, gentle, scented like bubble bath. Sophie lay asleep on her back with limbs splayed, her hair sprawling in a curly halo. Ellie curled herself into a tight ball, a fetal position. In sleep, both their faces were soft and angelic.

Nora wandered out of their room. Where was Dave? She descended the stairs, escaped to the kitchen, and reheated a cup of the morning's coffee. Maybe she should call him. It was her right, after all, to know what he was doing and whether he was okay. But she didn't call. She trusted him, didn't want to be "that wife" checking up on her husband. So she waited, keeping busy to make time pass. She straightened up the playroom, ran a load of laundry. She checked the clock, stared at her phone, scolded it for not ringing. Picked it up and absently scrolled through mail, opening nothing.

Where were they? What were they doing? *It's happening faster than we thought. She and the boys will go this week.* Probably they were moving clothes or buying furniture for a new place. Or signing a lease.

At this hour?

Yes, at this hour. Dave wouldn't lie to her.

She ought to go to bed. Read, watch television, doze off. When she woke up in the morning, Dave would be there, beside her. It was a good plan. Except that, as she started up the stairs, the doorbell rang.

Dave. He must have lost his key. She hurried to the door but stopped, her hand on the knob. What if it wasn't Dave? What if something terrible had happened and a stranger—a police detective—was outside, coming to inform her.

Oh God.

She braced herself against the doorpost. Took a breath. Opened the door.

It wasn't a detective. "You're home."

Nora's mouth opened, but she made no sound.

"Sorry to alarm you." Paul cleared his throat. "I'm not sure you remember me. We've met, but it's been a while. Paul Ellis." He extended his hand. "Barbara's my better half."

Nora's hand rose, weightless, to shake. His grip was practiced and firm. His smile was tight.

"Of course I remember you." She smiled just as tightly. What was he doing there? What did he want?

"Sorry to intrude at this late hour. But I'm looking for my wife. I haven't been able to reach her. I would have called but, though I know where you live, I don't have your cell number. Actually, would you mind sharing it with me? For situations like this..."

Paul certainly wasted no time on amenities. His brashness surprised her. Did he always behave this way, practically ordering others around, demanding what he wanted? And was she really supposed to give a man who beat his wife her phone number? Uh, no.

"Of course." Nora recited her number, reversing two digits.

"Excuse my abruptness," Paul continued while he punched the wrong number into his phone, "but where is she?" He peered over Nora's shoulder into the house. "Is she here? Inside?" He raised an eyebrow.

"Barbara? Here?" Nora's face burned. Why was she blushing? She took a step back.

"Yes. Her note said she was spending the evening with you. Something about a girls' night."

Wait, she'd left him a note using Nora as her cover? Well, hell. Why hadn't Barbara or Dave clued her in? Now she'd blown it.

Paul watched her. Tall, fair-haired and elegant, his features were perfectly symmetrical except for that one eyebrow that was still raised. No one would suspect him of violence.

Nora's smile was still pasted across her face when Paul reached for her arm and guided her into her own home. As he closed the door, Nora glimpsed a couple walking their dog around the cul-de-sac. She had the urge to call out to them but stifled it, not sure what to say.

Incongruous with his hand-tailored slacks and unchewed, imported Italian loafers, Paul smelled like Old Spice. The smell brought Nora the image of high school, her first boyfriend, Bobby Baxter, and his beat-up old Jeep Wrangler. She recalled the awkward impossibility of making out even semi-comfortably in that car, and the thrill of being with Bobby, co-captain of the football team. And, even as their steamy breath fogged the windshield, the nagging certainty that Bobby would never have been with her if Tommy'd still been alive.

The scent, the memories it evoked, were jarring. So was the physical contact. Paul's hand gripped her arm firmly, with entitlement. Probably, that same hand had caused Barbara's bruises. But surely, Paul wasn't going to hurt her. He wouldn't dare, couldn't risk bad publicity. Still, Nora's breath was short, her chest tight with fear. Where was Dave? When would he be home? Oh God, what if he and Barbara walked in now, with Paul here? She had to make him leave.

Paul steered Nora directly into the living room. She pretended she was his hostess, inviting him in. She flipped on the light switch.

"Have a seat." She smiled, tried to take charge.

He didn't release her arm. His hand felt solid and lean. Decisive. Had she and Paul ever touched before? Had they hugged hello or goodbye at rare New Year or Fourth of July parties? She didn't think so, no. She would have remembered. Paul was movie-star beautiful, a celebrity. A public figure. The few times they'd met, Paul had seemed aloof but charming, as if perpetually on a campaign stop. If he'd greeted Nora at all, it would have been with an impersonal nod in her direction. But now, here he was with her, alone in her living room, his hand gripping her, his body smelling like an old boyfriend. She glimpsed his clear nail polish. His Rolex. His simple gold wedding band. He was so close that his breath brushed her face. She wondered if his nose had always been perfect or if it had been cosmetically enhanced like Barbara's. And she noticed an almost imperceptible scar—pale, thin, and spidery—under his left eye.

You don't know him. He isn't who he seems to be.

"So, tell me. Where is my wife really?" He released Nora's arm, perched on the arm of the sofa, crossed his arms. Was he trying to seem casual?

"Actually, I'm not sure." She backed away, placing distance between them. Aware of his eyes on her, the intensity of his attention.

Paul rubbed his chin, scowling. "You know nothing about a girls' night?"

"I didn't say that," she improvised. "A bunch of us went out, but I got a headache and came home early."

Paul peered into her eyes. Had she sounded at all believable? She looked away, hoping he hadn't detected her lie.

"I'm surprised to see you. I thought you were out of town campaigning." Nora changed the subject, eyed the wingback. Hesitated to sit. She hoped the girls wouldn't hear voices and come down.

"I had a change in my schedule and came home early. I texted Barbara about it, expected she'd be there to greet me." He stood, took a breath. Stepped closer. "Nora, can we speak frankly?" He studied her. "Even though we've only met a few times, I feel as if

I know you well." Paul's gaze was heavy, penetrating. "Barbara talks about you so often. She considers you one of her closest friends."

He stood only inches from her, looming. Nora tried not to squirm. She wasn't prepared for scrutiny, certainly not by a man as stunning as Paul. She hadn't tweezed her eyebrows lately. Hadn't put on mascara today. She felt flawed and exposed, nowhere near as perfect as Barbara. But why should she give a damn what Paul thought of her? He was a wife beater who'd shown up at her home late at night, uninvited. Nora cleared her throat, swallowed. She kept up her standard smile, her go-to, unthreatening, noncommittal facial expression.

"Well, I don't know where they went after I left, but I'm sure Barbara will be home soon. She might be tipsy, but I'm sure she'll be glad you're home." Nora started for the door, hoping he'd follow.

"Wait, Nora." He sat on the sofa. "There's more. You and I need to talk."

Talk? About what? Did he suspect that she knew he was an abuser? Or—Oh God—that Barbara was about to leave him? He must. Otherwise, why would he want to talk?

"Do you have—would you mind if I had a drink?" Abruptly, Paul's demeanor changed. His brows furrowed and he gazed at the floor, looking worried. Or wounded.

Nora smiled her smile but wanted him to leave. She didn't want to get him a drink. "It's late and, like I said, I have a headache—"

"Just a quick one?" He was relentless. "Sorry. I know I'm being pushy." He backed off, smiled dashingly, almost bashfully.

"No, it's fine." Nora sighed and stepped over to the Chinese lacquered liquor cabinet.

"Scotch, please."

Everything sounded harsh and unfamiliar. The clink of glass, the slosh of liquid. Nora poured two fingers into two glasses and handed one to Paul.

He took a sip, closed his eyes as if savoring the heat. And opened them again. "Now then. Let me ask, where's your husband?"

"Dave?" Nora stammered. Stupid question. What other husband could he have meant? "Oh. Working late. On a legal case." Stupid stupid stupid answer. Of course it would be a legal case. Dave was a lawyer, what else would he be working on? Other than helping Paul's wife leave him. Outside, a car circled the cul-de-sac. Oh God. Was it Dave and Barbara? He'd said he'd be home as soon as he could.

"Join me?" Paul gestured to the sofa.

Nora remained standing. How was she going to get rid of him?

He sat back, looking up at her, comfortable and entitled, as if he had every right to be there with his Old Spice wafting cloud-like around her. "Does your husband often work this late?"

Damn. Did he suspect that Dave was with Barbara? Nora took a drink, felt the burn of alcohol sliding down her throat. "When he has to."

Paul sipped, his eyes digging at her, making her blush. Or maybe it was the scotch.

"I like you, Nora. Of all my wife's friends, you're the only one who seems worth her time. Even so, I'm trying to decide whether or not to confide in you."

Nora took another drink, dodging his scrutiny. Confide in her? Why would Paul want to confide in her? She thought of Barbara's bruised arm. Of her warning, "You don't know him. He isn't who he seems to be." Nora glanced again at the door. It seemed miles away.

"I want to pick your brain."

"My brain? Why?" Nora stiffened.

"As you know, my campaign has been demanding. I've had to travel quite a bit these last few months: pressing flesh, raising funds, giving speeches, talking to the media, kissing babies. You know the drill. It's been a very stressful time, and I haven't been home much. My wife, well. Barbara has not been happy about that. I'm sure she's talked to you about it."

Nora gave a patient smile, didn't know what to say.

"In any event, I'm worried. I think my prolonged absences have taken a toll on her. My stress has spilled onto her. Bottom line, my sweet Barbara hasn't been herself lately." His eyebrows peaked. They were honey-colored, a shade darker than his hair.

"What do you mean?"

"Has she seemed, well—moody to you? Depressed? Perhaps a bit secretive?" Paul sighed. "Nora, I found pills."

Pills?

He leaned forward, watching her, his eyes burning. "Why is Barbara making up stories, lying to me about where she is and what she's doing?"

"She wasn't lying."

"Spare me. Of course she was. We both know you weren't out drinking earlier. You're a terrible liar. So, yes, Barbara lied. And she's hiding pills. Don't cover for her. Because I think—no— I'm pretty damned sure that Barbara's in trouble."

Yes, Barbara was in trouble. But probably from bruises more than pills. *He'll never let me leave.* Nora hesitated, figuring out how to reply. She shook her head. "Really? She seems fine to me."

"I see." He studied her face, assessing her reply. "Actually, that's no surprise. She's good at covering things up." Paul looked into his glass. "You wouldn't know this, Nora. But Barbara isn't who she seems to be."

Nora shivered. Paul had echoed Barbara's words, just turned them around.

He swirled his scotch. "Today, she's the epitome of class. The perfect political wife. But when I met her, that was hardly the case." He smirked as if remembering. "Far from it. Barbara ran with a decidedly questionable crowd. Big time gamblers. Low-lifes. Connected guys. I'm talking about seriously rough, criminal characters. She partied hard, indulged in drugs. I have no doubt she had regrettable sexual relations—"

"Please, Paul, that's not my business."

"Which thing? The sex? Or the fact that she received payment for it?"

"How do you know that?"

"How do you think I met her?"

Nora took a breath, then a gulp.

"That's shocking to you." Paul's smile was thin. "Despite that, I saw something in her. She stood out, shining like a rough diamond. I saw her potential, and I fell for her. Hard. I was certain that, with the quality of life I offered her, she'd put her sordid past behind her and blossom. But now, with me being away so much..." He looked at her and sighed. "I think she's lonely, maybe even depressed. My fear is that she's fallen into her old ways, reconnecting with old habits, even old acquaintances."

He paused again, watching Nora, who searched for an appropriate response. Should she nod sympathetically? Shake her head doubtfully? In the end, she mimicked Sophie, tilting her head as if in a question. She bit her lip to look concerned. That seemed to work; Paul continued.

"I'm convinced she's struggling, trying to handle her problems on her own. I wish she would come to me for help. Because I swear on all that's holy, I'd do anything for that woman. Anything." Paul's voice tightened, became metallic. His gaze moved to the painting above the fireplace, a sailing ship being tossed in a roiling sea.

Nora felt queasy, as if on that ship. Was Barbara really taking drugs? And—oh my—had she really been a hooker? Nora had never known a hooker before. God. What had it been like, taking money to have sex with strangers? How had Barbara done that, with her perky spirit and freckled nose? It didn't seem possible.

But then, neither did it seem possible that Candidate Paul Ellis would beat the crap out of his wife.

Paul chugged the rest of his drink. He set his empty glass on an end table, looked at her. "You know something about this. I can see it on your face. Tell me. Whatever it is, I can handle it. Is it an affair? With Richie What's-his-name, that slimy coke dealer? Or—" He slapped his forehead. "How have I not thought of this before? I bet one of those creeps is blackmailing her." He sat back, stared into air.

"Paul, you're inventing—"

"That would explain everything. Because until now, Barbara's kept a low profile in my campaign. But we plan for her to become much more prominent as election day nears. I bet someone's threatening to sabotage my candidacy by exposing her past. That's probably what she's doing tonight. Meeting the blackmailer, paying him off. That explains why she left a note saying she was with you, so I wouldn't worry." A vein on his forehead pulsed. His nose seemed sharper, more severe than before. His eyes gleamed. "Nora, tell me. Am I right?"

Tears welled in his eyes, almost but not quite convincing. He was no longer the confident candidate for Senate. He was now a desperate husband, creating outlandish scenarios to explain his wife's lie. As if he'd somehow forgotten that, a couple of days ago, he'd given that same wife a purple arm and black eye.

Nora took a breath, softened her smile, and tried to sound reassuring. "I honestly don't know, Paul. But I don't think she's being blackmailed."

"Really? Then where is she?" Paul's tears disappeared, his gaze hardened. "For God's sake, Nora. She's taking pills again. Hell, I'm scared to Christ she'll end up in the hospital." His voice became a whisper, "Or worse." He leaned back, pressed on his eyes and sniffed.

Oh God. Was he crying for real?

Nora sat next to him and put her free hand on his shoulder. "I don't know where she is. But I know that she's okay. She's with a friend."

When he looked up, his lashes were wet, his breath shallow. "Who?"

Her smile was wearing thin, but her face wouldn't do anything else. She tried not to let her eyes shift as she lied. "I'm not sure. She has so many." Did he believe her?

Paul frowned. Sighed. Stroked his jaw. Finally, his gaze drifted away. "Okay. I understand your position." His voice was toneless, emotionless. "No need to say more, Nora. I despise being lied to, so I won't press you further. I won't waste my time. As long as I have your word that she's safe."

"You do."

Paul held her eyes for a moment, then stood.

Nora made no comment as she led him to the door.

"You're a good friend, Nora. Barbara's lucky to have you." He leaned down, and his whisper tickled her ear. "We'll talk again."

Nora watched him drive off. When his taillights' red glow was out of sight, she moved to the liquor cabinet and poured another scotch.

There was a dent in Dave's pillow, and the covers on his side of the bed were rumpled. Nora sat up, looking for him. The bathroom door was open. Behind her temples, a headache pulsed. Oh God. Paul. He'd been in the house. And then she'd sat up alone with a bottle of scotch.

"Dave?"

No answer.

Where was he? The clock said eight-twenty. Had he left for work already? Without even waking her up? And the girls—the camp bus would be there in minutes.

"Girls?" Nora flew out of bed and checked their room. "Girls?" She ran down the stairs.

Ellie was in the kitchen, finishing a bowl of Frosted Flakes.

"Ellie, where's Daddy?"

Ellie regarded her spoon. "Gone."

"He left for work?"

"Yup." She lifted the bowl and drank the remaining milk.

Nora called to Sophie who was getting dressed in front of the TV. Nora told her to hurry because the bus would be there any minute. She made sure their swim bags were packed, slapped peanut butter and jam onto whole wheat, threw fresh nectarines and chocolate chip cookies into sack lunches, and silently fumed.

Dave had come in after two a.m.—when she'd last looked at the clock—and he'd left this morning without a word? Without explaining where he and Barbara had gone, what they'd done last night? Without hearing about Paul?

Paul had cornered her, rattled her. He'd made her uneasy in her own home while her husband had been off somewhere, oblivious, with Paul's wife. Putting her in the middle. Well, Dave's departure was not okay. As soon as the girls left for camp, she'd call him at the office and have a word with him.

Meantime, she smiled and kissed the girls. Told them to have fun. When the bus pulled up and she walked them outside, the phone rang behind her.

It had to be Dave. Good.

She waved to the bus and ran to answer, grabbing her phone before it would go to voicemail. "Hi there. Did you get any sleep?"

"Not really. My wife didn't roll in until three."

What did Paul want from her? What was wrong with him?

Nora tensed, pushed her hair away from her eyes. She stared at the window. "Well, I told you she'd get home safe. Look, hey, I'm kind of in the middle of something—"

"By the way, the number you gave me didn't work. I got the correct one from Barbara's phone."

Oh. Nora said nothing.

"Listen, Nora, you and I have to talk."

The edge in his voice chilled her. "Why?"

"Don't insult me. Stop pretending you don't know."

"Know what?"

"Oh please, Nora."

"I'm sorry?"

"We have to meet." His voice was hushed, almost a whisper. "Today. Privately. I'll clear an hour. How soon can you get here? It's imperative."

Imperative? "I'm busy today."

"Please. It's for your sake as well as mine. I'm pleading with you."

Nora sunk onto a kitchen chair and moved Ellie's empty cereal bowl aside. How had she inherited Paul? Until last night, she'd barely ever spoken to him. Now he wanted her to meet with him privately? What should she do? Hang up on him? Tell him to get lost? Warn that he was irritating her husband?

And speaking of her husband, why hadn't he called? Why had he left so early without a word?

"Sorry. I can't—"

"Believe me, Nora. You have to."

"Honestly, whatever's going on between you and Barbara, I can't help."

"Actually, you're probably the only one who can."

Nora rolled her eyes. Why was Paul hounding her? "I've got to go."

"Listen, Nora." He paused. "I've learned the truth." His voice was guarded, shadowed. "Because I've been worried about Barbara, I hired someone to be my eyes while I was away. I've just received his report. So, now I know. And you need to know, too."

Wait, eyes? Someone had been following Barbara. Watching her. Had the "eyes" figured out that she was preparing to leave? "This doesn't concern me."

"I'll explain face to face, Nora. Not on the phone. Before I take action—well, you and I need to have a conversation."

A conversation? "Like I said, I have plans."

"Change them."

Who did he think he was? "How about later in the week?"

"Nora. My schedule is obviously far tighter than yours. I'm in the midst of a Senate campaign for God's sake. If I can clear my schedule for an hour, surely you can clear yours. I'm sorry for being so pushy, but this cannot wait."

She imagined Paul in the study at his home, hunching over his phone, whispering so Barbara wouldn't hear. Or maybe he was at campaign headquarters surrounded by volunteers and campaign posters bearing his face and name. What was so important that it couldn't wait? Why didn't she just say no and hang up?

"I'll send a car for you at noon. We can talk over lunch."

Damn. She'd hesitated too long. Paul had taken her silence as a yes.

"No. I won't be here," she began. But he'd already hung up.

SATURDAY, OCTOBER 23, 1993

S aturday afternoon. Nora wanted to get her math homework out of the way so she could go to Annie's later. It was
tedious review, multi-digit decimals to multiply and divide.
0.7592 x 8.36 =?

She had her calculator. It would be easy peasy.

She opened her book bag, unzipped the compartment where
she kept her calculator.

"Nora," Marla called. "Come here."

Nora rolled her eyes and headed down the hall to her parents'
bedroom. Her mom probably wanted advice on eye shadow or
the shade of her stockings. Marla was all aflutter about some
black-tie affair she and Philip were invited to that night. The party
was all she'd talked about for days. She'd had Philip's tuxedo
cleaned and bought herself a new dress.

"Have you seen my dress?" The question came from her parents' closet. "I can't find it. It has to be here."

Nora joined her at the closet door. Her mother had thrown
half the hangers off the rod; her clothes were strewn on the floor
in a heap.

"I hung it up in here. I know I did. I took it out of the bag and
hung it right up." She was bereft, tugging at her hair. "Did you
move it?"

"No. Why would I—"

"Because if you did, just bring it back. I won't be mad."

"Mom, I haven't seen your dress. Are you sure you hung it
here? Maybe it's downstairs in the coat closet."

"No, I wouldn't have done that. I put it in here."

"Nora!" Tommy bellowed from downstairs. "Somebody's here! Come down!"

What?

"Now what?" Her mother frowned. "Who's here?"

Nora shrugged. "Dunno."

"Oh, never mind. Go on." Marla dismissed her with a wave of her hand. She bit her lip as she regarded the pile of clothes on the floor.

"I'll look in the coat closet. Just to be sure." God. Why did Marla assume Nora would know where her stupid dress was—as if she'd taken it? *Just bring it back. I won't be mad.* Seriously?

"What's with Mom?" Tommy stood on the steps, watching her.

"She's freaking out because she can't find her dress." It wasn't until then, talking to Tommy, that Nora wondered who'd come to see her. The front door was open, but Tommy hadn't invited the person in.

He followed her. "Which dress?"

What did he care? "The one she got for tonight. That party." She passed the coat closet. "Hey, can you see if it's in the coat closet while I go to the door?" She jogged down the rest of the steps and swung the door wide.

Annie's arms were crossed, and she wasn't smiling.

She'd seen Tommy.

Nora stepped outside, carefully closing the door behind her.

"I was riding my bike. I thought I'd stop over, see if you wanted to ride with me."

Nora hugged herself, felt her face burn red, stared at the grass, didn't dare look up.

Her life was imploding. She wanted to disintegrate. To die. How could she face Annie now? Annie knew everything. She knew that Nora had lied about the house renovations. And worse, she knew about Tommy, that he lived there. That the neighborhood weirdo, freak, creep was Nora's brother. Worst of all, she knew that Nora had publicly pretended not to know him.

"So. That was your brother?"

Nora didn't look up, just nodded.

"Why didn't you ever say so? Is he the only one? Do you have sisters, too?" Annie didn't sound mad as much as curious.

Nora told her that he was her only sibling. Annie asked a lot of questions: what Tommy's name was, how much older he was, whether Nora knew why he and Craig fought all the time. Was it just because of Craig's mean streak? Although, Craig was sweet to Annie, and she thought he was cute and built. Didn't Nora think so, too?

Gradually, Nora dared to move her gaze up from the grass to Annie's knees, then her waist, and eventually, her face. Annie didn't look angry. She wore her usual half smile, as if she might laugh.

Nora agreed that the kid who beat up her brother was cute and built. But she couldn't agree to sweet. He was a bully. "About Tommy." She took a breath. "I should have told you about him." Nora's tongue felt stiff, had trouble forming words. "But we—he and I—I mean, I just don't talk about him."

"I get it. I don't talk about my sisters, either." She nodded toward her bike. "So, want to ride to the river?"

Nora shook her head. "Can't." She could barely face Annie, let alone ride bikes with her.

But Annie didn't give up. "But we're on for tonight, right? A sleepover?"

Nora assessed Annie's tone. Her question was as light, as lilting as always. Was it possible that she really wasn't mad?

"Thing is, my annoying sisters will be home. Can we stay at your house this time?"

Nora stopped breathing. Her parents would be out at their party. She and Annie would be home alone with Tommy. Nora would have to make him swear to keep his bugs to himself. And warn Annie about them.

"Let me ask my mom." She led Annie into the foyer and ran up the steps to Marla's room.

"Nora, guess what?" Marla sang from her closet where she was rehanging her clothes. "You were right! Tommy found my dress. It was in the coat closet, just like you said. I was sure I'd hung it in here, but no. I guess I'm losing my mind."

"Mom—"

"But now I have another crisis—my black heels don't fit right. It's been an age since I wore them. My feet must have shrunk. I tried them on, and my feet slip in them."

"Mom," Nora tried again. And this time Marla listened long enough to say, sure, fine, invite a friend over, just don't get on your brother's nerves.

"Absolutely not."

"Dave, will you just listen—"

"No. Under no circumstances are you to meet with him."

Nora had called Dave immediately after she'd talked to Paul. But Dave had been in a meeting and hadn't called back until almost eleven. His reaction was immediate, intense, and insistent.

"Really? I wasn't aware I needed your permission. Especially since you've been out all night doing who knows what without my knowledge, let alone my approval."

"Okay. I'll rephrase. Please don't go. Is that better?"

It was, except for the sarcastic tone.

Nora sat at the kitchen table, still in her pajamas. Out the window, branches swayed in the wind. The clouds were thickening, the sky darkening.

"He's sending a car for me. What am I supposed to do, turn the driver away? Not answer the door?"

"Yes. Exactly. Do not answer the door. Do not even speak to the driver, or to Paul. If Paul calls again, hang up. Have no contact with him whatsoever. Especially now, with everything falling into place."

"I have no idea what that even means. What happened last night? Where were you?"

"I can't go into it now, Nora. I'll tell you everything later."

"No. Tell me now."

He let out an exasperated sigh. "It's happening imminently, like the day after tomorrow. We need to keep things normal until then. Which means don't go see him."

"Don't you even want to know why he wants to see me?"

"No."

"I'm serious. Maybe I can help. I can find out what's so urgent and what, if anything, he knows. If he suspects that Barbara's planning to leave, I can reassure him. I can be like an undercover agent."

"I don't want you involved, Nora. He's not a nice man."

"Oh please, Dave. What's he going to do? We're having lunch. We'll be in public, probably in a fancy restaurant in the middle of Center City. I'm a big girl. I'll be perfectly safe."

"I don't like it." But his tone had softened.

"I'll be fine."

He paused. "Actually, it would be good to know what he's thinking."

"Yes, it would. So, I'll find out." Nora was on her feet, heading upstairs.

"Nora. Be careful. I'm serious."

Of course she would. She was always careful.

"And call me. The minute you leave. I mean it. The very minute."

Nora promised that she would. When she hung up, she felt empowered and included. Useful. She showered and flitted around her room, picking an outfit that wasn't too mommy-ish. Her black dress was too severe, the floral too flighty. The grey culottes worked, the ones she'd worn to her cousin Becca's bridal shower. Yes, with the white linen top. She took her time selecting accessories, making sure that they weren't too costumey. Not that she was competing, but she wanted Paul to see that he wasn't the only husband who adorned his wife with jewels. So, she slid on the solitaire engagement ring that she usually saved for dinner parties, and the gold chain with the diamond drop, and her diamond stud earrings. As she misted herself with cologne—a years-old gift that she'd never even opened until now, made by Dior and aptly named "Poison"—she realized she hadn't paid this much attention to getting ready for a man since she'd been single. She thought of Bobby Baxter and the scent he shared with Paul.

The doorbell rang at precisely noon. Nora dabbed her lips with gloss and fluffed her hair. She went out to the limo just as the clouds broke and it started to rain.

SATURDAY NIGHT, OCTOBER 23, 1993

*A*nnie came over around eight, after Marla and Philip were gone. Nora led her upstairs to her room so they could change into their pajamas before making popcorn and watching a video downstairs. She'd set cassettes out on the coffee table: *The Shining, Friday the 13th, Dirty Dancing, Ghostbusters.* Old favorites. But Annie wasn't interested in movies. She had ideas of her own, had brought with her a bagful of makeup and hair gel, a razor and shaving cream, her sisters' old bras. Cigarettes. A bunch of tiny, airplane-sized bottles of Johnny Walker. And a list of cute boys and their phone numbers.

Nora didn't know what to do. She'd gone along, doing that kind of stuff when she was at Annie's house, but she hadn't anticipated that Annie would bring it to hers. The cigarettes freaked her the most. Even in his bedroom with the door closed, Tommy would smell the smoke and definitely tell her parents. What if he saw them wearing makeup and drinking liquor? The sleepover was out of control, and it had barely even started. Annie was already taking off her top and choosing a bra.

"Wait," Nora put her hands up, not sure what she could say to slow things down, but the words came just in time. "I'm starving."

She delayed with pizza. But pizza, even with pepperoni and extra cheese, was good only for about an hour. And even during that hour, while they waited for the delivery guy, Annie stood at the bathroom mirror, smearing eye shadow on her lids, applying mascara, dabbing gloss onto her lips.

Nora stared at Tommy's door, trying not to let on that she was nervous. Hoping that Tommy wouldn't come out and bother them. Or see what they were doing.

Nora chewed her pizza slowly, stalling. How could she get Annie to change her plans? Annie was relentless, pouring liquor into their sodas and telling Nora to drink. Nora drank.

And by the time they were done eating, Nora was less anxious. Why had she been so uptight? After all, what was the big deal if they put on makeup and shaved their legs? Nothing. There was no big deal. About anything.

Upstairs, Annie poured more Johnny Walker into their cups of soda. They drank as they took off their shorts and tops and sat on the side of the tub, foaming and shaving their legs. They put on bras and stuffed them with tissue. They redid Annie's make up and then fixed Nora's, heavy with eyeliner and dark purple shadow. They restyled each other's hair. They drank more soda spiked with Johnny. They laughed because everything was funny.

Annie wanted to smoke, but Nora pointed a wobbly finger at the hallway. "Tommy. He'd tell." Her tongue was thick. Words felt fat.

"What a dick." Annie frowned. "My sisters and I don't tell on each other. Ever. We made a pact." Her last words blended together, sounding like "Wemmedda pack." She held an unlit cigarette, then gave one to Nora. They didn't light them, but stood in their underwear and stuffed bras, striking poses with cigarettes, trying to be sexy and saucy, embracing each other and feigning kisses, breaking into fits of giggles. They imitated movie stars. They took turns pretending to be a boy and practiced kissing. Nora felt giddy, elated. She had Annie all to herself for the whole night. Annie, the coolest girl in her school. Her best friend.

Nora was having such a good time that she even stopped worrying about Tommy. She distantly heard his door open and the ensuing creaks, clicks, and huffs. His footsteps going upstairs to the attic.

After a while, and more spiked soda, Annie and Nora began calling boys. They sometimes said who was calling, sometimes made the boys guess. They teased coyly, flirted openly. And when Annie dialed Bobby Baxter, Nora wasn't too shy to talk to him. In fact, Nora gushed words that she wouldn't remember later, and that, mortified and hungover, she would question Annie about relentlessly.

At some point, they made it back to Nora's room and fell asleep on top of her double bed, still in their stuffed bras and panties.

In the morning, Nora woke to Annie's high-pitched screech.

"What is this!" She held a photograph to Nora's face.

Nora moaned, unaccustomed to hangovers. She strained to focus. Annie's hand was shaking, but Nora saw the photo, the image of Annie in her underwear and heavy eye makeup, posing suggestively with a cigarette in her hands.

"Look!" She held out another picture. This one was of them both, their legs coated with shaving cream, seated topless on the side of the tub, butt to butt. She held up more. "Did your brother take these? Did you plan this with him, Nora?"

"Are you crazy?" Nora's heart slammed into her throat, tried to fly out her mouth. "No. Of course not. I had no idea—" Nora sat up too fast. Her skull hammered so hard that she had to close her eyes, let the pain settle.

Annie was ranting. "Really. You had no idea?"

"No." She reached for the pictures Annie was holding. "Let me see them. Where'd you get them?"

Annie threw them at her. "They were on your dresser."

Nora leafed through them, adrenaline and fury surging with each image. Tommy had spied on them, taken pictures of the two of them not just shaving their legs topless, but primping in stuffed bras, posing in underwear with cigarettes, kissing each other with feigned passion.

"What's he planning to do with these? Because if he shows them to anyone—Oh shit, he won't, will he?" Annie was talking too loudly. If she woke up Marla or Philip, they'd want to know what was going on.

"Shh! Annie. He won't."

No, Tommy wouldn't show them to anyone. Would he? God, Nora wanted to kill him. He was such a loser, such a twisted, disgusting, freaking loser. She finally asked a friend to sleep over, and he had to ruin it, peeping on them, sneaking snapshots of their personal, private business. Now Annie would never come over again. She might not even be her friend anymore, and who could blame her?

"I promise, he won't show them to a soul." Nora tried to sound confident. "Tommy's annoying and strange, but not mean. He probably thinks they're funny."

"Funny?" Annie's makeup was smudged and runny; her eyes seemed to be melting.

"Like I said, he's strange."

Annie fumed. She sat beside Nora and went through the pile of pictures again. Her hair was knotted and tangled, and her bra hung loose around her chest, the tissues having fallen out. She slammed the pictures down and stood, pulled on a T-shirt and shorts.

"I swear, I'll kill him." Annie headed for the door.

"Wait. I'll go with you."

Together, they burst into Tommy's room. He was sitting at his desk, holding tweezers, working on mounting a beetle. He looked up when they came in, eyebrows raised as if annoyed at the intrusion.

"Tommy, what the hell—" Nora began.

But Annie interrupted. "Tommy, that's your name, right? So, you're a pervert? A peeping Tom? Spying on your sister's friends for jollies?"

Tommy's grin was smarmy, self-satisfied. "Jollies? Like anyone would get excited by your pitiful little bodies?"

"You don't know me, Tommy, but here's the thing. I'm not someone you want to mess with." Annie's hands were relaxed at her side. She stepped further into Tommy's room, her voice low, buzzing like a wasp about to sting. "So, here's what you're going to do. You're going to give me those photos and the negatives. Every copy of them. If you don't—if anyone outside this room ever sees even a single one of them—I swear you'll be sorry you were ever born."

They waited a few long moments, but Tommy was unfazed. He chuckled, leaned back in his chair and folded his hands behind his head. "What are you going to do, have your thug buddy Craig beat me up? Because guess what? He already does." He scratched his mop of black hair. "Actually, whatever your name is, I don't think I'm giving you those negatives. No. Here's what's going to happen. I'm keeping those pictures. And you and my dear little sister are going to do whatever I say, or else they show up in your parents' mailbox, on doorsteps, and all over your school."

"You wouldn't dare!"

"For starters," Tommy continued, "you're going to tell Craig that you think I'm the hottest guy in town and you want him to kiss my ass."

"You're insane!" Annie lunged at Tommy, pounding his head. "Give me those negatives, you piece of shit, bastard freak—"

"Annie, don't!" Nora tried to stop her, didn't want things to get out of control. She pulled futilely at Annie's waist, knowing that the attack was fruitless and counterproductive. Anger only fueled Tommy and incited his outrageousness; indifference was the only way to handle him. Besides, compared to Craig, Annie's flailing fists were nothing.

As if catching a firefly, Tommy finally snapped his hands out, grabbed Annie's wrists, and held on, snickering as if amused. Annie struggled for a while, but he just smiled until she stopped.

"You done?" he asked.

"Screw you," Annie huffed.

"Be careful. You don't want to make me mad. I can mail those babies out this afternoon. Now get out." Tommy released her wrists and busied himself with his bug, dismissing them.

"This isn't over. You'll be sorry, you perv." Annie stormed past Nora who hurried after her, apologizing, afraid of Annie's rage. She'd never seen it before, didn't know how to calm it.

Annie was fuming. "He won't really mail those pictures, will he? Because my parents will kill me."

"He won't." But oh God, what if he did? Annie would never speak to her. And what would Nora's parents do when they saw the liquor? The kissing? Fuck Tommy. She ought to kill him.

Annie wouldn't stay, wouldn't talk anymore. She packed up her things quickly, silently, angrily. The air was so brittle; Nora couldn't breathe.

At the door, Nora tried again. "Annie, please. I don't know what to say."

"I know." Annie's voice was flat. "I get why you never talk about him, and why Craig can't stand him. Your brother's a disgusting sicko. I feel sorry for you, having to live in the same house as him. But even if he's your brother, I promise you he's going to regret this little prank. If he does anything at all with those pictures? He's done. I mean it, Nora. Toast."

Nora watched Annie disappear around the corner. Then, she went back upstairs. Her eyes narrowed and her skin burned. What could she do to get back at Tommy? Break his framed tarantula? Set his dark room on fire? In her room, she kicked at the wadded tissues scattered around the floor, and when she flopped onto her bed, crying, her pillowcase smelled like makeup.

TUESDAY, AUGUST 14, 2018, 12:15 P.M.

Campaign headquarters was a storefront in a South Philly strip mall, once a large video rental store. Paul's face was plastered everywhere. The walls were papered with larger-than-life posters of it. Desks were buried under stacks of brochures, bumper stickers, doorknob hangers—all advertising it. There were lawn signs galore. Whiteboards covered with marked abbreviations and coded numbers. A huge flat screen television tuned to whatever Congress was doing. A monstrous coffee urn, and a folding table laden with donuts, cold cuts, protein bars, bagels, apples and bananas. The room was buzzing. Staff members, mostly young and glued to cell phones, scurried about organizing volunteers, assigning tasks, wearing buttons with Paul's face and name.

The limo driver guided Nora through the maze into a corridor, through a back doorway into the candidate's private office. As Paul rose from his desk to greet her, a preppy young woman dashed in, reminding him that he'd have to leave for the Junior League no later than two. He thanked her, saying that he was not to be disturbed until then, and locked the door when she left because, he explained, "Otherwise, they'll all be in and out and not give us a moment."

Paul gestured at a sleek leather sofa, offering Nora a seat. She sat and surveyed the room. A glass-topped coffee table displayed an arrangement of succulents, the morning's Inquirer, and a large crystal dolphin sculpture. Silver pendant lights hung from the planked ceiling. The floor was faux aged wood, partially covered by an ornate oriental rug. The walls were dotted with fine art—a Wyeth that looked real, and was that an actual Chagall? Nora stopped herself from gawking, even from commenting on the decor. She didn't want to appear impressed. She hadn't come by choice, but at Paul's insistence. And she was there, not as an admirer or supporter, but as a spy. Still, she was stunned that just a door and a short hallway separated this tranquil space from the clamor and hullaballoo of the outer office. She strained but couldn't hear even a whisper of the hubbub. Vivaldi played softly.

"Wine?" Paul asked. "I've chilled some Pinot Grigio." A full bar lined the far wall.

"Not for me."

"Coffee then? Cappuccino?"

"Cappuccino. Thank you."

Nora slid back on her seat. The leather was smooth, the cushions oversized. If she sat all the way back, her feet wouldn't touch the floor. She scooted forward, keeping her feet grounded and her back straight, and watched Paul as the Keurig whipped up her coffee. His hand lingered over her cup as if dropping something in.

But that was ridiculous. What was he going to do, poison her? Drug her? Right here in his campaign headquarters? No, she'd imagined it. Ice clinked. Paul returned with her foamy coffee and his scotch on the rocks.

"What did we do before Keurig?" He sat beside her, close enough that their knees bumped. He grinned and his teeth glistened, eyes twinkling. He really was spectacularly handsome. "Thanks for coming, Nora. I know you were hesitant."

Nora was uncomfortable. She crossed her legs, but that was worse, so she uncrossed them, leaned forward and sipped her coffee. It tasted bitter. But of course it did. Coffee was bitter.

Bitterness didn't mean arsenic or a roofie—isn't that what they called those date rape drugs? Still, she faked taking another sip, then held her cup on her lap, reluctant to swallow more. Oh God. What was she doing there? Why had Paul wanted her to come?

Don't look for trouble. Don't rock the boat.

Paul set his drink on the coffee table without using a coaster. He had no concern that his glass would leave a mark. Paul moved with ease, with entitled confidence, gliding fluidly from spot to spot, pose to pose. Practiced, like a dancer. A Broadway star.

Stop ogling him, Nora scolded herself. The man had caused Barbara's purple arm and swollen eye.

Paul sighed and met Nora's gaze. "So. You're wondering why you're here. There's no easy way to say it, so I'll just say it." He paused and cleared his throat, watching her as if assessing whether she was strong enough to hear what followed. "Nora, my wife and your husband are having an affair."

Nora didn't move. Her coffee cup jiggled in the saucer. She swallowed. "I'm sorry?"

Paul nodded, then repeated. "They're having an affair."

Nora knew that wasn't true. There was no affair. Dave had sworn it. As had Barbara. Paul was wrong. She set her cappuccino cup on the table and shook her head. "No. You're mistaken. Barbara would never—"

"Oh, but she would. And so would your husband."

"No."

"No? I suppose there's only one way to convince you." He went to the bar, unlocked a drawer, pulled out a manila envelope. "As I mentioned earlier, I've been so worried about Barbara that I hired someone to keep an eye on her while I'm away."

Nora took a breath. Of course. Paul's private detective must have seen Barbara with Dave and assumed they were having an affair. She almost relaxed, almost smiled, but didn't. Because what if the detective had found out that Dave and Barbara had been arranging for Barbara to leave? What if the detective had found bank withdrawals or stock sales?

Paul handed her some photos from the envelope. They'd been taken from odd angles, at stealthy distances, in lighting that was too bright or too dark. But what they showed was clear. Barbara and Dave in a dimly lit booth, heads together, his hand on hers. Dave holding Barbara, her head against his chest. Dave and Barbara putting boxes in her car. Dave coming out of Paul's house, hugging or kissing Barbara, holding her tight. There were dozens of the same ilk. Nora went through them, one by one. They seemed incriminating. Paul had reason for his conclusion. Just a few days ago, she'd reached the same one. But now she knew better.

"Drink this. It'll help." Paul handed her the cappuccino. Watched her. "Go on."

Nora needed time to think. Why was Paul watching her so intensely? Why was he pushing her to drink her cappuccino? What did he want from her? Uneasy, she held her cup to her lips and feigned another sip.

"Pictures don't lie. There's no doubt what's been going on."

Even with Dave's explanations and denials, Nora felt stabs of jealousy. Hot, sharp ones. She eyed a shot of Dave with Barbara in his arms. His eyes were shut, as if he was savoring the embrace. Why was Dave pressing himself against her?

She could imagine his explanation. "Oh, come on, Nora. It was nothing. I was comforting her." She was crying/scared/worried/overwhelmed/something-that-would-justify-a-big-too-close-hug.

Fine. He'd been comforting her. He'd had a legitimate reason for the hug. But really, had he needed to enjoy it so much? She pictured Barbara's enhanced breasts against Dave's chest and clutched the cup and saucer so tight that her knuckles turned white. She simmered. Nora was fine with Dave secretly helping Barbara, but the pictures showed more than mere help. They showed them constantly touching. A hug here, a peck there, a hand on a shoulder or an arm or the small of a back. And it wasn't just the touching that bothered her. It was also the way they looked at each other, the familiar, comfortable, private gazes they exchanged. The photographs jostled her, almost made her forget her purpose in being there. Almost made her believe Paul's assertion of an affair. They certainly made her understand how hurt and angry he was.

Paul stood, refilled his drink. "In fairness, with me being away so much, it's understandable that Barbara would be lonely and seek companionship. Especially since she struggles with depression."

Depression. He'd mentioned it before, but Barbara never had. And she hadn't seemed to be suffering from it. Then again, married to an abuser, Barbara might well be depressed.

Paul kept talking, but Nora was distracted, still looking at the pictures. Dave's wedding-ringed hand on Barbara's back, too close to the curve of her butt. Her highlighted hair against his cheek. She had to stop, take a breath. She set the photos and her cappuccino on the coffee table, envying Paul's scotch.

"Are you all right?" Paul watched her, sitting again. Again, too close.

"Of course." She was, wasn't she? She blinked, wishing he'd sit farther away.

"You don't need to pretend," he said. "Not with me." His stare was fixed on her. "Finish your cappuccino. You'll feel better."

Nora glanced at her cappuccino cup. Why would he care if she finished it? Had he actually drugged it? No, of course not. Why would he? She shifted in her seat, avoiding his gaze. She should leave. She'd done her job. In fact, she'd found out more than she'd needed to. She'd report to Dave the good news, that Paul had no clue about Barbara's plans to leave, and the bad news that he'd been having Barbara followed, and had a stack of photos that seemed to implicate her in an affair with Dave.

Behind Paul's desk was an exit leading directly to the parking lot. She'd go out that way, avoiding the hullaballoo of the front office. But what could she say to draw the visit to a close? What would a woman do in a situation like this, having just been told that her husband was cheating? Would she faint? Cry? Run away? Nora wanted to seem credible.

"I can't believe it." She intended to go on to say that she wanted time to think, that she needed to be alone. But Paul interrupted.

"Nevertheless, here we are. The victims of cheating spouses. Pathetic, aren't we?" His smile was twisted, more of a grimace. "You don't know me well, Nora, but be assured that I am a man of action. I don't tolerate being crossed by anyone. I asked you here in part to share information. In part because I've determined what I believe is an appropriate way to proceed."

Proceed? To where? Paul used too many syllables. Nora had lost his meaning, tried to concentrate.

"Am I right in assuming you want your marriage back?"

Back? The question bothered her. Her marriage wasn't gone. She tilted her head, confused.

"Nora, believe me. I want mine back too. But I won't tolerate being lied to, let alone betrayed. Not in business. Not in marriage."

Paul's jaw tightened, his gaze narrowed like some sleek, blue-eyed predator. A wolf, maybe. Or a fox. Did foxes have blue eyes? She repeated his words in her mind, but they passed her by, like breezes, like strangers. Present for a moment, then gone. What had he said again? His eyes were so blue.

"Nora, you and I have a mutual problem. By cooperating, we can achieve a mutual solution."

Nora had no intention of cooperating. But she would listen, for Dave. For Barbara.

"Honestly, I don't see how Barbara and I can move forward. Infidelity isn't something one can simply forgive. There have to be consequences. A broken vow must incur some kind of retribution, don't you agree?"

Retribution? As in punishment? Like getting spanked? Or grounded? Or going two weeks without a cell phone? Or beating Barbara to a pulp?

She nodded, yes, pretending to agree with him. She was a spy, after all. Spying on Paul, who was still talking and seemed to be closer to her than before. When had he moved?

"For example. Say your husband came home and said, 'So sorry, Nora. I cheated on you, but the affair is over. Let's move on.' What would you do?"

Well, actually, he'd done just that. Five years ago. Dave had made his tearful confession, and she hadn't told anyone. Paul was speaking purely hypothetically, didn't know anything. No one did. Unless Dave had told Barbara and she'd told Paul. But no. Why would Dave do that? He wouldn't.

"Would you say, 'Fine, dear,' and simply move on? I'm betting that, no. You wouldn't, because one can't simply forgive such a thing."

But she had forgiven it. At least, she'd tried. Eight months pregnant with her second baby, she'd ached to believe Dave when he swore that he'd never lie or cheat again.

"I know I can't. The trust is broken, the betrayal too deep. So how do we move on? I'll tell you how. We restore the balance."

Nora had lost the thread. Paul's reasoning was almost but not quite rational. Her mouth was open, but she couldn't feel her lips. She licked them, but no. They were numb. When had that happened? Those photos. Had they affected her more than she'd realized, sent her over the edge? More likely it was the coffee, but she'd had only had a sip. Was that enough? Had he actually drugged her? She pressed her lips together, felt a dull, sensual throb. Wow. What if she'd finished the drink? Would she have passed out? Paul's words were clumping together now, and the edges of his face blurred. Nora was definitely woozy. Was she going to be sick?

"Paul, I really should go." Her enunciation seemed slow. She shimmied forward on the leather cushion, grabbed her bag, and attempted to stand. But Paul, rich, aloof, suave, sexy Senate candidate Paul, with his blurry square jaw and over-bright, gleaming blue eyes, eased closer. He didn't smell like Bobby Baxter. His scent was unfamiliar, saltier, harsher, and more aggressive than Old Spice, except for his breath, which smelled like scotch.

"Not yet, Nora. In order to restore equality, it's clear what must be done." His lips grazed her neck.

His hand was on her knee. Nora moved to push him away, but Paul's hand proceeded under the hem of her culottes and slid up her thigh.

"Stop—" She swung to slap him, but his free hand simply grabbed her wrist and shoved it away. "Don't!" She squirmed and wriggled, but Paul pressed on.

The hand not occupied in her culottes cupped her breast. She tugged at it, tried to remove it, but he leaned onto her, pushed his mouth against her deadened lips. She resisted, turned her head to escape his tongue. His cologne burned her nostrils.

Paul released her breast to hold her closer while his other hand persisted, pressed up her thigh. His lips snaked into a smile, and he hissed into her ear. "This ain't the minor leagues, Nora dear. If a man dares to have his way with my wife, he'd best believe I'll reciprocate."

His fingers darted beneath her underwear and jabbed into her body, invading, violating her. Thrusting, digging, twirling.

"Stop—" she roared. She arched her back but couldn't pull free. "No!"

"Don't resist me, Nora." His breath tickled her neck.

No, this couldn't be happening. She had the sense of exiting her body, watching from above, maybe from that light dangling from the ceiling. She saw more than heard Paul's words, their fiery colors. She felt their scorching heat.

"This is going to happen, so you might as well relax." His fingers moved inside her. "After this, you won't be a victim anymore. You and your husband, I and my wife—we'll all have committed the same betrayals, the score will be even. Balance restored, our marriages can move forward."

He pressed Nora backward into the sofa. When had his shirt buttons opened? Or his pants unzipped and lowered around his hips? His free hand was at her chest, and the buttons to her linen shirt, the one with the ruffle, came open, one by one.

Even overpowered, Nora raged. She struggled to resist Paul, but he swatted her attempts like harmless house flies. When she tried to strike him, he flung her arm away so hard that it propelled onto the coffee table, knocking his scotch glass into her delicate cappuccino cup, breaking it. While Paul fumbled with her waistband, she felt around for anything she might use as a weapon, fingering objects on the coffee table, measuring weight, shape and girth, identifying the crystal dolphin. She strained to grip it. Lift it. Bash Paul's head with it. Nora mustered her strength and willed herself to heft it an inch, just one tiny inch off the table, but couldn't. The thing was too heavy, wouldn't budge. Her forearm lacked the strength, and her fingers failed, dropping limply into the puddle of spilled scotch and cappuccino, onto the slim, jagged edge of the cappuccino saucer.

Nora grabbed hold of it. With a growl from someplace deep inside her, she swung the shard at Paul's head with all her strength. Her strength wasn't very strong, though. Her fingers slipped and, too soon, before she'd finished digging the edge into Paul's skull, the broken saucer fell from her grasp.

Paul cried out.

He released her and raised his hand to his temple. Blood swelled from a jagged gash and streamed down his face. He stared at the blood on his hands as if he couldn't understand what had happened.

When his weight shifted, Nora lifted herself onto her elbows and worked her way out from under him. Paul was distracted, dazed, dabbing at his wound with his shirtsleeve. Nora tried to move quickly. Grasping the sofa for balance, she grabbed her pocketbook, pushed to her feet and stood unsteadily, eyes on Paul as she dared to take a step, then another. Carefully, she let go of the sofa and edged away from him, past the coffee table with its broken cup, spilled drinks, and crystal dolphin knocked onto its side.

When she looked back at him, Paul seemed stunned, one side of his face streaming red. He fumbled with his pants, cursing, blinking through blood, and groped in their pockets for a handkerchief.

"What have you done?" he croaked, his voice as raw as if it, too, were bleeding.

Nora secured her bag under her arm and raced in slow motion. Each of her steps was too short, taking too long. She hiked up her culottes and struggled with shirt buttons—so many buttons that she abandoned the effort and kept moving toward the door. Except, no. That door led to Paul's campaign offices, to his entire staff. Paul would chase after her, bloody and raging, and his staff would charge her like an angry mob. So she pivoted, aiming for the back door to the parking lot. But she spun around too quickly, and a wave of crippling dizziness almost brought her down.

"You fucking bitch!" Paul pressed the handkerchief to his temple. "Look what you did!" He stared in disbelief at all the blood, ribbons of it flowing from his head.

Nora didn't look. Turning might make her dizzy again. Instead, she estimated how far it was to the door. Fifteen steps? Twelve? It might as well be miles. Her mind felt sluggish, her movements heavy and ineffective. But she had to move. At any moment, Paul was likely to get up and grab her. Hurry, she told herself. Faster! She held her breath and kept plodding ahead, braced for Paul to pounce.

When she dared to glance back from the door, though, Paul hadn't moved. He remained huddled and groaning on the sofa, bleeding onto his fine, hand-tailored shirt, but he saw her looking at him.

"Nora, stop!" He billowed to his feet as if hoisted from above, as if about to sail across the room and catch her.

Nora froze. There was no sense trying to escape. It would take him no time, just a few sweeping steps to tackle her.

"Do not move!" He started forward.

Nora stiffened and closed her eyes, preparing for impact.

But impact didn't happen. At least, not to her. When she heard the crash, Nora opened one eye and turned her head toward Paul. He had thundered to the floor, knocking into the coffee table and landing in a heap of succulents, newspapers and broken glass, his ankles tangled and trapped in his expensively tailored, unfastened slacks.

Nora tried to open the door. It wouldn't budge. Her pocketbook slipped to the floor. Slowly, leaning against the door, she stooped to pick it up, looking back at Paul.

He was on his knees, wiping blood from his eye with one hand and pulling his trousers up with the other, bearing little resemblance to the charismatic candidate she'd come to meet.

She tried the door again.

"Nora, wait. Listen." Paul spoke softly, like a wolf. Like a snake. "I thought you'd be on board with this course of action. I never anticipated that you'd object. But since it didn't work out, let's agree, no hard feelings?" He stumbled to his feet and touched his forehead. He blinked at the wet blood on his fingertips and sank back onto the sofa. "Damn, this won't stop bleeding. But listen, how's this? I won't report you for assault if you agree to keep our little liaison to ourselves. All right? Come sit. Let's talk. I won't do anything you don't want me to. I just want to make peace so we can discuss what to do about our spouses. Please. Come sit."

Nora didn't go sit. She closed her fingers around the doorknob yet again, turned and pushed. The door still didn't open. She pulled, but that didn't work either. She leaned against the door, trapped. What could she do? Risk sitting with Paul again as if there were no hard feelings? Take her chances running through the outer office? Hopeless, Nora leaned her head against the door. And saw the dead bolt. Oh. No wonder. She wasn't trapped after all. But she had to hurry, couldn't take time to look at Paul again, couldn't waste even an eye blink. She plunged ahead, pushing with all her strength, feeling a click as the bolt gave way. Nora reached for the doorknob, grabbed it, twisted, anticipating escape. But before she could get out, something whizzed past her ear and exploded against the door. Tiny shining sparkles erupted in the air around her head, floated snow-like to the floor.

The crystal dolphin lay shattered at her feet.

Behind her, Paul said, "That was a warning, Nora. Keep this to yourself or you'll face consequences. Nobody crosses me. Nobody. Understood?"

Nora swung the door open and barreled outside.

"Answer me, you pathetic cow!"

The rain had stopped. Puddles dotted the asphalt of the parking lot, reflecting white sunlight. A pair of aides wearing campaign T-shirts and carrying posters passed her on their way to the office. They stopped and stared. Damn. Did they know she was running from Paul? Were they his people—would they accost her and force her back to Paul's office?

"Ma'am?" one of them said. "Are you all right?"

She didn't trust them. "I'm fine." Her words sounded wrong, as if someone else said them, but she kept moving, leaving them standing there, frowning and whispering. What were they staring at? Did she have Paul's blood on her? Or was her hair messed up? Oh God. Was Paul charging after her, bloodied and simmering? Nora didn't dare look back. Holding onto her bag, she kept inching toward the street, one step after another, until she made it to the curb and stopped to lean against a light pole. Hailing a cab, she realized that her blouse was unbuttoned, hanging open. She managed to overlap the collar, holding it closed, by the time the driver stopped.

She half fell into the backseat. When the driver asked her where she wanted to go, she managed to articulate her address. He eyed her from the rearview mirror, probably assumed she was drunk.

As he pulled away from the curb, Nora risked looking back at Paul's office. The candidate was nowhere to be seen.

The cab driver watched her in his mirror, asked if she was all right. She nodded. Talking, explaining what had just happened, was beyond her capability. So was comprehending it. What had happened? Paul drugged her—probably? And tried to rape her—definitely. How was that possibly actually true?

After the cab had dropped her off, Nora stood in her driveway feeling disconnected from her body. How much time had passed since she'd entered Paul's office? An hour? Less? How long until the girls would get home from camp? Oh God. She couldn't face them, not after what had happened, what he'd done. She would call the police and report him. With each step toward her house, she felt his claw-like fingers inside her. The man was a predator. An abuser. He deserved to have his campaign aborted. He deserved to be in jail. Yes, she would have him arrested.

But not until she had a bath.

Nora made it to the front door, then her bathroom. She drew a bath, pulled her clothes off, put a foot into the water, and remembered something about bathing after sexual assault. About destroying evidence? Wait. No, that wouldn't apply. Because Paul hadn't left any sperm behind. All Paul had left was the repeated, endless shock of his fingers, and a constant, aching, rawness whenever she took a breath. She felt unclean, scuzzy, contaminated, dirty, unfit to greet her children or even touch them until she had scrubbed enough to somehow undo what had been done to her.

She got in the tub carefully, sunk down into water so hot she could barely endure it, and concentrated on holding the soap, on sudsing her body with it.

The phone rang almost immediately and she let it go, certain that it was Paul calling to repeat his threat. As soon as the phone finally stopped ringing, it started again. Again and again.

Despite the hot water, Nora shivered. She kept seeing Paul's twisted grin, his feral blue eyes. Why was he calling? What did he want from her? She dunked under, felt the heat engulf her. Opened her eyes and saw the tiled walls, wavy through the water. She stayed there, holding her breath until, with a jolt, she realized that maybe it wasn't Paul, but Dave, who'd been calling repeatedly. She'd forgotten to call him after her visit with Paul. He must be frantic that he hadn't heard from her, especially since she hadn't been answering her phone.

But Nora couldn't call him back. Couldn't let Dave hear her unsteady voice, couldn't risk having him find out what had happened.

"Damn it, Nora!" he would yell. "I told you not to go." Then he'd slam the phone down, furious, the vein in his forehead throbbing, fists tightening. Who knew what he'd do to Paul? Dave might end up getting hurt—or arrested. So, she couldn't talk to him yet. Instead, Nora grabbed her phone from the counter. Slowly, she manipulated her trembling fingers, texting him that she was home and okay and that they'd talk later.

The phone rang again as soon as she'd sent the text. Not Dave's number. Oh God. It had to be Paul's. Reflexively, she threw the phone, sent it skittering across the bathroom floor.

You looked for trouble. You found it.

Nora closed her eyes and lay back, took deep uneven breaths, felt the sways and sloshes of the water responding to her slightest movements. Over and over, she replayed the scene at Paul's office. Paul's unbuttoned shirt, unfastened pants. His explanation, "There must be some kind of retribution, don't you think?" His bloody head. Despite all her scrubbing, she smelled his cloying cologne. Despite the soft embrace of hot water, she felt his cold, viselike grasp. Time passed, but she didn't move.

Nora was still in the tub when the camp bus pulled up. The girls stampeded up the steps, calling for her. She wasn't ready. She hadn't prepared a way to greet them, hadn't fixed snacks or planned an after-camp activity. She sat bolt upright, as if caught doing something shameful, and reached for a towel.

"Mom, I have a new friend!" Sophie burst into the bathroom, her face flushed. Or maybe sunburned. Had Nora forgotten to pack sunscreen? "Her name is Madison. Can she come over? Please?"

Behind her, Ellie dropped her camp bag on the tiled floor and chewed her fingernail.

Nora's phone rang.

"Mommy, want me to get it?"

"Nope. Let it go." She dabbed her face and smiled brightly, reached for a towel and pulled the plug. Water gurgled and spun, sucked helplessly down the drain.

SUNDAY, OCTOBER 24, 1993

Nora's whole body raged. She couldn't stay still, couldn't lie down or sit up, couldn't even manage a good cry. She burst out of her room and into Tommy's.

"How could you do that?"

He glanced up from a butterfly he was working on as Nora charged, intending to sweep the mountings off his table and destroy all his precious specimens. Tommy turned and reached an arm out, his hand catching her midriff, stopping her, knocking the air out of her lungs. Gasping, Nora swung her fists, pounding at him, spewing words and tears.

"I hate you!"

"What else is new?"

"Give me the pictures or I swear I'll smash your camera, your dark room, and all your stupid bugs!"

"Try it." Tommy grinned. "I'll break all your bones." He grabbed one of her flailing arms and twisted.

Nora winced in pain. She forced herself to stop struggling and spoke calmly. "You're making a mistake. Trust me, you'll be sorry."

"Sorry? For what? You should thank me."

He released her and leaned back. Lowered his brows, eyed her with something like pity. "I took those pictures for your own good. So you'd see for yourself, with your own eyes, what bad choices you're making."

"My choices are none of your business."

"God, Nora. Do you really want to be one of them? Part of that mindless, superficial horde? That girl you had over, she's one of the worst. Stuck up. Cheap and trashy—"

"She is not!"

He chuckled, pleased at getting a rise out of her. "She's so cheap and trashy that she's practicing being a slut even before she's even grown tits."

"You're disgusting."

"Me? You're the one with cigarettes and liquor, kissing another girl while you're half naked."

"Shut up! It's none of your freaking business." Blood rushed to Nora's face. Her heart raced.

"Think about how she's changing you. Do you really want to be like her? Look who she hangs with. Guys way too old for her, like that asshole Craig. If she's not trashy, why do you think that he's so eager to see her?"

"Because she's cool. Which is something you wouldn't know about, loser."

For the briefest moment, Tommy's eyelids quivered. Then he uncrossed his arms and went back to his butterflies. "Fine, Nora. Blend in. Be mediocre. Don't dare to be different or have pride in who you are. Be like those trampy, dime-a-dozen, 'cool' girls. But remember, once you're known as cheap trash, you're cheap trash forever."

Something sharp and cold cut through Nora's chest. "Shut up, Tommy. Just shut up. You don't know what you're talking about. Annie's my friend. You don't know what that means because you don't have any."

"If having friends means acting like those *cool* pieces of shit, I'd rather be alone."

"Well, good. Because you are. And you always will be." Nora spun around and left, slamming the door behind her.

And came face to face with Marla.

She was just standing there in the hallway.

Oh God. How much had she heard? Would she ask about the pictures? Nora's mind went blank. How could she explain?

"Nora, what's on your eyes?" Marla squinted and grabbed Nora's chin, looking closely. "Are you wearing makeup?"

Damn, shit, damn. She hadn't washed it off. Now Marla would lecture her about growing up too fast and making smart choices. Blah, blah, blah. First Tommy, now her mother. Everyone was telling her how to live her life. And it wasn't even nine in the morning.

But Marla didn't lecture her. Instead, she shrugged and said, "I guess that's what girls your age do at sleepovers."

Wait. She wasn't mad? Marla put an arm on Nora's shoulder, guiding her down the hall, back, into Nora's room. They sat side by side on her unmade bed.

"A word to the wise," Marla said.

Nora braced herself for a barrage of Marla clichés. At the same time, she forced her face to look unworried, unbothered, unmortified, unfurious, as if there wasn't a stack of half-naked photographs, as if she weren't being blackmailed by her perverted asshole brother, peeping Tommy.

"You get what you give," Marla said. "From what I just heard, you're giving anger. Anger begets anger. Tommy's only trying to be protective."

Protective? What planet did Marla live on?

"You're his little sister, after all."

Duh. Wasn't that the whole entire freaking problem?

"And you're growing up. You're in sixth grade, not exactly a little girl anymore. That's hard for him to adjust to. He's your big brother, and he worries about you. That's natural. Just like it's natural that you'll experiment with things like makeup and friendships. Tommy's trying to look out for you."

By spying on her? By taking pictures of her and Annie topless and doing each other's hair and drinking mini-bottles of whiskey? Of Annie teaching Nora how to kiss? "No. He's trying to ruin my life."

"Nora, how can you say a thing like that?"

How? Seriously? Clearly, Marla had no idea what went on between her kids. Nora didn't answer, didn't know where to start.

"It isn't easy, is it?" Marla's shoulders slumped. She gazed at the floor, sighing.

What wasn't easy? Nora watched her mother, the gray strands sprinkling her brown hair, the errant curls escaping her loose bun. The paleness of the skin on the back on her neck. The colorless tone of her wool robe and the tightness of the shoulders underneath. God. What did she want? Why was she sitting there, staring at nothing?

Marla cleared her throat and checked her rose painted nails. "Life doesn't always turn out the way we expect it to."

Wow. A new cliché to add to the list. Nora grabbed a pillow, braced for more. *You'll attract more bees with honey than with vinegar. If you get a lemon, make lemonade. Family comes first.*

"For example, I never imagined having a son who was a genius."

A genius? Tommy was an idiot.

"But as brilliant as he is, Tommy's never had good social skills. He hasn't made many friends. I suspect he's kind of jealous of yours."

Nora rolled her eyes. Tommy wasn't jealous. He was a turd whose parents overindulged him, believing that he was the world's smartest kid, feeding his bug obsession by buying, among other things, a mini-freezer, microscopes, mounting materials, a fancy camera, enlargement equipment, an entire freaking dark room.

"Friends are an issue for him. He won't talk about it, but I suspect kids his age bore him. Sometimes they get on his nerves so bad that he starts picking on them. And when Tommy gets mad, he loses control and gets physical."

Wait, hold on. Marla thought Tommy got physical? That he was the aggressor?

"As you know, he's given and received more than a few punches and gotten into trouble at school. Dad and I took him to a counselor, but that led nowhere. Tommy refused to admit he needed help. And he flat out denied ever bullying or picking on anyone."

Nora searched Marla's face for traces of a lie, a joke, a willful distortion, but found none of those. Did her mother really believe that Tommy—withdrawn, introverted, slouchy, twerpy Tommy—could be a bully who started fights? That he dared to pick on anyone besides his little sister?

She ought to say something, set her mother straight, but how could she tell Marla that Tommy was not the occasional instigator, but the perpetual victim? That Tommy was ostracized, universally despised, and a loser that bullies picked on for sport? She couldn't. She didn't.

"Here's my point," Marla went on. "Try to step into Tommy's shoes. And remember, friends come and go, but family is forever. So, give him a break. He's your big brother for life."

For life. Nora held onto her pillow. Oh God. Breathing hurt. Nora wanted to rip out her hair. Marla had no idea who Tommy actually was—an outcast, a sneak, a sicko peeper, a lowlife blackmailer. She ached, worrying about what he'd do with the photos. She wanted to strangle him.

Marla put a hand on Nora's leg. Those rose-colored nails, the glittering stones of her mother's wedding ring made Nora's temples throb. Her skull wanted to pop. The moment stretched.

"So. You and Annie had fun?" Marla straightened her back, put on a smile.

"Yeah. How was your party?" Nora changed the subject before Marla could ask more.

"Great." Her eyes lit up. "Too great. Dad's still sleeping it off." She squeezed Nora's hand and, after sharing a too long, very uncomfortable, deeply penetrating look, said she was glad they'd talked, and went downstairs to make coffee.

Nora replaced the pillow and lay back. She closed her eyes, trying to digest what had been said. When she opened them, Tommy was standing in the doorway, aiming his camera at her, smirking.

Dave came home early, unexpectedly. He barreled into the playroom, and even as the girls jumped on him with cries of "Daddy!" and reports of their day at camp, he kept his eyes on Nora.

Nora tried to smile, to act normally. She stood to greet him as she would have on any other day. But after smiling 'hello,' what was she supposed to do? Her mind buckled, blank. Why couldn't she remember her usual way of greeting Dave? What had been their routine before another man had shoved his fingers between her legs? Had she gone to Dave with a kiss? Waited for him to come to her? Had there even been a kiss, routinely, or just a welcoming grin? Why couldn't she recall this frequent and mundane event? Dave was still watching her, expecting something. But what?

Sophie asked Dave if he'd take them to the park. Elle hung on his sleeve. Somehow, he freed himself, squatting to give them kisses and hugs. "Before we do anything, your mom and I have to talk."

Of course. That was why he'd come home early. To talk about Paul. Her visit. Nora bit her lip. What should she tell him? She stalled, picking up loose beads from the necklace Sophie had been making.

"Nora." He stood at the stairway, waiting.

"You girls okay for a few minutes?" She glanced at Sophie, then Ellie, who was chewing her thumbnail and pulled it out of her mouth as soon as Nora looked her way.

"They're fine, Nora. We'll just be upstairs."

Dave hadn't wanted her to meet with Paul. He'd warned her that it was a bad idea. She should have listened. But that was useless to think about. She'd gone and now she needed to figure out what to tell him. She watched the girls, delaying. Sophie worked on her beads. Ellie was drawing.

Nora's phone rang. She let it go. Tasted blood on her lip.

"Nora?" Dave sounded impatient.

Nora crossed the room, still unclear about what to say, or even how to greet her husband. Still feeling that her body was not quite her own.

Dave was waiting. She felt it, the weight of his gaze on her. Was she taking too long? Was she moving slowly, or was her sense of time altered? He didn't tell her to hurry, didn't seem concerned that she was acting oddly. In fact, when she approached, he stepped close and kissed her mouth, then led her to the kitchen table where he pulled out her chair and sat beside her with probing, expectant eyes.

"So? What happened? Tell me."

Tell him? Tell him that Paul's mouth had smashed her lips, or that his breath had steamed her face? Nora smelled Paul's harsh cologne, though she couldn't place where it came from. She saw his bare, ginger-haired chest, the blurring ceiling lights, the cappuccino cup. She felt his thrusting, swirling fingers. She closed her eyes. Tell him.

"At first, he was cordial." She didn't look at Dave. She examined the saltshaker and the half-full coffee pot. The refrigerator door covered with the children's drawings. "His office is swank. It's got art. And a full bar—"

"That's nice. Why did he want to see you?"

Why was she avoiding the truth? Was she embarrassed? Should she be? Did she think the assault was somehow her fault, that—Oh God—she had somehow encouraged Paul? Had she given signals that she was attracted to him? Lots of women were, after all. Most of their friends were open about finding Paul drop dead gorgeous—for sure, Patty did. And Alex. But no. Nora needed time to process it, was still in shock, but she hadn't done anything. Paul had plain and simple attacked her. He'd tried to drug her and force her to have sex.

But she couldn't tell Dave any of that. If she did, his face would harden, eyes steely, jaw rigid. He'd call the police, but not right away. Not until he'd gone and beaten the bloody crap out of the honorable candidate for Senate. She pictured Dave in a jail cell, arrested for an assault.

She couldn't risk it. Besides, Nora doubted she could make herself say the words out loud. He raped me. With his fingers. She cringed, unable to even think the truth. Besides, what good would saying it do? Words were finite and simple, gave no hint of what had actually happened, the humiliation, invasion, fear. The disbelief. The rage.

At least she knew about rage. She'd learned long ago how to contain it within a smile.

She fiddled with a cereal crumb, pushing and rolling it beside a placemat.

"Nora? What's going on?"

"Sorry. I'll make it short. Paul told me that you and Barbara are having an affair."

Nora's phone rang again.

"Shit." Dave chewed his lower lip. "What gave him that idea?"

"He hired a private investigator to watch Barbara while he's off campaigning. He's got pictures of you together." She paused and met Dave's eyes. "There's a lot of body contact."

Dave's brows rose. His eyes shifted ever so slightly. "No way."

"You do touch each other a lot. Your hands are always on her."

"Horseshit."

"Dave. I saw the pictures. Shots of you going into and out of their house. Hugging. Kissing her goodbye at the door—"

"Kissing?" He frowned. "Pecking maybe. A friendly 'hello' and 'goodbye.'"

She studied his face, saw no deceit. "Okay." She gave Dave's hand a reassuring squeeze. "But I couldn't tell him the truth about why you've been spending so much time together or taking boxes out of their house or pecking her face. He assumes it's an affair. Understandably." She nodded, then met her husband's eyes. "And he's hopping mad. He scares me, Dave. He's nothing like his family-man, all-American, nice-guy public image. He's mean. Evil. He vowed that there'd be consequences. And I believe him. We've seen Barbara's bruises." She shifted in her chair, easing her lingering soreness.

"You're right." Dave took out his phone. "I better check on her." He punched in a number, drummed his fingers on the table, waiting. His eyebrows furrowed. "No answer." He set down his phone, scowling. "This isn't good."

Nora folded her hands. Maybe Barbara was at the hospital with Paul, having the gash on his head stitched. How had Paul explained the wound to his campaign workers? And to Barbara? Oh God. If he'd told Barbara that Nora had hit him, Barbara would for sure tell Dave that Nora cut Paul's head open. And Nora didn't look forward to explaining why.

"She's probably busy."

"I called before I left the office. She didn't answer then either." His eyes darted from spot to spot, thought to thought.

"She might be at the hairdresser. Or the gym."

"No. He thinks we're having an affair, and you said he's furious and looking for revenge. My guess is he's taken her phone so I can't reach her. He's putting an end to our affair." Dave leaned back, crossed his arms. "And if he's taken her phone, God knows what else he's doing. Damn."

Nora pictured Barbara's bruises, heard Paul's warning. *Cheating isn't something one can simply forgive. There have to be consequences.*

"Should you go over there? I'll go with you."

"No, no. That would just aggravate him and make it worse. Look, the guy's an abuser, but he's also in the public eye, running for the damned Senate. He won't risk doing anything extreme to her in the middle of his campaign. I think for now, we should lie low and not antagonize him." His eyes narrowed and his jaw clenched. Then he took a breath. "Let him think he's in charge. The lease begins Saturday. We just get through the next couple of days and Barbara and the kids will be out of here—free and safe."

"Why not bring them here?" Nora didn't like the "couple of days" part. "We could make sure they're safe until Saturday."

"Believe me, I've tried." Dave shook his head. "I've asked her to stay here, or in a hotel, or with other friends. She doesn't want to go anywhere until she can be gone for good. She's afraid he'll find a way to stop her."

"But that was before he—" she stopped, mid-sentence. She'd almost slipped, almost said *before he assaulted me.* "Before he talked to me about your affair."

Dave rubbed his eyes and sighed. "Right." He thanked Nora for finding out what Paul was thinking, pecked her cheek, and headed upstairs to change.

Nora's phone rang again. She went to pick it up and shivered when she saw Paul's number on the screen. What did he want? Was he afraid she'd file a complaint against him? Did he want to apologize? She turned off her phone, but not before checking her missed calls. Paul had called half a dozen times.

"Mommy, are you done talking yet?" Little voices flew up from the playroom. "We're hungry. What's for dinner?"

Nora called out, "Strip steaks."

But she didn't start dinner. Instead, she sat for a while, moving that crumb around with her finger, her heart heavy with the weight of her secret, smelling Paul's cologne. Seeing blood streaming down his face.

A broken vow must incur some kind of retribution, don't you agree?

THURSDAY, OCTOBER 28, 1993

*A*nnie had changed.

Nothing overt or dramatic. Not anything Nora could name. But she was different: slightly removed at lunch, a tad distant when they sat together on the bus. Even on the phone. In fact, unlike in the past, Nora seemed to be the only one making the calls, and the calls were shorter, less confidential, as if Annie was just going through the motions of talking, skimming over who wore what and which girls liked what boys.

Annie's aloofness ate at Nora. So, she decided to appease Annie by answering the question Annie had been asking for weeks and admitted that she liked Bobby Baxter. But Annie hadn't seemed to care. Worse, she hadn't reciprocated. She had left Nora hanging with a secret exposed.

Annie was shutting her out.

That night, Nora lay in bed, worrying about her friendship. She comforted herself by thinking about the past. The good times: Annie taking her that first time up to that bathroom cluttered with her sisters' towels, hairdryers, brushes and lotions. Annie's fingers gently steering the skinny disposable razor through the mounds of foam on Nora's legs, under her arms. Annie dabbing purple shadow onto Nora's eyelids or teaching her to slow dance. Even now, she could hear Michael Bolton. How was she supposed to live without Annie?

Nora turned onto her side, forced her eyes closed, but the memories kept coming. Annie telling her about kissing. Instructing her.

"Keep your lips soft and a little open in case he wants to put his tongue in." She'd shown her. Nora had said, "Ew." Annie had laughed, called her a baby, and demonstrated, first on Nora's hand, then on her mouth. And laughed some more.

Nora had learned Annie's cool way to laugh, head back and nostrils flaring. She'd learned to wear Annie's amused, knowing hint of a smile while others talked. To walk with Annie's nonchalant, unhurried swing to her hips. Annie was her guide, her role model. Without Annie, Nora would still be that awkward girl wearing the totally wrong kind of clothes and childish style of hair, standing at the side of the room, saying the totally wrong things—if she even had anyone to say them to. If she lost Annie, she lost everything.

All because of Tommy.

Nora tossed. She rearranged her pillow. How was she supposed to fix things? It wasn't her fault Tommy had taken those pictures. She couldn't undo what he'd done, and she'd apologized a hundred times. What else could she do? She wanted to talk to Annie about it but getting her alone wasn't easy. At school, kids always clustered around. On the bus, other people could hear. And on the phone, Annie had been distant. She needed to see Annie's face, to have Annie see hers. It was her only hope.

The next morning, Nora left for school without breakfast, her homework unfinished because she'd been unable to concentrate. Her chest felt raw, her stomach twisted. She went to school in a wounded haze, waiting for an opportunity. Finally, between English and Math, she saw Annie at her locker.

"Can we talk?" Her voice was paper thin, too high-pitched.

"What's up?" Annie waved to some girls walking by, then worked the combination on her locker door.

"Nothing. It's just…"

Annie's locker door swung open. She knelt, putting books in, stuffing others into her bookbag.

"Is something wrong?"

"Wrong?" Annie stood.

"I mean, it seems like, I don't know. Are you mad at me?"

Annie stepped up to Nora, their noses inches apart. "Hmm. Let me think. Why would I be mad?"

Of course she was mad. What a stupid question. Nora went on blabbering, sounding dumber and dumber. "It wasn't my fault. And I said I was sorry."

"Sorry's worth shit."

Nora couldn't breathe, felt punched. Her body wanted to cave in on itself.

"We could do what he said and talk to Craig."

"Are you serious? Do you know Craig at all? If we tell him to lay off your brother, he'll want to know why. And I'm sure not telling him. Besides, it would probably backfire. Instead of easing up, Craig would beat the shit out of him. Which wouldn't upset me at all. But then, who knows what he'd do with the pictures."

Nora bit her lip. "So, no Craig."

"Of course not." Annie's voice became a hiss. "Nobody finds out about this, Nora. Not Craig, not anybody." Her face hardened, and her eyes turned to ice. "Look, it's been four days. You haven't done shit. What's so complicated? Why's it taking so long? You want me not to be mad? Get those pictures. All of them. And the negatives."

Nora could barely make a sound. "I'll try."

"Trying's crap."

"I'll get them."

"Good. Bring them to my sleepover Saturday."

"Sleepover?"

"Come around eight."

The locker door slammed and Annie sauntered off, waving to some eighth-grade boys.

Nora stayed behind, absorbing the news: Annie had almost not invited her to her sleepover. Had almost not mentioned it. Annie was going to drop her unless she could get Tommy's pictures. But once she got them and gave them to Annie, things would be normal again. She and Annie would go back to how they'd been. They would. For sure.

Nora called Barbara at seven and nine. Dave called her at eight and ten.

All the calls went to voicemail.

"Bastard took her phone away," Dave fumed and cursed. "That's the only explanation."

Nora didn't agree. There were lots of other possibilities. Barbara could have lost her phone, or forgotten that she'd turned it off, or dropped it into the bathtub. But she saw Dave's point. The likelihood of something innocent happening to Barbara's phone on this particular night was low.

After the ten o'clock call, Dave's forehead veins were pulsing. His breathing was rapid and erratic.

"Want me to fix you a drink?"

He didn't answer, just sat, breathing and pulsing. His right hand made a fist.

Nora and Dave sat in the family room, the television tuned to some complicated British mystery that neither of them was following.

"So should we go and check on her? Or call the police and have them check?"

He bit his knuckle and stared at his phone. "I don't want to stir things up. We have to wait."

They did? Nora wasn't sure. But Dave said to wait, so she waited.

Waiting didn't feel right though. She watched the clock above the fireplace, its second hand hopping forward in measured bits.

Each hop linked time to space but went nowhere, just around and around. And around.

Of course, she didn't have to wait just because Dave wanted to. She could call the police on her own, could report Paul's assault. The police would go arrest him then, wouldn't they? And with Paul in custody, Barbara would be safe from his arm-twisting, eye-punching temper. Nora pictured it, the police sending someone to her house to follow up. An overtired detective with a crew cut and a pot belly would look her up and down, probably rating her a five, or at most a six, as he asked her what had happened. Sophie and Ellie would peek from the stairway, having heard the doorbell. Nora would ask Dave to take them back to bed, but Dave would want to know why the policeman was there. So she'd make up an excuse, just something to get Dave to go upstairs with the girls. When Dave was gone, she'd take the detective to the kitchen and offer him coffee. He'd say no and start to ask questions, politely at first, then more pointedly. He'd make her repeat details, looking for inconsistencies.

What time did you say you went over there? What were you wearing? How much alcohol did you drink before the alleged assault? Was there actual intercourse? No? So, you're alleging, what, that he kissed you?

She'd have to describe exactly what Paul had done to her. The cop would twist his mouth and eye her with unsubtle doubt, struggling to imagine Paul Ellis—dashing, elegant, wealthy, powerful, charismatic candidate—bothering to stick his fingers up the panties of a five- or six-rated house frau like Nora. He'd suck his teeth and ask why she'd waited so long to call police.

"All this time later, you understand, it's too late to test for many types of drugs that you claim he put in your coffee, so we have no evidence. All we really have, ma'am, is your story."

So, no. The police might not go to Paul's house even if she reported him. At least not immediately.

"Let's wait until morning." Dave stared at the television screen, or maybe the wall above it.

At some point, they went to bed. They must have said goodnight, must have kissed. It was their habit, but Nora wasn't paying attention. She kept her distance, staying on her side of the mattress, grateful that Dave was preoccupied, because if he touched her, she was sure he'd sense that something was different, something was wrong. He'd want her to explain. So she made sure her body was not touching Dave's, giving him time alone with his thoughts. Taking time for hers.

When Nora closed her eyes, she saw Paul hovering over her, his eyes snakelike, lips snarly. So she got up and turned her phone on, tried Barbara one more time, even though it was after midnight. When Barbara's voicemail clicked on, Nora went back to bed, lying with her eyes open, hoping Barbara was all right, watching the window for the first rays of sunlight.

When morning came, though, she was finally asleep, dreaming that Dave was making pancakes. Who dreamed about breakfast? Unless it wasn't a dream? She smelled pancakes. And bacon. Still, her limbs didn't want to move, nor did her eyelids. She pulled up the comforter, drifted toward slumber until voices interfered, smooth and professional, like newscasters. Were the girls watching television? The news? Surely not. And why was volume up so high? She curled her pillow around her head, muffling the sound. Even so, Sophie's voice blasted loud and clear up the steps.

"Daddy, where's the remote? We want to watch Paw Patrol!"

"Downstairs," Dave yelled back. "Look under the couch cushions!"

"We did. It's not there!"

"It's nowhere!" Ellie screeched.

Nora gave up. Sleep wasn't going to happen. She lay still, collecting herself for the morning, recalling fragments of the day before. Paul's office. His scent. His fingers. His words. *If a man dares to mess with my wife, he'd better believe I'll reciprocate.*

A wave of revulsion passed through her. She had to stop thinking about Paul, had to stop reliving that humiliating, disgusting, infuriating incident. Had to get up and start a new day.

Don't cry over spilt milk.

She pushed herself up and out of bed. In the bathroom mirror, she examined her face, checking to make sure it gave away nothing. Saw tangled hair. Hollow spaces under her eyes.

Nora splashed herself with cold water, brushed her teeth. Fluffed her hair. Good. She was reviving. A smile would squish the hollow spaces.

After breakfast, she'd call Barbara again. And if Barbara didn't answer, she'd call Paul as if nothing whatever had happened in his office, as if she'd never even gone to see him. She'd say that Barbara's phone didn't seem to be working and ask if she could please speak to her. Good plan. Why hadn't she thought of it last night?

As she headed downstairs, Dave came out of the kitchen carrying a tray of pancakes, bacon, and coffee, pouting when he saw her. "You're not supposed to be up. I'm bringing you breakfast—"

"Daddy!" Sophie interrupted, charging up the stairs from the playroom, Ellie right behind her, yelling over each other's words.

"Mommy! Daddy! Guess what?"

"Auntie Barbara!"

"Just now! We saw Auntie Barbara—"

"—on TV!"

"She's on the news!"

WEDNESDAY, AUGUST 15, 2018

The news flash was that Barbara Ellis, wife of Paul Ellis, candidate for United States Senator from Pennsylvania, had died. Her car had gone into the Schuylkill River some time during the previous night.

The girls began to whimper, asking questions, orbiting Nora, clinging to her robe. Sophie stared at the TV, her eyes wide, head tilted.

Nora couldn't think. Couldn't absorb the information, let alone explain it to her children.

"Dave?" She hoped he'd know what to say to them.

But Dave was silent. Still holding her breakfast tray, he stared at the screen. His jaw was tight and rippling, his eyes wild.

"Dave," she said again. She needed him to steady her, to help her make sense of this horrible development.

But Dave plopped the tray down on the coffee table and ran up the stairs, skipping every other step.

"Where are you going?"

"Daddy?" Ellie cried.

Sophie and Ellie clutched Nora's arms and waist. They hung on her, asking questions she had neither the wisdom nor the strength to answer.

Where had Dave gone? And Barbara—Barbara was dead? How could she be dead? Nothing made sense. Nothing.

"Let's eat, girls." The words came on their own. "Breakfast is getting cold."

Her daughters headed for the kitchen, probably glad to follow routine. She took her tray and they sat at the table as a normal family would, eating pancakes and bacon. Ellie poured a river of syrup over her stack. Sophie chewed warily, her eyes on Nora.

Nora gave them a gentle, patient smile. "Aunt Barbara had a terrible accident. It's awfully sad but try not to worry. Everything'll be okay." Her voice sounded empty.

Dave burst back in, breathless and holding his laptop. He took his seat at the table and punched up the news. Nora got up and read over his shoulder. Barbara gazed back at her from the screen, alive and glamorous. Smiling. Paul was there, too, in a sleek campaign shot. Then there was a third image: Barbara's BMW being towed out of dark water, still half submerged.

The girls remained unnaturally silent. Nora folded her arms around her middle, reading the words in spurts. The car had swerved off the road. Had entered the water from the pier on River Road in Gladwyne. Officers had responded to Paul Ellis's call late Friday night. The distraught candidate had reported his wife missing. Had stated that Mrs. Ellis had been suffering from severe depression Had threatened to harm herself. Specifically, by driving her car into the river. Within the hour, police located the car. Mrs. Ellis was locked inside, unresponsive. Declared dead.

Dave scratched his head and wandered out of the kitchen. He didn't answer when Nora called for him.

Nora's phone rang. She heard it but made no move to answer it.

Sophie said, "Mom! Your phone!"

When Nora didn't move, Sophie ran and got it, handed it to her.

"Mom!" Sophie's eyes were frantic. Her world had been turned upside down. First Auntie Barbara was dead. Now her mother wouldn't answer the phone. It stopped ringing.

Sophie was beside herself. "Why didn't you answer it?"

"I don't feel like talking right now." The breakfast table, the coffee and bacon, even her family seemed intangible. She forced a weak smile.

Ellie said, "Mommy's sad, Sophie."

Sophie waited a beat and nodded soberly, then gave Nora a hug. "Everything'll be okay, Mommy." She sat again and resumed eating, eyeing Nora as she chewed.

Breakfast progressed. Ellie wanted more bacon. Or was it orange juice? Distracted and consumed with thoughts of Barbara, Nora wasn't sure, hadn't been listening. She passed both the pitcher and the platter.

The news reports had indicated that Barbara's death had been either an accident or, as Paul had implied, a suicide. But Nora disagreed. She was certain, positive beyond the tiniest shadow of a doubt, that Barbara's death had been neither. She didn't know how he'd done it, but somehow, for sure, the candidate for Senate had murdered his wife.

THURSDAY, OCTOBER 28, 1993

The door to Tommy's room had been closed since dinner. Nora put her ear against it and listened for hints of what he was doing. She heard nothing, but Annie's ice-cold warning echoed in her head. "Get me those photographs."

Nora lifted her fist to knock, but hesitated, rehearsing what she'd say. She took a breath, ribs aching. What if he refused? What if he laughed and told her to get out? What would she tell Annie? She imagined showing up at the party without the pictures. Annie wouldn't make a big deal of it. She'd just ignore her. Nora would be cast out of Annie's circle. Friendless. Alone.

She contemplated the door, the flat wooden barrier to her brother's world of weirdness, a world she'd prefer not to enter. But she had no choice. Steeling herself, she banged on the door, too fast, too hard.

"What?"

You'll get more flies with honey than with vinegar.

Nora took another breath, slowing down. "Can I come in?"

"Why?"

Asshole. Why did he think, to deliver a pizza? "Just to talk."

He didn't answer right away. She waited, jittery, staring at the door. It was Thursday night. The party was just two days away. Not a lot of time to convince him. What was taking him so long? Why didn't he just tell her to come in? What was he doing in there? What if he wouldn't even talk to her? She put her ear against the door again, heard a rustle of fabric, a closet door slide shut, the creak of the floor.

Maybe she should knock again. She lifted her fist, but the door opened. Tommy, in an old T-shirt and sweatpants, allowed her to follow him into the dimness. He sat at the desk, leaving his bed as her only choice, unless she wanted to stand while they talked. Use honey, not vinegar. It would be cozier, sweeter, more sisterly to sit. The room smelled stale and musky—shadowy, like secrets.

"What?" He sat with his shoulders slumped. His desk lamp was the lone source of light, glaring over stacks of framed insects, spare pins, hunks of foam board, glass slides, jars of glue and chemicals. A large dead moth, pinned with its wings splayed. And in the corner, Tommy's camera.

But no photographs.

Nora put on a smile. "Is that what you were working on?" She nodded at the moth.

He blinked. "What's it to you?"

"I'm interested, that's all."

"Since when?"

What was wrong with him? They both knew she didn't give a fig about his damn bugs, but couldn't he accept her question as a friendly gesture? A kind of peace offering?

She walked to the desk and looked closer at the poor creature. "Did you net this?"

"No. It got caught in my trap." He turned to look at it. "But it panicked. See? Its wing got torn." He pointed. She leaned in. The thing was pathetic, lying there helpless and dead, spread-eagled. She scanned the rest of his desktop and saw no sign of the pictures—no envelope, no box that they might be kept in. She glanced at Tommy. His lips looked red and irritated, a little swollen, even bruised. Why?

"But I'm mounting it anyway because of the great markings and its size. It's not perfect, but—What are you staring at?" He scowled and touched his mouth.

"Nothing." She backed away. Felt her fake smile waver.

"Bullshit. You were staring at me."

"No, I wasn't."

Tommy glowered. "What do you want, Nora? We both know you don't give a flying fuck about me or my collection." He stretched his legs out, crossed them at the ankles.

"I'm trying to make peace, that's all. So we won't be at each other as much. I mean we're family."

Family is forever.

"Uh-huh." He didn't move.

"And it's stupid how we, you know, do things to make each other mad."

He crossed his arms.

"I thought if I got to know more about the things you like, it'd be a start. You might do the same, and—"

"Okay, enough. The answer's no. You can go now." He laughed at her, his braces glimmering.

"What do you mean no?"

"You're so transparent. Do you think you can just hop in here and sweet talk me into giving you those pictures?"

How did he know?

"I already told you. I took them for your own good, so you'd think twice about what you're doing and who you're doing it with."

"Where are they, Tommy? You have to let me have them."

"Not happening." He turned back to his moth.

"Tommy, please. Please. I'll do anything. I'm begging you—"

"Leave. Close the door after you."

She stood for a minute, watching him ignore her. The cowlick. His thick, matted hair. She ought to grab a baseball bat and smash his head in. But Tommy didn't have one. He didn't play baseball, and she couldn't very well smash his head in with a butterfly net.

What could she do? Nora closed the door behind her and leaned against it, trembling. Without the pictures, her life was ruined. Over. From inside Tommy's room came a faint rustling, like swishing fabric.

D ave sat silent in front of the family room television, massaging his temples.

Nora had to tell him what she suspected, that Paul had killed Barbara. She called him into the hallway, away from the children. "Can I talk to you a minute?"

Dave held up his hand, fending her off.

"Dave, I need to tell you—"

"Not now." He rushed past her and disappeared into his study.

Nora followed him, but the door closed in her face. She stopped, stunned. Dave had never shut her out like that before. She bit her lip, fought tears. Did he think he was the only one who was hurting? She'd lost a friend, too. She stared at the door that separated them, resenting its sturdiness. It was solid pine. Or maybe oak. She didn't know much about wood. But it was respectable and thick, promising bookshelves, leather chairs, soft lighting, and pipe smoke, a comfortable room beyond. Nora raised her hand to the knob. Never mind that Dave had shut the door, she could still go in. It was her house, too. She had every right. But she didn't turn the knob. Maybe it would be better to knock. She considered it. In the end, though, she took her hand away from the door, neither knocking nor going in, deciding that Dave wanted to be alone. Or at least apart from her.

Nora's eyes filled. She smeared tears away, annoyed with herself for crying over a closed door when she hadn't shed one tear for her dead, probably murdered friend. She pictured Dave in the study. Was he weeping? Pacing? Downing a shot of whiskey? Maybe all of those things? But picturing him in there, she realized that he hadn't intended to hurt her by shutting her out. No, Dave just needed to be alone with his guilt. Clearly, he blamed himself for Barbara's death. If he'd gone over there last night or arranged for her to move a week, even a day ago, Barbara would still be alive. Paul wouldn't have had the chance to kill her.

Nora wanted to reason with him, remind him that he wasn't at fault. She knew Dave wouldn't listen. She put her hand gently on the door and let it rest a moment before she walked away.

The girls weren't ready for the camp bus. Nora waved it away, then bundled them into the car and headed to Patty's. They were somber and quiet on the ride but, when they saw their friends in the back yard, they perked up, running to join them.

Alex, Patty, and Katie were sitting around the umbrella table. They greeted Nora with hugs and raw, teary eyes. For a while, they all sat silent, watching the kids dart around almost as if it were a normal day. But nothing was normal. To Nora, the sounds of the children at play—their squeals, shrieks, and shouts—were sharp and jarring. The sunlight was cloying, the blue of the sky painfully bright. Nora stared at an empty lounge chair, sorely aware of the friend who wasn't there.

"I couldn't believe it when I saw the news," Alex said. "Did you all see it?"

They'd all seen it.

"The news said Barbara was depressed." Patty's eyes were red and puffy. "Like they want people to think it was suicide."

"It's crazy, isn't it?" Alex's mouth hung open.

"Totally. Since when was Barbara depressed? She had an amazing life. What did she have to be depressed about?" Katie dabbed her eyes with a paper napkin.

"Nothing." Patty fought with her hair, tried to force it into a rubber band. "She wasn't. No way it was suicide. I don't buy it."

Nora lay on her lounge chair, thinking of Barbara's last minutes. Had she been conscious at the end? Had she known that she was going to die, that Paul was murdering her? Had she watched the water rise around her, felt its chilling grip? Nora closed her eyes, and the person trapped in the car, banging on windows was no longer Barbara but Tommy, and water was rising over his neck, his chin, his nose. Nora blinked him away, gripping her armrests.

The others positioned their chairs in a circle and talked in hushed tones that no one would hear, especially the children, not that the children were listening. They—all of them, including Ellie—were preoccupied with their construction project in the sand box.

"I don't get it," Katie said. "Even if she was depressed, that's not a reason to kill yourself. You see a shrink. You take pills. You don't drive into the river."

"Wait a second, what did I miss?" Alex added ice to her mimosa. "Does everybody agree that she was depressed? Because I don't. She seemed to love life. And she had everything."

"She seemed to have it all, but maybe she didn't." Patty shrugged.

"Huh?"

"I'm just saying I don't think Barbara liked herself all that much. Like, she was always trying to improve her looks. The boobs. The lips—"

"She did her lips?" Katie's eyebrows lifted.

"You didn't know? Last winter. Remember, for a while they looked inflated? Kind of like Polish sausages."

"No," Katie frowned.

"I remember," Alex said. "I thought she had herpes. Cold sores."

"No, uh-uh." Patty shook her head. "It was lip enhancement. I think she got a tummy tuck, too. She never actually said, but nobody who's had two kids has a stomach that tight."

"She looked perfect," Katie added. "She had money. Her husband was about to be a Senator so she'd meet everybody—The President. The who's who of money and power. My God, the parties she'd go to. Tell me, what did she have to be depressed about?"

Alex dabbed her eyes, sniffed. "No idea. None."

"She looked like she had everything, but I'll tell you one thing she didn't have: self-confidence." Patty squeezed sunblock out of the tube.

"Please." Katie searched for her sunglasses. "Are we talking about the same Barbara?"

"I'm serious. Barbara never went to college. I don't think she ever once read the book club books. She wasn't sophisticated or intellectual." Patty slapped sunblock onto her legs. "And then her husband starts pulling ahead in the polls, so she would've been thrown into the country's most elite circles. Like you said, Katie—the who's who of power and politics. I bet she was terrified."

"Terrified of what?" Alex looked skeptical. "It wasn't like people were going to quiz her. Men became idiots around her. She was flat out stunning. That was enough."

Patty shook her head. "Maybe it wasn't enough for Barbara. Maybe being stunning was her way of covering up her feelings of inferiority."

"Bullshit. I can't believe that she didn't feel good about herself." Katie took the sunblock tube from Patty. "It wasn't just her body that was perfect. Look at her house, clothes, jewelry, cars, kids. And my God, her husband. Paul's rich and powerful. Not to mention that he looks like Brad Pitt—"

"Brad Pitt?" Alex interrupted. "No way. Paul Ellis is much more refined looking. His features are elegant and chiseled where Brad's are blunt—"

"I don't believe you don't see it. They definitely look alike. Paul could be Brad's brother." Katie was adamant.

Nora thought they were both right. Paul was longer and leaner, but, yes, she saw a definite Brad Pitt resemblance. She shifted in her chair, imagining Brad Pitt drugging and pawing her, felt her stomach churn. She turned her attention to the kids, focusing on small bodies in motion.

"Anyway, Katie, how can you assume that being married to Paul meant she felt good about herself?" Alex scolded. "How we feel about ourselves isn't determined by who we're married to." She swirled her drink. "Patty's right. Deep down, I bet Barbara didn't feel worthy of Paul and all his trappings. We all know how she grew up with nothing and went to work in the casinos. Between us chickens, I've always suspected that her past was, well, a little sordid."

"She was a blackjack dealer," Katie said. "What's sordid about that?"

"A dealer?" Alex's eyebrows rose.

Patty struggled again with her hair. "That's what she claimed. But I'm with Alex. I think the dealer story was a cover. I always thought she was an escort."

"Stop. Just stop." Katie looked at Nora for support. "You're ripping Barbara to pieces. We were supposed to be her friends. And she's dead. Am I the only one who's devastated? Can't you show some affection? And respect?"

Alex spoke up. "We're all upset, Katie. We're just trying to sort it out. Okay?"

Nora's head throbbed. She rubbed her temples. "Honestly, nobody should give a rat's ass about her past. She was our friend."

"The point is," Patty's voice tightened, defensive, "we're trying to figure out why she'd kill herself. And I'm thinking maybe it's about her past and low self-esteem."

Katie squinted in the sun. "So, you're suggesting she was pretending to be someone she wasn't?"

"Possibly." Patty sipped her mimosa.

"But lots of women have low self-esteem. We all think our bodies suck and we're fat or ugly." Katie jiggled the flab on her upper arms. "Look at these. Plus, my thighs are pure cellulite—"

"No, they're not, Katie," Nora cut in. "You have an adorable figure."

"No," Katie said. "It's sweet of you to say so, Nora, but I don't. Even if I did, I wouldn't know it. I'd only see the flaws because like most women in our screwed-up culture, I never feel good about myself. We all feel like we aren't good enough. But we don't do what Barbara did."

Right, Nora thought. And neither had Barbara. But she couldn't tell them that, because then she'd have to explain about Paul, about what she knew.

In the yard behind them, the children played tag. They ran and squealed and seemed to be having fun, not focusing on death. Nora watched them, imagining Tommy in the backyard, catching bugs.

She tried to relax, to let go of both Tommy and Barbara. She got up to admire the foliage edging Patty's deck. Rosebushes. Boxwood hedges whose dense, shadowy branches almost hid a giant black spider in its web.

"I just don't see it." Katie picked up the conversation where they'd left it. "To me, Barbara was more confident than any of us."

"Okay. Then maybe it wasn't about who she was," Patty suggested. "Maybe she killed herself because of something she did."

Alex blinked. "Like what?"

"I don't know. Something scandalous. Like having an affair." Patty took out her thermos to refill mimosas.

"Seriously? Married to Paul Ellis?" Alex shook her head.

"I agree. She'd never," Katie said. "If you have a man like Paul Ellis, you're not looking at anyone else."

Nora sipped her drink. What would her friends say if she told them that Perfect Paul had been abusing Barbara? That just last week, he'd turned Barbara's arm purple and blackened her eye? That he'd had Barbara followed and photographed while he was out of town, that he'd made her call him every two hours to report her whereabouts? Or that, when Nora had gone to see him, Paul had assaulted her? Would they believe her? Doubtful. To them, Paul was a superstar, the ideal man. They giggled in his presence like gawking, star-struck teenagers. Nora tried not to wince, recalling his slithery hands on her thighs. She crossed her legs, folded her arms. Couldn't stop the images. Blood pouring from his forehead. The walls wobbling as she inched toward the door. The anger, the entitlement in his voice, *Come back here, you pathetic cow!*

Her friends had gone quiet. Kids voices made background sounds. Nora imagined Tommy wandering off near the bushes, gazing at beetles or bees. The spider spun its web. On the trees, leaves fluttered in the breeze.

"Then again, it might not have been suicide." Patty said. "Might have been an accident."

Or murder. Nora sipped her mimosa.

"But how?" Alex said. "The car went all the way from the street, through the parking lot, across the pier, and into the river—how could she go that far by accident?"

"And besides," Katie said, "if it was an accident, like the car went out of control and she tried to stop, they'd have found skid marks, right?"

"Says our resident CSI," Patty smirked. Her hair had come loose yet again, locks falling around her face. She undid the rubber band and tried again to make a ponytail with hair that was too short.

"I learn a lot from TV shows, Patty. Skid marks would mean she tried to stop before she went into the water, which she wouldn't do if she was committing suicide."

"But I guess they didn't find any." Alex reached for the pitcher and refilled everyone's glass.

Nora took a sip, leaned back, closed her eyes. Saw Barbara's car careening into the water. *There have to be repercussions, don't you agree?* He'd killed her. He'd done it, somehow, with or without skid marks.

Katie began talking about suicide, people she'd known or heard of who'd killed themselves. A former neighbor had shot himself, a classmate had taken pills.

Small hands landed on Nora's stomach. Her eyes popped open. "I'm thirsty," Ellie said, and before Nora could stop her, she picked up Nora's glass.

"Wait!" Nora reached for it, but too late. Ellie drained the glass.

"Your juice was sour." Ellie set the empty glass on the table and hurried back to the game, still somewhat steady on her feet.

Nora sat with her mouth open, staring after Ellie. And then because she didn't know what to do, she copied what the others were doing. She laughed.

Dave greeted them outside. He seemed almost normal, actually glad to see them. As he hugged the girls, he said, "I'll grill burgers, Nora. Go relax." He didn't talk about how he'd spent his day.

Maybe cooking was his way of apologizing for his gruffness that morning. Maybe he was feeling better. She tried to read his face, but he kept moving, not staying still long enough for her to get a good look. While he unloaded the car, he assigned tasks for the girls: helping him peel the husks off corn, forming hamburger meat into patties, setting the table. He had everything under control. Nora went upstairs and took a shower, thinking about Barbara, about drowning. She held her face under the shower head and let water stream into her eyes, inhaling it into her nose until she began coughing. She imagined not being able to pull away, not getting air.

When she came downstairs, Ellie was folding napkins.

Dave came in with a platter of burgers and corn. "Chow's on," he said. But he didn't say anything about his day.

During dinner, he chatted and made small talk. And still didn't say what he'd done all day.

He helped the girls melt marshmallows over the dying coals. Ran their baths and tucked them into bed, addressing the girls' inevitable questions about Aunt Barbara.

Sophie's chin wobbled. "Graham said she's dead and never coming back."

Ellie curled into a fetal position and chewed her fingernail.

Dave dabbed at their tears. Nora backed away, letting him take over, not sure she could handle the conversation. She didn't know what her daughters understood about death. She'd never discussed it with them, even though Mindy's dog and a number of people close to them were dead: Dave's father, both her parents and her brother. But Ellie and Sophie had never really known any of them. So whatever they'd learned about death had been indirect—from television or stories, maybe from other kids. Or maybe they knew about it innately without having to be told. Maybe all animals did.

Dave talked gently, his voice fluctuating in singsong. Nora leaned against the wall and didn't interrupt or join in, even when his explanation veered far from what she'd have said. Heaven, for example. She didn't believe there was such a place. She and Dave had a policy of not lying to their daughters—not even about Santa or the Tooth Fairy. But now, Dave was elaborating about how Aunt Barbara was happy and safe and with God and the angels. Really? Was he abandoning their honesty policy? Or did he actually believe what he was saying? Either way, how was it that she didn't know? Why hadn't they ever shared their beliefs about death, let alone how to discuss them with their children?

Dave described heaven as a perfect place where people never had to worry, and Nora imagined Barbara flitting around with a newly-fitted pair of designer wings, an 18-karat halo shining on her head. Would she have to wear a white robe and plain brown sandals? Were there no glam heels and sleek tight pants in heaven? What would she do all day without mani-pedis, tennis games, personal trainers, and happy hours? Sing? Is that what they did in Dave's heaven? Sit on clouds and sing? Dave couldn't possibly believe what he was telling the girls. Could he? Did he also believe in a fiery hell with Satan and legions of demons? How could she have lived with the man for over a decade and not known these fundamental things about him?

Unless she did know. Of course she did. Dave was probably just comforting his little girls with a story in which Aunt Barbara was okay. His voice was like a nursery rhyme. When he finished, and she went to kiss them goodnight, Sophie's tears were dry and Ellie was calm.

But even then, when they were back in their room, Dave didn't say anything about his day. He took a shower.

Nora sat in bed, waiting, debating what to talk about first. She wanted to ask if he even remotely believed what he'd told the girls about heaven. She also wanted him to explain why, that morning, he'd closed the study door in her face. Most of all, though, she wanted to tell him what she suspected about Paul. But she didn't talk about any of those things. Because, when he came out of the shower, Dave finally talked about his day.

"You what?"

"I reached out to a guy in homicide."

"Homicide?" So Dave agreed that Barbara was murdered.

"Informally. Lou and I have known each other for years. He's arrested a number of my clients, but I still say he's a good guy. So, I bought him an omelet and asked his opinion about a hypothetical case."

"Hypothetical."

"Completely." Dave crossed his legs and spoke like a lawyer. "'Imagine it, Lou,' I said. 'A well-known politician is secretly a wife abuser.' He was intrigued. So, I told him that the hypothetical politician's wife is so desperate to escape him that she's going to the extreme of planning her disappearance."

"Did he know which politician you were talking about?"

"Don't know. Maybe not yet. I said, 'Let's say, he notices something's up with his wife. He has her followed and mistakenly concludes that the something is an affair. In reality, the guy's just a friend, but the politician becomes irate, promising he'll deal with it. The very next day, the politician's wife is found dead—an apparent suicide.'"

"So? What did he say?" Nora swung her legs over the side of the bed and sat hip to hip with Dave.

"He didn't say anything. Actually, he laughed."

"He laughed?" What kind of laugh? Was it a dark, ironic chuckle? A stream of knee-slapping giggles?

Dave flopped back onto the mattress. "He said I had to be joking."

"And when you said you weren't?"

"He basically said I was out of my gourd. 'Effing Paul Ellis?'" Dave imitated Lou's south Philly accent. "'That's who you're f-ing talking about? You gotta be f-ing kidding me.' He went on to say that Paul Ellis is the darling of the state, that no one would ever believe my bullshit. And there's no way Barbara Ellis's death was anything but a suicide. Then he sees how I'm not smiling. And Lou knows me. We respect each other. So he says, 'Look. I don't know about any domestic abuse.' And if there had been complaints on file in such a high-profile case, he'd know."

"Of course there were no complaints. She didn't dare report him."

"Bottom line, there's no record of abuse." He stared at the ceiling.

"But what about the bruises on her arm? They must still be there. And her black eye?"

"There's no proof that Ellis ever touched her. But there is proof that Barbara was taking anti-depressants and drinking. And testimony stating that she was desperately lonely with her husband gone so much."

"Testimony? From whom? Anyone besides Paul? Because that's bull. She was thrilled when he was away."

"Nora. Paul Ellis is a rock star. Women swoon when he walks by. Men admire him. Publicly, he promotes his beautiful wife, happy marriage, and loving family. No one's going to believe that his wife despised him."

"What if I tell Lou what she told me about how controlling he was? How he hurt her. How terrified she was of him."

"You're all alone with that assessment, Nora. Her other friends would swear she was gloriously happy. And they're not alone—the whole damn state believes that."

Dave was right. Paul had created an impeccable public image. Nora remembered his hands between her legs. She pictured Barbara's car plunging into the water. Had Paul been there? Had he watched from the road?

"So that's it? Lou won't do anything?"

Dave sighed. "I told him she'd been so scared that she'd hired me to help her with logistics—the new identity, the move, financial details. I gave him my files."

"And?"

"And he took them. Made some notes, but that was it. Lou's attitude was that lots of marriages end with lots of tragedy—even suicide—and that this one was sad but not noteworthy."

"But he'll look into it, won't he? You showed him that Paul had motive."

"The cops are convinced Barbara was a troubled woman who killed herself. And Paul Ellis would be crazy even to sneeze in the middle of his campaign, let alone murder his wife. I'm sure my file is in the bottom of Lou's junk drawer."

"So he won't even talk to Paul?"

Dave's jaw tightened. "Lou already talked to him. He said Ellis seemed completely blindsided and messed up over his wife's death. Which, he reminded me, had occurred while she was alone, driving her own car. So, while he thought it was interesting that she planned to divorce her husband, that fact changed none of the evidence surrounding her death. They're convinced it was suicide."

Nora bit her lip, picturing how it had been for Barbara. The car flying off the ramp, the splat of impact, the gurgling and gulping of the river. Barbara strapped in behind the wheel, cold and wet, watching dark water rise. Had she struggled to get out? Seen Paul watching from the riverbank? Begged him for help?

"They're wrong." Nora frowned. "He killed her. I don't get why, though. Because even though he wanted to punish her for having an affair—he called it retribution—Paul was adamant about wanting his marriage to survive."

Dave said nothing, didn't move.

"Dave? Forget the affair. What if Paul found out she was leaving? Because if he knew—Oh God. She said he'd never let her go. Maybe that's why he killed her."

"Christ, Nora." Dave sat up. A hand went to his forehead. "Don't you think I've agonized over that possibility? What if he found out she was leaving because I slipped up somehow?" His voice was thick. "Her death would be on me."

"No, it wouldn't." Damn. Why had she said that? "It's on him, only him, no matter what set him off. Dave. Please. Don't blame yourself."

She reached for him, but he walked out of the room. She heard his footsteps going down the stairs. A moment later, the study door clicked shut.

THURSDAY, OCTOBER 29, 1993

Tommy had retreated into his attic dark room. Nora sat on her bed, listening, waiting for Marla and Philip's squabbling to transform into snores. Even then, she waited a while longer, making sure they were deeply asleep. Not that they'd get out of bed to ask what she was doing, not that they'd even hear her moving around. Still, she wanted to be sure that no one knew, that no one would notice even a footstep.

While she waited, she kept replaying the day. Annie's coldness, her ultimatum, her threatened consequences if she didn't get the pictures. Nora's life would be hell. She'd go to the cafeteria at lunchtime and see Annie sitting with all the glittery popular girls, and nobody would make room for her to join them. Nora would stand, tray in hand, having nowhere to go. Would she have to sit alone? With dorky kids she didn't even know? Or with Natalie and Charisse and their dweeby, immature friends from elementary school? No way. She'd sooner throw her food out and skip lunch altogether, forever.

For sure, Nora needed to get those photographs. Without Annie, she'd be as friendless as Tommy. Her tears dropped onto her pajamas. It was so unfair that he was her brother. Weirdo. Creep. Freak. Because of Tommy, Annie was slipping away.

Or already had.

But with any luck, she could fix it. She wiped her face and got out of bed. Cautious and silent, she crept down the hall to Tommy's room. The door, of course, was closed. She knocked softly, making sure he was still upstairs, and when he didn't answer, she tiptoed inside. The stale air, the heaviness of his scent, almost made her gag. Being there, invading his private space, felt wrong, even shameful. But hell, he'd invaded her privacy, hadn't he? He deserved to be invaded back.

Nora snapped on the lamp. On the desk, she scanned clusters of broken insect parts, loose pins, a stack of small foam boards, the microscope. If she were Tommy, where would she stash the pictures? In the overflowing dresser? The cluttered closet? In the mini freezer with his bugs? Under the mattress or the bed? He had a thousand possible hiding places. She turned in a circle, trying to choose.

She started with the dresser and opened drawer after drawer, feeling the contents for pictures or negatives, anything that wasn't fabric. She touched his T-shirts and sweaters, his underwear. Felt something smooth among his socks, pulled at it. Strange. An old stretched out pair of Marla's pantyhose must have gotten tangled in the laundry. She threw them back into the drawer and kept searching.

In his closet, she stepped over a mountain of blue plaid shirts and found a shoebox stuffed not with shoes, but photographs. Jackpot! She almost screamed with joy, certain that she'd found what she was looking for. She took the box to the lamp and began going through it.

The photos were extreme close-ups of grasshoppers, flies, moths. Cicadas. Nothing of her and Annie. But there had to be. She dug deeper, pulled out more. Found shots of Marla. Candid shots of women Nora didn't know. Close-ups of women's hands, earrings, eyebrows, shoes, hair, lips.

But not one of Nora and Annie.

She was still rifling through the photos when the ceiling creaked. Tommy was moving around upstairs, probably closing up his darkroom. Nora hurried, tossed the photos back in the shoebox and shoved it into the corner of the closet where she'd found it, behind the pile of laundry and a Lord and Taylor bag with something dark—maybe a shiny purple scarf—rumpled on top. Weird. Never mind. Tommy was clumping down the steps. She darted for the door, quietly shut it, dashed to her room and jumped into bed where she remembered that—oh God—she hadn't turned off Tommy's desk lamp.

She lay on her bed, listening, waiting, listening to see if Tommy noticed the light. If he'd accuse her of going into his room and snooping. Minutes passed. When he didn't burst into her room, she began to relax. Except not really, because she hadn't found the photos, and Annie's party was just a day away.

SUNDAY, AUGUST 19, 2018, 1 P.M.

Barbara's memorial service was standing room only, packed with politicians, judges, community leaders, business executives, state and local VIPs. The governor was there, as was Henry Brady, the incumbent senator Paul hoped to replace. Throngs of people gathered in the foyer of Langston Memorial Chapel, buzzing around the widower like a hive, offering condolences, embraces, kisses and whispers amid competing clouds of importance and colognes.

Barbara's boys, Colin and Harry, wore somber, dark little suits, ties, and shiny shoes. They behaved perfectly, seated in the front row with their nanny and some tanned, silver-toned people Nora assumed were their grandparents.

Enlarged photos of Barbara in an evening gown graced aisles and entrances. Attendants handed out prayer cards with her picture on the front.

Katie and her husband, Stan, had arrived early and saved an entire pew for their friends. Nora hadn't seen the husbands in a while. When Stan greeted her, she was startled by the dark gray curls sprouting on the outer edge of his ears. Alex's husband Ed had changed, too. He looked worn, his eyes sinking into sacs of dark, ashy skin. Did Alex notice those sacs? Did she worry about Ed? They all said it had been too long, things like that. And Patty's big husband Ronny was reaching to hug Nora. He didn't look like himself, either, sporting a ginger-gray beard. Ronny shook Dave's hand, then rotated his shoulders, visibly uncomfortable in a suit.

"Barbara never acted like she knew so many big wigs," Patty said. She held an embroidered handkerchief on her lap, prepared for tears. "Look. There's Jim Slade, the news anchor. And the guy from Channel 3—what's his name? Oh look—that's Mayor Weber!"

"Barbara didn't actually know all these people," Alex said. "Paul does."

"But she didn't care that he knew celebrities," Katie said. "Barbara would have married Paul if he'd been a street sweeper. They were so in love, a perfect couple."

Nora glanced at Dave, his tightly-set jaw. They'd discussed the service, how there would be endless, unbearable praise of Paul, the devoted husband and father. Dave had promised not to react, but she could already feel him tense.

"Poor Paul," Alex sniffed. "Look at him. Even with all those people around him, he looks so lonely without her."

"You can almost see her by his side, even now."

Nora said nothing. What was the point? Dave shifted in his seat, looked at the ceiling. Nora squeezed his hand.

"Is that a bandage on his head?" Katie leaned sideways to get a better look. "I wonder what happened."

Patty and Alex strained to see, but people blocked their views.

Nora didn't have to look. She knew what it was and exactly where it was. She wondered how many stitches he'd needed, what excuse he'd given for the injury.

For a moment, their row sat quietly, women beside their husbands.

"Where is she, anyway?" Katie piped up again. "Isn't her casket supposed to be here?"

Stan put a hand on Katie's shoulder and gestured toward the front of the chapel. "See that golden urn?"

Katie gasped. "No."

He nodded. "Barbara's ashes."

"She was cremated? Already?"

"Shh!" Patty frowned, signaled that the people in front of them could hear.

"The lilies are lovely, aren't they?" Nora tried to steer the conversation, make it normal.

Patty commented on the boys' suits. Alex pointed out the mayor's wife, how nice she looked.

Ed spotted Henry Brady. "Now that's class, forgetting about the campaign for a day." He leaned forward to connect with Stan, Ronny, and Dave. "See that, fellas? Doesn't Brady have class?"

"Enough to make you vote for him?" Ronny grinned, but noticed Patty's glare and sank back into his seat.

Organ music swelled and receded. The pastor asked everyone to stand for a hymn.

And the service began. The pastor led the 23rd Psalm. Everyone remained standing for another hymn. Everyone sat. A childhood friend of Barbara's read a poem, something sad, telling mourners that Barbara wasn't really dead, she'd simply become the morning breeze or flowers or a cloud in the sky. Patty and Alex sobbed. Katie sniffled. Nora was determined not to get emotional. She held onto Dave and steeled herself, refusing to think about the loss of Barbara and her pert freckled nose, her bawdy laugh, her bangling gold bracelets and massive diamond rings, her bouncy highlighted hair. Her husky voice confiding, "Paul will never let me leave."

And then Paul stood at the podium, tall and imposing, his expression appropriately sad, his charismatic charm projecting through the room. His bandage noticeable. He thanked everyone for coming, for helping him and his sons through the last few nightmarish days. His voice broke when he mentioned Barbara's name, and he paused, collecting himself. He appeared to continue off script, speaking not from his prepared speech, but from the heart. It was his fault, he said, that Barbara was gone.

Nora drew a breath, saw Dave leering at Paul with open loathing.

Paul went on, saying that he'd known about his wife's fierce battle with depression and, despite his better judgment, had honored her request to keep it secret even from her parents. At this point, Paul addressed the elderly couple in the front row. "I'm so sorry, Edna and George. I should have opened up to you. If I'd have known how badly-off Barbara was, I would have. I'd have done a lot of things differently."

Nora swallowed. Dave sat rigid, grinding his teeth, blinking fast. The audience was rapt.

Paul continued, blaming himself for letting his wife's condition deteriorate beyond all hope, for putting public service first and traveling for his campaign without realizing that his wife desperately needed his undivided attention. For presenting not just his friends and family, but his constituents with an idealized public image of a happy, healthy family even as a mental illness was secretly and steadily destroying his beloved Barbara.

Paul took a deep breath and drew himself up, as if dignified in his grief. Dave shifted onto his haunches, as if ready to dash.

"Depression may have caused Barbara to take her own life, but the real fault for her death lies with me, her husband. I should have had a better understanding of her suffering. I should have made certain that she got treatment. I should have let her know that she was not alone and that there was hope. I did not do any of those things, and I will regret my omissions all my life. It is those very omissions, though, which lead me to make a promise here, today, not just to all of you, but to Barbara's memory. Whether or not I am elected to the Senate, I will remain committed to the cause of mental health. And today, in honor of Barbara, I announce the establishment of the Barbara Renee Ellis Foundation for Mental Health. I promise to do my best to ensure that no other family endures a loss like the one mine struggles with today."

He kept talking, but Nora didn't hear what he said because Dave muttered a curse, yanked his hand from hers and stood, causing some commotion as he stepped over people's feet to get to the aisle where he turned and stomped out of the chapel. Nora considered going after him, but Alex reached over and squeezed her hand, comforting her. Whispering, "Who knew her middle name was Renee?"

SUNDAY, AUGUST 19, 2018, 3 P.M.

Dave refused to go to the reception, didn't trust himself around Paul. Nora almost went home with him, but Patty wouldn't hear of it.

"Come on, Nora. Barbara would want you to be there."

Dave was still blinking too fast, and the small muscles around his eyes were taut. Would he be all right by himself?

"Go ahead." He squeezed her hand. "Patty's right. You should be there."

"Are you sure?" she began, but Dave was already headed to the car.

At the house, Paul welcomed each guest at the door. Nora moved with the line of people waiting to shake his hand, offer condolences. She stood behind Patty and Ronny, hoping to slide in with them and avoid contact with the bereaved husband. But Paul stopped her.

"Thank you for being here, Nora." He took both her hands.

His grasping fingers and the scent of his distinct cologne awoke memories. Reflexively, Nora recoiled.

But Paul took hold of her and drew her close, whispering, "Honestly, it means a lot to me that you're here. You're the only one who understands."

"I came here to honor Barbara." Nora leaned away from him.

"Of course. We all loved her. I, more than anyone. If only I'd known…"

"Save it." She locked eyes with him. "I know the truth, Paul."

She pulled away before he could reply, and Paul was embraced by the next person in line.

Barbara's house was filled with boisterous drinkers in black and silent servers in black and white. Important people mingled. Nora wandered away from her friends, weaving past clusters of strangers, wondering what Barbara would think of this extravagant event, the opulent floral arrangements, the abundant gourmet food. There were bar stations in the living room, family room, and rear patio. Waiters darted through the crowd, offering stuffed mushrooms with crab, peanut chicken satay, and mini egg rolls. Platters graced every linen-swathed table with antipastos: olives of all varieties, cheeses, sliced sausages, and grapes. In the dining room were honeyed ham, poached salmon, bread baskets, vegetable medleys, potatoes au gratin, Caesar and green salads, berries, pecan squares, brownies, and carrot cakes. It seemed more like a wedding feast than a funeral.

Nora stopped to grab a martini. The olives were stuffed with bleu cheese. What did this excess have to do with Barbara? With death? She moved through the family room onto the deck and looked out on the layered garden, the pool two tiers below. A red cardinal flew back and forth over the water, repeating his trip as if looking for something. Maybe his mate. Maybe she'd left him. Did birds leave their mates? Nora had heard that ducks mated for life. Or was it geese? Maybe cardinals were different, fickle, always cheating and leaving the nest. Maybe he was looking for his mate so he could kill her for cheating. There have to be repercussions.

She should have gone home with Dave. What was he doing, home by himself? Drinking? Blaming himself?

All around her, people bent their heads together, talking into each other's ears with urgency. Discussing what? Plans for the campaign? For business? Certainly nothing concerning Barbara. From the deck, Nora saw Alex and Patty chatting and munching, clearly impressed by Paul's spread—his circus. She swallowed the rest of her martini and chewed an olive. Looked back at the pool and pictured Barbara sunning on a lounge chair, her long legs shimmering. Decided it was time to go home.

"Come with me," Paul appeared from behind and took her elbow.

Nora didn't budge.

"It's okay." He grinned and his teeth gleamed, unnaturally white. "I promise I'll behave." He touched the bandage on his forehead. "I learned my lesson."

His eyes were steady, confident, as if what he'd done to her was nothing of significance. He didn't bother to feign grief. "Please." His smile was crooked, almost boyish, self-conscious. "I want to talk to you. Just a few words."

Nora looked around, saw Patty and Ronny in the family room, the scattered catering staff, the sea of important people. Paul would be insane to assault her again with so many others around. And, come to think of it, given the opportunity, she could say a few words to him too. Words like, "abuser" and "murderer."

"I don't think so." She darted away from him, zigzagging through clusters of twos and threes, hoping to lose him among the crowd, finally slipping into a powder room to disappear. But when she swung the door shut, Paul caught it with his shoe. He shoved his way in, closed and locked the door, leaned against it. Swirled a scotch and sighed as if he were tired. Or losing patience.

"I'll scream." Nora reached for the doorknob.

Paul blocked it. "Please don't. All I want is to talk."

Nora stepped as far away from him as she could, her backside against the sink, her hands latched onto its porcelain rim. Her eyes moved side to side, taking in the mirrors, the small antique vanity, the birds and branches on the wallpaper.

"When you came in you said you know the truth. What did you mean by that?"

Really? This was why he'd followed her into the bathroom?

"Nothing," she fudged. "Just, you know, about Dave and Barbara. About the affair."

Paul's lips formed a slithery grin. "Nora, please. Lying isn't your forte."

Nora moved sideways, bumped the toilet. Oh God. How had she let him isolate her? There was only one way out, and he was blocking it.

"I meant that I know the truth. There was no affair."

He watched her, unmoved.

"And that I know Barbara didn't suffer from depression. You made that up."

If he came toward her, she'd scream. People would come running. How would he explain his presence in the powder room with her?

Paul's eyebrows rose. "Well, if that's what you meant, you're mistaken. On both counts." He sipped scotch.

"Look, I need to get going." She eyed the doorknob. "My husband's expecting me."

Paul didn't budge. "Why do you still doubt that there was an affair?" His voice had softened, become powdery.

The mirrors on opposite walls repeated their reflections dozens, hundreds of times; his frame towered over her. She tightened her grip around her empty martini glass. If he came within arm's reach, she'd smash it and cut him again.

Paul pressed on. "I'm curious. What do you think they were doing all those hours they spent together? You saw the photos. But if they weren't enough to convince you, how's this? The night she died, Barbara admitted she'd been unfaithful. She begged me to forgive her."

He was lying. "No. That didn't happen."

"It did. During our argument. My wife admitted that she was involved with someone. She wouldn't identify him, but that didn't matter as I already knew who he was."

Nora frowned. Why would Barbara tell Paul she was having an affair when she knew he'd become enraged—and when she wasn't even having one?

"After she confessed, Nora, the most incredible thing happened: The bubble burst. Poof. In a momentary flash, clarity set in. I had a revelation. I was, for the first time in years, free of her spell. No longer in love with her. In fact, I was repelled. I told her to pack and leave."

Paul had to be lying. Just days ago, he'd been insane with jealousy and possessiveness, desperate to keep his marriage intact. But now, he claimed he'd told her to leave?

He was lying—about everything.

Paul sipped his drink, continued to lean against the door.

Except, what if he wasn't lying? Barbara might have confessed to an affair in order to hide the truth about Dave and why she'd been seeing him. *Paul will never let me leave.* Maybe Barbara had admitted to one kind of betrayal in order to conceal another.

But there was no reason for secrecy anymore. "Here's the truth, Paul. There was no affair. Dave was spending time with Barbara to help her prepare to leave you." She watched him.

He frowned. "So. To be clear. You're saying there was no cheating. And Barbara wanted to leave me. Oh—And she wasn't depressed?" He smirked, rubbed his chin. "Do I have it right?"

Nora didn't answer, held onto her empty glass.

"You are fascinating, Nora. But completely wrong." Paul shifted his weight, leaned against the mirror by the door. The reflection looked as if he was shoulder to shoulder with himself. "Here's what's true. Barbara would never have chosen to leave me. She depended on me, completely. I saved her from a whore's life and made her into a goddess." He crossed his arms. "So, whatever your wandering husband told you, whatever far-fetched cover story he made up is just that—a cover story. Your husband lied to you to conceal their tawdry affair. But it doesn't matter now. Barbara's gone. Their affair is over. And I don't give a rat's ass about any of it. As to you? Well. Believe what you want." He waited a beat, then turned to leave.

Nora's face burned. She couldn't breathe. She watched the back of Paul's elegant black hand-tailored suit and as he reached for the doorknob, she heard herself spit out the question she had intended not to ask.

She expected him to spin around and attack.

But Paul turned slowly and merely raised an eyebrow. "Seriously, Nora. The question isn't whether I killed her. It's why? Why would I kill her?" He scowled. "The answer is that I wouldn't bother. We argued that night, yes. After the unpleasant incident with you—for which I sincerely apologize, by the way— I ended up in the hospital getting stitches, and I realized the low point to which that woman had brought me. How badly she'd disappointed me. And how, despite the wonders of modern plastic surgery, time was devouring her. Her skin was beginning to shrivel and sag. Jowls were forming." He grimaced. "The point is that I saw that Barbara was, for lack of a better phrase, a used up, dried up, cheap old tart. After that realization, I didn't need to kill her. To me, she was already dead."

Nora couldn't speak. How could Paul be so callous about anyone, let alone the woman he'd married, the mother of his children? Paul isn't who people think he is. She sunk onto the vanity stool, stared at the pretty bottles of lotion and cologne, amenities Barbara had laid out for guests.

Paul continued. Pieces of him, his shoulder, an arm, the side of his face were reflected in the mirror. "Our argument was admittedly rather ugly. I told my wife flat out that I'd become bored with her and wanted a divorce. She didn't believe me at first. She couldn't imagine that I, who've doted on her for over a decade, simply no longer cared for her. When I insisted that I did not, she became vindictive, promising that our divorce would be scandalous and ruin my political career. I reminded her that we live in the 21st century. Divorce is well tolerated by the vast majority of the electorate. Hell, half the voters are divorced themselves. I assured her that my campaign would be unaffected by our split, but that, due to our prenuptial agreement, she'd receive not one cent. I suggested that her lover might support her, but failing that, she might return to the—shall I call it a profession? A trade? Either will do, I suppose, for the way she supported herself when I met her, except that now, being substantially older, she'd be far less marketable. And, given her circumstances, she'd never get the children.

"She did a good deal of yelling and crying, but in the end, I told her to pack up and go, as I couldn't endure the sight of her anymore. That was the last thing I said to her. She ran out of the house sobbing. I heard her car speed off." Paul looked into his drink. "I didn't follow, just let her go. How could I have known where she headed?"

Paul's gaze became momentarily vacant, then he took a drink and looked at Nora quizzically. "I behaved monstrously to you that day. Is that why you think I'm capable of murder?"

Nora doubted everything he'd said. "Tell me how you did it."

"Really? I know I was out of line, but murder?"

Someone tried the doorknob, knocked.

Nora considered asking the knocker for help, but stopped herself, picturing the chaos that would ensue. "I'll be right out," she called.

Nora drew herself up and met Paul's eyes. "Tell me," she repeated.

With her back straight, her chin raised so she could look into his eyes, she stepped closer to him. She didn't falter. She didn't back down, didn't even blink, not even when she stood close enough to inhale his scotch-drenched breath. She was actually confronting him, refusing to be bullied. And, somehow, she wasn't afraid.

"Nora, I'd never hurt Barbara. I was finished with her, but why would I physically harm her?"

"Oh please. Paul, you physically harmed her all the time. I saw the black eye, the huge bruise on her arm."

Paul's eyebrows furrowed. "What are you talking about?"

"Last week. Have you forgotten beating her up?"

"Beating her up?" His face twisted. "That's absurd. I have no idea—Oh, wait. I know about the bruise, but you've got it all wrong. I found Barbara with a knife, about to cut herself. I tried to take it, and she fought me. I grabbed her arm and twisted until she dropped the knife—That could have caused the bruise."

Nora shook her head, amazed at the ease of Paul's lies and the quickness with which he spewed them. Barbara hadn't been about to kill herself. She'd been about to leave and start a new life. She'd been excited for her future.

"And the black eye?"

"I'd assume that happened during our struggle as well. I might have elbowed her. I don't know. But Nora, I am not a violent man, let alone an abuser. I never laid a hand on Barbara."

Nora studied his face but found no signs of lying. Paul was smooth, practiced. She remembered how he'd forced himself on her, the gleam in his eyes. *He's not who he seems to be.*

Paul finished his drink and set the glass on the vanity. "Believe what you will, but even the police say she died by her own hand. And think about it. If I'd wanted to kill Barbara, would I have done it so clumsily? Don't you think I would've have made sure she was never found?"

"Sure, if you'd planned it. But you were angry, not thinking clearly. Acting on impulse."

"I wasn't angry, Nora." His voice was calm, almost gentle. "I was indifferent and bored. Finished. That's why she did what she did." He glanced at the door behind him. "Look, I have to get back. People must be looking for me."

Nora waited, but he didn't leave.

Instead, he watched her, as if deciding whether to say more. Then his lips curled into a smile, or maybe a snarl. "Fine. Let's put this to rest. For the sake of argument, let's say I killed her. How did I do it?"

Nora stepped back, knocked the stool. "Maybe you drugged her like you tried to drug me. And put her into the car."

"I see." He met her gaze. "So, I laced her drinks with crushed sleeping pills, rendering her all but unconscious." He put a finger to his lips as if thinking. "Then I put her into the car and drove to the pier where I then rearranged her in the driver's seat, belted her in, put the car into drive and her foot on the gas, somehow accelerated, and slammed the door just as it went flying into the water." He shook his head, seemingly at how preposterous the scenario was. "Do you honestly think that would have been possible? That I could have pulled it off leaving no witnesses, no evidence? That I would have taken that risk, especially now when I have so much to lose?"

Nora's breath caught in her throat. The description sounded far-fetched, but Paul's details were disturbingly exact. She thought of Barbara. Of how much Paul had to lose. "Yes. I do."

His broad grin was wrong, inappropriate. "But why kill her? I have a lot to lose, and a divorce would have cost me nothing."

Nora chewed her lip.

"I've got to get back. Come out and get a refill." He winked at her empty glass, unlocked the door and left.

SATURDAY, OCTOBER 31, 1993, 8:30 P.M.

Nora arrived at Annie's party wearing last year's French maid costume. She had clammy palms and no photographs, and half expected Annie to kick her out, demanding that she hand them over or leave. But when Nora joined the others in the rec room, Annie didn't even look up. She was busy whispering with a girl in a Daisy May costume whom Nora didn't know.

In fact, of the ten girls Annie had invited, Nora recognized only four: Meg, Lynne, Jen, and Jasmine who sat at their lunch table. The others clearly knew each other, though. A few wore coordinated cat costumes. Two huddled in the corner, a vampire restyling a cheerleader's hair. Nora tried to mix in, laughing when everyone else did, pretending to know what or whom they were talking about, overhearing chunks of conversations that she assumed concerned boys.

She shouldn't have come. Annie had moved on, made new friends. She was part of the cool, fast clique, while Nora didn't fit in—never had, never would. Nora watched Annie and pitifully aped her gestures, facial expressions, and posture. Nora longed to be home in her own room where she could be by her dorky, uncool, solitary self.

The Exorcist was playing on the big console television, but the sound was either off or overpowered by an Aretha Franklin oldie blasting from the stereo. A few girls were dancing. Nora didn't join in, didn't feel comfortable. The ping pong table was covered with a plastic tablecloth and food—pizza, chips, dips, and sodas. Meg told her that there was a handle of vodka behind the wall to the laundry room. Nora pretended to know what a handle was and tagged along with Meg, smiling as if she knew what she was doing while Meg poured.

Nora drank, nibbled, sat in various poses, modeling her behavior after Annie's, all the time waiting for Annie to ask for the pictures. Finding the party a big fat bore. After about an hour, Nora began thinking up excuses to leave. A toothache? Or maybe cramps. Something that Annie would believe and not blame her for. She sipped her vodka and Diet Sprite, watched girls in stupid costumes, and listened to irritating, loud music.

"Well? You got them?" Annie came up behind her. Her nose nuzzled Nora's cheek.

Nora's heart beat louder than the music. She wanted to cry, to beg for more time. "I tried. Really hard. I looked in his room, but—"

"So, no. You don't have them."

"Annie, I'll get them. I will. But I need more time. I can only look when he's not around." Nora was about to say that she wasn't feeling well and had to go home, but Annie slid an arm around her shoulder and spoke softly.

"See, the thing is, Nora, that that's not okay. We agreed you'd bring them tonight."

Except that, no, Nora hadn't agreed; Annie had insisted. She knew better than to argue though. "I'm sorry. Look, I'll get them as soon as I can. I promise." Her heart ricocheted against her ribs. She waited for Annie to throw her out, to completely reject and shun her.

Instead, Annie smiled charmingly. "Oh yes, Nora. You will. I know you will." Annie slid her arm off Nora's shoulders and started to walk away, but stopped, leaned over and whispered,

"By the way, Nora. Remember when you told me who you liked?"

Of course she remembered. Nora hadn't wanted to tell anyone, but days ago, trying to win back Annie's favor, Nora had finally, reluctantly revealed his name. As soon as she'd said it, while the last consonants still resonated on her tongue, she'd regretted it. Her face had heated up with embarrassment and dread. Would Annie tease her for liking a boy who was only a year older, not a hot shot in high school? Or—oh God—would she get back at Nora by telling him? Annie might, just for spite.

"Why?" Nora's stomach flipped.

"You'll see." Annie winked and tweaked Nora's chin. "The party's not even started yet." And she flitted off, joining some girls getting food.

Nora's stomach wouldn't settle. She still wanted to leave, but Annie had urged her to stay, and she didn't want to risk displeasing Annie, further straining their friendship. So, she hung around, pretending to be having fun, drinking vodka to calm her nerves.

At about ten, Nora found out why Annie had wanted her to stay. The boys paraded in through the sliding doors on the deck. She recognized most of them from school. A few were older, though. A couple were even in high school. Why were high school boys there? Maybe to see Annie's sisters? Except, no. Her sisters weren't around. And, oh God, Craig was there. Despite their age difference, he and Annie were friends. Nora remembered Craig beating up on Tommy, then stopping to talk with Annie through the school bus window. He sauntered in, a bigshot in his leather jacket, exhaling smoke from his cigarette. Nora tensed, wanted to hide. She'd had no idea older kids would be there, let alone Craig. Then again, Craig wasn't always a bully. He'd actually been nice to her on the camp bus. She watched him greet Annie with a big, white-toothed grin, and was so focused on him that she almost didn't notice the clean-cut, preppy seventh grader who came in behind him. Bobby Baxter.

Nora froze, her gut somersaulting. Bobby Baxter was there? That must have been why Annie had needed to know who she liked, so she could invite him. Maybe Annie wasn't as mad as she seemed. But now what? How could Nora get his attention? How should she act? Should she talk to him? Wait and see if he talked to her first? Except—oh God—what if she was wrong? What if Annie hadn't invited him because of her, and Bobby had come there to hang out with one of the other girls? Maybe he liked someone else or someone else liked him—someone much cooler than Nora.

Nora scanned the room for Annie. Annie would tell her what to do, how to be. But Annie was in a clump of kids, laughing at some guy telling a story. Craig was in the clump, too. So was Bobby. He was also laughing.

Nora backed against the wall. Maybe Bobby hadn't seen her, didn't even know she was there. She edged her way to the laundry room and poured more vodka, drank it down, felt it sear its way through her insides. A little woozy, she sidled to the bathroom where she stayed, examining her stupid, costumed self in the mirror, fiddling with her hair, deciding that Bobby Baxter would never like a girl as uncool as she was. *Misfit. Oddball. Freak.* She sat on the floor, hiding, and might never have come out if someone hadn't banged on the door.

When she emerged, red-faced and certain that everyone was watching to see who'd tied up the bathroom so long, the first person she saw was Bobby Baxter. He was looking right at her, smiling. Was she supposed to smile back? Wave? Nod? Oh God.

She was such a loser. She wanted to disappear, to just dissolve into nothing.

"Hey," he said.

Nora almost looked behind her, to make sure he wasn't talking to someone else. But she stopped herself and managed to utter, "Hey."

He stepped closer. Bobby was tall. She had to crane her neck to see his face.

"So, what are you, a waitress?"

Her face burned. "French maid."

He laughed. Not a mean laugh. The kind of laugh that acknowledged how silly costumes were. "I almost didn't come, but Annie said you'd be here. So I figured it'd be okay."

What? Music pounded, so it was difficult to hear him. Had Bobby Baxter just said he'd come because she'd be there? Had he actually said that? "Well, anyway. Here we both are." Ugh. What a stupid stupid stupid thing to say. Plus, because of the music, she'd shouted it.

Idiot. Weirdo. Creep.

Bobby stuck a hand in his pocket and shuffled a little. When he slouched to talk into her ear, she inhaled his cologne. "Thing is, I heard Annie throws some crazy parties. I didn't think you'd come if it was going to be that kind of thing."

What kind of thing? Nora shrugged and smiled but had no clue what to say. "You smell good." Oh God. She was so lame—how mortifying.

"Old Spice." He half-smiled, cowboy-like and oh so cute. "Glad you like it."

She stood still as a rock. She couldn't think. Had nothing, no inkling of how to proceed.

But Bobby didn't seem to notice. "Honestly? I don't know what to expect tonight." He shifted from foot to foot, his voice low and husky. "But if it gets weird, just stick with me, okay?"

Stick with him? With Bobby? She managed a nod. "Sure."

Bobby grinned, put his arm around her and led her toward the laundry room. Nora couldn't absorb what was happening. Bobby Baxter, who sat across from her in math, woodshop, and art, but never actually talked to her. Bobby Baxter, her crush with the big hazel eyes, long lashes, and shaggy brown hair, who she'd never imagined even noticing her—that very same Bobby Baxter was walking with his arm around her to get a drink. Of vodka. After asking her to stick with him. She beamed. She glowed. She floated as if in a dream.

But then, Annie shouted, "Game time!"

Bobby rolled his eyes. "Here goes." He squeezed Nora's shoulder before leaving her to join the circle. Boys sat on one hemisphere, girls on the other.

Nora tried to fade into a corner, but Jasmine saw her and patted the carpet next to her, making room for Nora to sit. Nora sat. She didn't look at Bobby Baxter, but felt his presence. He was—oh my God—so cute and cool. His touch still warmed her shoulder. The scent of his Old Spice lingered on her costume. She felt dazed. Someone handed her a new drink. She gulped it, and asked Jasmine if she knew what the game was.

Jasmine figured spin the bottle, for starters.

A kissing game. Oh God. Nora's stomach twisted, her hands got sweaty. Was that what Bobby had meant when he'd said Annie's parties got crazy? Well, no way she would play. She remembered the mall and the boy with the wet, wormy lips.

"Seven minutes in heaven!" Annie called.

Everyone murmured or laughed. Nora had no idea what this game was but guessed that couples would spend seven minutes kissing. Seven whole minutes? Annie passed out paper and pencils and told everyone to write their name down. Nora thought she'd throw up. She eyed the bathroom again and sent Annie telepathic messages, begging for her help. But Annie didn't even look at her as she collected the names in a bowl.

"Hurry up, everyone. Write your names down."

As Annie approached, Nora had a brilliant idea. Instead of her own name, she scribbled "Annie" and put it into the bowl. No one would notice if Annie got picked twice. They were all tipsy. And, for sure, no one would notice if Nora didn't get picked.

"We'll alternate picks. Boy, girl," Annie instructed.

And the game began. A guy with big shoulders and glasses named Mark picked Jen's name and the two disappeared behind the sofa. Meg picked Joel and they went under the staircase. Adam picked Jasmine, led her into the storage room. Then Annie drew her own name which meant it was her turn to choose. She scanned the circle, eyeing the boys, then locked eyes with Nora. Why was she staring that way, holding Nora's gaze so long and silently with her jaw set and chin high? The room hushed while everyone waited for her choice.

Finally, Annie smiled smugly and said, "Bobby Baxter."

Her eyes remained linked with Nora's. Nora stopped breathing. Annie had to be joking, must be playing a trick on her. But no. Bobby Baxter stood, flustered and bashful, and Nora understood that this was no joke. Annie flat out knew that Nora liked him. Why, of all the boys at the party, had she chosen him?

Nora already knew the answer. Annie had chosen Bobby precisely because Nora liked him. She'd chosen him out of spite. Annie was punishing Nora for not bringing the photos. She didn't give a rat's ass about Bobby, couldn't care less about kissing him. She'd picked him merely to display her power, to let Nora preview the hell Annie could tailor just for her.

Nora trembled as she watched Annie lead Bobby to the patio where they would spend their seven minutes, or who knew how long, pressing their lips together. So much for his offer to stick together. Nora would have to sit there alone, staring at the silent television, listening to the thumping music, all the while imagining what they were doing. Would anyone notice if she walked out? Why had she even come to this damned party?

"I pick Nora."

She looked up. Craig was grinning at her, holding a piece of paper. He gestured with his thumb. "Let's go."

What? How could he pick her? She'd written "Annie" on the paper. It had to be a mistake. She should refuse. Demand that he show her the paper.

"Yo." Craig reached for her with his big, thick hand, the same big, thick hand that had more than a few times crashed into her brother's face. Somehow, she was on her feet, watching herself as if from outside her body, somewhere on the ceiling. She was aware of Craig's fingers, huge around hers. His body beside her. Tall, solid. Hard. His smell heavy with cologne and harsh with tobacco.

How had Craig picked her? What was she supposed to do? Run, she told herself. She glanced at the sliding doors to the patio where Bobby Baxter had gone with Annie. To kiss her. "If things get weird, stick with me," he'd said. But things had gotten weird and he was gone. Annie had taken him away, just because she could.

Craig led her to the laundry room. Nora felt limp, didn't resist. He backed her against the wall, his pelvis pressed against her. Oh

God. Nora's mouth went dry. Her throat clamped shut. What now? Was he going to kiss her? He was in high school. Boys that age did more than just kiss. She stared at the tile floor, keeping her lips out of his reach.

"Annie told me you're the shit bag's sister. Who'd of guessed?"

Annie had told him? Of course she had. Annie and Craig were friends. Buddies. That was why Craig had chosen her, because Annie must have told him to.

"Pick Nora," Annie would have said. "You'll have a blast. She's the sister of your favorite creep."

Pairing Nora with Tommy's tormentor was another part of Annie's show of power—a taste of how miserable she could make Nora's life.

Nora was caught between Craig and the wall, couldn't breathe.

Craig pecked at her neck with quick sharp nips that made her shiver and almost gag. He stopped and leaned back, grinning.

"Hey. That piece of crap ever tell you how he keeps getting locked in his locker? Or how his stinking sneakers disappear from gym class?" He laughed. A hoarse, barking sound.

Push him away and leave, Nora told herself. Just go. Now. But she didn't move except to shudder.

"Freshman year, I made him buy my lunches for like, a whole semester. God, what a fucking loser." He grinned, shook his head. "Oh, yeah. Your brother and me? We go way back. We got what they call history." Craig examined her closely, breathing on her face. With his thumb, he stroked her nose, chin, lips, cheeks.

Her stomach turned inside out. She pushed his hand away. "Stop."

He didn't. "You, on the other hand, you're not a piece of crap like your brother. No. You're a piece of something else altogether. And Annie said you like a good time."

Craig came at her fast, his mouth hard against hers. His lips were dry, and his tongue darted in and out of her mouth, lizardlike. He stopped, laughing out loud. At what? Her? Her brother? Did Craig think she was going to let him do stuff to her? Oh God. Where was Bobby Baxter? Was his tongue in Annie's mouth? What else would Annie do with him?

Craig started again, his hands gripping Nora's backside. His teeth nibbled Nora's lips gently. Then less gently.

When he punctured her skin, Nora yelped. Tasting blood, she shoved him hard. Was he trying to bite her lip off? Was that even more fun than trapping her brother in his locker? Craig was a pig. She fled through the family room, past shadowy, heavy-breathing couples, to the garage door. Behind her, Craig was laughing, but she didn't look to see if he was following her with his beefy fists, razor lips, and sharp, white teeth. At the driveway, she didn't stop or slow. She raced down the street, around the corner and up the block. Tears streamed, her chest burned, and still, she ran. Nora ran as if she had hope. As if there were somewhere safe to go.

Nora went downstairs, past the waiters and mourners, and out Paul's front door. She walked all the way home found Dave in his study, sipping whiskey in his easy chair. He didn't move when she came in.

"He killed her. I'm sure of it." She planted herself on the chair's leather arm.

"Yep." He still didn't move.

"We have to do something."

"Like?"

"Like talk to the police."

"I've done that, remember?" His jaw was tight.

"Right."

"And I gave the police all my files. Everything."

"So, he's going to get away with it?"

Dave took a long drink. "Not if I can help it." His tone was grim.

"What's that supposed to mean?"

He didn't answer.

"Dave?" She nudged his arm. "Tell me what you're thinking."

"Nothing. I'm not thinking anything." His eyelids twitched, giving him away.

Nora waited but Dave said nothing else. She'd intended to tell him about Paul and his smug description of the murder, but Dave was withdrawn. Was he hiding something? She slid into his lap and put her head on his chest, needing to hear his heartbeat, feel his breath, reconnect. After a while, Dave wanted another drink, so she had to let him up. Other than that, neither of them moved until the front door opened and, with shouts and hollers, their daughters thundered into the house, home from the neighbor's house.

SUNDAY, AUGUST 19, 2018, 6:15 P.M.

Nora was drained. Her face hurt from faking smiles, her throat ached from forcing a lilt into her voice. She wasn't in the mood to cook, deal with sibling bickering, or listen to details of their day. But she had to. Dave hadn't come out of his study and was probably still drinking, brooding about Paul. Blaming himself for Barbara's death. So, Nora cooked, waiting for him to appear and help with the girls. When they asked for him, she said he was working and would join them as soon as he finished.

While the chicken broiled, she decided to go get him. She stood outside the closed study door, listening, hearing nothing. Why was she hesitating to knock? He was her husband. She should be able to talk to him any time. How could Dave be so self-indulgent, withdrawing from the kids and family responsibilities just because he felt bad? What about how she felt? She'd lost one of her best friends, but she still had to cook, plan play dates, converse, wash camp clothes, give baths.

What was really going on with Dave? He'd made a spectacle at the funeral, storming out while Paul spoke. He was acting as if he were the only one affected by Barbara's death, the only one who thought Paul had killed her, the only one who wanted to see the bastard in jail. Why did he feel entitled to mope and sulk all day? What was he doing in there? Had he fallen asleep? Or passed out from drinking? Was he catatonic, staring at the wall? Or worse...

She didn't knock. A single stained-glass lamp was the only light on in the study. With his shirtsleeves rolled up, Dave sat in the same place she'd left him. His shoes were off, feet propped on the ottoman. When she came in, he looked up from his drink, red-eyed and somber-faced.

"Nora?" He seemed confused, as if he'd forgotten where he was, or was startled by not just her entrance, but by her existence.

"Dinner's almost ready."

He sat up, set his feet on the floor and his glass on the end table. "Okay." His hair was disheveled, and he blinked repeatedly. "What time is it?" He lifted his wristwatch close to his face and stared at it as if he couldn't read what it said.

"Almost six."

"Seriously?" He stretched his neck. When he looked at her, he seemed altered. His gaze seemed faraway, walled off.

She crossed her arms. "Seriously, Dave. You need to spend time with the girls. They need to know everything's okay."

"Right. Sorry. I didn't mean to stay in here so long. Must have dozed off for a while." His words bled together. How much had he had to drink?

"You can be with them now. At dinner."

"Of course. I'll be right there." He didn't move. "Look. I know I shouldn't be sec—" He stopped, stuck on his word, paused and tried it again. "Secluding myself in here. But, truthfully," he enunciated each syllable, careful to say 'truthfully' without a slip, "I'm not fit company. I honestly don't trust myself right now. Not with the kids, not even with you."

"What are you talking about?" A chill ran up Nora's back. Even a bit hammered, Dave's words alarmed her.

His voice was low and flat. "I let her down." He closed his mouth, his jaw rippled. He looked at the wall. "She counted on me."

"Dave, it's not your fault. Paul's the one who killed her."

"I know." His eyes were empty, defeated.

"Come have dinner, spend time with your daughters, and let's all go to bed early, okay?"

Dave stared at his glass. "I'll be right there."

Nora went back to the kitchen. Ellie was folding napkins and Sophie was setting out silverware. Nora took the chicken out of the oven, put the mashed potatoes, green beans, and salad on the table, and reminded Ellie to stop chewing her fingernail. Dave joined them, eyes red and swollen, and feigned cheerfulness as he dished out portions. The family sat quiet, the girls pouty and subdued, Dave withdrawn and morose. Nora searched for peppy conversation. But about what? Sophie's new camp friends? Ellie's lack of them? Dave's policeman friend, Lou? Barbara's funeral? Or Paul Ellis's description of a murder?

Nora swallowed chicken and counted. One. Two. Three. She blanked her mind and eyed the trashcan. "I spy, with my little eye. Something yucky."

And miraculously, as if they were a normal family at a regular dinner, the game was on.

MONDAY, AUGUST 20, 2018

When she heard the front door close, Nora tried to convince herself that the sound was part of her dream. That she should roll over and drift back to sleep. Yet, even half asleep, she had to admit that, no, it hadn't been a dream.

She opened her eyes and found Dave's side of the bed unrumpled, unslept in. He hadn't come to bed again. Had probably spent the whole night sulking and drinking. How long was his self-blame, self-pity party going to go on?

The clock said twenty to six. Had she really heard the front door? Normally, Dave didn't leave for work until eight, even eight-thirty. Nora went to the window just as his car backed out of the driveway in the rain, windshield wipers whapping back and forth. She grabbed her phone off the nightstand to call him, find out what he was doing. She punched in his number.

And heard his phone ring downstairs.

A chill rippled through her as she moved into the hall. She gripped the bannister, gazed down the staircase. Saw Dave's briefcase in the foyer, his phone on the table beside the front door. Dave hadn't gone to work.

"Mommy?" Sophie stood in her doorway, curls messed, pajamas askew, head tilted. "Where did Daddy go?"

Nora had no answer. "Not sure," she tried to sound less frantic than she felt. "I guess he had an early appointment." Was that answer believable? Would it satisfy Sophie? Sophie frowned, studying Nora. Sensing the lie?

Ellie broke the tension, bursting from the bedroom. "Sophie, it's raining. No swimming today."

Sophie considered this news.

Ellie pulled on Nora's arm, asking if she could have French toast.

They all headed for the kitchen. Nora focused on making breakfast, helping small hands crack eggs into a ceramic bowl and whisk them with milk, soak the bread. She praised her children at every step and focused on the sizzling hisses of butter melting in a cast iron pan, the warm smell of cinnamon. The intent faces of her daughters as they mastered their tasks, cooked their own meal. She answered all the questions about why there were yolks and whites, about whether eggs were really baby chickens. Nora struggled to remain in the moment, but her mind kept drifting toward Dave, who—damn it—must have been up all night, drinking and lathering himself into a fury.

While the girls ate, Nora made their lunches. She was taking out slices of white bread when she realized where Dave had gone. The chill of her bones told her. The adrenaline surge in her veins told her. She knew the where, and only guessed at the why because what he intended to do there was too terrifying to consider. Her hands were unsteady as she spread the peanut butter, as she packed peaches and yogurts into lunch boxes. Her heart thundered as she packed camp bags. But when she kissed the girls and watched them splash through the rain to the camp bus, she smiled and waved as if everything was normal and their father was perfectly fine.

As soon as the bus drove off, she tugged on jeans and a T-shirt and hopped into her car. She drove, sloshing through wet streets, never doubting her destination.

Sure enough, Dave's BMW was in front of Paul's house. Not in the driveway. In the street. Parked helter-skelter, at least a yard from the curb. Had he been too angry to pull over to the curb? Nora pictured him running through the rain to the door, confronting Paul, pushing a finger into the candidate's chest, accusing him of killing Barbara.

She didn't want to picture Paul's reaction.

She parked her car in front of Dave's, jumped out, and hurried up the long, winding path through banks of firs and Chinese maples. She smeared rain off her face, heard fat drops splattering the greenery, the slate walkway. Where was Dave now? Was he okay? Heart clanging, Nora tried not to slip on slick wet slate. Reminded herself to breathe. Told herself that when Paul answered the door, she'd simply say that she'd seen Dave's car out front and needed to talk with him. She wouldn't need to explain. Paul would probably be relieved—

A sharp crack pierced the air. Nora froze, spun around. A squirrel darted up a nearby tree trunk. It must have snapped a twig. No big deal.

Except that the lawn, the foliage, every twig on the trees was soaked. And wet sticks wouldn't crack.

Nora hurried to the house, ran up the steps to the front door. And stopped. The door hung open. Paul would never have left his door open. No, it was open because of Dave. Oh God. What was he doing in there? What had he already done? She listened, but heard no heated voices, no struggle, just the soft, steady splat of raindrops.

Cautiously, Nora stepped into the foyer. She stood there, dripping onto the marble floor, deciding what to do. Should she call out to Paul? To Dave? No, better to stay quiet and take a look around. She started toward the living room but stopped, startled by another sharp, sudden crack.

This time, she knew it wasn't a twig.

SATURDAY, OCTOBER 31, 1993

Her lip was swelling. She should probably put ice on it, but why bother. Who cared if her lip ballooned like a sausage or if it got infected with Craig's germs and killed her? She flopped onto her bed. At this very minute, Annie was wrapped in Bobby Baxter's arms, engulfed in a cloud of Old Spice, kissing his sweet, soft lips. Nora covered her face and groaned.

How could Annie betray her so deeply? Taking Bobby Baxter just to punish Nora. And, as if that weren't punishment enough, she'd turned Craig the beast loose on her? Nora still felt Craig's teeth pecking at her. She shivered and curled onto her side, hugging her knees to her chest. Why was Annie being so evil? Was it just because of Tommy's stupid photographs?

Maybe it was that simple. Maybe Annie was so pissed and afraid that her parents might see the pictures that she didn't know what to do except make Nora's life hell. If that were the case, and if Nora gave her the photos, then Annie would relax and be her best friend again, and everything would go back to the way it was.

Right. And maybe Tommy would be class president.

Still, it was a possibility. Nora's only hope of getting Annie to ease up was to produce the pictures and negatives—and soon.

Nora knew what she had to do, just not how to do it. Her tongue played with the cut on her lip until the sting became too intense to bear. Then she sat up, frustrated, figuring out what to do. She'd heard Tommy moving around in his room, so she couldn't look there.

Then again, if he was in his room, then he wasn't upstairs in his dark room, which meant she could look there. Probably, he wouldn't have left them anywhere so obvious, but it was worth a try. Searching was better than lying in bed picturing her best friend making out with Bobby Baxter, kissing him the way she'd taught Nora, with her lips parted just a little, her head turned ever so slightly so her nose wouldn't bump his, letting him press his hands against her backside. Shit. Shit. Shit. Nora's heart crackled and burned. Their seven minutes must be up by now. After making out with Annie, Bobby Baxter must be back in the party room. Did he even notice that Nora was gone? Nora sniffed, refusing to cry anymore. But tears welled anyway, blurring her vision. The party games and Bobby Baxter would go on without her.

This was all Tommy's fault. God, she hated him. Why why why did she have such a shithead for a brother? *Life isn't fair. Make the most of what you've got. When you get lemons, make lemonade.* Nora wanted to rip Marla's face off, pull out her hair. What kind of mother was she? How could she dismiss Nora's whole life with her asinine clichés? Why couldn't Nora have a normal family?

Nora raged. Her chest boiled. She was on her own, without allies, and she would do what she had to in order to survive, which meant she'd find the pictures that night, whatever it took. She tiptoed down the hall to Tommy's room, listened. Cracked open the door, his mustiness smacking her in the nose. His desk lamp was on, spotlighting a newly-mounted moth, it wings spread akimbo on foam board. Tommy was sprawled on his bed, sleeping on top of his blankets, still in his clothes. His face was relaxed, without a care. She wanted to clobber him. Instead, she snapped her fingers, testing to see if the sound would wake him up. When it didn't, she raced up the steps, assured that the sounds of her footsteps in the attic wouldn't wake him up either.

MONDAY, AUGUST 20, 2018, 8:15 A.M.

The bang had come either from above or from the rear of the house. Or someplace to her right? The domed ceiling played tricks, rolling sounds around, confusing Nora's sense of direction. But somewhere close by, someone had fired a gun. She was sure of it. Not that Nora was familiar with the sound of gunfire. She'd heard it only on television. But the sound was unmistakable, couldn't have been anything else. Her body reacted, heart rate speeding, adrenaline pumping, brain struggling to comprehend. Someone was shooting at someone.

"Dave?" His name burst from her like a roar, not just once, but again and again as she ran from room to room, searching for him, passing an upended wingback chair, a table lying on its side. A brass sculpture knocked off its base.

Nora grabbed a thin-necked porcelain vase off a table and carried it like a club. It was better than nothing. She could throw it. Or bash Paul's head again, hit the same spot as last time, reopening the wound. Was he really shooting at Dave? Maybe she could sneak up behind Paul, slam him with the vase while Dave—while Dave what? Stood there, watching? Lay on the floor, shot and bleeding? Oh God. What if Dave was already dead?

No. He wasn't. She would find him, and he'd be fine and happy to see her. He'd kiss her and lead her out the door and together, they'd go home, away from this nightmare. She chewed her bottom lip, tasted blood. Crossed the hall and, vase in hand, passed through the swinging doors to the kitchen. Saw shards of broken dishes scattered on the floor. God, what had happened there? She stepped over crumbled stoneware to a knife block on the marble counters and exchanged her floral vase for a heavy, solid, carving knife. And then, clutching it, ready to swing, Nora crept back into the hallway and proceeded to the rear of the house.

No one was in the family room with the bar, pool table, cushiony modular sofa and theater-sized television screen. Nora stood still, uncertain where to go next. Upstairs? The sound might have come from there. She started for the steps, but stopped when, faintly, she heard a laugh.

From a man.

But where was it coming from? She hurried to the sliding glass doors and looked out at the rainy deck, the layered gardens, the pool. Saw no one.

Another laugh, louder this time—mocking and hostile. The kind of laughter that Tommy used to inspire. Don't get distracted. This laughter had nothing to do with Tommy.

Somewhere, a man spouted words too faint, too muffled to understand. The voice seemed to come from Nora's right, but couldn't have. To her right was the outer wall of the house. Were they outside? She yanked open the sliding doors and stepped out onto the rain-soaked deck. Saw a grill, an outdoor bar, potted plants, but no Dave. No Paul. No one.

Back inside, she eyed the interior wall. The voice had definitely come from its direction. She stepped over to it, touched it, put her head against it, and listened. Waited. Her fingers ached from clutching the knife. Her body was rigid, flooded with adrenaline. Dave was here and alive. She knew it. She sensed him. Her ears ached from listening. Her skin prickled. Wait, what just touched her neck? She swung her arms, whirling around as she slapped at an unseen attacker. What was that shadow? Was something moving behind the sofa? Nora spun in circles, mouth dry, heart galloping.

Call the police. Tell them you heard gunshots.

Oh. That idea actually made sense. The police would certainly be more help to Dave than she would, even with her knife. But, damn, her phone was in her bag, and in her frantic rush, she'd left the bag in her car. She should go back for it. And she no doubt would have if a man hadn't begun talking again.

His voice was definitely coming through the wall. Was it Paul? Yes. Definitely Paul. And however improbably, his voice was coming from inside the wall. She strained to make out what he was saying but couldn't. Listened to hear Dave, but didn't. She searched for an entrance to a hidden room, tracing the walls inch by inch, top to bottom, from the corner near the deck doors to the bookshelves beyond the fireplace. Even on her second try, she almost missed the small button on the side of the mantle. Almost overlooked the faint, unsealed seams stretching floor to ceiling behind the easy chair.

But she didn't. Her fingers found thread-like breaks in the wall paneling, and when she looked closely, she saw one segment that was almost invisibly out of alignment with the others. A door? She pressed her ear to the miniscule gap, straining to hear voices.

"You're not..." Paul said something else she couldn't make out. Something about a "man"? He was speaking fast, maybe nervous. Maybe out of breath.

"No?"

Nora's eyes filled at the sound of Dave's voice. Dave was alive, talking. So he hadn't been shot. At least, not fatally.

"But I bet you've never even fired a gun..."

Nora almost didn't recognize Dave's laugh. It sounded harsh like a bark. "You're right."

Clutching the knife, Nora edged closer to the mantelpiece and examined the button. Maybe it would open the door.

Paul was talking again. "Why not be a gentleman and call the police? Go ahead. Have me arrested."

Dave didn't answer.

Paul's voice got louder, more urgent. "Look, we both know you're not going to kill me. We're civilized men, not the sort to shoot one another. When I fired before, my intent was merely to scare you off. Obviously, I didn't intend to hit you. If I had, you'd be dead."

Oh God. Had Dave been hit? Nora should run for her phone. Call for an ambulance. She looked into the hall that led to the front door.

Paul kept talking. "Why don't we resolve this situation? Tell me, Dave. What exactly has got your panties into such a knot? Surely not my misguided attentions to your wife? I'll admit that I was out of line, and I've apologized to Nora. But really, what I did was nothing compared to what was going on between you and Barbara."

"What the fuck are you talking about?"

"Oh. So, this isn't about Nora? What then? Barbara?" A pause. "What about her? Let me guess. You doubt that she killed herself. In fact, you're convinced that I killed her. Your wife believes that, too, by the way. Well, let me point out that neither of you has an ounce of proof. The idea is preposterous—"

A gunshot interrupted him.

Instantly, Nora pushed the button. The wall beside the fireplace slid away, revealed a tiny bunker-like room with metallic walls. At first glance she took in bunkbeds, mini-fridge, desk, computer. No windows. No door. Nora had heard of rooms like this. Secret spaces for rich people to escape burglars or hitmen—survival rooms? Panic rooms? Something.

Paul huddled in the middle of the floor, his hand-tailored shirt bloodied, his chiseled features battered. Dave faced away from her. He held a gun.

"Dave?"

At her voice, Dave turned, and Paul jumped, grabbing for the gun.

Nora leapt at Paul, tackled him and hung on, still holding the knife, kicking and punching to knock him down. But even with Nora clinging to his waist, Paul kept launching himself at Dave.

The bang was explosive. It rattled Nora's bones, hammered her skull, bounced off the steel walls of the tiny room so that even the air reverberated.

Paul staggered backward and collapsed onto the area rug, his body splayed over Nora.

Nora pushed Paul off her legs and stumbled to her feet. A crimson stain was spreading on his shirt. She looked at Dave, at the gun he still held, at Paul who wasn't moving. Still clutching the knife, she hugged herself and rocked back and forth, staring at the blood.

I told you. I told you. I told you not to look for trouble.

Dave came and took the knife, prying her fingers from the handle, checking that the blood on her face, clothes, and arms wasn't hers.

His lip was swollen and split. His cheek was red, his knuckles raw. His arms enclosed her. Dave clung to her, silently buried his face in her hair. Again, she heard the gunshot crack, felt the shudder of air and the thud of Paul hitting the rug. Oh God. Again and again, the sequence repeated. *Crack, shudder, thud. Crack, shudder, thud.* The walls swayed. Nora leaned against Dave, who leaned against her. *Crack, shudder, thud.*

Paul lay still and silent, and Dave began talking, his mouth making sounds Nora couldn't hear. The walls sped up their whirling, the floor melted away, and for a moment, just an eye blink, Nora couldn't hang on and felt herself drop away. Crack. Shudder. Thud.

Y*ou made your bed, now lie in it. Haste makes waste.* Her mother was chattering, spurting clichés. *No use crying over spilt milk. What goes around comes around. What's done is done. If you get a lemon*—

"Enough!" Nora's ears were ringing. She covered them, but the shrill clanging didn't stop, sounded like it came from inside her head. But that wasn't possible. She lay still, gradually aware of other senses. The hard surface beneath her. And smells—Old Spice? And something else, metallic and coppery. Something like blood. She opened her eyes, remembering. Dave stood over her, his eyes hollow, his face gray. When she looked at him, he took a step back, arms limp at his sides, gun dangling from his hand.

What had happened to her? Had she passed out? She stared at the gun, trying to remember, and even as the ringing persisted in her ears, she made herself sit up. Dave stood by uselessly, not moving to help.

"Dave?" She grabbed his hand, tugging on it as she pulled herself to her feet. "Talk to me. Say something."

"You told me I'd already said enough."

She had? She thought back, recalled hearing her mother nagging. Yelling at her to stop. "No, I didn't mean you." She moved closer.

Dave stared at Paul, said nothing.

"You okay?"

For a long moment, Dave remained silent. Finally, he sank onto the bottom bunk, set the gun beside him and hung his head.

He didn't sob, didn't make a sound. Silent tears streamed down his cheeks.

Finally, he said, "I fucking killed him."

Nora looked down at the body. Paul's nose was twisted and bloodied, probably broken. The flesh around his eyes was swollen almost shut, his stitched-up wound had reopened. She closed her eyes, counted to clear her mind.

"You had no choice," she said.

Dave faced her. She didn't recognize him. The ballooning, torn lip, the lopsided jaw, the puffy bruise darkening his cheek bone, the desolation flooding his eyes. His gaze drifted. Was he in shock?

"Dave, tell me what happened?"

"I was telling you until you yelled, 'enough'."

"I'm listening now."

Dave stared at the dead man on the floor. Nora took his hand, held it, and waited.

"Like I said, I came here to confront him. It got out of hand. Fast."

Apparently. The candidate's face was a mess; he'd sustained a lot more damage than Dave.

"For God's sake, Dave. What did you think you'd accomplish?"

"Maybe a broken jaw. A few knocked out teeth. Son of a bitch had it coming. He killed Barbara and was getting away with it. I had to do something."

Nora had nothing to say. She couldn't stop staring at the swollen lids of Paul's dead blue eyes.

"Damned if he didn't admit it, too. When he had the gun, he openly bragged about making it look like suicide. He flat out told me he drugged her with pills and put her in her car. Then he drove to the river, positioned her in the driver's seat, and pressed her foot on the gas, jumping away and slamming the door as it went into the water."

An icy shiver snaked along Nora's spine. Paul had described that very scenario to her, but not as a confession. As a sarcastic denial. A way to ridicule Nora's suspicions and make murder sound preposterous. Nora heard the splash and gulp of the river, the water swallowing the car and its passenger. Paul lay still, his face rearranged but indifferent.

"What about his kids, Nora? I made them orphans."

The children. Nora hadn't thought about them. Would Colin and Harry come home from camp and find Paul's body?

"Dave, the kids'll be home—"

"No, I asked about them before I punched him. They're at the shore. Grandparents took them with the nanny after the funeral."

Thank God.

"I sat up all night, thinking about settling up with that sick fuck. But I never thought I'd kill him." Dave didn't look at her. He was trembling. Dave—her gentle Dave, who was never violent, who'd been furious with her for killing even a spider—how had that same Dave gotten into a brutally physical bare-knuckle fight for the sake of "settling up"?

"I tell you what though," Dave nodded in Paul's direction. "That guy might have been rich, might even have won the election, but shit. He had no timing, no technique. No fight. His fists fluttered at my face a few times, but I decked him in a minute, tops. He hit the floor so hard I thought he was out cold. But when I went to check, he sucker-punched me and ran like a cat on fire to get into this room."

"What is this? A hideaway?" The shiny steel walls felt like a prison.

Dave shrugged. "A place to escape to."

"But why would he need this? Did he have enemies?"

"He didn't get where he was by being nice. He was prepared though. He told me it's bulletproof, soundproof, and fireproof, with its own air supply. And it seals up tight as a vault." He looked at her. "How'd you find it?"

"I heard your voices. I followed them and found an opening. The door wasn't completely shut." She covered her mouth. "God. If I hadn't come looking for you, what would have happened?"

Dave was shivering. "Simple. He'd have locked me in here. Maybe he'd have shot me first, maybe not. Either way, I would've have died here."

God. She'd nearly lost him.

For a moment, they sat silent.

"Well," Nora tried to sound positive. "I found you, and you didn't die."

"No." He paused. "God, Nora, I killed him."

"Yes." She put a hand on his shoulder. "You had to."

"I chased him in here, and the next thing I know, he pulls a gun from the desk. And without a word, he shoots at me. I dodged but it was close. I felt the bullet whiz past." Dave stood and opened a desk drawer. His hand shook, holding up a box of bullets. "Shit. He's got dozens of these." He opened another drawer.

"Dave, stop touching everything."

"Why?" Shivering, he rifled through some files.

"What happened after he shot at you? How did you get the gun?"

"Oh." He stopped messing with the desk, hugged himself as if to get warm. "His shot missed me, but I dropped like I was hit and lay still. When he knelt down to check how bad off I was, I jumped him and took the gun. I didn't plan to shoot him. But when you came in, you saw how he charged at me. Damn. It happened so fast, like a reflex. Goddam mother fucker. I fucking killed him."

"It was self-defense."

"Doesn't matter." Dave stared at Paul's body. "Here's what does. The police know I was helping Barbara leave him. They know I got her a new identity, new bank accounts, new apartment—the works. I told them that the suicide story was bull and that he killed her. They know I hated the son of a bitch, which is motive. And they'll figure out I had means and opportunity."

"But I saw it. I'll tell them what happened."

"Great." He took a breath. "That'll work. You're my wife so they'll believe you for sure."

Cold sweat beaded on Dave's forehead. He sat beside Nora on the bunk—four elbows on four knees, four eyes watching Paul's dead, lanky body. They didn't speak. Air blew slow and steady through a vent. Seconds, minutes, passed. Nora thought about Tommy, about Barbara. About killing. About what she'd have to do, about what she'd already done.

Nora couldn't look away from the clotted blood on Paul's nose. And in her mind, Marla's torn and ragged voice scraped like sandpaper, like cement on bare knees. *How could he do this? Why? Why? Why?* Her father, bereft, said nothing.

Nora saw herself, preteen, gangly and awkward, trying to look stunned, to create tears as policemen had appeared in her parents' living room. One with a bulging belly, dark skin, and bumpy sores where he'd shaved sat next to her on the sofa, his eyes sharp, prickling her from under big heavy eyelids. How had she gotten along with Tommy? When had she seen him last? Did she know his friends? Had anything happened lately to upset him? Nora was convinced that he knew what she'd done, that he would arrest her and take her to jail. But Philip had interrupted and explained about Tommy, his involvement in solitary activities and tendency to remain distant from others, even his family. His lack of close friends. The detective had eyed her even while her father talked, as if he's seen past the words and into her brain. As if he'd known the truth.

Paul's death had roused that memory, and it bubbled up in all its hideousness. Nora resisted, though, focusing on Paul's corpse instead of Tommy's, on the present crisis instead of the past. On Paul's open, staring eyes. Had Tommy's been open like that when they'd found him? She couldn't recall. But Tommy's death hadn't been unexpected like Paul's. No, it had been deliberate and planned. Probably he'd closed his eyes in anticipation.

His coffin had been carved from blonde, creamy wood.

Nora glanced at Dave. Didn't recognize the expression on his face, the twist of his lips, the tautness of his facial muscles. Was he panicking? Feeling remorse? She thought back to Tommy's death, trying to remember whether she'd felt either.

All she remembered was a great unburdening. A sense of relief. The realization that, without Tommy weighing her down, she'd be free to be her own person, not labeled as the weirdo's sister, never subjected to his hostile moods and sneak attacks again. She could invite friends over without worrying about what he'd do. She could have parties. Maybe even invite Bobby Baxter.

Now, looking back, she realized that she'd never really grieved for her brother. Her initial numbness had been followed by disbelief. And, God forgive her, outright elation.

Tommy. Who would he have become if he hadn't died? Sophie and Ellie's Uncle Tommy would be in his forties. His thick mat of hair would be thinning, or gone. For sure, he'd have lost that cowlick. And his acne. He'd probably still dress in khaki pants and plaid shirts, at least by day. Nights, who knew? He might work at a club. In a smoke-filled lounge, holding a microphone, belting out something from Cats. But Tommy was distracting her, and she couldn't let him—not now. She had problems to solve.

Like what to do with Paul, whose once handsome, now bludgeoned face was already sinking into his bones. Dave was blinking too fast, rubbing his palms back and forth over his thighs.

"Take deep breaths," she said.

Dave didn't. He took his cell phone from his pocket, began to punch in a number, fingers unsteady.

"What are you doing? Don't!" Nora grabbed his hand. It was cold, his knuckles raw from the fight. "You're calling the police?"

He yanked his hand away from her and punched in more numbers.

"Stop!" She snatched the phone from him, ended the call.

"Nora." His voice was hollow. "I have to report this."

"No. Think a minute. It will look bad. Your career—"

"Is over. Don't you get it? Everything's finished. I'm a killer. Christ Almighty, Nora! The kids'll grow up with the stigma."

"Not if you don't report it."

For the tiniest moment, he hesitated. "I've got no choice. I'm an officer of the court." He reached for his phone, but Nora sat and shoved it under her hip. She gripped his icy hand.

"You're not calling." She faced him. "Dave, look at me."

Dave didn't. His eyes darted from her hip back to Paul.

"Funny," his voice quivered. "I thought coming here and punching his lights out would make me feel better. Who'd have guessed this would happen?" He was physically quaking, teeth chattering, big bones rattling, breathing fast and shallow. He stared at Paul.

"Dave." Nora repeated his name until he turned to her, but his gaze was vague and unfocused. He'd been traumatized, must be in shock. What did you do for someone in shock? In high school, Nora had taken a course in first aid. So, shock. She tried to remember. Was she supposed to elevate his head? Lower it? Have him drink water? Damn. She had no idea, but since he was shivering, she grabbed a blanket off the top bunk and wrapped it around him, wondering even then if any loose hairs or fibers would transfer onto it. And how they'd ever explain their presence to the police.

She wrapped her arms around Dave, felt the familiar bulk of his shoulders, his back. She smelled him, stale and unwashed. He allowed the hug but might not have noticed it. Nora let herself sink into the embrace and felt how unnerved, how fragile Dave was. How he needed her to take charge. She took a breath and counted, preparing for the role, gathering energy.

Then she squared her shoulders and summoned the quiet, nurturing voice she'd used with the children. "Everything's okay, Dave. You're going to be okay."

When had he drifted into stunned silence? He'd been fine just minutes ago, bragging about how he'd fought with Paul and chased him across the house. Maybe the gravity of what had happened had sunk in while they'd been sitting there, while she'd been thinking of Tommy. But he needed to pull himself together. She needed him to focus.

"Dave," she said again. This time he seemed to see her, though from somewhere far away. "You need to go home."

For a moment, he gaped at her open-mouthed. "Home?" He reacted as if the idea were absurd, as if she'd said "Paris" or "the North Pole," and he answered slowly, sounding final. "I can't leave. Nora, I killed him."

"No, you didn't. Dave. You didn't kill him. In fact, you haven't even seen him." Nora cupped his face in her hands and held it, looking into his eyes. "Listen to me. We're going to erase this. It never happened. You never even came over here."

His face said the idea was absurd, not worthy of a response.

"Do what I say, Dave. Go home." She studied him, assessing his state of mind. Gently, she leaned over and kissed his sore lip. "You're not making any calls. You're driving straight home. Take a shower and get rid of your clothes and the blanket."

"What are you saying?" He blinked at her.

"Just do what I said. And don't worry."

He argued only a little, probably too exhausted or shocked to think. Probably grateful to be told what to do.

Nora helped him out of the panic room, walked him to the front door and out to his BMW. She tossed the blanket onto the front seat beside him and watched him drive off.

Then she went inside and began cleaning up. She scrubbed blood from Paul's fists, removed his spattered shirt. Used a clean corner of it to wipe the gun clean. Retracing their path from the front door, she swept broken dishes into garbage bags, righted furniture, and wiped clean everything that may have been touched. She searched for fallen hairs, stains, drops, shoeprints, any signs of Dave or of her.

When she finished, she began again, redoing what she'd done, then wiping down every single miniscule smudge on the wall, the bunk bed, the desk drawers, the mantelpiece, the bullet boxes, the button that opened the hidden door. Finally satisfied that she'd removed all traces of her and Dave's presence, she took a last look at Paul, his shirtless chest, his long, awkwardly splayed legs, his swollen and disbelieving blue eyes.

If she'd come looking for Dave a half hour earlier, would Paul still be alive? Would Tommy be alive if she'd gone after him? So many ifs. So many wrong choices and disastrous consequences.

Move on. What's done is done. You made your bed, now lie in it. We do what we have to do.

Wrapping her fingers in a clean swatch of Paul's shirt, Nora walked out, pressed the button that closed the hidden panel, and shut off his secret room.

MONDAY, AUGUST 20, 2018, 10:30 A.M.

They didn't talk about what happened. When she got home, Nora simply said that everything had been taken care of. She told Dave not to worry, fixed him a martini and pampered him. When the girls jumped off the camp bus and came running through the front yard, Nora hugged and kissed them as if they'd been away for weeks. She explained that Daddy wasn't feeling well, that they had to let him rest and keep their voices down, hushing them with quiet praise when they presented their projects of painted baked clay—Ellie's, a bright, sky blue cow, Sophie's, a cat splashed with gold and pink. Nora listened as Sophie talked about their day and Ellie interrupted to correct her. "No, it wasn't a dive, it was a belly flop. No, we didn't play soccer all afternoon, just for a while before arts and crafts."

Nora marveled at their healthy color, the glow of their skin. She fixed them a snack of melted cheese on mini bagels while humming "You Are My Sunshine." She took them to the library and read an Amelia Bedelia book to them in the children's section.

Later, she was still humming while she marinated chicken breasts. She thought of Paul in his panic room. By now, rigor mortis must have set in, making him stiff as a mannequin, even the fingers that had invaded her. Even his penis. Nora winced and cut into a cantaloupe.

She kept an eye on Dave, fixed him another martini and made sure he drank it. During dinner, though, he barely ate and didn't joke or talk with the girls as usual. When they asked why his lip was swollen, he lied, saying that he'd been to the dentist and that now he was very tired. Though it was false, Nora considered this answer promising. "Tired" was curable, a condition that would pass.

That evening, Nora bathed the girls, read stories with them and tucked them in. She kept the routine going on her own, realizing that she'd have to allow Dave time to recover. He wasn't as tough as she was, at least not in this arena. He'd had no experience with killing, let alone with discrepancies between intentions and results, goals and achievements. He would need help.

That night, when the girls were asleep, she ran the bathtub again and led him upstairs. He didn't stop her when she undressed him. Didn't resist when she guided him into the steaming tub and began to soap him. When he was covered with suds, she dropped her own clothes and joined him. He reached for her. His face was bristly against her skin, but Nora didn't mind. She lowered herself onto him in hot water and closed her eyes. Everything was going to be all right.

SATURDAY, OCTOBER 31, 1993

Nora crept up to the attic, testing each step, avoiding any creaks that might awaken her brother. Scarcely breathing, she opened the door to Tommy's dark room, turned on the overhead lightbulb, and came face to face with an oversized housefly in black and white, one in a row of photographs hanging from a clothesline.

She rotated, scanning the shelves where he kept his paper and chemicals, the sink, gloves on a hook, pans filled with whatever it was he stuck paper in for developing. Snakelike coils of negatives dangling from beams. Counters buried in photographs. Shadowy nooks stuffed with file boxes.

If Nora found their pictures right away, she might still be able to get them to Annie tonight, and they could burn them, making certain that no one ever saw them.

"We look like lesbians," Annie had gasped. "If my parents see these—You have no idea, you don't know. They'd kill me."

Nora had assumed that Annie was being dramatic. Her parents couldn't possibly be that strict. But Annie's eyes had flashed steely, maybe with terror.

But finding the pictures wouldn't be easy. Tommy had photographs piled everywhere. Hundreds of them, scattered on tables, stored in files, packed in boxes. Most of them pictures of bugs, every kind, size, color, and shape, taken from every distance, magnitude, lighting level, and angle. Grasshoppers. Locusts. Ladybugs. Mosquitoes. Wasps. Bugs she didn't know the names of.

Nora dug in. She leafed through half a dozen piles, took boxes off shelves, rifled through one, then another. One box held shots of their family. Marla opening a Christmas gift, modeling a new beaver coat. Philip buried in sand. Marla and Nora splashing in the ocean. The box held hundreds of pictures she'd never seen before. There was Grandma Ida, her white hair tied into its usual bun, at some long-ago birthday party with a forkful of cake suspended mid-bite. Nora could almost smell her—that mixture of toilet water and moth balls. But she was getting distracted, had no time for nostalgia. She opened another box, found shots of Tommy's old ant farm, wasp's nests, gypsy moth nests, beehives.

The next box didn't contain what she was looking for either. But what it did contain made her stop breathing and drop to her knees, at once revolted and mesmerized. She stared at the first photograph, confused by the image. She closed her eyes, looked again. Squinted and stared until she was certain of what she was seeing. Even when she was sure of the first photo, she wasn't sure about the others, and examined them, one by one, until her eyes burned. She pored through them yet again, selecting the most dramatic, or the most unmistakable, or maybe the most shocking, until she had just a few, and slid them into a manila envelope to keep them safe. No question, Tommy would surrender the ones she wanted to get these photos back. They weren't the ones she'd been looking for, but surely they'd be good enough for Annie, to prove that Nora was nothing like her brother, that she was on Annie's side.

Annie's party was still going strong when Nora got back. The rec room was pitch black and reeked of marijuana and booze. The music was so loud that Nora had to shout, asking kids if they'd seen Annie. She found her on the patio, smoking pot.

"I've got pictures," Nora kept her voice low as she pulled Annie aside.

"It's about time. Give them—"

"No, wait. These aren't the ones of us."

"This is bullshit, Nora."

"Listen. You have to trust me. He'll give us anything we want to get these back."

Annie grabbed for the envelope, but Nora held it just out of reach. "This is just between you and me, okay?"

"Sure." Annie took the envelope, opened it, and took out a picture. "What is this? It's too dark out here. Does anyone have a light?"

"Annie, no!" Nora scrambled to get the picture back, but Annie snatched it away. Nora grabbed the envelope and Annie tugged it, a standoff, until Craig stepped over, shining a mini flashlight on his keychain into their eyes and taking the envelope from them both.

"Hey, what's this?"

Nora's stomach lurched. What was Annie doing? Craig wasn't part of the deal, never had been. Annie, only Annie, was supposed to see the pictures. Nora lunged for the envelope, clawed at Craig's arm, but he laughed, holding it high over her head, teasing, telling her to jump for it. Again, Nora reached for his arm, but he spun around, dashing away. In an eyeblink, the struggle for the envelope was over. It was gone. Craig had opened it, was already examining the pictures, holding the light over one, then another. Annie leaned in to see, her jaw dropped.

"Is this for real?" Annie shrieked. "Oh my God."

She looked at Craig, and they both exploded into knee-bending, thigh-slapping laughter.

"Can I have them back now?" Nora tried to sound cool, like she didn't care much. She reached slowly and casually for the pictures and almost got them, but at the last second Annie moved them away. Nora stepped back, stung, and let her arms drop helplessly to her sides.

"Are you kidding me?" Annie choked on her words, she was laughing so hard.

"This is—That's who I think it is, right?" Craig bellowed.

"Annie. Give them back."

They ignored her.

"Yo, Donny, you gotta see these." Craig pulled his friend over and Annie handed him the pictures.

"Stop, no!" Nora reached for them but Annie played keep-away, passing them to Craig who held them in the air.

"You want 'em back, Nora?" Craig's eyes glowed. "Come get them." He taunted her, ready to pounce if she came too close.

Her lip still throbbed where he'd bitten it. "Just give them to me. Please." Her voice trembled.

"Don't be a party pooper," Annie scolded.

"She's right, Nora." Craig spun around and went inside with Annie right behind him.

Nora watched in silence while events spun out of control, as if she'd lit a match and a house had caught fire. No, not just a house, a whole forest. And not just a fire, a disaster, a conflagration.

In the rec room, Craig flipped on a light and turned down the music. His voice boomed, "Yo, boys and girls. Wait'll you see what Nora brought."

Bobby Baxter was there, quieter than the others. What did he think of Nora for bringing pictures like those? Did he know that the photographer, the subject of the photos, was her brother? Weirdo. Freak. Creep.

Annie helped Craig pass the photos around the room. She couldn't stop giggling, and danced around with Craig, gleeful at the reactions, lots of oh-my-god's and you're-shitting-me's. The party-goers slapped foreheads, and their eyes bugged out as they gradually identified the heavily rouged woman posed dramatically in a frilly negligee, then a long floral frock, lingerie, high heels, a swimsuit, and finally, that new black cocktail dress Marla had recently bought. Drunk and stoned, the other kids hooted and whistled, shouting out sex acts they'd like to see performed on the pervert in the pictures, finally deciding to plaster the photos all over their high school, to share Tommy's secret unappreciated glamour with the world. Weirdo. Creep. Freak.

Nora didn't fight them, didn't demand that they stop. *Family comes first. Your brother is your blood.* She faded into the shadows, silent, passive, and ashamed. Stunned at how drastically out of control events had spun, how her intentions had gone so wrong.

TUESDAY, AUGUST 21 – WEDNESDAY AUGUST 22, 2018

Days went by, not one at a time but as a continuous, rolling motion of waking and sleeping, motion and stillness, noise and silence, anxiety and calm. Nora held on, riding the cycles, letting them carry her through time.

On Tuesday, the mailman brought packets from school telling the girls which classroom they'd be in and who their teachers would be. Calls went back and forth between friends to see who was in the same room. Trips were made to buy final school supplies and more school clothes. Haircuts were scheduled at the salon. Nora met with the other room mothers to plan decorations, events, and healthy snacks for the first day of school.

Dave went to work, following routine with clients and cases, coming home on time for dinner. The conversations he and Nora had about Paul were cautious and late at night.

"Have you heard anything?" Or, "Any news?"

"No," and "No."

But late Wednesday afternoon, when the girls were coloring in the family room and Nora was unloading groceries, her phone rang. The screen said Patty was calling. Nora answered with the phone in one hand and a bag of frozen peas in the other.

"Nora? God, have you heard?"

Nora's throat clamped shut. She dropped the peas on the counter. Hugged herself. They must have found Paul. But how? She pictured him on the floor of that secret room. Had he begun to rot? Was his belly bloated? Were maggots eating him?

Patty continued, "It's Barbara's husband—Paul Ellis. He's missing!"

Missing? Not dead? Not found murdered? Nora relaxed a tad. Allowed herself to breathe. "What?"

"He hasn't been heard from since right after the funeral. The nanny and the kids got back this morning from his parents' house down at the shore, but the house was empty. They said on the news that the mail was piled up. Paul's car was there, but no sign of Paul."

Patty paused. Nora knew it was her turn to say something. "My God."

"I know. No one's seen or heard from him. His campaign must be going nuts, explaining his no-shows and canceling events. His campaign manager's been making excuses for him. I guess he thought Paul was going off script because of Barbara's death and he kept things quiet, expecting him to show up eventually.

"Rumors are flying. Some say he killed himself out of despair about Barbara. Another theory is that he's been kidnapped by terrorists or political extremists."

"My God," Nora said again. It seemed to be all she could manage.

"It's crazy, right? Go put on the news. It should be on the five o'clock. What time is it? Five. I want to go watch. Talk to you later."

Nora thought about watching the news, instead she continued to unpack groceries. Apples, avocadoes, arugula. Two percent, American cheese, whole wheat bread.

Minutes later, Dave came home with his eyes wild, his skin gray. She didn't need to ask if he'd heard. His face was as clear as a newspaper headline.

"Have you…" His voice was hoarse and full of whispers.

"I already know." Nora kept her answer balanced, unshakeable. "Patty called and told me that Paul's missing. It's shocking. They're saying he might have been kidnapped." She continued putting away groceries, reminding Dave through her actions how they were going to handle this development. They were going to go on as usual.

Dave stood near the stove, arms at his sides, staring at nothing.

"Okay, fine," she said. "Tell me what's going on."

Her words seemed to revive him. He blinked, cleared his throat. "It was on the news."

For a heartbeat, Nora panicked. Reaching to put the corn flakes on the highest cupboard shelf, she flashed back. Had she forgotten anything in that secret room? Had she left behind an identifying eyelash or fiber? A fingerprint? A micro-drop of blood? Would their presence be discovered? No, not possible. She'd been thorough, had gone over every inch of the place twice, three times. No, there was no evidence. They were fine. Besides, Paul was missing. Nobody had even found him.

"Homicide knows I was working with his wife." Dave had that pasty look again, as if his face lacked structure and could be remolded at the slightest touch. "They know I despised him. They'll want to talk to me."

Sophie appeared then. Her little hands and forearms were splotched blue and green from the markers. She wanted to go to the playground and complained that Ellie wasn't fun. Ellie trailed in behind her, somber, biting her fingernail. She asked when it would be time for supper and whether they could have hot dogs.

Nora juggled groceries and girls, handling both. She assigned tasks so that her children would help put away the remaining food, fold the bags, and take out ketchup, mustard and hot dog buns. Nora proceeded to fix dinner. Hot dogs? Yes, why not? Grilled, with melted cheese on top. And cut up melon. And potato salad. The girls scampered around: getting paper plates, napkins, paper cups from the cupboard. All the while, Dave's eyes remained flat and aimed out the window, his hands flaccid on the counter, like slabs of a quartered chicken.

"Okay. So, they'll talk to you." She wanted to prepare him, help him rehearse what he would say. "You know nothing."

He gave the slightest of nods, continued to stare outside. What was out there? A deck that needed restaining. A lawn that needed mowing. Bushes that needed trimming. What did he see?

"Dave. It'll be all right." A huge fly buzzed around the kitchen window. It banged its body against the screen, like a messenger from Tommy.

"What'll be all right, Mommy?" Sophie asked.

Oh God. Why did Sophie hear everything? "Everything, honeybunch." Nora smiled, but Sophie tilted her head, looking doubtful.

WEDNESDAY, AUGUST 22, 2018, 11:50 P.M.

That night, long after the girls were asleep and the lights were out, Nora lay next to Dave, listening to him worry. Dave's breathing was quick and shallow. She could almost hear the flapping of his eyelids, the clenching and unclenching of his fists, even the troubled pounding of his heart.

It was obvious Dave was suffering, wrestling with guilt. Still blaming himself for not saving Barbara, then for killing Paul. How long would it last, this self-blame, the sorrow and dread? Couldn't he see that he'd done everything he could for Barbara? That Paul had left him no alternative. If Dave hadn't killed him, he'd have killed Dave—and probably her as well? And even if Paul's body were found, Nora had made sure that his killer wouldn't be?

Dave sighed and tossed, tossed and sighed. She reached over, put her hand on his shoulder.

"Am I keeping you up?" Dave started to get out of bed. "I'll go downstairs."

"No." She took his hand, stopping him. "Stay. We need to talk."

"About what? Unless—do you think someone saw us at the scene?"

A witness? How long had he been worrying about that? "No one saw us, Dave. There's only one other house on the cul-de-sac. Plus, it was raining. Plus, the house is surrounded by foliage."

"I hope you're right." His breathing was still short. "You'd think I'd feel some closure now that he's dead. But I don't. Killing him didn't fix anything. Didn't bring Barbara back. It just made me a killer, the same as Paul."

"You're nothing like Paul."

Dave sat for a moment, then stood and walked out of the room. She heard him going down the stairs.

"Dave," Nora kept her voice low so she wouldn't wake the children and followed him. "Wait."

Dave didn't wait. He turned on the lights and took the Bulleitt Rye and two glasses from the liquor cabinet. Poured a few fingers in each and handed one to Nora. Then, slumped on the wingback chair, he lifted the glass in a toast.

"Here's to me for fucking everything up." He drank, then stared into his glass.

"You didn't." Nora gulped anyway, savoring the burn as the whiskey flowed down her throat.

"God, I am so fucked."

Nora sat in the chair next to him. When he finally looked at her, she was close enough to see little red capillaries in the whites of his eyes, striping them like a barber pole. Dave looked thin, fragile, and exhausted. He was angry one minute, sad the next. His shoulders sagged constantly. She needed to convince him that they were, and would be, fine. But how?

Maybe she should go all in and prove that she understood how he was feeling, that he wasn't alone. That life would go on. Did she dare?

They sat silent, drinking. Dave finished his glass and poured another, topped off Nora's.

"I keep seeing him go down." He swallowed more rye. "I hear the gunshot, again and again."

"I get that you feel bad."

"Bad? Fuck, no. I'm glad he's dead, the son of a bitch. If I had the chance to do it over, I'd kill him again."

"Then what are you saying?"

"Just that... I can't stop reliving it. He's alive. Then he's dead." He stared at his hands.

"You were traumatized. You've probably got what soldiers get—post-traumatic stress."

"Nora, stop. You don't get it. You don't have a clue what it's like to take a life."

Nora picked up her glass and downed the contents. It felt so smooth, warming her insides, softening the edges of walls and windows, time and truth. How about fear? Did it soften fear? What would happen if she told him?

Don't look for trouble. Don't rock the boat. Leave well enough alone.

"I know more than you can imagine."

"No, Nora. You don't." His tone cut the air, swiped at her.

A heartbeat passed. Another.

"I have something to tell you." Nora refilled her glass and focused only on the amber tones of the rye. That way, she wouldn't see Dave's revulsion when he heard about Tommy, and the truth of what she'd done.

MONDAY, NOVEMBER 2, 1993

Long after her parents had gone to bed, Nora was still awake, unable to sleep. She sat up in bed, picturing and re-picturing and picturing again what had happened Saturday night. Her so-called friends, the people she wanted most to impress, had become a wild-eyed mob as they passed around the pictures of her brother in drag—all of them, except for Bobby Baxter. Bobby Baxter, in his soft wool sweater and Old Spice, had watched it all. What had he thought of Nora for sharing those pictures of her own brother? He must have understood something about her intentions though—she'd kept insisting that the pictures were meant for Annie's eyes only. But maybe Bobby couldn't have cared less about her or her intentions. Maybe he'd been disgusted with everyone and just wanted to stop the bullying. After all, he'd stood up for Tommy, shouting above the riot of voices in the rec room.

"Okay, everybody. You had your laugh. Now give them back to Nora," he'd yelled.

Craig had stared at him, amazed that a mere seventh grader would challenge him, even a tall, preppy one like Bobby.

"You talking to me?" Craig faced Bobby, nose to nose.

"Give them back to her," Bobby repeated, not backing down. "That kid's not hurting anybody, so let him alone. What he does in private is his own business."

Craig had flicked Bobby's shoulder and turned back to his raucous friends, as if Bobby hadn't said a word. But Bobby had spoken up for Tommy even when no one had listened, even when Tommy's own sister had abandoned him.

But what could she do? Nora punched her pillow.

Had Craig and his band of bullies really done what they'd threatened, tacking up the photos of Tommy all around the school where everyone would see them?

Probably. Because when Tommy had come home, he'd locked himself in his room and hadn't come out for dinner. Hadn't answered Marla's, or even Philip's knocks on his door. So she was pretty sure Craig had done what he'd promised.

Nora fell back onto her mattress and stared at the ceiling, tears sliding down her temples into her ears. Tommy Tommy Tommy Tommy. Why should she feel so bad? It was Tommy's own fault for withholding the pictures he'd taken of her with Annie. He'd given Nora no choice but to search his dark room, and besides, he shouldn't have taken those pictures of himself in the first place. For sure, he shouldn't have been wearing their mother's clothes. She hated him for dressing up like a girl. She hated the kids at the sleepover for laughing at him. She hated Annie for having the party to begin with. And most of all, she hated herself for having her life, for being trapped in it.

At some point, the floor creaked. A door opened. She got out of bed and stood just inside her door, listening. The stairs to the attic shifted, groaning under Tommy's—it had to be his—weight. She should go after him.

But hell, what would she say? Sorry, I messed up? What good would that do? He'd probably had, by far, the most unimaginably unbearable day of his entire miserable life. No wonder he hadn't come to dinner. Everyone he knew, kids he didn't know, his teachers, the principal, the janitors—they'd all found out his secret. They'd seen his glossy red lipstick and wavy blonde wig, his flirtatious poses as he'd flashed a thigh or puckered up for the camera lens. And it was all her doing.

Pity and shame rushed through Nora. She hurried out of her room and whispered to him as he trudged up the steps to the attic.

"Hey."

He stopped but didn't turn or answer.

"Tommy, wait." She wasn't sure what else to say.

When he finally turned around, she saw the wreck that his face had become. His eyes had both been blackened, one so puffed up that it was nearly closed. His nose was bruised and swollen, caked with scabbing. His bottom lip bulged and made his whole mouth crooked.

"Your friend was supposed to call Craig off."

"I'm so sorry."

"I doubt that." His swollen lips didn't enunciate very well. "Since you're the one who gave out the pictures."

"No, they took them from me. I didn't mean to. I found them while I was looking for the pictures of Annie and me, and I thought you'd swap—"

"They're under my mattress. Take them."

Nora couldn't stop staring at Tommy's brutalized face. "Who beat you up? Was it Craig?"

"What do you care? You hate me too."

"I don't hate you. You're my brother."

"Like that matters to you. I told you, Nora. I warned you about those people, that girl Annie. You made your choice."

"That's not fair."

"I got suspended."

Why? "For what?"

"Who knows? Maybe fighting. Maybe the pictures. Maybe just because they all hate me." His chin quivered as if he were about to cry. He paused, controlling it, forcing a harsh laugh that sounded like a bark. "That asshole vice principal acted like I was the one who put the pictures up. He blamed me. Warned me about being a degenerate. Doesn't matter. I learned my lesson." His eyes wandered, looked distracted.

"What lesson?"

The question seemed to confuse him. "What?"

"You said you learned your lesson."

Tommy shrugged. "Oh. To stay away from people like them. Not let anyone get to me ever again. Not even you."

For a moment, they just stared at each other. Nora knew she should say she was sorry again or at least tell him how terrible she felt. But something in Tommy's posture silenced her, made it clear that he was beyond listening to anything she'd say. She eyed Tommy's swollen face and ached to beat up Craig and his tough-guy friends, to tear their limbs off.

"I'm going on up," Tommy lifted his hand in mock salute. "Well. Bye, Nora." He turned and climbed the rest of the attic stairs.

Nora stood alone, replaying his words, their hollow tone. Tommy had learned his lesson and wouldn't let anyone get to him ever again?

And she knew.

No. She was being overly dramatic. He wouldn't do anything so final.

Except, yes, he would. And was going to.

Oh God. She hurried up the stairs after him.

"Tommy!" Nora called, but he'd already locked the door.

She stopped, staring at the two inches of flat, dead wood that separated her from her brother. She didn't bang on it or shout his name again. She didn't move to get help or fight to change his mind.

Instead, Nora sat on the steps, listening, waiting, wondering. What was he up to? When would he do it? And how? Would she know when it happened? Wasn't she going to try to stop him? Why was her heart pounding as if anticipating some remarkable, life-altering, climactic release? Long, silent minutes passed and finally, she went back to bed.

At some point, she must have dozed off, because screams woke her. Her father's? Nora bolted upright, stared at a ray of sunlight beaming through a curtain gap. Footsteps pounded the ceiling overhead. Her father was yelling, his voice high-pitched and broken. Nora dashed from her room. Marla was in the hallway open-mouthed and wide-eyed, holding her belly as though she'd been punched.

Nora knew he was dead. She'd known before anyone told her, before the police had been called, before she'd climbed the stairs to see him hanging from a beam beside black and white shots of lightning bugs. Tommy was dead, and it was because of her, because of what she'd done, and because of what she hadn't done. No one accused her, but Nora knew. She had killed Tommy as surely as if she'd strung him up herself.

And she felt fine.

66 *A*fterward, I replayed our final conversation again and again. There were blatant clues that something was off. But I made excuses and pretended that I hadn't known. That I couldn't have prevented it even if I had tried. In the end, I made a choice. I did nothing." Nora bit her lip. Why had she told Dave? What had made her think it was a good idea, after a quarter century of silence, to say the words out loud? No one, in all this time, had suspected the truth. No one had blamed her. Until now.

"My God, Nora." That was all Dave said.

At first, Nora couldn't look at him. She kept her gaze trained on her drink, then her wedding ring. The ring and the drink were almost the same color in this light, both shades of rosy gold. Oh God. What had she done? Why had she told him? Would he think less of her? See her as self-serving and cold-hearted, even stop loving her?

Dave finished his drink. Poured another and refilled hers. Drank some more. Did he need alcohol before he could even look at her?

Nora's face burned. Her heart flew into her throat. Damn. She shouldn't have told him. What she'd done was far worse than what Dave had done. Tommy had been a kid, not a fiend like Paul. Some secrets should never, not ever, be revealed.

Seconds tick-tick-ticked. Or was it her pulse? The walls, the liquor cabinet, even the too-expensive light fixture that Dave had said would make a statement and bring the whole room together, all of them lost their edges and blended together, smooshing like clumps of Silly Putty.

Tommy had risen from the grave, and would get his revenge by destroying her marriage, her life. A lump grew in Nora's throat. She watched Dave, the motionless muscles of his face. He stood. Where was he going? Was he leaving her? Because of what she'd done?

She made for the front door. She'd run before he got the chance, even though she hadn't considered where.

Dave grabbed her wrist, stopping her. "Nora, stop. Where are you going?" He wrapped his arms around her and kissed her cheeks, even though they were salty and wet, and her lips ever so gently. "Sit. You're not going anywhere." He guided her back into her chair, then kneeled in front of her and stroked her cheek, smearing tears until she met his eyes. "How have you lived with this all by yourself?"

Nora tried to turn away.

"Look at me." He guided her chin upward until their eyes met.

She could sense Tommy watching in the distance, his face battered and eyes blackened. She concentrated on Dave, tried to ignore Tommy.

"You were a kid. What were you, twelve years old? You were struggling to fit in with your peers, trying to figure out who you were. You couldn't have realized the gravity of your actions, let alone what their outcome might be. You certainly didn't intend for your brother to be hurt, never mind to die."

How could Dave be so sure? Nora knew better. "I wanted to be free of him, to get even with—"

"Enough. The self-blame stops now, tonight. You were a child. You were not responsible for Tommy's pictures. Or his cross-dressing. Or any of his other issues. And above all, not for his death. A lot of factors converged—"

"Don't be a lawyer. That last night, I let him go up to the attic alone. If not for me, he'd be alive."

Dave's capillaries snaked around his irises, exhaustion, or something darker, shadowing his brow. He pulled her close, holding her too long and too tightly. Even when he released her, he clasped her hands, not letting go.

"So, like I said," she said, "I know what it feels like to take a life."

"No, you don't. Tommy committed suicide. You didn't kill him, Nora. Listen to me. You. Did. Not. Kill. Tommy."

Nora nodded. No use arguing the point. Dave hadn't been there. He hadn't known how desperate she'd been back then. He would never accept that she'd been fully aware, even at age twelve, of the gravity of her choices. She'd known that posting those pictures all over the school might be as lethal to Tommy as a gunshot, but she hadn't fought to stop Craig and his friends, hadn't really even tried. She'd known when Tommy called her by her actual name, not something like shithead or pisser. She'd recognized the futility in Tommy's voice—*Bye, Nora*—but she'd left him to his despair. She'd known and had deliberately and purposefully done nothing.

Dave leaned close, his eyes teary. "Thank you," he whispered. "I'm glad—No—I'm honored and moved that you've finally trusted me enough to tell me." He planted a kiss on her mouth, gentle and feathery, the way he'd kissed her after she'd labored through childbirth.

Nora wanted to cover her face, run up to bed, and pull the covers over her head. She wanted Dave to stop staring at her. God. Was this what openness felt like? Naked, with every flaw and scar exposed? She couldn't bear feeling so bare. Why was she punning? Obviously, she needed to make light of the situation, make it seem less significant. But Dave was still watching her. How long would this last? When would Dave be himself again and stop gaping at her in rapt amazement?

"So." She put on a cheerful smile, began talking in the soft authoritative tone she used with the children. "Now, we know each other's darkest secret. We're even. Balanced. We each have one killing."

"Except you didn't kill Tommy—"

"But that's all we get." She ignored his distinction. "One apiece. From now on, we live right. We raise our kids. We stay honest and open with each other. And we move on. Okay?" Her smile made her face ache, but she held it.

Dawn was only a few hours away when they climbed under the covers. They made love silently, tenderly. Afterward, Dave's breath deepened in seconds, but even with the late hour and the quantity of rye in her system, Nora stayed awake. *You did not kill him, Nora. You did not kill Tommy.* Was that possibly true? More likely, it was what Dave needed to believe.

THURSDAY, AUGUST 23, 2018

In the morning, Nora was greeted by Dave's empty pillow and a gnawing sense that she'd done something awful, the memory clawing its way from her belly to her brain. Now, Dave knew she was a sociopath pretending to be a stay-at-home, cheerful, suburban mom. He'd seen beneath her skin, witnessed the raw writhing reptile that coiled there. What had she done? Why had she told him?

Openness, she reminded herself. It had been her idea, so that Dave could forgive himself for what he'd done to Paul. So he could see that he was not alone, that she understood. She and Dave were unique, closer than most couples. They could share the truth no matter how difficult.

Shrieks of laughter flew up the stairway along with the aroma of coffee. Nora looked at the clock. Almost ten. Ten? Dave had let her sleep in. But why was he home on a weekday? Why wasn't he at work?

Getting up and brushing her teeth took effort. Normal tasks like face-washing required deliberate concentration. Nora's life had shifted. Her movements, her routine, felt altered, as if the whole world had taken a step away from her, making her former relationship to space and time obsolete. She made her way downstairs carefully, then stopped at the kitchen doorway to watch her family from a distance.

Dave was at the stove in a T-shirt and boxers, fixing eggs, the girls buzzing around him. What would happen when she joined them? Would Dave look at her differently? Would the girls notice a change?

"Mommy's up!" Sophie spotted her and pulled her into the kitchen.

"Daddy's making breakfast." Ellie withdrew her fingernail from her mouth.

Dave grinned, spatula in hand. "Morning, honey."

Honey? Dave never called her that. Not sweetie or dear, either.

"You're home?" she asked.

"Taking the day off. We deserve a family day." His smile was too big, too bright.

Nora moved toward him slowly, cautiously. She studied his face, watching for tiny muscle twinges, for involuntary tics of revulsion. She saw none. When she came close enough, he grabbed her for a kiss. A real one, not a quick peck.

"Daddy, can I put the toast in?" Ellie held bread slices.

"I want to!" Sophie tried to grab the bread.

"Take turns. Two slices each." Dave flipped the eggs, completely in charge.

Nora sipped coffee, watchful. Especially of Dave, who was acting cheerful and funny, painting faces on the toast with jam and blueberries. Was this real? What happened to his grief and guilt? Was he pretending for the children's sakes?

He set a plate of steaming breakfast in front of her. She chewed, swallowed, forced scrambled eggs and bacon down her throat. Smiled at her family and laughed when they laughed. She demonstrated that she was happy and loving, living in the moment. Feeling fine.

Dave winked at her as the kids stuffed their mouths. His jolliness didn't quite fit. It flopped, sloppy and loose, like a borrowed suit.

When everyone finished eating, Dave had the girls help clear the table. Nora joined him at the sink, and he kissed her forehead. As he put the pan in the dishwasher, Nora noted chunks of egg sticking to the surface. Normally, she'd have taken the pan out and scraped it off. But today, she swallowed her words. Why was Dave staying home and playing happy daddy? Was he overcompensating? Pretending not to be disgusted about Tommy?

Finally, Dave turned off the water, dried his hands and turned to her. She was relieved to see that his smile was gone, his brow furrowed. She waited, expected him to say something poignant, something profound.

"How about," he said, "we all go to the zoo?"

The girls ran circles around the table, shrieking, naming animals that they wanted to see.

Who was this giddy, manic, overzealous man? How long before he'd let her real husband come back?

It was her own fault though. She shouldn't have told him.

LATE SEPTEMBER, 2018

Days became weeks. Dave's forced ebullience gradually subsided, but he remained altered. When they were alone, he seemed somber, lost, his eyes walled off and distant, even when they didn't avoid hers. His needs were intense. Deep in the night, he'd often reach for her, pulling her to him with a desperate, but somehow impersonal hunger. During the days, he'd touch Nora whenever he could. Physically, he clung to her, embracing her unexpectedly from behind while she was cooking or putting dishes away or even brushing her teeth, his arms appearing as if from nowhere, enclosing her, clutching her as if she were an anchor that would keep him from drifting—no— a life raft without which he'd drown. Just like Barbara had.

Nora told herself that Dave's seesaws of highs and lows, exhilaration and dejection, would pass, his neediness would fade. He was, after all, recovering from the trauma of killing Paul and failing to save Barbara, while simultaneously enduring the tension of waiting for Paul's body to be discovered. She was determined to remain patient with his recurring moody silences. She endured his needy, hungry hands, the unfamiliar look in his eyes, and the tight, insistent way he shut them when they made love.

The pattern of Nora's life continued until school started. Abruptly, with her daughters gone all day, she was alone with empty time. But within days, she developed a new routine. She began each morning by scanning the newspaper for news of Paul's disappearance. When she found no mention of his body, she looked for reports of other murders. Any murders, all murders. Shootings, stabbings, stranglings, poisonings, beatings, in places all over the city, the country, the world. She read accounts of these crimes closely, repeatedly, focusing especially on descriptions of the murderers. These descriptions comforted her, assured her that she and Dave were not alone with their brutal truths.

Having finished with the paper, Nora tuned the television to the cable crime network and left it on as a soundtrack for her day. Without her children to distract her, killing took over her thoughts. She remembered Paul bleeding, imagined Barbara drowning. Tommy hanging. Eventually, she came to see herself as a natural killer, a person who murdered regularly. Pulling weeds from the ground, squashing a house fly, spraying a wasps' nest. Cooking lamb chops. Letting her brother go upstairs to hang himself.

By midday every day, Nora resolved to resist her grim proclivities and resume a normal life. She made phone calls, sent email, went to the gym. Volunteered at the school, helping in the office, chairing the PTA book fair committee, acting as room mother for Ellie's class. When she could, she met Alex and Patty for walks or coffee, but they weren't often available with little ones still at home, and Katie was working full time. Besides, when she got together with them, especially at book club, Barbara's absence weighed heavily, even when they talked of other things.

By Thursday of the third week of school, she was ready to pull her eyelashes out from boredom. She folded laundry, checked Dave's shirts for loose buttons and sewed them tight. She picked up a novel but caught herself staring at dancing letters and went to the kitchen for a cup of coffee, not because she wanted it but because she had nothing else to do. She considered cleaning out the front closet. Lord. How would she survive the empty days and weeks and—oh God—years ahead? The hands on the kitchen clock jerked and paused, jerked and paused, marking seconds until, in five hours and ten or so minutes, the three-thirty bus would bring the girls home and she would reanimate. Nora might have stayed in the kitchen, watching the clock for all five hours if the phone hadn't rung.

"They took the kids away." Patty blew her nose, weepy.

"What? Yours?"

"God, no! Colin and Harry. Their grandparents took them to live with them. I think they have a place in…"

Oh, thank God. Patty's kids were fine. Patty was talking about Barbara's.

"It's for the best, isn't it?" Why was Patty so upset?

"Well, no, I don't think so. The boys have been with Anna, the nanny, since they were born. But, with Paul missing, Barbara's parents fired her."

"How do you know this?"

"Anna called me. I thought she was calling to schedule a play date. But she wanted to say goodbye. She was sobbing. It was awful."

More endings, more goodbyes.

Nora watched the second hand move from the seven to the nine. Then, with an unflinching voice, she said, "Maybe Paul will turn up and rehire her."

"Seriously? You think he's still alive?" Patty's voice had tensed. "His campaign's come to a halt. And the media act like he's gone for good."

That was true. The news reports, when last Nora saw a mention of Paul, had hinted at his likely death. If he were alive, they'd said, why had no one heard from him? If he'd taken off to clear his head, surely, he'd have left word with his campaign, or at least

368 · MERRY JONES

for the nanny and his children. If he'd been kidnapped, wouldn't there have been a ransom demand?

Nora chewed her upper lip, deciding how to answer without reflecting what she knew. "What do you think?" There. She'd thrown the question back, dodged a comment.

"He's got to be dead. Honestly, Nora? I think he killed himself. He was devastated by Barbara's suicide. I bet he blamed himself."

Rightly so, since he'd killed her.

"Still, if he's dead, why haven't they found him?" Nora tried to sound baffled. She picked up a cloth and rubbed invisible stains off the countertop.

Patty was quiet, probably pondering the question of where Paul's body could be, but her answer never came. A child in the background called for mommy just as Patty's phone beeped with another call. Nora said a quick goodbye and a see-you-at-book-club. Then she stared at the clock for a full minute, or maybe two, before getting up to dress for the gym. It was important to keep moving.

DECEMBER, 1993

Nora had assumed that after Tommy's funeral, life would get better. But at home, it got worse. Her parents were consumed by heaviness and grief. Marla shrank into her herself, wandering rooms and hallways silently with vacant eyes, staying in days-old nightgowns, not talking or eating, swallowing only prescription pills. Her father's shoulders collapsed. He forgot to shave and smelled of sourness and whiskey, wandering off to work early and coming home late, reeking like a bar.

For her own sake, Nora stayed away from home as much as she could. The house drooped, the walls sagged. It was depressing there, overflowing with death. Tommy's room still had all his stuff, his bugs, his khaki pants and blue shirts, even his stale musky scent. The room's dark door remained closed, its contents untouched. His absence dominated the house, sucked the life from it. The lack of Tommy was larger, more pervasive than his presence had been.

But school was the opposite. There, life blossomed. Nora was suddenly popular. The friendships she'd craved when Tommy had been alive were now hers. At the age of twelve, she had a following. Everyone knew who she was and sought her out, even high school bullies, like Craig. Kids cleared a path when she passed through the crowded halls. Girls clamored to sit at her lunch table or ride with her on the bus or just hang out.

Overnight, Tommy's death had made Nora a celebrity. She heard—no—she felt their whispers. "That's the girl whose brother died. Did you see her family on the news? She's brave about it, isn't she? It's not like she mopes or expects special treatment or anything."

Bobby Baxter asked her to be his girlfriend. He called her every night and walked her to classes during school days. He kissed her hello and goodbye. Nora wasn't sure if he liked her for herself or for her notoriety, but, either way, everyone knew she was Bobby Baxter's girlfriend.

Nora ended contact with Annie. She cut her off completely and suddenly, like a rotten tree branch or a reeking, gangrenous limb.

Life was good. Nora put on smiles when she didn't know what else to do. Laughed when others did. She adapted to her role as the girl whose brother died, the girl who was handling a tragedy so bravely and so well.

Most of all, she blended in.

Underneath, she carried a curious void where Tommy had been. His absence fascinated her. At night, when her parents were asleep, her mother having taken pills and her father too much whiskey, she sometimes crept into Tommy's room and climbed into his bed to see what he'd seen. The mounted butterflies and moths. A framed scorpion. A blown-up photograph of a grasshopper. What had drawn Tommy to these hideous creatures? What had he seen in them that Nora could not? After a while, she'd get off his bed, stand in the middle of the room and picture him there, showing her maybe a butterfly, maybe a cockroach. Or holding up his latest trapped bug, something he'd found in the yard freshly dead or still struggling. Why had he wanted her to see his creepy-crawly specimens?

Now and then, she'd take one of his blue plaid shirts and wrap it around her shoulders. She'd lived with Tommy for all her twelve years. He'd been a burden to her, an outcast who'd thwarted her life, who'd preferred bugs to people. But despite all their time together, her brother had remained a stranger. A mystery. A nagging riddle she couldn't solve.

Night after night, in her own bed, Nora would see Tommy's feet dangling as he choked on his last breath. Night after night, she thought of what she'd done and what she hadn't. But when she weighed his life against what she'd gained since his death, never, not once, did she regret her choice.

SATURDAY, OCTOBER, 21, 2018

Book club was to meet at Nora's house on Saturday. On Friday morning, she was chopping walnuts for banana bread, thinking of that day's newspaper article about the college student who'd died falling out of a window. Had it been an accident? Suicide? Had someone pushed him? She pictured him in a flannel shirt and jeans, his hip leaning on the sill, arguing with his roommate or maybe his girlfriend, someone who hadn't intended to kill him, just to poke him in the chest and tell him something, maybe to shut the fuck up, and who watched in confusion or disbelief as he fell to the ground, arms flailing. Splat.

As she measured the flour, Nora wondered about the roommate or girlfriend, how they were managing. She wished there were a support group for killers, a non-judgmental place where they could unburden themselves and seek community. She glanced at the clock, saw that it was almost time for *Murderer Next Door*, her favorite true crime show, so she got her bread dough into the oven and went to the family room to watch television. She got flour on the remote, so she was distracted, wiping it off, when she noticed that Paul's face was on TV.

Nora stopped breathing. Oh God. Something must have happened. She'd caught the anchor mid-report. "... early this morning. Details concerning the cause of death have not been released." Nora swallowed air. "Once again, the body of Paul Ellis, missing Republican candidate for Senate, has been found in his Villa Nova home."

Nora didn't move. The anchor kept talking, and the screen showed police cars in front of Paul's house, but she couldn't follow the words. Her mouth hung open, her heart slowed, blood barely flowed. They'd found the secret room. Who? And how? And now what? The anchor must have ended his report because a game show popped on with bright colors and buzzers and jubilant contestants and a buoyant, friendly host.

They'd found him.

The secret she'd shared with Dave for so many weeks was out, public knowledge, which made Paul's death somehow more real. Her hands trembled. Damn, flour had gotten everywhere, into all the spaces around the numbers of the remote.

So. They'd found him. What had she expected? They were bound to, sooner or later. But how had they found him? By the smell? What had he looked like? Not handsome and smarmy anymore. He must have had a bloated belly, a decaying face. Bulging blue eyes.

Her phone rang, jolted her. Must be Dave. She ran for a dishtowel, wiped her unsteady hands, took a shaky breath, and answered the phone.

"They found him." Dave's voice was too fast and too thin. "It's all over the news. Nora, what now? What should we do?"

"Nothing. We don't do anything." Nora paused to slow the conversation. "This has nothing to do with us, right?"

Dave was breathing too fast. She imagined wet stains under the armpits of his dress shirt. "Right. Of course not. You're right." Still breathing fast. Still sweating.

"It's good they found him. Now people will relax and move on." Speaking slowly, she recited calming and reassuring phrases until his breathing settled. She suggested that he come home, but he insisted that after talking to her, he was fine. The news had just shaken him.

"Nora," he sounded calmer now. "Thank you."

"What for?"

"You know what. For talking me down when I get nervous. Again and again. For getting us through this. Honestly, I don't know what I'd do without you."

"And you'll never have to find out." Nora made light of his comment, but the words made her glow. Dave had never before acknowledged her help regarding Paul. He must finally be feeling better, and life would go on as it used to be.

Nora changed the channel to the *Murderer Next Door*. The narrator's voice soothed her as she stepped back into the kitchen. Time to check the banana bread.

SATURDAY, OCTOBER 21, 2018

"**S**o, tell me…" Patty chewed a mini Italian hoagie. "why'd it take a whole month to find him if he was in the house the whole time?"

"Maybe he wasn't," Alex suggested. "Maybe the killers moved him there."

Nora sipped pinot noir and passed the tray of small sandwiches to Katie.

"No," Patty said. "Uh-uh. It's been locked up. No one would risk going in there."

"Besides," Katie said, "they said he was in some secret room nobody knew about."

"I heard that too." Alex took a turkey on wheat and passed the tray. "I keep going through the house in my head. I can't imagine where it could be."

"Let alone why he had it." Patty took another bite. "I mean, what was he, a spy?"

"Think he was in the CIA?" Alex asked. "Nobody knew what he did, other than being rich and running for Senate. They call him a businessman. What the hell's that? I bet he was a spy, killed by other spies."

Laughter barreled up from the playroom. Patty had brought James and Graham, who sometimes picked on Ellie. Nora was on edge, hoping Ellie was fitting in.

Charlotte was back after several missed meetings. She piped up, sharing theories she'd heard about the murder. One was that Paul was a spy, not for the CIA, but for Russia, which was trying to get him elected so they'd have clout in the Senate. And the CIA, wise to the plot, killed him.

Alex had heard that, too.

Patty had also heard that he'd been killed by right-wing extremists or the Mob—some organized group because, against the majority of his party, he'd spoken openly about supporting gun control.

Katie heard that he'd been killed by a rival, but not a politician. "Oh my God. Do you guys think another man was in love with Barbara?"

Patty shook her head, doubtful. "Remember what she said about affairs? Something about how she'd never do it."

Nora didn't answer. She drained her glass and refilled it as if no one had said anything about Barbara and her love life. She walked around the room and topped off her friends' drinks.

"Do you like the sandwiches, Charlotte?" she asked.

"They're great. I love the bread." Charlotte chewed. "Where'd you get them?"

"Wawa." Nora smiled. "So. Anyone want to talk about the book?"

No one answered.

"I wonder if his death is connected to Barbara." Alex chewed.

"I bet it was," Patty said. "I bet he killed himself because he couldn't live without her."

"But they said he was shot in the chest. That doesn't sound like suicide," Katie said. "They said he might have been shot trying to get to his secret room."

"And what about the stuff they found in there?" Alex spoke carefully. She'd had a few refills of wine and gestured as she spoke, splashing wine against the rim of her glass. "Jump drives with records. They think they might prove illegal campaign contributions. Money laundering. Damn. We all thought he was such a stand-up guy."

"They think they might prove. *Might*," Nora said. "They haven't proved anything yet."

"But they wouldn't have said anything if they weren't pretty sure." Charlotte took another sandwich.

"Think Barbara knew what he was into?" Katie asked.

"Doubtful." Nora twisted her wedding ring. "How many women know what their husbands do at work? I sure don't."

Patty chuckled. "Really, Nora? The worst your husband would ever do is sneak off to play golf."

"Which is bad enough." Nora smirked.

"Well, I don't worry about Stu," Alex said. "I know exactly what he does."

"Only because you work together." Patty rolled her eyes. "Unless you're right there with them, you can't know what they're up to. So, I say Barbara didn't know."

"And yet, they both died within, what?" Katie asked. "A few days? They say he's been dead about a month."

"Well, I hope they catch the guy," Alex said. "It's creepy that somebody got killed right in the neighborhood."

"A Senate candidate with top-notch security in his house." Charlotte shook her head. "If he's not safe, who is?"

Everyone nodded or made some sound of agreement.

"Plus, they have no suspects? His security cameras were off? Seriously?"

"Yeah. That's why they think the killer was a pro. He left no clues."

Again, Nora emptied her glass.

"You're quiet, Nora." Patty said.

"Just listening. Thinking."

Patty leaned over, squeezed her shoulder. "It's good to get the club together again, isn't it? Even without Barbara."

Nora smiled. She made it a sad smile, though, in honor of Barbara. She set her glass down and stood. "I'll go check on the kids. Be right back." She grabbed a plate of banana bread.

On the steps to the play room, she heard Sophie talking softly. "James is just a bully, Ellie. You're not what he said. Forget him. I'll play with you."

Nora froze.

Weirdo. Freak. Tommy's feet didn't touch the ground, and the single lightbulb elongated his motionless dark shadow.

But Ellie wasn't like Tommy. She was just shy. She would blossom in time.

Nora brought the tray downstairs, gave Ellie the job of passing out the snack. Gave James a simmering glare.

On her third mug of coffee, Nora stood at the counter, gazing at the breakfast dishes in the sink. The leftover bits of frozen waffles. Clots of syrup. Splats of milk.

Dave hadn't eaten, said he'd grab something at the office. In the month since Paul's death, Dave had dropped ten pounds. His clothes hung on him. He'd gotten substitutes for his tennis games every single week. She wondered what to do for him. Obviously, he couldn't go to a therapist and talk about what was wrong. "I killed a guy and I feel terrible." Time would help. Dave's devastation about Barbara, his guilt about Paul—all of it would fade with time.

Until then, she'd keep cooking comfort food. Roasted chicken and potatoes. Soothing food. Certain dishes made life seem normal and safe: meat loaf, roast beef, spaghetti and meatballs, chicken pot pie. She was listing the foods that she found reassuring when the doorbell rang. Nora set her mug down beside Sophie's half-empty glass of chocolate milk. Was it the police? Had she left some thread of evidence in Paul's secret room? A fingerprint? Were they going to arrest her? Or Dave? Both of them?

Nora bit her lip. She could run out the back door. Or not answer the bell. Just stay silent and quiet by the breakfast plates with the uneaten waffle pieces and not move, not breathe, not make a sound until they went away. But what if they had a warrant? What if they broke the door down and found her standing by the kitchen table? Or was that just on television? Speaking of television, they probably could hear hers through the door. Probably assumed she was home, since it was on.

The bell rang again. They weren't going away. How could she answer now? She'd waited too long. It would seem suspicious to answer entire minutes after their first ring. *Never mind.* She could say she'd been upstairs and hadn't heard the bell. Or she'd been washing dishes, and the water must have drowned out the sound the way it had drowned Barbara. Then again, if the sound had been drowned out, she wouldn't know that she'd missed their first doorbell ring. She didn't need to explain anything.

She started for the door. And stopped after a couple of steps. Oh God. If they arrested her, what would happen to Sophie and Ellie? Would Dave confess to killing Paul? Would they both go to jail? Dave's brother would take the kids, so the girls would have to move to Jersey and be raised by Sheila, his whiny wife. But maybe she wouldn't go to jail. Dave would get them a good lawyer. For now, she'd just answer the door, play innocent and helpful. Find out what they knew and figure out a reasonable explanation for whatever evidence they'd found. It was doable. She could do it.

The walls, the hallway, the furniture shimmied, telescoping the front door, large and stark and ominous. She drew a breath, let it out. Floated forward. She reached out, turned the knob and pulled, closing her eyes for a moment, and opened them, prepared for a plain-clothes detective with tight buttons and bumps from shaving, or two detectives, both grim faced.

But no one was there. No detectives or uniforms. The porch was empty.

Out front, an engine revved. Nora leaned out the door, saw a FedEx truck pull away.

And on the stoop, a package.

The package was addressed to Dave. Had he ordered something online? New shirts maybe? She checked the return address, expecting something like L.L. Bean. Instead, she saw the address of the Philadelphia Police Department.

The police? Nora tossed it onto the foyer table as if it were a hot coal, as if her fingers were burning. She ran a hand through her hair. Blinked at the package.

It wasn't large. Felt dense, as if it contained a book or papers. Documents.

Of course. Dave had given Barbara's documents to the police, hoping his files would convince them that Paul had murdered her. But with Paul dead, there would be no need to pursue it. The police were probably returning Dave's property. Closing the case.

Still, Nora didn't move. She chewed a thumbnail, watching the package, unable to walk away.

In the next room, the television blared. A gunshot fired. Ominous music followed. A narrator asked a question: "Was it suicide? Or murder?"

Dave and Barbara. *I'm helping Barbara with some confidential matters. Personal matters.* Their plans for Barbara's escape were all in that envelope. Where had they arranged for her to go? What name had she planned to use? How much money had they squirreled away? Had they included proof of Paul's abuse? Was there other incriminating information about Paul? *He's not the man he seems to be. He'll never let me leave, he's proved that time and again.* Barbara and Dave.

The package glowed. It pulsated and danced, teasing her. "Open me. I'll tell you all about how your husband was helping Barbara."

And why shouldn't she open it? Barbara was dead, so there was no need for confidentiality, was there? Poor Barbara. Pretending to be the happiest, most fulfilled woman on the Main Line while loathing her violent, egomaniacal, controlling, politically-ambitious husband. Funny how Nora had always been jealous of Barbara, her flashy looks, her glamour, her status and wealth, her high-flying husband. Barbara's life had looked magical, but in reality, it had been hell.

And poor Dave was finally recovering from his guilt over Barbara and her hell. The package, when he got it, would rile it all up again. Whatever healing he'd achieved would be scraped raw like a ripped-off scab.

In the family room, a woman screamed. Music slashed. Someone said they'd known him but never suspected a thing. He was a good neighbor who'd always shoveled their walk when it snowed.

She could protect Dave from having to resurrect all his pain. She could hide the package, even destroy it. He'd never know it had come. Even as she reached for it, though, she knew she wasn't going to throw it out. At least, not until she'd seen what was inside.

Nora carried it gingerly, as if it were stolen merchandise. Well, it was. She brought it into the kitchen and set it next to the newspaper, still open to the obituary page. She sat, her warm coffee mug cradled in her hands, looking at it. Was she really going to do this, open something addressed to Dave and then dispose of it?

What you don't know can't hurt you. Don't look for trouble.

But she wasn't looking for trouble. She was taking care of her husband. Protecting him from needless pain. She assured herself that she wasn't snooping as much as performing an act of tenderness, of love. She picked up the package and, in one swift motion, ripped it open.

The stack of files was neatly labeled. One file folder contained car things. Copies of her new driver's license, tags, title and insurance cards for a navy-blue BMW convertible. The driver's license and car title were assigned to Kelly Ann Benson.

Kelly Ann? Not a bad name. It suited Barbara. Nora pictured Kelly Ann riding in her new car with the top down and her hair flying in the wind. But along what streets?

Nora leafed through the files, found one containing rental papers for a four-bedroom, two-bath home in Rockport, Maine. Wait, Maine? Hadn't Dave said they'd been looking in upstate New York? She read through the lease, checked out the amenities. Would they have met Kelly Ann's standards? Skylights, upgraded kitchen, hardwood floors, laundry. Overlooking the pier. Oh wow.

At first, she didn't notice the initials on each page of the lease. They almost skipped her attention. When she first saw them, she thought that the set that wasn't Barbara's must belong to the leasing agent, that it was just a coincidence that the second set matched Dave's.

D. W. It didn't mean anything. Maybe lawyers routinely initialed leases with their clients. Maybe Dave had had power of attorney for Barbara or had cosigned the lease for some legal reason.

Nora eyed the initials as if the squiggles were dangerous, as if they might leap off the page and poison her. Indeed, as she stared, the letters lost their hard edges and came alive, squirming like centipedes, scurrying like Tommy's ants.

The automatic ice maker dropped cubes into the freezer tray. The coffeemaker clicked, shutting off. The refrigerator hummed. In the next room, a commercial played, telling her to call the law firm of Meyer and Sheridan if she'd been injured at work, urgently repeating the phone number. Nora was aware of these simultaneous sounds, as well as that of her own heartbeat, of blood rushing through her veins. And she watched the initials scurry in frantic circles, daring her to come close enough for them to sink in their fangs.

Obviously, she was overreacting. Dave had explained, and Barbara had confirmed what he'd said, had even apologized for their secrecy. She'd seemed genuinely sorry.

Nora was probably mistaken about the initials. The handwriting looked like Dave's, but how could she tell from just two letters? Most likely, the leasing agent shared Dave's initials. It was just a coincidence. Until, there it was, on the last page.

Nora's hands were in her hair, over her eyes, clutching her stomach. Her mouth opened. Her throat closed. The kitchen spun and blurred. Dave had signed the lease. Oh God. What a sap she'd been. Everything made sense now: Dave's secrecy about his work for Barbara. His profound rage and pain at her death. His need to exact revenge on Paul. His weeks of deep mourning. Dave hadn't just been helping Barbara escape her vile marriage. No. He'd been planning to escape with her.

I told you not to look for trouble.

A TV announcer introduced a program called *Lovers Who Kill* and kicked off an episode about a black widow who'd met her first husband at a New Year's Eve party in Stamford, Connecticut.

Nora's heartbeat, the rush of her blood almost drowned out the voices. She had to think, figure out what to do and how to go forward. Who was Dave, anyway? She'd forgiven his earlier affair, taking him back not because he'd begged and pleaded, but because he'd sworn he'd never lie to her again. *I gave you my word that I'd never lie to you. I promised I'd never cheat again.* But now he had done both. He'd looked her in the eye and lied about it. Repeatedly.

The truth was, he'd plotted to leave Nora and their children. He had been planning all along to live with one of her supposed best friends, that lying, hussy bitch Barbara, aka Kelly Ann. That whore deserved what she'd gotten, sinking into the cold dark river, helplessly feeling it snake into her nostrils, over her eyes, and through her mother-fucking highlighted hair. Nora's hands clenched. Her jaw tightened.

She pictured Dave and Barbara signing the lease, toasting the future, celebrating. Had they laughed about her gullibility? Her hands were in her hair again, grabbing and pulling, unsure where to go or what to do.

What a chump she'd been, helping Dave hide Paul's body, nursing him through his grief. Being his crutch.

The folders were still stacked on the table, except for the open one containing the condo information. How toxic those papers were, spread out on the table where her children ate, sullying the placemats. She scooped them up, scooped up the whole pile and the envelope, and held them away from her body as if they were garbage, or a stinking dead animal. Or radioactive waste. She headed outdoors to the trash, stomping through fallen leaves in the yard. The chill autumn breeze nipped at her neck as she dumped the whole stack into the metal can. She went back inside, searched the junk drawer for matches, pawing over Scotch tape rolls and tangles of rubber bands, packages of batteries and pencils. She found them under a toothpick box. On the way out, she grabbed lighter fluid off the barbecue grill. The leaves crunched as she passed through them again, and the breeze bit at her nose and fingertips. As she doused the files, she looked down into the can. The pile of papers had come apart, exposing random pages of the lease with two snaky inked signatures at the bottom. One was Kelly Ann Benson. The other she recognized without having to read.

The signatures burned in her mind as she doused the files, and the dangerous chemical smell of lighter fluid seared her senses. She lit a match, tossed it into the can, and in a whoosh, felt the heat as flames flared and smoke rose. The fire soared and crackled, but Nora didn't move. She didn't step back from its hunger or its hiss. She stood still and watched, waiting until every flame, every ember, every trace of fuel burned out and the metal trashcan held only dust and ashes.

If she'd have asked him about the signature, he would have had an explanation. A glib, smooth, completely sensible one. Just like his answer about Barbara. *I've been consulting her. She needed a co-signer. There never was an affair.* Confronting Dave would achieve nothing. He would deny deny deny. Lie lie lie.

She stared at the ashes, wondering what she was supposed to do. Leave? Divorce him? And then what? She'd be alone with the children, fighting over custody and support for years. They'd become a scandal, the topic of neighborhood gossip. "Did you hear about Nora Warren? Dave moved out. He was cheating on her." Her friends would stay away, as if being cheated on and getting divorced were contagious. She'd be ostracized from her cozy club of comfortably married women.

The air smelled of burnt paper. Nora's breath shortened, her skin felt clammy. No, she didn't want a divorce. It would be so public, so shaming. But what else could she do? She couldn't stay, but how could she leave? She tried to make sense of the impossible, to sort the facts she'd just discovered. Had Dave planned simply to leave with Barbara and let Nora wonder where he'd gone? Had he planned to say goodbye before he went? How had he lain beside her night after night, proclaiming his love, while he'd been carrying on with Barbara? How could he have done this to her, breaking his word, treating her like she was nothing, not once, but twice? No. It was over. Dave was an imposter. She could never forgive him, never trust him again.

Nora's mind scrambled, struggling to deny what she knew, unlearn what she had learned. Maybe she was overreacting. Maybe staying married wouldn't be so bad. After all, Barbara the bitch-slut-whore was dead and out of their lives. Dave had moped for a while, but he was starting to get over her. Maybe they could pretend it never happened. Nora imagined how it might be: waiting for Dave to come home late from work, kissing him, sniffing him for traces of perfume, checking his phone and email, listening for his lies.

She couldn't do it. Not again. The marriage was over.

Oh God. Standing by the trash, staring at ashes, Nora hugged herself and counted until she cleared her mind. She felt oddly calm, grounded by the truth.

Nora closed the trash can and went inside to take a bath. She poured hyacinth-scented oil in the water, stepped into the tub and lay back, assessing her options. Dave didn't know about the package. He had no idea that it had arrived or that she'd opened and read the truth. So, unless she told him, he'd never know that she knew. The meaning of that sunk in slowly, warm like the bath.

What Dave didn't know made all the difference. If he didn't know, he wouldn't be defensive or angry. They would endure no bitter confrontation, no accusations, no visible damage to their marriage, no talons clawing each other's hearts. No divorce. For all the world to see, they would go on being Mr. and Mrs. David Warren, a devoted couple with two lovely children.

Nora ran a soapy luffa along her leg. Luffas reminded her of childhood, of that girl Annie who'd taught her how to shave her legs. Annie made her think of Tommy, his sad pathetic existence. His sad pathetic death. She thought about how well that death had worked out for her, the attention it had brought. The cool girls clamoring around her, vying for her friendship. Bobby Baxter asking her to go steady. No question, the tragedy had elevated her status.

Bubbles floated and popped beside her. Slowly, she dunked under the water and looked up through the bubbles to the wavy light, listened to the silence of water until her lungs ached and she burst back into the air. Shampooing her hair, she thought more about Tommy. As she concentrated, picturing his dead, dangling legs, the future began to take shape, opening before her like a map—no, like a golden, glowing pathway.

When she stepped out of the tub and patted dry, her mind continued along that pathway. What if she volunteered to drive the girls to Dave's mother's house on Saturday? What if, while they had cookies and milk, Nora visited the bathroom and opened the medicine cabinet? Surely, Nana Edith wouldn't miss a handful of heart pills. She took so many medications, she couldn't keep track of all of them. Edith was over eighty. Her memory wasn't what it used to be.

MONDAY, OCTOBER 29, 2018, 10:40 P.M.

That night, Nora did her best to act normal. In bed, she returned Dave's kisses, reminding herself that that they would be among his last. She went through the motions of lovemaking, an actress playing a well-rehearsed role. His loving lies burned like acid, his breath was heavy on her skin, and his persistent thumping, banging, huffing, pounding annoyed her entire being. Did he even notice her distance? Did he interpret her sighs as passion rather than boredom? She closed her eyes, waiting for him to finish, thinking about the drug. Propanol? No. Propranolol, double the "ol". She'd refilled it for Edith several times, noting the warning on the label, never imagining that she'd ever need to know that an overdose would cause, rather than prevent, a coronary. What did it taste like? Was it bitter? Would it blend into mashed potatoes? Or maybe a cheese omelet wolfed down before tennis? Wouldn't it be tragic if he collapsed on the court?

With a moan and a final thrust, Dave was done. He slumped on top of her, kissed her a final time, rolled off and looked at her.

"You okay?" His eyebrow raised, waiting.

"Just tired." Hell, if he could lie, so could she.

"Tired?" He watched her softly, touched her face as if he cared about her. "Well, then. Get some sleep. Good night." He propped on an elbow to kiss her again, then settled onto his pillows.

Nora turned off the lamp and stared into darkness. Not the tennis court. She wanted to be there. To see it. But not alone. She wanted people there to swarm around her, offering sympathy and support. But where? Maybe they'd invite people over. Yes. Patty and Ron. Sheila and Dave's brother, Don. One or two other couples. Maybe one of Dave's law partners. Never mind, she'd decide later. And she'd arrange a sleepover for the girls, so they'd be out, safe at Alex's or Katie's.

But what should she serve? Something Dave would eat every bite of, like pork loin with blackberry sauce. She'd hire someone to help her serve, and plate everything in the kitchen herself, so that she could prepare Dave's personal dish.

Nora heard the *clink* of silver against china. She saw the glitter of crystal and pouring of cabernet or pinot noir. She ran her fingers over the crocheted table cloth and linen napkins. Flowers—maybe irises? The night air sizzled with the heady aroma of grilled meat and the buzz of a few martinis, just enough to cushion nerves and steady hands.

Then what? Would it happen right away? How long would it take? If it took a while, she wouldn't be able to sit still, much less talk to anyone. Never mind. While her helper cleared the dinner plates, she'd go to the kitchen and arrange the mini carrot cakes on a tray. Oh, better yet—crème brulee. Perfect. Sad, though. Because what were the chances that anyone would actually eat dessert? Maybe she should go with something more mundane. Well for now, for tonight, she'd go with crème brulee, but it didn't matter since, in the commotion, no one would eat it. But she'd be in the kitchen, listening and waiting, while, in the dining room, voices would bump and spill over each other, a sea of jabber. Ron would be slurring, his voice booming over the others.

"No—let me tell it, Patty." Ron, half drunk, would insist on finishing some joke his wife would undoubtedly be ruining.

Simultaneously, Sheila would squawk about her pregnancy. "He's due on April Fools' Day. Can you imagine his birthday parties?"

Nora would strain, listening for Dave. Would she hear him? Would anyone notice him becoming quiet, holding his chest? Grimacing?

Who would scream first? Patty? No, Sheila. She'd be alert, the only one sober.

"Dave!" she'd shout. And then others would notice him slumped at the head of the table.

"Oh Christ," someone would say.

"What happened? Dave?"

"Is he breathing?"

"Somebody call 9-1-1!"

His brother would pull him to the floor and pound his chest, starting CPR.

Dave would lie still, his face darkening, his teeth exposed.

Eventually someone would shout, "Where's Nora?"

Guests would call, "Nora? Nora!"

She'd rush out of the kitchen with a question on her lips— what is it? No, wait. She'd rush out with the crème brulee tray in her arms, and when she saw Dave on the floor, she'd drop it in shock and despair. Yes. Nora envisioned the clatter of the silver tray, the chaos and destruction of fine dessert, and then... Then what? How should she react? Should she run to Dave? Stand frozen in stunned disbelief? Somehow both. First the latter, then the former.

His skin would be purple, his eyes bulging as if not believing that this was his end.

The girls were the only snafu. She didn't want them to suffer, and they would, inevitably. Kids always suffered, but they were strong, resilient. And this option was probably the kindest. A wound caused by a swift cut was easier to heal than one caused by slow, repeated slashes.

Dave's coffin would be walnut. Or cherry wood. Something dark and distinguished. Oh, and she'd need to buy a black suit. New black pumps, too. A hat? Did widows wear hats with veils? Patty would know. God, she had so much to do.

And when it was all over, what then? Would she grieve for him?

"You okay?" He was groggy, mostly asleep.

She nodded and snuggled under the warm comforter. No, she wouldn't grieve. Because for her, Dave was already gone. A memory. A ghost. His actual dying would be a mere formality, followed by surging attention and loads of community support. His death would unburden her. It would make her free. Just like with Tommy.

"Dave," she nudged his shoulder before he was completely asleep. "What would you think of having a dinner party?"

SATURDAY, APRIL 8, 2019

Derek was by far, the kindest and most insightful widower in the grief support group. Not to mention the best looking. The coffee date had been his idea.

The grief support group had been Patty's.

"You're stuck." She'd begun nagging Nora just weeks after Dave's death. "You can't isolate yourself, Nora. You need to reach out to others who can help you heal." Patty had done the research, found the non-denominational, open-to-anyone-who'd-lost-somebody group that met at the Baptist church on 18th Street. "Just go, see what it's like."

The truth was that being a widow was lonely and boring. So, after a few months, Nora followed Patty's advice. She might as well go check it out. How bad could it be?

Don't dwell on the past. What's done is done. Move on.

Across the table, Derek looked over the menu and absently stroked his beard. The beard suited him: meticulously trimmed, yet soft. "You like pie?" He looked at her, the questions in his eyes asking about more than just pie.

Nora had spotted him the minute she'd walked into her first meeting, two months ago now. She'd been immediately drawn to him, not so much to the beard as his intense blue eyes, Harris tweed blazer, and striking, yet gentle, demeanor. She'd later learned that he was a widower of three years, a tenured history professor at the University of Pennsylvania, the father of two girls, ages six and nine.

At that first meeting, Nora had been wary, taking a seat near the door, ready to flee if she felt the urge. Who were these grievers, these strangers who got together biweekly to talk about, dwell upon, and share details about the worst pain of their lives? And what was she doing among them, given that her loss of a spouse had been her own deliberate choice? Was she like the others at all? Was she even grieving?

Stupid question. Of course she was grieving. But not for Dave, the lying, cheating, deceitful bastard. No, she was grieving for herself, for the life she'd thought she had, for her identity as Mrs. David Warren. Oh, yes, she mourned that person deeply. So, she attended the grief meetings, commiserating with the others.

Still, sitting among them, Nora had felt like an imposter, keeping her eyes on Derek, the striking stranger in Harris tweed, while the others dabbed their eyes and sniffled. Unlike the others, widowhood had treated her well. As soon as the autopsy had determined Dave's death natural, by heart attack, his fat life insurance policy had paid out, and his firm had bought out his partnership, leaving Nora and the girls flush for life. She'd enrolled them in Baldwin, an elite private school, and bought herself a Lexus. Life was good. Almost.

In truth, Nora sorely missed having an "other". A partner. A spouse.

"You seem distracted." Derek lowered his head, gazing up at her.

"Sorry." She looked at his sweet blue eyes, felt tongue-tied. "It's just…" Just? Just that I don't know how to act? Just that I haven't been out with a man other than Dave for more than fifteen years? Just that I'm a misfit, weirdo, freak who's unable to make simple conversation.

Derek covered her hand with his. "Relax, Nora. With me, there's no pressure. We're just here for pie."

No pressure. Just pie.

Derek. Even at the meetings, surrounded by broken people, he always said the right thing.

Like what he'd said to that guy who'd lied to his kids. "For weeks, I told them that Mommy was in Florida, visiting cousins. I told myself I was sparing them the truth. But, to be honest, I wasn't sparing them. I was sparing myself from saying, 'Mommy's dead'."

It had been Derek who'd given perspective, assuring him and the others that there was no good way to share traumatic news, that it was enough to do their best. Nora had drifted, recalling how she'd sat down with Ellie and Sophie and told them that Daddy had passed away, that he wouldn't be with them anymore.

She'd watched their eyes, the confusion, the dawn of comprehension, the onslaught of tears. Then, she'd soothed them with Dave's own explanation. "Daddy's okay, though. He's up in Heaven."

Sophie had furrowed her eyebrows and tilted her head. Then her eyes had brightened. "Ellie! Daddy's in Heaven with Aunt Barbara."

Nora had almost choked. Had pictured Dave strolling hand in hand with Barbara in sunny, green meadows with birds chirping, bunnies hopping, and bees buzzing around their happy, love-dazed heads.

Maybe they'd gone off together after all.

Well, damn them both. Sophie had been wrong; Dave and Barbara weren't happy, they couldn't be. Nora was the happy one, the winner, the survivor. The inheritor of Dave's assets. The planner and executor of a standing room only, not-a-dry-eye-in-the-place funeral, the receiver of endless sympathy and admiration from Dave's friends, family, colleagues and acquaintances. She was the one who was still breathing, moving ahead, going out for coffee on her first date with a handsome new man.

Nora smiled at Derek, fascinated by the very un-Dave-like slender length of his fingers on his coffee cup. Imagining them touching her breasts. Yes, she was the winner. For once, she was free. No one to betray her. No one to bully her or take what was rightfully hers.

The waitress brought the pie and refilled their coffee.

"Can I have a bite?"

Wait.

The voice in her ear. It wasn't Derek's. And Derek wasn't interested in tasting her pie. He was telling her about his younger daughter's amazing math skills and digging into cherry pie.

The hand she saw on the table beside hers was thicker, stronger, hairier than Derek's. Nora's blood chilled. She didn't dare turn her head.

"Sorry, I'm talking too much," Derek said. "Your turn. Tell me about Nora Warren."

"Ha!" Dave said. "Go ahead. Why not start with how you killed your husband?"

Nora stiffened. "Not much to tell."

"Like hell."

Nora tried to shove Dave from her mind. She steadied her hands and took a hefty bite of pecan pie, shifting the subject. "So. Did you grow up around here?"

Derek swallowed coffee, nodding. "Bryn Mawr. The second of four boys. How about you? Any siblings?"

As if on cue, Tommy plopped into the booth beside Derek. He held a jar of beetles, or maybe roaches.

Great. They were both there. She forced another smile. "Nope. I was an only child."

Tommy glared at her.

Dave reached over and scooped a dollop of whipped cream off her pie. She wanted to slap his hand. What was he doing there? Where was girlfriend Barbara? Why wouldn't he just go be dead? Tommy set his jar down next to Derek's pie plate, and bugs began crawling out the top. Derek didn't appear to see them. He kept talking, and Nora tried to stop staring at the creatures and pay attention to what he was saying. Something about single parenting?

"...and your daughters are about the same age as my little one. Maybe we could make plans for all of them. Like the zoo. Or a museum?"

Tommy suggested the Natural History Museum. He loved their exhibit on Extreme Bugs.

Dave became livid, insisting that Nora keep Derek away from the girls. "They shouldn't have to meet every dude you hook up with."

Really? Dave was the one who'd hooked up with someone the girls knew. But Nora didn't react. She kept wearing her smile, as if Tommy and Dave were not right there at the table interrupting, provoking, and commenting. Because they weren't. They were only in her mind.

Finally, pie and coffee were finished. Derek took Nora's hand as he walked her to her car. Tommy wandered off to find more bugs, but Dave strolled along, checking out her new Lexus. When they said goodbye, Derek kissed her lips lightly, slowly, gently as the brush of a feather.

Dave stood close, watching, judging. "Seriously? He calls that a kiss? I used to kiss you so hard your knees would cave."

Nora pulled away, her face hot.

"Sorry," Derek said. "Too soon? I didn't mean—"

"No, it's fine. It's just... I haven't kissed anyone since..." She looked away. Dave puckered up and kissed his middle finger.

Derek touched her cheek, gazed into her eyes. "Well, then, I'm glad we got that first one out of the way." He leaned close and kissed her again, more deeply.

Dave repeated Derek's words, mocking him.

Nora said goodbye and drove off, but was shaking so badly that, after a few blocks, she had to pull over to the curb. What the hell was wrong with her? Seeing Tommy and Dave? Hearing them? Tommy was no surprise. He was a pest that had never let her alone. But Dave? She'd never had him show up before, not once, ever, since he'd died.

Until today, when she'd had her first date.

Damn. Was Dave going to nest in her head like Tommy, appearing at whim? Never letting her go? Never letting her be alone with another man? She thought of Derek, his sweet steady eyes, his kiss.

Her hands clutched the steering wheel and she stared at the open road.

Don't dwell on the past. What's done is done. Move on.

Nora simmered. It wasn't fair. They were parasites, both of them, feeding off her, living in her head. Dave and Tommy. Tommy and Dave.

In the back seat, Dave leaned back, held up a scotch and toasted her.

"Go away, damn you!" Nora slammed her forehead with the heel of her hand. She closed her eyes. Counted until she was sure he'd gone. Then she took a breath and checked the back seat.

No Dave.

Nora sat straight, started the car, and headed home. The girls would be back from school soon, and there was dinner to fix. Maybe she'd whip up a special dessert, finally get to eat some of that crème brulee.

ACKNOWLEDGEMENTS

Heartfelt thanks to Myra Fiacco and Jess Moore at Filles Vertes for their encouragement, energy, insight and enthusiasm, and especially for Jess's careful, thoughtful, and detailed editorial comments which helped refine the book.

Thanks also to:

Lanie Zera, Janet Martin and Nancy Delman for their consistent, long-lived support,

Kimberly Leahy for her generous and thorough read,

The entire Philadelphia Liars Club, especially Oddcast co-podcasters Jon McGoran, Gregory Frost, Kelly Simmons and Keith Strunk for being models of perspective, persistence, humor, irreverence and determination,

The regulars at the Main Line Coffeehouse for sharing battle stories and hard-earned wisdom, and rooting for each other's success,

And especially Robin, Baille, Nick, Zoe, Neely and Daniel. You are the cream in my coffee, the sun in my sky, the breeze on my river, the light in my eye, etc.